The
OTHERS

A SCIENCE FICTION NOVEL

Margaret Wander Bonanno

ST. MARTIN'S PRESS
NEW YORK

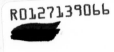
Design by Judy C. Dannecker

Library of Congress Cataloging-in-Publication Data

Bonanno, Margaret Wander.
    The others / by Margaret Wander Bonanno.
        p.   cm.
    "A Thomas Dunne book."
    ISBN 0-312-05140-9
    I. Title.
    PS3552.0592508 1990   90-37282
    813'.54—dc20   CIP

First Edition
10 9 8 7 6 5 4 3 2 1

For Uncle Don, who dared give a girl-child her first astronomy
   book
For the real Rau, who saved my life
And for "Patsy," regardless of how it ended

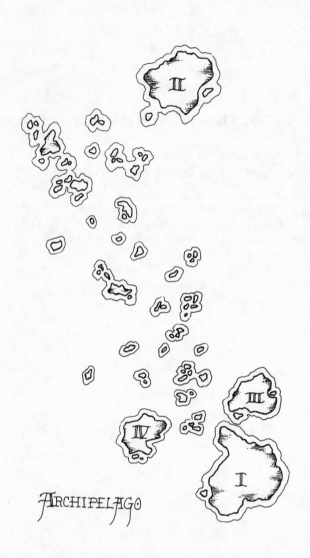

ARCHIPELAGO

THE OTHERS

"Dilemma"
(from *Essays of WiseLiiki Philosopher*: T-Y871)

Has ever a species been presented with the dilemma confronting us? Forbidden by circumstance to examine more than the smallest fraction of the world whereon we dwell, clearly different from that species which dominates the whole of it, we are left to seek our ancestry in one of two directions.

Either we assume that, because our blood resembles nothing so much as that of the presapient sea creatures whose realm surrounds our Archipelago, we must perforce be akin to them. Therefore did we on one temperate primeval day, our innate curiosity sparked into instantaneous intelligence, haul ourselves up out of the sea where we had flourished for countless eons and, fully formed, possessed of fingers and thumbs and the large and many-faceted brains which are our optimum feature, proceed with neither setback nor evidence of failed effort, to build our multi-layered cities upon the land?

Elsewise, refusing to accept a possibility so miraculous and without proof, we base our entire science upon a Legend—obtuse, obscure, poorly rhymed and badly written—which yields us in its circumlocutory fashion the surprising speculation that we were brought here from another place.

The difficulties with the Legend are twofold. Even in its entirety it never told us who it was who purportedly brought us here or why and, whether fortuitously or no, so much of it was destroyed during the early zealotry of the Thousand-Year.

We are able to trace our oldest artifacts to an era five hundred thousand years past. Meticulous examination of every portion of our islands reveals no older trace, nor indication of how these tool-using beings who were our forebears chanced to evolve. Was that evidence lost beneath the volcanoes which even now continue to re-shape our realm, or did these events never transpire upon this world?

1

one

I t is said we are not alone here in the bowl of the sky.

There are those among our WiseOnes who from their studies have extrapolated certain precise and complex data which indicate that the conditions which support life on the World can be duplicated on approximately forty thousand of the estimated billions of worlds in our part of the universe. (Though I, having failed abysmally in the sciences in all my skillscans, pretend no true comprehension of the more sophisticated of their findings.) There is also the Legend.

Whatever speculative value any of this may at one time have had, we are in fact remote from the nearest star, and offworld travel was only theory when the present troubles began. In short, it offers no possibility of escape. However, it possesses still a certain philosophical allure, coupled now, on the verge of our annihilation, with a kind of irony. If we have kin among the stars, it might have been gratifying to record our presence for them before the People succeeded in eliminating us.

That is the reason I have begun this chronicle. The Telepaths have confirmed that our present segregation is only the beginning. The People, having taken from us all that they found useful (which we freely offered, perhaps unwisely), have concluded that they no longer need us. Our appearance and our Way have always made them uneasy, and since we cannot alter the first and will not the second, they find justification in eradicating us . . .

But as I reread what I have written thus far, I am ashamed. Lingri the Chronicler, Lingri so-named WiseOne, has confirmed that she is no more than the Lingri Inept of her childhood, which was so very long ago. It was intended, it is imperative, that this be the last, best chronicle of my species. Yet it begins as a shambles. An indication of the desperation of our plight and of how far I, at least, have lost the Discipline. It is unworthy of my kind, who have entrusted this to me. It is unworthy also of those of the People who sheltered me, instructed me, cherished me when even my own considered me, frankly, peculiar.

That I have not eaten for four days, that my hand trembles so violently I can barely hold the stylus, is no excuse. There is also insufficient light for proper writing. *They* now control the power plant and have seen fit to provide us with power only intermittently, primarily, I think, to try our patience. Since we are no longer permitted to venture out of doors in daylight . . .

But I must not continue in this vein! To lose Discipline is to lose everything. Let me begin from the beginning.

I am about to tell you a tale of two species: one which evolved independently on its world, one which in a time before time was "seeded" on that same world from some distant place.

The first lived on a great land mass which covered nearly all of a hemisphere, evolving into a robust feudal society of many small nations constantly at war, each with each. The other dwelt on an archipelago in the middle of a vast sea,

4

turning its energies away from war to build beautiful cities and a most advanced technology.

The first, unable to venture far from shore in its clumsy sailing vessels, did not know the second existed. The second, able to pass over land or water in silent skimmercraft, observed the first without being observed, saw that its numbers and abilities increased and grew wary, watching and waiting.

The first sang and danced and made wonderful music, embraced and quarreled and embraced again, killed and made peace and plotted how to kill again, coupled and bred in prodigious numbers undaunted by famine, plague, or the ever-present threat of yet more war.

The second turned its eyes within, studied and meditated, perfected its sciences, lived by a complex code of duty, protocol, and obligation, kept its population constant, and while its members were immune to most disease and seemed to live forever, it was also true that they had forgotten how to laugh.

I will tell you, if you care, how the two encountered and intermeshed for a time, combining their strengths to construct a world greater than the sum of its parts. I will tell you, too, how this glorious experiment became nightmare, and where all evidence indicates it will end. That done, my chronicle is done, ending with ". . . and some eighty years later, they killed us all." Then I shall put down my stylus and join those who remain, awaiting the inevitable. Even so, I suspect that the Council, which has given me this duty, will not be satisfied with the manner in which it is done.

Gayat has arrived to peer over my shoulder as I write this last. I do not mean this literally; he is too well Disciplined to be so overtly rude—I think. He has in fact only crossed my threshold, bringing with him the aroma of broth in a covered tureen held gingerly between his two uncalloused hands. But Gayat is a Telepath and son of Telepaths; his very presence is sufficient to raise the hair on my neck and slam the doors of my mind in self-defense, as I hasten to gather what stray thoughts may be rebounding off the walls in this small space. I accomplish all this without moving a muscle; it is quite a feat, actually. Gayat is aware of this mental slamming—it has characterized our relationship throughout his brief life—and waits.

"Well?" I greet him without turning.

"Well, yourself," he replies, with little respect for the seventy-five years I have lived before him. He sets the tureen down just beyond where I might be expected to spill it; I have that reputation. "There has been a food consignment, and the Council deems it necessary for even a chronicler to eat."

Ordinarily I would praise him for his irony, but the times are not ordinary.

"Have the children eaten? And you?"

"Yes to the children, and mine is being kept for me." He changes the subject with a Telepath's obliqueness, which is so sudden it seems no change at all. "You have yet to tell them who you are. Who *we* are."

He has been peering over my shoulder, mentally at least. I put down the stylus and recite the Discipline before I trust myself to speak.

"Gayat-*la*, I have yet to determine to my satisfaction who *they* are or will be, if they exist or will exist at all. Far less am I able to find a common frame of reference adequate to explain to them who we are. I have drawn upon all of my knowledge and experience, yet I still have not an inkling how truly to begin this. Would you care to try?"

He responds with an eloquent negative gesture.

"I must be going. However, I will first remind you that the morrow is a Blue day."

I answer this by not answering it. As I will be seen by no one on the morrow, the restored tradition of the Color Days holds no significance for me. I resume my stylus as if Gayat were already gone. Nevertheless, I must recite the Discipline three times more before I trust my thoughts to fly free again.

* * *

6

Gayat is correct, of course, but so am I, and the burden of the chronicler is to always see every side of every issue. Little wonder never a one of us has ever been elected to the Council, though there have been Matriarchs who would perhaps have made better chroniclers. Gayat is correct, in that I must tell you who and what I am, who *we* are, before I can go further. It was my intention to do precisely that when that son of a Telepath stepped into my mind, though I will not give him the satisfaction of telling him.

But even as I write this, I struggle futilely to understand who *you* are.

We are—or were, until this recent age—the People. Doubtless every intelligent species has a name for itself, a word which in its language means simply "the people." This at least was what we called ourselves until that second species, who of course referred to *them*selves as the People, arrived on our shores eighty years ago. We, being far fewer in number and consequently less inclined to argue, agreed to allow ourselves to be called the Others, in order—*they* said—to avoid confusion. That the name remains the same in our tongue is a subtlety which even now most of them do not know.

Yet I wonder now, with the infallibility of hindsight, how much we surrendered in so minor-seeming an acquiescence?

I am, therefore, an Other, one of that species of island dwellers who came from a far place, longer-lived and "different," who learned to skim the surface of the World while the People were still ankle-deep in its mire, who learned early to calculate the paths of stars, memorize a hundred pages on any subject in an afternoon, "read" the weather, polar magnetism and occasionally Other minds, and commune with the creatures of the sea, but who never dared to dance or sing or laugh aloud until I met the People. These were but some of the differences between us.

As to the similarities:

Must I specify that both species are bipedal, land-dwelling, oxygen-breathing, large-brained, divided predominantly into

7

two sexes, possessed of opposable thumbs and therefore tool-makers? If you are not at least some of these as well, will our story hold any interest for you? And if you are none of these, what are you? To answer this I must defer to the greater wisdom of my grandmother, the WiseOne Loriel, and to a conversation which transpired over ninety years ago.

"If they were not—at least land-dwellers and toolmakers—they would lack the technology and probably the interest to venture into space, do you see?"

Loriel was attempting to explain in terms accessible to a nine-year-old—and one with a reputation, already, for thick-headedness—one of her all-consuming obsessions, which was the search for life on distant worlds.

"If they were sea-dwellers, for example, they might have as much interest in the sky and what lay beyond it as we would have in adapting to a permanent life in the depths of the sea—entertaining in conjecture, perhaps, but not practicable."

Ironic, this, considering what ultimately became of Loriel.

"Alternatively, if they were methane-breathers, for exam-ple—you *can* surmise the properties of a methane-breather, can you not?"

I nodded vaguely, grateful for her choice of words. Anyone, even thick-headed Lingri, could *surmise*, but if she had asked me if I *knew* . . .

To know anything, in an Other sense, is to understand it as thoroughly as finite reason permits. To say I knew the properties of a methane-breather, even a hypothetical one, would be to say that I could deduce from the chemical prop-erties of methane and the conditions which created it the phys-iological, mental, and psychological traits of an intelligent being which utilized it as we did oxygen. In addition, I must be able to describe a world whereon such conditions existed—a vast and continuous swamp, perhaps—down to the flora and fauna which shared it with this intelligent, ostensibly tool-making, potentially spacefaring species.

If I were not an Other it would have made my head ache. Yet I *could* picture it—I who could not so much as recite the chemical composition of methane as most of my peers could. What did this mean?

Loriel has said nothing in the minim or so it took me to wend my way through this, though her not-speaking said much about her patience.

"Methane-breathers . . ." she reiterated, her obsidian-sharp eyes observing me mildly, ". . . might consider us too different to merit study, might perhaps find it inconceivable that an oxygen-breather possessed sufficient intelligence to *deserve* study. Consider this."

Consider it I did, but arrived at nothing. It must have been evident on my face.

"Oxygen-breathers, then," Loriel continued, as if I had answered intelligently, "for the sake of simplicity. As to the number or nature of their limbs or mouths or eyes or fingers, these are finally of no consequence, though there is a theory of parallel evolution which postulates that certain norms are constant within the same galaxy. Bipedalism may be such a norm, but an upright biped could have wings in place of hands, or—"

"What about a brain?" I interrupted, caught by something flashing across my consciousness with such clarity I forgot the breach of protocol in interrupting an elder. "Could there be beings that evolved until they were nothing but brain?"

Loriel looked at me for a long moment without speaking.

Permit me at this juncture to explain that I was in disgrace again, having wreaked havoc for the second time with the skillscans designed to direct Other offspring toward the optimum choice of profession, and while my mother, the Councillor Jeijinn, had gone to smooth matters over with my tutors yet again, she had made it clear that she would appreciate my absenting myself for a time from her awareness. This had happened before and, as before, I betook myself to Loriel.

Serious thought was being given, should I fail the 'scans a third time, to training me for a handcraft rather than one of the science tracks, but this was assuming a 'craft could be found suitable to my general fumble-fingeredness. No one yet knew of my true gift. It was too "different," and I was too baffled by it to recognize it as a gift, much less to reveal it to anyone. Yet in asking my grandmother so fanciful a question, I was in danger of doing precisely that.

No doubt WiseJeijinn, Matriarch and Councillor, over-achiever from a race of overachievers, found a certain justifi-cation in foisting her disappointing offspring off on Loriel; my grandmother in her day was as much an anomaly in her realm as I was in mine. (Though she has long since been professionally "rehabilitated," so much of her theory having subsequently been proven fact. I will not have similar honor. My anomaly and my rehabilitation will die with me and mine. Loriel foresaw that, too.)

She oversaw my arrival in the observatory from the very top of the dome, where she was locked into the motivchair and engrossed in some elaborate piece of machinery whose func-tion I could only guess at. With her silver-gray garments and her silver-gray hair (her only affectation, when I knew her—to my knowledge she never cut it, managing somehow never to get it caught in things; it hung nearly to her ankles, held at her nape with a single intricate clasp, shimmering like a waterfall), she might have been invisible, an extension of the array of equipment rising from where I stood at ground level to where she was, five storeys above my head. Except for those black eyes, which sparkled at me even at that distance.

"I see you have found your way unhindered," she greeted me and detached herself as if reluctantly from her work, lowering the motivchair to where I stood craning my neck, giddy with watching despite my being the one with feet on the floor.

Her statement so puzzled me that whatever greeting I might have prepared died in my throat. Did Loriel too consider me inept?

A characteristic of Others which People have always found particularly sinister is our total spatial recall. An interaction between polar magnetism and the electrolytes in our blood enables us to remember any route once traversed, and we cannot lose our way. Even at my tender age, having been to the observatory more than once in the company of either parent, I could have found it blindfolded. My only concern had been whether Loriel had given me security clearance to pass the scanners. Or was that what she had meant?

Hovering no more than a handsbreadth from the floor in her 'chair, she saw all of this in my face, though I had thought myself well masked behind my Discipline.

"As to the latter . . ." she said, reading my thoughts though she was no Telepath; none of my family were, ". . . I had you approved for scanner clearance. Hereafter you may come here whenever you wish. Unlike your mother, I conclude you are mature enough not to break or stumble into things."

Before I could either express my gratitude or explain that I was not quite as inept as Jeijinn thought me (the two concepts wrestled for dominance in my brain; I was a chronicler in spirit even then), she went on.

"As to the former . . ." The motivchair bobbed slightly, whimsically, as she maneuvered it nearer. ". . . it was an irony, nothing more. Though ill-placed, I daresay. One whose skill-scans have failed her is in poor humor for such pastimes. Shall we talk?"

"Grandmother . . ." I began helplessly, finding words for the first time, but she gestured me to silence.

"Too many minds are at labor here." She pulled me into the chair beside her, activating the mechanism as she indicated her associates—Loriel never had subordinates—astronomers, meteorologists, technicians, silent and seemingly unlistening as they went about their tasks on the various levels leading up to the dome. "We must not disturb them with our idle talk."

Trust Loriel to make it seem we were doing them a service, rather than removing ourselves from their curiosity.

I tried desperately not to look down. In fairness, the 'chair ran smoothly and silently; I might not have been conscious of its movement at all save for the sight of level after level dropping away before us. When we arrived with the smallest lurch at the top of the dome, my grandmother focused my attention away from my uneasy insides onto the viewer which had so absorbed her attention when I arrived.

It was a telescope; I had surmised that much correctly.

"What do you see?"

"Stars," I said at once. "But, Grandmother, in the daytime? How?"

She embarked upon a soft-voiced explication of the principles of light refraction, which any ordinary first-level candidate could master, though I was third-level and had not, and for the first time they became clear to me. Instructing me to keep my eyes on the viewer, Loriel described precisely which stars I was seeing and their known properties, slipping in a question now and then about my skillscans until, bit by bit and painlessly, the debacle was told. Was it wishful thinking or mere recklessness which made me then interject my question about beings who were pure brain?

"From where does this thought derive?" Loriel asked me, a look of actual surprise escaping the careful mask with which anOther habitually meets the world.

I searched myself. Whatever else it might be, my answer must be truth.

I state here, in the event your species differs from mine, that anOther cannot lie or, rather, that we find it metaphysically simpler to speak truth, most of the time. This is a given of our nature, and prior to our contact with People there were no words in our tongue to denote that which is deliberately untrue. Only our discovery that some People can twist a truth so deftly it is almost an art form awakened us to the many permutations of untruth.

This is not to say that truth itself is a simple thing. There are greater truths and lesser truths, truth-within-truth, truth-seeming-untruth and a host of truths unspoken. But these are gloss, marginalia, a part of the fabric of our being which will come clearer, I trust, in my narration. Certainly they were nothing of what was in the mind of the nine-year-old seeking a truth unsullied to present like a gift to her grandmother.

"I do not know," I at last answered Loriel's question; it was the only truth I had. "I simply opened my mind and the thought was there, waiting for me."

"Curious." Loriel activated the mechanism to lower the 'chair. "Perhaps your tutors are 'scanning you for the wrong skills."

"What should they be 'scanning me for, Grandmother?"

It was all I could do to match my stride with hers as we left the observatory. We were going, I hoped, somewhere special for midmeal. Loriel's pace was vigorous despite her great age.

My grandmother was well past the midpoint of her second century. She had been in her sixties when she bore my mother Jeijinn, and Jeijinn, for her own peculiar reasons which I was never entirely to understand, was past a century when I was born. This was not extraordinary, for Other females could bear children well into their hundreds, though most preferred to replicate themselves far younger than this. Thus while an-Other's average lifespan was two hundred years, and most lineages could contain as many as six living generations, ours yielded only three.

"You simply opened your mind and found it there—this being which was pure brain? Pure thought in physical form, if you will?" Loriel frequently answered a question with a question, worrying at it as if it were something profound. Perhaps it was; I surely could not know.

"Yes," I answered truthfully, though by now my truth was set about by doubt. "Grandmother? Have I done something . . . unDisciplined?"

It was possibly the worst offense anOther child could accuse herself of.

"Not at all." A faint bemusement tugged at the corners of

Loriel's mask. "But, presented with the theoretical possibility of a being who was pure brain, any one of your peers—or any of mine, for that matter—would become entangled in explication and never find an answer . . ."

We had entered the main crossways by now, and my grandmother deliberately lengthened her stride so that I must struggle to keep up; even in this she was growing me.

". . . they would become absorbed in how it might move, find sustenance, reproduce, defend itself, and so lose the point of the question. If their opinion were empirical, they would conclude that such a creature was an impossibility. If mystichemical, they would postulate that given an environment in which it could evolve unthreatened to maturity such a creature would need neither to move nor defend itself, and could manufacture its own nutrients out of enzymes which . . ."

She stopped, I think, out of simple compassion. I had fallen several paces behind in the orderly-moving crowds of Others, and was breathless and out of my depth in all respects. Loriel waited for me to come up to her.

"Forgive me," she said mildly. "I tell myself it is because you are of only nine years and as yet untainted by our close-mindedness, yet I think it is also something else. Something different. Something uniquely Lingri."

There was that word again—"different." Was it to characterize the whole of my life?

"What is that something, Grandmother?" I pleaded, holding rein on my distress lest it spill over into my voice. "What is it that makes me different?"

"I am only a WiseOne, Lingri-*la*," Loriel replied. This time I recognized the irony. "I don't know everything!"

At the very hour in which we walked the tranquil, sun-dappled ways in the heart of the City, entered the garden of Yaru in the shadow of the Citadel's spires and were given Loriel's accustomed bench by the fountain, half a World away a war was beginning. It was a smallish war, as such things go, in

14

which under cover of darkness the tribe known as Kwengii, a thousand strong, swept down on the weary fiefdoms of Hraregh to burn and rape and pillage. A troupe of traveling Players, with loyalties to both sides or to neither as the case might be, was caught between the swords of the former and the crossbows of the latter, and all but one were killed.

It was a scenario played out almost daily anywhere in the People's realm, or so the Monitors—those Others specially trained to pass among the People and observe—had noted in the course of several centuries. The significance of this particular skirmish was that the sole survivor of that troupe of Players—a child of nine years, like me and yet so unlike, who was to become so much to her People—was Dweneth.

Loriel and I concluded our meal and walked leisurely back to the observatory in golden sunlight, conversing pleasantly and admiring the *kressha,* which were then in bloom, trailing over the garden walls. The child Dweneth, bleeding and frightened into stuttering silence, fled through the cold and friendless dark of a strange land, the slaughter of her mother and three siblings stark in her memory, the slim hope of reaching her father in a far province the only thought that sustained her.

At virtually the same time that Dweneth, wrapped in her particolor Players' cloak against the damp, her terror yielding at last to exhaustion, gave way to deep and dreamless sleep beneath the leaves of a forest the Hraregh call simply Gloom, I labored in sunlight, doing garden chores and eavesdropping on a debate which before day's end was to offer direction to my addled life.

The contrast between our two lives at this precise moment is significant. If the People as a whole have been called primitive, even savage, might it not be because so much of their lives is given over to mere survival? And if Others can be accused of being effete and distant, may it not be for the opposite reason?

But, to retrace my steps: I was pulling weeds.

It is something that with all our technology we might have found a less arduous way to do—with selective defoliants, perhaps, or some complex tool—but anOther does not exist who does not relish the texture of soil between the fingers, the sound and fragrance of growing things. Old Tagal had sensed this in me, and saw fit to employ my youth and energies among the *gli*flowers.

WiseTagal, who was older even than my grandmother, had appointed himself caretaker of the observatory grounds despite his many degrees and vast wisdom, because he refused to either work in the laboratories or attend conferences after yet another falling out with Loriel—a not-uncommon occurrence, legend had it, over the past hundred years. This I could well believe, considering their divergent temperaments and anOther's passion for argument—the only fallibility, besides our insatiable curiosity, which no Discipline could cure. I did not, however, accept the companion tale, never meant for my ears, which suggested that Loriel and Tagal had once been bondmates.

It was quite possible that Tagal, ever absorbed in his work and never having had consort, might not have realized that the time was upon him. Too, Loriel was long unpartnered following Liiki Philosopher's rebirth and before she chose Jei-jinn's father, and then again long after. And yet, Loriel and Tagal as lovers? This I could not accept, not only because a child will not permit its elders the privilege of passion, but because they were so unlike. Adversaries, indeed; lovers, no. But I was decades away from learning how readily the two can be one and the same.

"It is madness, you know, this obsession of hers!" Tagal muttered in his cracked voice as he sat on a bench in the shade, luxuriating his gnarled old toes in the warm, fragrant loam, watching me work. Like most webtoes, he seldom went shod.

I labored on my knees among the flower beds beneath the

conference room's long casements, out of which an occasional snatch of voice wafted to me on the soft air.

"Time-consuming madness, when we have little time to consume!" Tagal shifted his walking-staff in his hands. "Legat's Parallel proves to my satisfaction and any Other's that we evolved here, from this very sea, whether prototypes are found or no. Why does she persist in this star-searching?"

The "she" in Tagal's diatribes could never be any but Loriel. "The conclusions she draws are not even her own. Had she not been Liiki's chosen, she would never have thought these things through herself. Madness!"

"My grandmother says Legat's Parallel is too full of flaws and suppositions," I ventured, tugging at a weed whose runners were longer than I'd expected, wishing my hands more callused. I was only repeating what I'd overheard, but Tagal pounced on it.

"Indeed? And what do you think, Your Wisdom?"

I tugged. "Tagal-*al*, I don't understand any of it."

"Don't you? Mind that runner—it tangles about the *gli*. No benefit derived from damaging the latter in uprooting the former." I complied, aware of his eyes upon me, his thoughts probing at mine. He was an old one; I must allow for that. "Have you not studied the Legend? Can you not see its inadequacies? I thought you were at second-level?"

"*Third.*" I yanked, the runner came free, and I dumped the prodigy unceremoniously in my weed basket. The *gli*flowers' plaintive scent told me I had damaged them after all. I patted the soil down around them gently, trying to make amends. "I am Loriel's grandchild, am I not? Of course I have studied the Legend. And absorbed its subtexts and the Apocrypha with my mother's milk. It does not mean I understand it."

"That's been said of you," Tagal observed—querulous, critical. Carefully I weighed his age into the equation of our dialogue so as not to take offense at his words. He raised himself slowly from the bench, shaking the soil from between his toes, leaning over me on his walking-staff. "It's said you

17

dream instead of listening. I'd hoped it was not truth. This is a time for listening. Grave change is imminent, and yours is the generation which must countenance it. A hundred WiseOnes and as many Matriarchs cannot decide what to do when the Violent Ones land on our shores. What will you do?"

He did not wait for me to answer, not that I could have. The shadow of the People had loomed over our Archipelago since before my birth. If WiseOnes and Matriarchs knew not what to do, who, then, was I?

"This is a time for listening," Tagal repeated, trembling with intensity. *"Listen!"*

I did. What I heard, beyond a twittering of small birds and the trill of a lizard in the long grass, was the ongoing debate beyond the casements, where ten WiseOnes inquired and averred, proved and disproved, confirmed and contradicted, seemingly without respite but always within Discipline. No voice was raised, no insult hurled, no insinuation advanced, no composure threatened. From where I crouched amid the *gli* and the twining *kressha* the words were not clear, but if I were to stand directly beneath the windows . . .

I turned to Tagal, incredulous. He could not be suggesting I was actually to *listen?* The invasion of privacy was one of the more serious of the unDisciplines, sufficient to cause my grandmother to question her wisdom in allowing me the run of the observatory. But Tagal was contemplating larger matters.

"It is your right," he answered what I had not asked. "It is all our past, but your future, which they debate. Tell that to her if she takes it amiss!"

With that he was gone, slowly treading the raked path with no sound but the tap of the walking-staff. He had not entirely passed the curve of the retaining wall before I picked my way gingerly between the *kressha* vines, wiped my soiled hands unceremoniously on my jumper, and tucked my breeze-blown hair behind my oversize Other ears that I might not miss a word.

I could not see had I dared to try: the wide stone sills were well above my head. Doubtless I could have scrambled up the rough-dressed masonry to peer in at the open casement, but I was not so foolhardy, Tagal's endorsement or no. Tagal was, after all, no longer here to vouch for me, and if he and my grandmother were at odds again, his patronage could only work to my detriment. Therefore I contented myself with skulking beneath the sill, identifying individual WiseOnes by their voices; I was good at that.

There was of course Loriel and, ever eager to contradict her, the physicist Govin, his voice a low counterpoint to her sharp-syllabled lilt. Between them in both voice and opinion was the philosopher Frayin. These I knew personally, from their frequent visits to Loriel or in the company of my father Evere. Also, Frayin's son Chior was my schoolmate, and fair to equal his mother's brilliance someday, though I found him a bore, and more close-minded than the average Other even at our age. That he was my personal nemesis need not be mentioned.

Of the seven remaining, six were only disembodied voices, some of which I might have recognized from visicomm, but to none of which I could attach a name. The tenth had not spoken at all; I knew him by his Silence.

(A Silence, in telepathic terms, is a projection of the Telepath's mind outward to touch upon any consenting mind within proximity. Its effects are various. Upon a group as contentious as these particular WiseOnes it had the effect—usually—of gathering the disparate minds into contingency, of balancing and tempering what might elsewise become an unDisciplined verbal brawl. Others may long have abandoned war but oh, how we relish argument, and unenvied is the Telepath who must be focus for any formal debate!)

Seldom were WiseOne and Telepath contained in the same individual. The two Disciplines were simply too divergent. Rarer still was it to find a Telepath under a hundred years in the role of Focus. But Lerius was all of this and more, which was the why of all that happened that day when I, literally pulled into the room by the mind of anOther . . .

*   *   *

But if I do not stop myself here, I shall use up every scrap of paper to be found on One Greater Isle and yet fail in my task. For still we do not see each other clearly, you and I. I have, as my grandmother would say, lost the point of the question. Or perhaps, being a chronicler, I have learned how many points a single question may possess, and know not which one will choose me. I will persist in my way rather than Gayat's (for a Telepath does not see as everyone else does, any more than does a chronicler) to find my path to truth.

Therefore I surmise you, reader, to be one of a possible three. Either you are among those beings—limbed or winged or pure intelligence—whom Loriel sought among the stars her life long. Or you are one of our own starsiblings, winnowed out of a great deal of bad poetry in the Legend and come searching, but too late. Or, strangest of all, you are not from offworld at all.

Let us postulate that this is your world and always has been, and you have thought your kind alone upon it. Perhaps some footnote in your written histories makes mention of a holy war fought against some vaguely identified but incontrovertibly evil race which was therein annihilated. Perhaps your folklore contains tales of strange and magical creatures who were not People after all, and who are now no more.

What is this, then, which you hold in your hand—fiction, false history, fairy tale? It is if nothing else a moral lesson upon the fate of the "different" in any world. But is it, as told by one who has said she cannot lie, a version of the truth?

——————

"The Unlikely Candidate"
(<i>Monograph, Rau Monitor:</i> T-Y1013,
Codex129147189)

Our technology and the long-standing use of gemstones in industry yield the axiom 'The gem which does not fit the machine may yet have its uses.' While the literal meaning was intended as an endorsement of the wearing of decorative jewels no longer garnered by slave labor, this writer suggests it may also possess a not-dissimilar metaphoric meaning. One is asked to recall the traditional figure of the Balance Mechanism, that part of a machine—or of a social order—which bridges two incompatible forces in order that they may function in harmony. For the societal model, this writer suggests the use of the term Unlikely Candidate.

What is the Unlikely Candidate? It is nothing more than the least likely become the most probable—the gem which does not fit the machine, the individual who does not 'fit' the social order we have established since the Thousand-Year. These include the poets, the dreamers, the solitaries, those who engage in powers of mind neither 'practical' nor telepathic and yet having uses, perhaps, which transcend both.

This writer suggests an innate predisposition which evidences itself, despite social disapprobation, in these non-pragmatic modes, often at a very early age. Those who possess it are not many, yet they must be heeded. Why so? Because while our kind professes to allow its members total freedom of expression within given societal parameters [emphasis mine], it is the very inhibition of those parameters which reduces all but the truly radical of heart to a relative degree of acquiescent uniformity. But what of those who cannot— as opposed to those who will not—fit within the parameters?

Perhaps the most noteworthy example from the Ancient Histories is Saretha the Warrior Queen, who slew her rival Somar only to find his soul thereby subsumed into and fused with hers. No need to recount the transformation of Saretha's life or how it was reflected in ours. To her we owe the first awareness of the Inscape, the refinement of the powers of Telepathy. Balance of the Telepathy, Mother of the Way, Saretha was what we were to become, even at the cost of her life.

A more recent but perhaps no less dramatic instance is that of the unnamed child who, in unwitting fusion with a Telepath, gave us the key to our evolution, which had baffled generation upon generation of scientists before . . .

Finally, what is one to make of this Unlikely Candidate? From a scientific viewpoint, she may be seen as some evolutionary mu-

21

tation, the causative factor which elevates the species to its next stage. From a philosophical perspective, she is once again the Balance Mechanism, necessary to bring about the reconciliation of opposites, lest they annihilate themselves. Never in our history have we needed such a figure more.

———

"On the Disposal of the NonPeople"
(*Official Orders of the People's Purist Prae-sidium: 1637–38*)
*****EYES ONLY*****

. . . using the very same machinery and methods they taught us, to free ourselves of them. This was to include a three-step plan:

One: *Contain*
Two: *Reduce*
Three: *Eliminate*

Step One proved the most costly and time-consuming, since it was necessary to run extensive compuscan on elements of population we had not anticipated in the initial set-up phase. Problem: How to recognize anOther? How to weed them out, in a manner that was cost-effective, without causing too much stress to the People?

Had it not been for the Anti-Comp Riots of '33, we could have cross-referenced all POB's and had done with it, but four years later we were still picking up the pieces from that, so Place of Birth was not a reference point we could use. There was the added problem of sabotage, the 'dumped' files and tapeworm programs discovered as late as this year. Getting at all of these Others was not going to be as easy as we'd initially thought.

Names were only sometimes helpful, especially with the fad in recent years among certain fatuous segments of our own population of giving Other names to their children. This practice is now pun-ishable by stiff fines or imprisonment, and changing the child's name is mandatory. Anyone with no declared religious affiliation could be brought in on suspicion at any time, and this netted us a few

22

surprises. We also used medical records, since blood type is the final racial discriminator, even when physical appearance can 'pass.' But since very few Others ever required our medical facilities except for accidents and emergencies, this turned out to be a small-scale and costly exercise.

Finally we had to resort to city-by-city and house-to-house searches, stopping suspected persons in the street and subjecting them to body searches, blood tests, and so forth. While this was also very costly and time-consuming, it had the advantage of scaring a number of them back to their islands, which saved us the later bother of transportation. So much for Step One.

Step Two was at first to consist of simple on-the-spot executions, following show-trials and a lot of public air time. This was done successfully in certain more remote areas, but since the majority of nonPeople infestations were in major urban areas, their out-of-hand execution could have caused protest or outright rioting in such a setting. There was the added complication of certain citizens who took it upon themselves to protect and conceal individual nonPeople and sometimes whole families. There was also the regrettable incident involving the Mayor of Grenni, who led his entire citizenry to appear in the streets wearing Othercodes on their outer garments in defiance of the Praesidium. Mayor Golav was subsequently impeached, and the ruling junta has rounded up and eliminated the organizers of this ludicrous display.

Finally it was decided, regardless of the cost, to enact Step Two by transporting the whole surviving population of Others back to their islands before the final phase could begin. Costs were offset by giving the crews of the transport vessels the freedom to appropriate any moveable goods remaining on the islands, thereby filling the elsewise empty holds for the return trip. Items including furniture and jewelry, clothing, machine and computer parts, industrial-grade gems, artworks, made up the bulk of these transports, and the profits from sales on our side were divided according to rank among the crews.

Step Three has not yet been implemented, the dispute being whether to actively exterminate them, or to simply cordon them off and let them starve.

The Guard now patrolling the perimeter of the Archipelago is confident of keeping their prisoners in and rescue or supply attempts out, but the continued cost of maintaining the Guard, weighed against the length of time it may take the nonPeople to die out of their own accord, seems to indicate the need for more definite action. There is also growing unrest among some citizens who feel that, as long as Others never return to our world, they should be left alone. Such recidivist thinking is dangerous, and it seems that some more immediate means must be found, and soon, to achieve our desired end.

two

I write in near-darkness, with a handful of the best styli, which I am told the Council has had reserved especially for my use in this time of shortages. When these fail, there are ten children's drawing charcoals, honed to something resembling fine points, though still they have a tendency to crumble. I write on the last known consignment of real paper to be found anywhere in the Citadel, on the backs of discarded printouts, and whatever scraps I have managed to forage in my run-to-ruin birthplace. In the end I suppose I shall be reduced to scratching on the walls with my fingernails. Where once I composed whole volumes directly into microstor, I am reduced to this.

Yet hand-writing was, after all, how I began as a child, too shamed by my untried poetry to request computer time for it. It is good once more to return to my beginnings, to feel the words as they drip like raindrops one by one from my fingertips.

I must not dwell upon the fact that every word I ever did

commit to storage was erased, along with the entire written history of Others, when the Purist Party's dictates brought our computers down for the final time. Who am I to mourn the loss of my scribblings when everything that we were, everything we knew, was lost in the indifferent flick of a power toggle? It has always been easier to destroy than to create, so the People thought.

They did not know or had forgotten that our Telepaths have eidetic memories, and that all of us are trained in the Mnemonic Discipline as soon as we can speak, so that long before the current crisis a process of "living storage" was begun. As long as there are Others, we shall have a history.

My works, of course, were never considered for such memorization, and only what my own flawed memory retains survives. Why? Because my works were always intermeshed with People's folklore and their almost-forgotten ancient tales. Hence People erased them solely because they had been composed by anOther, whereas Others, in a rare display of pettiness, deemed them unworthy of preservation because they originated with People. Hence Lingri becomes a controversy even in nonexistence.

Ironically, it was Dweneth who insisted over fifty years ago that I also have my books printed up *as* books—as old-fashioned, paper-paged, clothbound replicas of the treasured tomes she trundled halfway 'round the World in her battered Players' trunk when we both were scarcely children. Perhaps a stray copy or two of those books survives. I do not know.

The broth Gayat has so conscientiously brought me has long since grown cold and savorless. Nevertheless, I consume it, for it is as much my duty to eat as it is Gayat's to see that I am fed. My hands no longer tremble, and I have engaged a Discipline which does not allow for fatigue. In a windowless, featureless cell, the confines of which would drive most People mad, I am content. Perhaps I have become like those beings of pure brain which Loriel and I once conjured up between us. All that I have left, all that I require, exists inside my mind, waiting to course through my veins and drip from my fingertips. I write.

Above me the city is inordinately silent for a place where presently three times as many live as lived before, for all surviving Others dwell here now, driven back from the wide World and all our scattered Archipelago to be contained upon this One Greater Isle. We were never more than a million, and no one will tell me how many of these still live; I suspect it is but a fraction, and diminishing. Small wonder the introspective silence of we who survive. Sand blows unhindered down the empty ways which once were scrubbed daily and teemed with walkers passing to and fro on Other business. In the worst of our past it was never thus.

We have prepared ourselves to the best of our many abilities, combining our skills for the benefit of all. Whatever comes, it will be met with dignity and without despair.

While we have food, it will be distributed according to precise calculations of each individual's need, as based upon age, metabolism, and optimal caloric intake. While all may know hunger, as long as there is food none will starve.

Overcrowding, a serious consideration for those as in need of privacy as we, has been mitigated where possible by housing compatible personalities together, and by setting aside certain places in the labyrinth of the Citadel where each may find a time and place for solitude and meditation.

Wherever it is possible to retain our former way of life, we do so. Teachers and healers move among children and elders, their skills more needed than ever before. Whatever information we can glean about events transpiring beyond the Archipelago, from whatever sources—intercepted radio broadcasts, rumor among the sea-creatures—is quickly spread throughout the City and shared by all. All who are able labor to keep the City clean and in repair as conditions permit.

We who can see in all but total darkness can avoid the Guards' patrols and move about by night, though the cost upon detection is profound. Our days are filled with the sound of flyovers and the rumble of tanks knocking corners off of buildings as they pass. The Guard patrols on foot as well, smashing and desecrating, setting fires out of boredom. These forays are sporadic, and mostly the Guard remains aboard their ships; nevertheless, we remain watchful. They delight in urinating and defecating in the ways and in the common rooms of emptied dwellings. We ignore their actions, and clean up their messes when they have gone. This infuriates them.

We have restored the tradition of the Color Days, where as an expression of solidarity each individual wears some garment or badge of a specified color on a given day. It is a minor thing, but it strengthens us.

Though the Purists have placed an interdict upon any form of assembly, both the Telepathy and the Council of the Matriarchy continue to meet in secret in the hidden places of the Citadel. The Council's session is intended to weigh all means to preserve our bodies; the Telepathy labors to preserve our souls.

Lingri alone is alone most of the time, by decision of the Matriarchy, doing what it is she has done her lifelong—snatching words out of the air and affixing them to paper, on the possibly mad assumption that they will someday, somehow, be read.

Why Lingri? Why did not the Council (if not the Wise-Ones with their instruments for measuring almost anything, down to the proportion of brain cells given to deductive versus inductive reasoning versus creative thought) choose a more exemplary member of our society—a WiseOne, perhaps, or a Telepath? In this entire sea of stars, has there ever been a species beyond our own which presumes to calibrate creativity with a slide rule? Would any but anOther wish to do so? I sometimes think that we are not so much a species as an aberration, a perversity, and the universe will be better off after we are gone; however, these fits pass quickly. Why run one's finger down the list of possible candidates and choose me?

I hyperbolize, of course. There is no such list. Other mores preclude it. Others value each member of society equally, regardless of gifts . . . at least in theory. That as a child one may yet be subjected to the silent sneers of one's classmates is not indicative of an inherent viewpoint, regardless of the pain it may engender. And the Pain Discipline, after all, is among the first anOther child masters. But by any standard of Other perfectability, Lingri—dreamy, vague, and given to spilling things, poet born of a race of scientists—is truly not whom I would have chosen.

"Why not a WiseOne?" I demanded of the Matriarchs when I was informed of their decision, and again: "Why not a Telepath?"

I was being difficult and we all knew it; the reasons were manifest. WiseOnes speak and write in terms so cerebral it is questionable whether they themselves comprehend one another, and some like old Tagal live lives more cloistered than the most solitary of Solitaries, so absorbed are they in their work. A WiseOne's perspective is too specialized, and will not serve.

As to Telepaths, I never yet encountered one who could compose a coherent sentence; many of the deeper ones can barely speak. These abilities have atrophied in them for lack of use. Those who can fly aloft on the complexities of thought find little merit in encumbering themselves with words. If a WiseOne's perspective is too narrow, a Telepath's is too broad to be contained within the confines of a chronicle.

(As a psi-passive classified nonTelepath—one who can receive only from a trained mind and send sporadically and with rare success—I am in no position to judge a Telepath, though perhaps to a degree I can understand. I am a qualified *bRi*-speaker, one of the last among us who can commune with those winsome proto-intelligent creatures who inhabit our seas and were once mistaken for our evolutionary ancestors. The sheer delight to be found in their tumbling, exuberant, syntaxless tongues exists in no air-swimmer's language. The danger of too-long contact with *bRi* is in that very delight; one is loath to reburden oneself with one's accustomed grammars thereafter. Perhaps I can comprehend a Telepath's incoherence after all.)

In my opinion the ideal chronicler would be a glass, possessing neither tint nor color, translucent if not transparent, that her story might shine through her unimpeded. Else she would be a mirror, so hard and polished and without flaw that her story would reflect back at its reader, lucid and lacking ripple or defect from the instrument which reveals it.

Instead, by order of the Council of the Matriarchy, she is Lingri—imperfect glass, defective mirror, but the chosen instrument nevertheless.

"It is hoped," WiseJisra Matriarch said to me, having charged me with this duty, "that your chronicle will reflect all that you came to know of People, offered without bias."

"Without bias?" The phrase almost causes me to stalk out of the Council chamber, refuse the commission. The People have robbed me of my consort, my child, every elder I ever knew, and my dearest friend. How, then, without bias? Is it bias to alter one's opinion in the light of changing conditions? I am being tested, and I know it. On the brink of annihilation, and after all these years, my own are skeptical of me still.

The Council, in choosing me, deemed me "most suitable." This is both truth and irony. Neither WiseOne nor Matriarch, neither Telepath nor teacher nor healer can be spared from the essential tasks of our survival, and I am none of these. Being the least useful, I become of the greatest use. My teacher Rau would have been delighted; I am his Unlikely Candidate yet again.

If it is not yet obvious that there are as many opinions as there are Others to possess them, I state it here. It is a compounding of our tragedy that as our numbers decrease, so do our opinions and our diversity.

*   *   *

Rau was my teacher, because I chose him. Tutors may be chosen for one in childhood, but with adulthood and the choice of profession, one's teachers are one's own to choose. It was Rau who took Tagal's weed-pulling urchin and transformed her into his emissary to the People. I came to him in my seventeenth year, my general degrees in hand, having postponed as long as possible a choice offered me in the garden of the observatory seven years before.

I had of course researched Rau thoroughly, gaining access to the Inner Archives, where I spent the greater part of two days scanning the qualify-files of all rated teachers in all areas of study, eliminating any who were too specialized or whose credentials were too intimidating. Only Rau seemed to precisely fit my needs. His only failing was in making his residence on one of the more remote outislands.

I made the journey in Jeijinn's skimmer; being as yet unprofessed I was not entitled to one of my own. First the spires and domes of the City, then the gently undulating suburbs of One Greater fell away beneath me, followed by the strait separating One Greater from Three Greater Isle and the scattered panorama of the Lessers. Some of these were no more than a reef or sandbar where even a solitary could not subsist; the rest were the rich foliage-clad cones of dormant volcanoes, the patchwork flatlands of the Agriculturals, the high Otherbuilt crags of the Industrials.

Banking to sunward, the skimmer passed over a great stretch of open sea, where *bRi* greeted its shadow with their frolics. Unable to contain my delight—I had never seen so many at once, and I was alone; who would reprove my unDiscipline?— I lowered the windscreen and shouted greetings to them. We exchanged pleasantries, and the *bRi* escorted me as far as their attention warranted, abandoning me at last as I neared the Outers.

Rau's tiny island might have been deserted. Except for the smooth-pebbled shingle where I set the skimmer down, the rain forest marched unbroken to the water's edge and I, urban

31

dweller accustomed to the more controlled and temperate climate of One Greater, acknowledged the tropical closeness of the air with some misgivings. If Rau and I proved compatible, I would have to live here for two years or more. But I must not anticipate what might not come to be.

He was there suddenly, among the trees, as he had not been when I first arrived, his hand-dyed garb blending with dappled shadows so that even my Other eyes had difficulty discerning him. I waited. Protocol dictated he was to come to me.

I watched as he made his sure-footed way down the shingle, bemused at the sight of him; he did not appear at all as the dignified teacher I had envisioned. The hand-sewn garments I had expected, as I did the full black beard in People's fashion, where most Other males were clean shaven. But Rau also varied considerably from the physical norm for our species, being short and stocky where most Others tend toward ectomorphy. This was a favorite topic for his irony.

"I am a throwback," he would claim, "or else a leap forward. A more practical adaptation to this world, which is undoubtedly quite different from the one whence we came."

Rau also subscribed to Liiki's scientific interpretation of the Legend, which was one of the several reasons I had selected him.

"A throwback," he would say. "As you are, sea-eyes."

It is a fact that most but not all Others are dark-eyed, as most are tall and thin and sallow and one in four has webbed toes, and more than half have tapered rather than rounded ears, but except for the last two, we share most of our outward characteristics with many People and, among them, we were often taken for Zanti or Tawa or even Lamorak.

Regardless, the Purist Party has codified these general characteristics into a racial "type" whereby they claim to be able to detect interbreeding, which is now a capital crime. In the early days of the dictates, many fullblooded People were rounded up and subjected to their so-named "purity tests," while a number of Others and the few rare Intermixes who did not fit the "type" were let slip. My sea-colored eyes granted me immunity until the final days, when my notoriety ran before me and my holograph graced every crossroads and comm-screen, whereas Joreth my son, whose blood tested "pure," may never have been discovered at all. But even this I do not know.

"Best the lot of us could do!" Dweneth Healer announced gruffly, settling Joreth's newness into the crook of my arm, naked, wet and slippery from the birthing-bath, tucking the drying-cloth absently about his robust, finicking limbs. "There's a great deal of effort vested in this lad; don't you forget it!"

"Beyond my own?" I asked her dryly; it had not been an easy birth. "I shall keep it in mind!"

His bud-mouth searched instinctively and I gave, watched won-deringly as he seized the breast hard and suckled, a look of the most extraordinary surprise on his small face. Was the taste as good as all that? What had he to compare it with? The face was a miniature of his father's, his grandsire's, but nothing of mine.

"I know," Dweneth answered what I had not asked, running one hand through her tousled curls, which the surgical cap always flattened. "Splicing's still tricky, for all the years we've been at it. Your man's of a fierce-resilient gene-pool; yours proved the more vulnerable in the grafting. So the son's a replica of his father—People inside and out, but for one tiny detail."

I had noticed Joreth's ears by not noticing them, until Dweneth allowed her fingers to trace their shape. They were as they should be, folded down like a pup's to protect his acute Other hearing at first; within a day or two they would unfurl to their normal shape like the petals of some exotic flower. Then it struck me. People's ears were not so. By his ears, at least, my son was Other.

"As to strength and gifts and lifespan . . ." I began. We had researched this, his now-absent father and I, using the limited sample of previous intermix birthings, before we dared this venture.

"He'll be no more Telepath than his mother," Dweneth replied ironically. "But as strong and, if possible, as stubborn. And like to live as long."

Her healer's hand rested lovingly on the small head; a single drop of perspiration fell from her brow to his in benediction. Joreth's vigorous sucking ceased, his father's green eyes questioned this new sensation, until the greater need took precedence and he resumed.

I dared not look at Dweneth; she was long past childbearing for her species, and there had never been time nor proper circumstance. I felt rather than saw her eyes brim with tears, and could not speak.

"You two can manage without me from here on!" Her voice was gruffer than before, and she turned away.

I fought the urge to follow her, to place my son into her empty arms. Was he not as much hers as mine? A great deal of effort, indeed.

As I watched my would-be teacher surefoot along the shingle toward me, something fluttered suddenly across my vision like a pain-colored silk, to catch on some snag in my brain and hold there for an instant before vanishing.

Was it some presentiment of a life entangled with People's— of friendship and sharing the wonders of the World, of music and the affairs of rulers, of passion and a two-breed son— ripped finally from the roots like a *gli*flower and left to ignominious waiting, winding down to death? Or was it a backward flash—imperfect recollection of an unkempt child screaming inchoate poetry before an assembly of WiseOnes, anchoring her fate in the past of Legend and hurling it forward into the future?

Was it at least a warning—to abandon what I was about to do, clamber back into the skimmer and flee before it was too late, choose some less harrowing life, if only that of a beachcombing solitary, as unconcerned with time and responsibility as the *bRi* who would companion me?

In truth, how could I? Written in inevitability before my birth was the People's lust for territory, a curiosity as insatiable as our own, a need to explore and push outward in their lumbering sailships toward the far horizon. Was I to wait, passive, while the People came to me? Or could I act, do something—not to postpone the inevitable, but to make it somehow more bearable for both sides?

Perhaps this was presumptuous, but if Others as a species are perverse, I was no exception. The very difficulty of a task has always drawn me; it is why I am a chronicler. In the time it took Rau to cross that small stretch of beach I was committed. The possibility that Rau might not accept me, or I him, did not occur to me.

"The skimmer is not yours." Statement, not question, and the only greeting he was to give me.

"It is Jei— my mother's."

"I see," was all Rau said. Who my mother might or might not be was of no consequence to him.

He motioned me to follow him. It was far cooler in among the trees than upon the open beach. The distant sound of a cataract grew ever louder as we followed the island's only stream to its source, and my first question would have been why Rau had chosen a place of such tumult, regardless of its pristine beauty, in which to set up his academy. For as such I took the replica of one of the poorest of People's dwellings, exact in every detail and abutting the very rock face from which the waterfall issued, to be.

"Because noise is endemic to the People," Rau addressed my puzzlement. "Inure yourself to that, and you have a beginning."

I followed him into the hut through its low, hide-covered doorway, as Rau explained that the "hide," as well as every article which appeared to be made of some animal product— the "furs" on the sleeping platform, the "bone"-handled cooking knives—was synthesized.

"But among People, one uses what People use." He watched me closely, to see if I would demur at this violation of our most basic Disciplines.

"But surely one cannot acquiesce to the eating of animal flesh?" I blurted. Rau was quick.

"How would you reconcile it?"

35

I considered the Alimentary Discipline: "Take for sustenance no more nor less than will best maintain life and health. Seek that which is simple before that which is complex, and take not animal life except to save your own."

I weighed this against what I knew of People's culinary habits, which were largely dependent upon the flesh of animals even, if they happened upon one sick or wounded close to shore, the skinned carcasses of our precious *bRi*. Surely one need not acquiesce to such customs in order to pass among People? What of the tribes in more remote regions that engaged in ritual feasting upon the flesh of conquered enemies?

". . . who would slay you for refusing their hospitality," Rau interjected mildly, following my thoughts, "and when they saw that your blood was not like theirs, would drink it and ingest your heart in order to possess your 'magic' . . ."

He had begun to lay a peat fire in the center of the hut's beaten floor, beneath a crude smokehole in the thatched roof. For the first time I truly understood the statistics on death by fire I had studied before coming here. This peat fire was the only source of heat or light in the hut's single room, though in my observation it yielded more smoke than either.

". . . though I did not have it in mind to send you among those in particular."

He spoke as if I had already accepted him as my teacher, and I would be halfway home to One Greater that night before I realized that I had. His eyes sparkled at me not unlike Loriel's, and I knew he was playing at ironies.

"Wherever you assigned me," I replied with the stiff seriousness of youth, "it would surely be possible to subsist on the native vegetation, roots and berries; I have passed my Survival Year. I believe I am capable of resolving such a difficulty as it arises."

"And if your hosts are offended at your refusal to share their cuisine?"

I thought hard. I had had answers to all of this when I'd left One Greater with the dawn; they seemed to have abandoned me here.

"I would say it was a . . . religious taboo," I suggested, rather impressed with my own cleverness. "That I have no religion as People understand it would qualify as truth unspoken, would it not?"

Rau brushed the dried moss from his hands and sat back on his heels to contemplate me.

"Excellent, to a point." He produced a fire-starter from its ornate box and worked it over the heap of moss. "And if they insisted upon converting you to *their* religion?"

He had me there. However opinionated, no Other would resort to such coercion, enforced by violence as Rau was suggesting. Research and theory were not enough; I must learn to think as People.

"One presumes I am here that you might instruct me in such nuances, Rau-*al* . . ."

"Before you presume anything—" His manner changed abruptly, like cloud across sun. It startled me. Other mood changes are subtle, when they are apparent at all. "—condition yourself on this valuable point: there are no titles here. I am Rau and you are Lingri, that is all. Unlearn Other respects, and you will be prepared to master People's."

"*If* I choose you, *Rau*." I matched my tone to his. "I have not decided that as yet."

"In fact, you have." He sparked the fire into sullen smokiness at last and turned the topic, giving me no chance to argue. "How many languages have you?"

"Four," I blurted, wishing I had not let this slip so easily. Rau knew of my two generalist degrees—the least gifted could achieve that much by my age—but I had hoped to save the linguistics degree as a kind of leverage.

"And they are— ?"

"Gleris Scholars' Written, Intertribe Trade Patois, Hraregh Dialect—Windward accent—and Werthan semi-literate," I recited breathlessly, as if any one of these had not cost me hours of painful study. "I had thought in light of their being the most widely used . . ."

"Good," Rau said, giving the word no more inflection than

37

a grunt. I realized he had spoken it in Hraregh, and that his accent was considerably better than mine for all my pains. "Before the year is out you will also master Droghian, Lamorak, and Mantuul spoken and written."

"Of course," I replied carefully, also in Hraregh and for the first time beyond a linguistics laboratory. Again the implication that I had already accepted him. We should see.

As I recall, we never spoke in anOther tongue after that day, but passed among all of the People's tongues we knew between us, according to which study we undertook on a given day and Rau's assessment of my need for greater proficiency. In fact I did master Droghian and Mantuul as well as the tongue-twisting Lamorak, with some Kwengii swear-words for seasoning, to see if my seeming-omniscient teacher could be surprised. He could.

But this was future unwritten as I sat questioning Rau before the peat fire, my eyes streaming from the smoke, the unceasing din of the cataract outside penetrating my very bones. I might have been prepared to accept him from the beginning, but Rau was less prepared to receive me. He was to dismiss me that first day—arbitrarily, I thought, and without appeal.

What did I need to know about Rau that his credentials did not already tell me? It was my right to interview him first, but I already had my answers. That he possessed all of the generalist degrees, had spent a certain period of time among the Telepaths and a further time among the *bRi*, that he had been a Monitor himself for twenty years before presuming to teach, were well known to me. That he was the author of several monographs, including the definitive study on prisons and torture in the Shadoward Quadrant and the theory of the Unlikely Candidate, indicated that he could teach me what I required. What more was I to ask? I confined my interview to general questions regarding the customs of the various tribes

Rau had lived among. At last, my throat constricted to a whisper by the smoke, I fell silent.

"Have you finished so readily?" Rau's voice held a twinkle, as did his eyes. The Disciplines always sat lightly on Rau; I was never to know if this was some residual of his life among People or something intrinsic to his nature. "Have you no curiosity about my teaching methods? How I manage to infiltrate my Monitors so that they go undetected? How they master truth-seeming-untruth for the sake of their lives? None of this?"

"All of your Monitors have lived to tell the tale." I knew this from the Archives. "I am content with that."

Rau grunted and served up two portions of something he had been concocting in an iron pot on a trivet over the fire while we talked. What his cooking lacked in appearance it possessed in flavor, and I said as much.

"From Llellaar Province," he informed me. "Certain of its religious cults are vegan. In times past some Monitors used this as their argument for shunning animal flesh."

"Then I shall use it also," I said with a confidence I did not necessarily possess. He might have told me this from the beginning.

"Dubious," Rau said mildly, concentrating on his food. "The cults have since fallen under interdict and most of their followers have been put to death."

Death, as I had discovered time and again in my preliminary research, seemed more important to People than life. But Rau's playing at ironies was growing wearisome, and I was tired of being tested.

"Shall we proceed with the interview?"

"Momentarily," he replied, gathering up the bowls and utensils and going to wash them in the stream.

This hiatus was as deliberate as all his actions thus far, and I took advantage of it to sit quite still, my eyes taking in whatever details of my surroundings I had not noticed before. This single room with its smoke-stained rafters, wattle and daub walls, and the worn, handcrafted artifacts, fitted everything our records, pieced together from the memories of perhaps a thousand Monitors, contained about the lives of those People who inhabited what we called the Shadoward Quadrant, where most Monitors were infiltrated. Why would anOther choose to live in this primitive manner in the between-times when he had no acolytes?

I wondered if there might be some special object, some unique memory-piece, which I might bring back with me to add to his store.

I would take with me neither recording device nor any manner of sophisticated Other equipment. It was not that we feared People's using such devices to harm us, but that the devices' alien strangeness might serve to confuse and frighten them. Monitors made their crossover into the People's world with only the clothes they wore and whatever could be contained within the confines of the mind.

Was my mind strong enough, my memory accurate enough, to serve this purpose?

There was that flash of warning again. Why must I persist in this? What perversity had caused me to choose, of all teachers, the author of the Unlikely Candidate?

For I had not needed to read Rau's monograph. I knew all there was to know about the Unlikely Candidate—the name of the child, and of the Telepath, the details of the event which once and for all had hurled Legat's Parallel back into the sea from which it had sprung, and gave us back our place among the children of the stars.

When he returned from his mundane chore, Rau's first question would no doubt be precisely why I wished to be a Monitor. Truthfully, how was I to answer him?

"*. . . a being such as you describe would have in ancient times been called a poet . . .*"

I was hearing voices again; this one had belonged to my second-level tutor.

"*. . . there are none such now. Poetry dwells too near the negative* *passions; it is no longer practiced openly. Those whose gift it is to write become instead archivists, essayists, chroniclers . . ."*

So preoccupied was I, Lingri Dreamer, that I did not hear Rau return—could not have, at any rate, above the roar of the cataract—looked up to see his short, round figure casting shadows over me from the doorway in the elongating rays of the setting sun. Whatever was to happen would happen now.

"Shall we proceed?"

With a gesture he led me outside where the light was stronger; I was grateful for the freshness of the air. A soft mist rose from the cataract and hung about the trees, and the noise of rushing water permeated everything.

"It will be necessary for me to examine you." He drew quite close to me for the first time, and I realized how much shorter he was than I, who am of only average height for a female of my kind. No questions, then? Only this? "Sometimes a simple physical anomaly can mark one as anOther. We dare not take that chance. I am celibate; you need have no concern."

No female of my species need fear sexual coercion from one of her own, and my age alone would indicate my unbonded, hence sacrosanct, status. As a celibate, Rau could suppress whatever ordinary sensual impulses might pass between us in the simple contact of fingers upon flesh. I acknowledged his disclosure, and began to undress.

First the boots. Webfeet are an immediate indication of Otherness. Fortunately, I did not follow the maternal webfoot line.

"You are nonTelepath?" Rau inquired softly as I worked the fastenings of my outer garments; his hands were thrust deep into his sleeves.

"Yes."

This pleased him. "Some will train a Telepath, but I will not. The dangers are too great, for all concerned."

"I understand," I said, and stood naked before him.

What did he see in this figure of an adolescent female, tall and slender like most of her kind, unremarkable either for

41

beauty or the lack of it, as free of physical flaw as advanced genetics and optimum nutrition and fitness regimens made possible? There is no shame in nakedness as Other knows it. My body, as yet undriven by any mating urge, passive beneath a celibate's clinical eye, was but a tool, a means to an end. If to People's eyes this scene beneath the mist-shrouded trees in fading sunlight held some erotic content, it did not for Rau nor me.

"It will be necessary for me to touch you," he said at last. Other does not touch anOther without permission, a consequence both of our Telepathy and our sense of privacy.

"As you wish," I replied, wondering if this, as all else in this place, were some manner of test. Females among People were frequently subjected to unsolicited hands; I must be prepared for this.

But Rau only examined the capillaries under my eyelids, where the different hue of Otherblood is most apparent.

"One must under all circumstances avoid leeching or bloodletting, as well as any attempt to examine the eyes," he said.

The light was almost gone, the twilit air chilling to unshielded flesh. I found my voice. "Assuming that is always possible."

"One must *make* it possible," Rau said evenly, and at the last moved to sweep my hair back from my ears.

A flicker of disappointment flashed across his eyes. I have unmistakably Other ears, and had kept them hidden beneath my waist-length hair in the spurious hope Rau would accept me on merit before they came to his attention.

"Unfortunate." He let my hair fall over my shoulders and disappeared into the hut.

"I can wear my hair down over them!" I called after him above the cataract, scrambling into my clothes, feeling suddenly more than naked. "Rau, if necessary I will have them altered!"

That brought him back through the doorflap, knife blades in his glance.

"Never!" he shouted. I had never heard anOther shout.

"That much is not necessary! You are anOther, always, regardless of the way that chooses you!"

A wiser individual would have known then that it was over, would have put on her boots and found her way back to the skimmer in the sudden dark, followed the *bRi* back to One Greater and returned to the Archives, either in search of a different teacher or of a different way. But I was not so-named Lingri Inept for nothing. I carried my boots in my hand, stumbling in my haste.

Rau was engrossed in rebuilding the fire, measuring the leaves of some fragrant herb into a tea-warmer; the aroma greeted me above the now-familiar stench of smoke. I stood in the doorway, letting the flap fall behind me, awaiting some acknowledgment. Rau was as oblivious as if some insect had blundered in to flutter about the fire. More, for he would have caught an insect and released it outside to prevent its immolating itself. I did not merit even this much attention.

"If it is only because of my ears . . ." I began.

Rau set down the tea-warmer and tucked his rough-cropped hair behind his own ears, which were if possible more Other than mine.

"It was a test, then. When I spoke of having them altered, it was only to emphasize the importance this holds for me. I will do whatever is necessary, for to become a Monitor is something I *must* do."

"All who seek a teacher are driven by what they *must* do, Lingri-*la*," Rau replied, and with his use of the respect I realized the interview was over. "It is always thus when one of your youth and advantage deliberately seeks so inhospitable a way. Doubtless there are teachers who will provide what you seek, but I can teach you nothing."

———

"Anticipations and Prognostications"
(Essay, WiseRavaine Healer: *Xeno-PsychNet*, T-Y1017, encoded)

43

... *The greatest of their distresses will not be their terror of our science and devices, for though these things will terrify at first, they will in time be assimilated as a kind of magic no stranger than the many magicks which are the People's everyday fare. To beings for whom so much of life is mystery unexaminable, either due to lack of information or technology wherewith to acquire it, or owing to religious taboo, such things are more common than we can properly comprehend.*

The "magic" of visicomm, of holography, of vehicles which run of their own with no beasts to pull them, will be ascribed to mysteries no more frightening than those of conjuring or spell-casting or the effects of aphrodisiacs, and our newfound visitors will adopt the use of these "toys" without properly mastering them or wishing to know why they do what they do. The "magic" of telepathy will in time seem no more alien to them than dream-reading or future-telling, practices widespread among them, and will be accepted with as varying degrees of credulity. Rather, what will terrify them, perhaps irremediably, will be the cultural and ethnological "magicks."

Why will we defy the "normal" course of things, and persist in living so much longer than they? Why will we persist in abnegating those very societal trappings which they insist are the only valid definition of a "true man"? That we have neither gods nor lawyers, soldiers nor clergy, kings nor tax-collectors, that we require neither coinage nor price-fixing on goods, that we refuse to brutalize each Other in the name of sport, that we neither covet our neighbor's consort nor her goods, will at first baffle, and finally enrage them.

Because they cannot see the Inscape which rules us, they will assume us lacking in structure, and this very seeming anarchy will so threaten their own structures that they will no longer be able to endure us. Our very existence will seem to them a mockery of their strictures and their curfews, their laws for the sake of laws. However strange each of them may seem to their neighbors, they will find us the stranger, and they will be forced, instinctively and morally, to turn on us.

As to how their abrasive, unsubtle People's consciousness will impact upon the integrity of Othermind, only time will answer this ...

three

Whether I managed to salvage some dignity in my departure from Rau's island, or simply bolted through the dark wood to the skimmer, slamming the hatch against the roar of the cataract, which still lingered in my ears, if only metaphorically, I do not now recall. Some instinct on my journey here had caused me to store the route in the skimmer's memory so that it could find its own way back to One Greater. My eyes could not be trusted on this journey; they were too filled with tears.

AnOther's mask does not eliminate emotion—to do so results in psychosis; it has been tried. It merely discourages its expression. It is truth unspoken that, alone and unobserved, one's emotions are one's own. Therefore, alone in the skimmer with none to witness, I wept—bitterly, blindly, childishly. As I understood what had just transpired, I had conclusively become what in my society theoretically did not exist: a failure. Worse, I did not even know why.

In such condition I dared not subject myself to Jeijinn's scrutiny; I left the skimmer in its underground bay and set

45

my feet upon the ways—to Loriel's, I thought at first and then, rethinking, decided my fragile Discipline could not withstand her irony this night. Instead I walked the long way around to the interisland telfer terminal.

The night deepened. Others were at late-meal in the soft glow of light behind the privacy screens. I was on my way to the Industrials. A failure I might be, but I could still call upon my father.

Life on the Industrials flowed along continuously overlapping workshifts, where each scientist and technician worked according to her own innate diurnal rhythms. My father, Evere, was nocturnal by inclination, yet one more factor which had driven him and Jeijinn apart after the brief and preoccupied bonding which had produced me. Likely his day would be beginning when I arrived, though the night was nearly over.

Thus I did not stop at his dwelling—he was rarely there anyway—but went directly to his workstation in the complex built into the side of one of the volcanoes harnessed to utilize its power, confident I would find him there.

Possibly the most gifted computertronics expert of his generation, though Others do not subscribe to the use of such superlatives, Evere had a single failing—a total inability to be taken seriously by his womenfolk. It was one of Loriel's favorite ironies, which had the effect of rendering Jeijinn quite livid, that Evere could hardly be responsible for my upbringing, having sired me, no doubt, during a fit of absent-mindedness.

My growing years had been divided between Jeijinn and Loriel, with little recourse to Evere in his hermitage, because as Jeijinn put it, "Unlike your father, I occasionally remember to feed you!"

To call Evere vague was to be imprecise. He was never vague in the manner in which his sole offspring is habitually credited with vagueness, and he could never be called inept. His reputation for precision was such that a discrepancy between his calculations and the computer's was invariably deemed the computer's error. Evere's difficulty, if you will, was more the difficulty Jeijinn and her ilk had with him than he with them: an inability to accept as reality any life which transpired beyond his computer screen.

I found him, not surprisingly, at his console, lost in some problem so complex I could not have begun to ascertain its nature. He had not changed unduly in the however-long it had been since last I came here. Perhaps he was thinner, more unkempt. His colleagues looked after him where they could, but he resisted their efforts by simply failing to notice them. His workstation was walled-around with the remains of meals unfinished, of projects pending or half-begun. There was a pallor on him, as if it were long since he had seen the natural light of day. The radiation burn down one side of his neck was more vivid than ever.

The scar was a curious relic of Evere's only act of heroism beyond the confines of a computer. The volcano harness had malfunctioned during a children's tour of the facilities; Evere had rescued several from the vicinity of the malfunction before the seal ruptured, spattering him with a minuscule amount of cooling lava.

"Sufficient," the healer who had treated my father remarked, "to sear flesh without reaching bone. WiseEvere was fortunate."

He could have had the scar healed or surgically removed, but strangely chose to retain it; I would catch him fingering it idly while he waited for his computer to catch up with him, as if it helped fix him to reality.

"You are, as always, pleasing to the eye," my father greeted me at last, embracing me with words as he could in no more conventional way. I had stood beside his console for nearly twenty minutes before he chanced to notice me.

In anyone else the statement would have been unvarnished irony. Between my travels and my tears I was nothing appealing, and more than one Other had chosen not to see me on the telfer journey. But Evere was incapable of irony; he meant precisely what he said.

("What he meant, idiot," Dweneth would chide me down the years, "was that he loved you, and the sight of you pleased him no matter what. But your kind is too perverse to say it plain!")

". . . yet I sense portentousness," my father observed, studying me thoughtfully. "You have something to tell me?"

He actually logged off and shut down his terminal completely, something he had never before done in my presence. Throughout my childhood he had offered me what attentiveness he could by stopping his work onscreen, but having it hover there in the corner of my eye had always hastened my narrative, garbled my intent, and threatened my Discipline. For the very first time no ghostly unfinished project intervened between us, and I began to weave my tale of failure until . . .

Until the chair I sat in, indistinguishable from the thousand like it in the complex, became an alien thing, and only Discipline prevented me leaping from it to sit crosslegged, like Rau, on the floor. And why, when I stopped speaking—no doubt in midsentence—and Evere tried to offer what counsel he could, did his words become meaningless? Or, rather, so fraught with a multiplicity of meanings that it was as if I were mentally linguanalyzing each individual phoneme, as I had in wrestling with People's syntaxes in preparation for my now-forbidden way?

There was no mystery in the stench of peat smoke lingering in my nostrils as on my person; I had brought it with me from Rau's hut. But by what illusion did I still hear the hoarse insistence of the cataract in this sterile, ordered room, where even the sound of the volcano's great heart was muted and only the computers hummed? And why, when I contemplated my father's flawed, familiar face, did I desire nothing more than to touch him—most unDisciplined, most unOther—to trace the ragged line of that scar as I had not done since . . .

Remembering when my father and I had last touched caused me to rise abruptly from that alien chair, to flee that ordered, sterile room, blundering as usual.

"Evere-*al,* Father, forgive me, but I must . . ."
In my haste I could say no more.

I returned to Rau's island with the sun and the *bRi.*

What I should have done, what any Other would have done, was to return to the telfer station and the tedious journey back to One Greater, there to retrieve Jeijinn's skimmer and retrace my route to Rau a second time. But I had need of sky and air and a beach to walk on before my second journey. Rau would accept me this time; he *must.*

The largest of our islands is not so vast that one cannot walk shore to shore within a day; I sometimes wonder if the constancy of such an insular existence has not shaped our Discipline overmuch. The yellow-pink suffusion of false dawn deluded the eye at the horizon as I stood at the tidal line; a queasy phosphorescence encrusted the tops of the waves, captivating, and a poem began to take shape in my mind, tucked away safe for later. I walked to the end of the jetty, thinking: I could all but walk to Rau's island, so great was my need. The thought must have projected; suddenly I was not alone.

"It's wanting . . ." observed a high-pitched sibilance at my feet. ". . . it's not asking . . . am I offering?"

bRi. I clambered down the rocks and stood waist-deep in the water to greet her. From childhood these creatures had companioned my solitary beach-walks, knowing me a speaker; their presence was often far less taxing than that of my own kind.

"It's wanting . . ." the *bRi* repeated; I wondered what she was doing here alone, this close to shore, without her podkin. She nudged me backward to indicate she would have me sit on the jetty, heaved her great body partway out of the water so that her kelplike mane trailed over my feet. Her huge head rested so lightly on my knees that I might not have known she was twenty times my weight.

"*bRi*-friend," I trilled, stroking her bloodwarm, green-gold flank in *bRi*-courtesy, "how know you what this one wants?"

49

"It looks adown the ways," the *bRi* explained. To her the sea was a map of crisscrossed ways, primevally knowable, that we poor airswimmers could not see. "There is wanting in its gaze. It is a distance?"

AnOther never asks a favor directly, as *bRi* never offer one. But if I could make my need clear in such a way that it suited the *bRi*'s purposes, she would assist me in whatever way she could.

"It is a distance, *bRi*-friend," I acknowledged, saying no more. It piqued her curiosity.

"Tell me!" she trilled.

I did.

"Good feeding there is . . ." she mused, as if the venture were her own idea, and swung her great head off my knees, nodding her pleasure at it.

Thus I came to journey over the sea astride her broad, salt-slick back, my hands entwined in her sluicing mane, my knees gripping her untiring flanks until I was beyond fatigue. Numb with cold and streaming wet, tumbling off more than once when the *bRi* in playfulness encountered pod-kin and forgot me, cavorting with her huge brethren until she might have crushed me had I not mastered her choreography and learned to move with it, I endured. Toward the last we were escorted by two companion males, flanking us in golden shimmering dance over waves long since spangled bright with sunlight.

They left me, depositing me as gently as a newborn on the very shingle where the treadmarks of Jeijinn's skimmer were still discernible. Sunblind, drenched, nearly paralyzed with fatigue having eaten but once and slept not at all in a world's turning, I lay on the warming, brittle rock, gathering strength sufficient to walk inland.

Did Rau watch me all that time? It did not matter. I was to learn that my teacher could watch within a certain distance whether he was physically present or not. Doubtless no one, not Rau himself, ever knew the full extent of his gifts.

He showed no surprise when this object vomited up from the sea swept aside the doorflap as he was making firstmeal, only offered me tea and some porridgy concoction as nondescript as yesterday's.

"There is something I must tell you," I announced after three cups of tea and the retreat of numbness from my extremities. "It may cause you to rethink your decision."

Rau responded to that by reaching up to a cache in the rafters where he kept his own rough clothes, tossing some down to me. Without ceremony I stripped off my own sodden things and selected what would fit, wishing I had left my boots behind to spare them water-ruin, and tied the rough-spun tunic tighter at the waist than ever Rau could. The gesture amused him; he poured us both more tea.

"I seldom rethink. Nevertheless, tell me."

I began the tale of a child and an old one in a garden of the observatory, of a conference and an open casement and the irresistible pull of a Telepath's Silence and, out of these disparate elements, an event worthy of a monograph.

One moment I was standing ankle-deep in *gli*flowers beneath the windows of the observatory, wondering in the wake of WiseTagal's departure whether I dared eavesdrop as he had urged me upon the debate within. The next I was clinging to the broad stone sill, my bare toes dug into the mortar as I listened with every atom of my being. Never had I heard a debate so fervid among my own.

(It was within my lifetime that our ethnological referents began to alter, to divide the inhabitants of the World into *us* and *them,* and a creeping apprehension began to trickle down to all levels of our society. Visicomm and the infonets carried it like static; Jeijinn my mother often brought it home with her from Council meetings, permeating the fabric of her being. All our lives were now lived in its shadow. No gathering of Others, however informal, could avoid some mention of the time when *they* would come, and of how we were to meet them when they did. Here, among the WiseOnes, whose recommendations, when they were listened to, would influence the Matriarchy's decisions, the debate was feverish.)

51

". . . the People are violent," the Philosopher Frayin stated the obvious in her rich contralto voice. I could see her kneeling in the light from the open casements, her person softened about the edges where it melded with the thought that consumed her; it made her beautiful. "We have cast aside the ways of violence for more than a thousand years. Are we to take them up again? How, and retain what we are?"

"How not, and preserve what we are?" countered one whose face I did not recognize but, from his tone and demeanor, no doubt a former Matriarch. "If we are no more, what are we?"

Our Discipline had never precluded defense of self, and every Other was schooled in the protective arts from childhood, though only very young children presumed or were permitted to lay hands upon each Other. But did this by extension permit us to defend ourselves as a species?

". . . with hands and bodies alone, or with weapons, and if with weapons, of what sort and limitation . . . ?"

". . . we have never before now been threatened with invasion, conquest, or death at the hands of a little-understood adversary. The question cannot be answered in the abstract, and no one of us has had need to confront it in the concrete. This is our greatest vulnerability . . ."

"By what right do we defend our place in a world which is not our own?" Loriel demanded, as she had since before I was born, bringing the debate back to its point of origin, which was our very lack of one. Had we evolved, as Legat's Parallel postulated, from the seas of this world, or had we been brought here on the wings of Legend?

"In the Beginning was the One . . ." the Legend began, "and the One was Origin of All We Became."

The Legend told of how the One brought his children out of the Bowl of the Sky in the storm that was the End of the Beginning. There was a great deal more, written in a hand or hands so ancient and shrouded in antiquity that they had employed the old Linear Script, which can be read in only one direction, rather than the more practical modern Alternating Script.

The poetry was in places so atrocious as to offend any Other's esthetic sensibilities even if we had not long abandoned poetry for science. In the initial stages of the Thousand-Year much of it was destroyed before an elder wisdom prevailed, but what survived was hardly a scientific document.

If the Legend had once served us as a manner of creation myth, it did no longer. We had come to know that the All of creation could not be contained within the finitude of any system of belief, and our steadfast lack of religion was to become one of the sticking points between us and the People.

As to the Legend, until we developed the theoretical capability for space flight, it had been relegated to the status of literary curiosity, nothing more. We had never attempted to construct or launch a spacecraft. How could we, without drawing the undesired attention of People to the source of so pyrotechnic a wonder hurling itself out of the sea into the skies? It was our very sensitivity to People's fears which eliminated what might have proven a means of escape in these last years. Nevertheless, the technology had existed in our memory banks, unused and unusable, from the year of Loriel's birth.

The initial formulae had been postulated by the brilliant radical scientist Liiki—Father of This, Mother of That—whose best pupil and last cherished bondmate, until Liiki made the Change, had been Loriel. Liiki's generation lacked the high-powered telescopes which Loriel's generation perfected; therefore, Loriel was able to build her technology on Liiki's and bring it to fruition. But the devotees of Legat's Parallel remained adamant, and the debate between the two factions was longer-lived even than the debate regarding the People, though the two were inextricably interrelated.

Loriel and the radicals were convinced from their star studies that life, and subsequently intelligence, on far worlds was not only possible but likely, and they interpreted the Legend in this light. The One to them was not a person, much less a god, but rather a metaphoric description of some alien inter-stellar device, its origins and purpose strangled in a great deal of bad poetry. The very name One was etymologically akin to our words for "star" and "traveler." But offer what proofs they might, the radicals could not convince those like old Tagal, or the pragmatist Govin, that the Legend was anything more than legend, until this day. Loriel had proposed an interdis-ciplinary experiment, with the consent of the Telepathy in the person of Lerius, and the technological assistance of my father, Evere, to offer a final proof.

"By engaging the Telepathy in a bridge between living and dead, to be impulse-recorded by WiseEvere's most recent engram-methodology . . ." she was explaining to her col-leagues as I listened. It was gibberish to me. I dug my toes into the mortar and tightened my grip on the window ledge. ". . . it is hoped we can reach beyond the Legend into the minds of those who wrote it, to encounter, it is hoped, at least the collective subconscious, if not the very mnemonic patterns of the long-dead, and the truth."

At one time Telepaths had been able to commune beyond the body's death, but this skill had failed in recent generations. The nature of Loriel's proposal caused a stirring, murmuring incredulity around the half-circle of WiseOnes, given voice by the ever-skeptical Govin.

"Telepathy is recognized as one of the arts; it is a spiritual Discipline!" he protested. "It has not to do with the pragmatic or the scientific!"

"It is precisely such tenuous and artificial subcategorization, WiseGovin, which has heretofore limited our research," Loriel answered dryly, a tight grip on her Discipline; Govin habitually infuriated her. "Any accurate methodology which arrives at truth is valid."

"One must be certain to guard against the dangers of psychic transference," a WiseOne wearing the healers' sigil cautioned from the far side of the half-circle. Her words were primarily for Lerius, though she did not expect him to heed them;

Telepaths keep their own counsel. "Any attempt to combine individual minds into a single entity is fraught with—"

Her words were lost beneath Govin's.

"The end justifies the means, then, WiseLoriel? Simplisticism and unDiscipline both, in one with your credentials, when we can ill-afford either . . ."

He might have gone on, and Loriel might have countered him, point and counterpoint until the second Thousand-Year, except that Lerius intervened.

He had begun subtly to extend his Silence, first to enfold the two combatants, then all in the room, stopping the words in their throats, the very thoughts within their minds. I could see him, kneeling on a mat like the rest but apart, his back to the half-circle, the better to avoid distraction and maintain the Focus. He had seemed asleep or else entranced, if not turned to stone in his incredible stillness. Yet even I, on the peripheries and, I thought, beyond his reach, felt the Silence touch its icy fingers into my mind. I gasped.

Which is how I was discovered. Totally caught up in the debate, I had begun to lean farther and farther into the room until, losing my grip on the window ledge, I tumbled sprawling headlong onto the meticulous parquetry of the warmstone floor, and began to scream.

" 'And the Second was called the Fountain'!" I shrieked, repeating the second verse of the first Canticle of the Legend as I had learned it from Loriel's lips as an infant, only now I was simultaneously writhing on the floor like a mad thing, " 'and the Fountain was Mother of All We Now Hold True'!"

The nine WiseOnes, taken aback by this untoward display, had risen from the half-circle and stood transfixed, uncertain what to do. They began to move toward me, except for my grandmother, and Lerius.

" *'There was also the Third, which was Thought Made Truth,'* " Lerius prompted me, not in words but in Silence, his body still turned away so that I could only imagine his white-irised Telepath's eyes, daunting things. Then he spoke, though the voice was not his own:

55

" *What have you to tell me, my beloved?* "

The appellation calmed me, I am told, and I responded to it.

" *The malfunction is irreparable, beloved, our ship without power . . .'* "

As the Lerius-voice was male, so mine was female, and far older than my years, far older, perhaps, than any Other. Voice, persona, movements, became something not-Lingri, not-Other. Had I then the knowledge I have now of theater and role-playing, what was happening might have seemed less strange. Yet, I had not willed this, and was not acting.

" *'. . . we are trapped in this jump-point forever, beloved. We can neither go forward, nor return, our fate oblivion, caught between the stars.'* "

" *Then we have failed . . .'* " Lerius-voice answered with such anguish that several of the WiseOnes must have stepped back, their Discipline threatened. For myself, I could not see but only hear that anguish. " *'Add your hand to mine, beloved, that we may implement the destruct as one.'* "

" *'Stay your hand, beloved,'* " Lingri-voice said. " *'For while it is agreed that we must die, what of those in our care? They cannot speak for their own fate. Must it be as ours?'* "

" *'The Dictate states that we may not leave the sleepers where there is already intelligent life . . .'* "

" *'The source which composed the Dictate is no more, beloved. Beyond this moment, we are no more. Only these, so very new to life, can hope to survive us. Can we rightly take lives which slumber so deeply they cannot know what we do in their name?'* "

"Sleeper ships!" somewhere outside me Loriel cried, exultant, no doubt in challenge to Govin. "Cryogenics—there's your answer!"

"What species could have possessed such knowledge five hundred thousand years ago?" I heard Govin object. Still I could see nothing.

"What matter? It is sufficient proof—"

"WiseLoriel," the healer's voice interjected, "there is a danger here . . ."

"I am aware. Fetch WiseEvere at once. Better the child awakens to her father's face than any one of ours . . ."

After that, Lerius and I began to speak in a tongue unlike any heard before. It was recorded, of course, but even with linguanalysis it took five years to translate. It was Loriel, of course, who compiled the final report:

Linguanalysis of the dialogue between Lerius and the child at last yielded the following:

The Speakers were without question of a species totally unlike our own or that of the aboriginal People. They were corporeal, not pure mind, as has been suggested in some quarters, for it is clear that they knew they would not survive the destruction of their disabled vessel. That they lived to a vast age—the male, to judge from his temporal referents, had achieved approximately 2,700 years; the female some 2,400—indicates that death was largely an enigma to them, and that their timesense was quite different from our own. Therefore, they were able to 'exist' in both the past and the present, and possibly even a manner of algorithmically projected future, simultaneously, and to survive the process of interstellar gravity-well 'jumping' without loss of psychological integration. It is impossible to say for certain, with what little dialogue we possess, whether the civilization which spawned them had been recently or anciently destroyed, but the implication of their dialogue is that they knew themselves to be the last of their kind.

The core of the dialogue is this: Their civilization had been engaged for an indefinite era in transporting less-advanced populations from their homeworlds and 'seeding' them on uninhabited worlds elsewhere. This function operated under a Dictate which forbade the 'seeding' of a second intelligent species on a world where a first—in this instance, the ancestors of People—already existed. But the cessation of that civilization, coupled with the immediate crisis of their ship's malfunction, made the deposit of their living cargo—presumably proto-Others—upon this world the sole exception to that Dictate.

As to how our ancestors were transported from a disabled space vessel onto the surface of the World, the question continues to plague our best scientists. Were the cryocontainers, either individually or enclosed in some manner of ferrycraft, capable of being jettisoned from the mothership to autopilot to a soft landing on the Archipelago? If so, why has no trace of refined metal dating from that era—specifically, the remains of those cryocontainers—ever been found in the most meticulous search of the Archipelago?

A suggestion has been made that some manner of matter-energy particle beam, which has in fact been theoretically compusynthesized in our advanced laboratories, would not have been beyond the capabilities of an interstellar species, and that this may have been the means of transport by which proto-Others were brought to this world. This might explain the frequent repetition of metaphors for flight and magic in the Legend. While it may be permitted to rejoice over the outcome of the dialogue and the knowledge it has given us, it must also be acknowledged that it raises as many questions as it answers.

When the dialogue ended, I am told I swooned. Lerius caught me, sweeping me into his arms, holding me to him, tears splashing onto my insensate face from colorless eyes which had never known tears. Only a Telepath's Discipline and sheer strength of will held him to the present as the alien presences faded, all but drawing us down into their oblivion as well.

I awoke in the Healers' Hospice to find Evere hovering over me. My child's hand traced the familiar scar on that welcome face, the only thing to hold me to the real and now. At the edges of my consciousness I could hear Loriel and Govin arguing still, though this may have been a result of the sedation given me.

When the healers deemed me fully recovered, Loriel subjected Lerius and me to brainscan, discovering a subtle alteration in our engram patterns which made them mutually compatible, as if those who had owned the voices now owned some part of us as well.

"You remember nothing more?" Loriel asked me more than once. "Can you not describe what you saw? How Lerius appeared to you, what manner of creature you had become? Were there names, memories, associations familiar or strange? Child, try to remember."

Hypnoscans yielded nothing beyond the engram alteration, and Jeijinn had intervened to categorically forbid any further telepathic meddling. Anything further to be gathered from the event must rely on my memory.

"I am trying to remember, Grandmother. But there *is* nothing more. Forgive me."

"Nothing to forgive you for!" Loriel said, uncharacteristically gentle. "If only you could conceive of how much you have done . . . But let us speak of different matters. How long have you been writing poetry?"

How did she know? Had someone gone through my rooms while I was in hospice? Even a child's privacy was sacrosanct. How did she know?

"You spoke of it following the trance," Loriel explained. "Recited a great deal of it, in fact. A result of the medication, no doubt."

"No doubt," I concurred with fledgling irony.

"As I am no judge of such matters, I will not tell you it was good," Loriel said, avoiding my eyes. "Say rather I found it . . . thought-provoking."

Could the aberration be explained away as resulting from the trauma of the recent event, or must the truth be known? Was I in disgrace again?

"None heard but I," Loriel assured me. "Be not ashamed of your innate gift, Lingri-*la*. Did I not suggest your tutors were 'scanning you for the wrong skills?"

"And you call yourself a race of scientists?" Dweneth was incredulous, years later, when I told her. "I'd have been with Govin. A lot of garble and bad acting. Try a stunt like that in my business and you'd be vedged right off the stage."

" 'Vedged'?" I had thought I knew the whole of Players' jargon by then, but this term was new to me.

Dweneth rolled her eyes at my ignorance and mimed the

59

hurling of rotten edibles at an unfortunate Player. As we were within the boundaries of my world, I could not permit myself the luxury of laughter.

"Etymologically intriguing," I admitted, "nevertheless, one cannot but consider the perspective of the food-bespattered Player."

"*You* cannot but," Dweneth said, laughing enough for both of us.

Others keep no secrets, only privacies. When the occurrence at the observatory hit the infonets, my name was carefully not mentioned. However, it was not difficult for any Other to ascertain my identity.

No mention of the incident was ever thereafter made directly to me. My tutors continued their arduous task of guiding me along the general degree track, for whatever changes might have been wrought in my brain, an increased aptitude in the sciences had not been among them. I was still Lingri, poet born of a race of scientists. Only now I could write my poetry without apology.

The scientific community was turned on its Other ear by the evidence Lerius and I had helped reveal, and experts from any number of fields delighted in luring either or both of us into as many tests and experiments as they could devise as I grew to adulthood. Only the Survival Year, which necessitated my leaving One Greater for the outislands, freed me temporarily from their curiosity. I wonder now if some of my guides on Survival were not overly observant as well.

Lerius and I never spoke again, though we frequently spent hours or even days in the same room, hooked up to the same machinery for testing or measuring this or that. He was a Telepath, I was not; there was no reason for him to speak to me.

Hence, regardless of lip-service paid to privacy, I became an object of at least mild curiosity throughout my growing years. Worse, Loriel fell under a manner of cloud. Though it had never been her intention to include me in her experiment, my presence on the observatory grounds at the time was her responsibility, and I was carefully scrutinized down the years for any alteration in character or intelligence. But as I remained Lingri, as I ever was, the shadow passed from my grandmother in time, until she managed all by herself to find some new controversy with which to stir Other minds and tongues and infonets.

As for me, I would clearly find no peace in my own world. Dare I seek it in the World beyond?

Rau stirred the fire when I had done and considered me solemnly.

"So it was you."

"Apparently."

"Why did you not tell me before?"

"I had hoped you would accept me as I am, without any coloration from my past."

"Is your past not your self as well? As much as your willingness to swim the seas in a night to bring me the story finally?"

"That was precipitous," I admitted, chagrined, "but it was the only way I could think of to make you see."

His eyes may have twinkled in the dim light. Then the doorflap was between us yet again. I followed him.

We labored together in his beanfields; he *would* cultivate them in primitive People's fashion—laboriously and by hand. The major events of my life, it seemed, were to be inextricably intertwined with the pulling of weeds.

"You cannot send me back," I presumed to challenge Rau's silence. "I cannot *go* back. Since that day of the voices I have been waiting, though until yesterday I did not know for what. Some part of me no longer belongs to OtherWhere. Shall I be that much a stranger among the People?"

He stood between the furrows, a stocky figure in dusty homespun, bunches of weeds in his fists, twigs in his beard. A comic figure, Dweneth would have said, but Dweneth often judged appearances.

"I have said I could teach you nothing," Rau said, seeming perversely pleased, "except possibly how truly to listen. I did not mean you could not learn. Nor perhaps teach me a thing or three, Lingri Acolyte."

"No question about it," Dweneth said when I told her, "Other-perverse, every bloody one of you. I'd have swatted him over the head with a hoe or something and gone home in a sulk. How'd he know you wouldn't throw yourself off a cliff the first time he sent you away?"

"I am anOther," I explained, though Dweneth swore it was more often excuse than explanation. "To commit suicide for so trivial a personal reason was not one of my options. Further, it was not Rau who sent me away, it was my own inability to see."

"Perverse!" Dweneth snorted, rummaging through her Players' trunk, which she kept with her even on One Greater.

"What were you doing at the time?" I wondered.

"Oh, I?" She was half-buried in the trunk; its contents muffled her voice, and the odd bit of colored stuff flew out from time to time as she rummaged. "Touring the provinces with the *Gorindel,* I suppose. Or was it *Hgree's Folly* that year? And fighting off Droghen's sweaty hands and still teaching myself to read. That was the year I bought the *Faerie*. Found it in a barrel of broken plate and rubbish at a weeksmarket. A good thing, too, considering how it saved your life.

"Anyway . . ." She abandoned her search in a shower of filmy garments, none of which was the one she wanted, slammed the lid of the trunk and sat on it, swinging her legs. ". . . that's all, I'm afraid. No Telepaths nor teachers, no skimmers nor sea-creatures. Nothing so glamorexciting as you, Dearheart."

I studied with Rau for two years without ever asking how he would infiltrate me among the People. The night before we left, I asked.

"In the usual manner." His eyes twinkled. "I shall sell you."

"On the Fourteen Tribes of the Known World"
(Monitors' Report/Compilation Code-6152118205514)

Taken from the perspective of lingual subgroups, there are four-teen tribes in the known world. By geographical subdivision, these are:

To Windward: Wertha, Kwengii, Lamorak, and Llellaar

To Sunward: Gleris and Kelibek

To Leeward: Melet, Zanti, Dyr, and Tawa of the Hillpast Wastes

To Shadoward: Mantuu, Plalas, Hraregh, and Droghians.

A rhyme once taught in Plalas, before its cultural decline, perhaps encapsulates best what the People think of themselves:

> *Werthan Flamehair, pale, befrecked*
> *Kwengii Sunhaired, armor-decked*
> *Lamorak Black-eyes, herd-humpers be*
> *Llellaar Grasseaters, unschooled, free.*
>
> *Melet Islanders, many-godded*
> *Dyr Dark-magicked forest-dwellers*
> *Tattooed Tawa, veiled and cryptic*
> *Zanti Scholars, deep-eyed, mystic.*
>
> *Mantuu Blueblood, thirsty killers*
> *Drunken Hraregh, wassail-lovers*
> *Kelibek Slave-makers, conquest employs*
> *Gleris whom politics destroyed.*
>
> *Droghia lives upon the waves*
> *And Plalas has seen better days . . .*

"First Person Accounts"
(from *The Approved History of People*, revised ed. Volume I: *Before All That*, pages
974-75)

*We could always spot 'em, even before we knew for certain they was
real. Hell's bells, why d'you suppose we made up all them tales of
faeries and whatnot, except to try and explain the strangeness?*

*It was something about the way they smelled, for instance. Not
like good, healthy sweat, which is the way a normal person's supposed
to smell, nor even like one of them new chemical-scent things, but
like—I dunno, like something you'd find on a beach, something
that's been washed too often for its own good. Even in the olden
days, when they'd try to live like us and washed as rare as we did,
they never stank the same. Some says it's because they don't eat
meat. Well, maybe. But I've got to think it's something more than
that.*

*So, see, we didn't need to look at 'em too close to know they was
ringers. Once you gave 'em a good squint, though, it was that
much easier. They never quite got the gist of the way we lived, never
got the routine down, if you know what I mean. There was something too neat in the way they spoke. Something too neat about the
way they'd hold onto a tool, say, like if they was just playing with
it 'cause they had something better at home, back 'on the Archipelago.' It gave 'em away every time. Can you blame us for wanting
to put an end to 'em, if only to stop 'em being so superior, and
spying on us?*

*So I don't care what anyone says about 'em slipping in among
of us for all those years—we always knew. Maybe we was just biding
our time, to find out how many of 'em was there, and whether they
was there to make war on us or only watch. So don't believe any
of them stories and 'Personal Histories'—we always knew. Any fool
could tell the difference between us and them.*

four

When it was time, Rau sold me to a merchant in plate and cooking pots.

My teacher had created a persona for himself in the ShadoWindward provinces: he was to all appearances a slave-dealer, traveling the coasts from Zanti up through Melet, Man-tuu, and what was left of Plalas, gathering castoff children and the skimmings of brothels and played-out mines and factures, to offer them for sale to likely masters in the more prosperous regions of Hraregh, Wertha, and Droghia. None of it was true, of course. How he ever in conscience managed to spin such patent untruths before him I do not know; more, he insisted upon dressing the part. Looking more a pirate than the most opulent of pirates, he had combed and curled his beard, decked himself in gaudy satins and fine hose, adding heavy rings to his ears and nose. Even I could almost be taken in by him.

For myself, I too looked the part I was to play—barefoot, clad in well-worn skirt and gipon, and with a plague tattoo etched into the inner side of one wrist.

We came ashore in Hraregh in a leaky plank boat, which suggested we had hugged the coast and not come far, when in fact a skimmer and the *bRi* had helped us here. As Rau steered, I sat in the bow, searching the morning mist for fishing vessels or the stray pirate craft. We encountered none, but the exercise put me in the proper state of alertness for what was to come.

"This wood is haunted, so the locals say . . ."

It was the first Rau had spoken to me since the announcement over morning tea that today I would make my crossover. No time to return to One Greater to make whatever farewells were suited to a journey from which one might not return. Perhaps it was better thus.

". . . a hundred years or more ago, the local warlord razed all the villages hereabouts and planted this wood, so that he might spend all his days in hunting . . ."

We dragged the boat up the strand.

". . . the villagers, bereft of their lands and homes, were turned out upon the roads. The warlord had no interest in them. Many starved, some turned to thieving and piracy, all were dispersed upon the winds . . ."

Rau fetched his travel-things from the bottom of the boat, gave them to me to carry—an artfully filthy carpetbag, a serviceable clasp-knife and, of course, the leg-irons.

". . . the first time the warlord hunted here with his firstborn son, they were slain in the deepest part of the wood by rustic-made arrows loosed by an unseen hand. Thus, the tale goes, the wood is haunted, both by the restless shades of the warlord and his son, and by those of the villagers who even in death seek to return to their burnt and ravaged homes.

"As a consequence . . ." Rau fitted the leg-irons around my ankles, and ran a length of light chain from them to the manacles I had been wearing for months, in order to become accustomed to their weight and presence, as if I had worn them all my life. ". . . none living ventures here. The villages stand with their backs to the wood, and most boats dock farther down the coast."

I made note of this; should I need a sure route of escape, I could come here unseen and call the *bRi*.

Rau motioned me to follow him, one step beside and one behind, as was proper to the female and servile in a society which made sharp distinction between either and the male and free.

"There are tales aplenty of elven and shades and beasts who speak to men," Rau went on; it was my part to remain silent. "Whether we have been responsible for any of this I cannot say, for while it is truth that Others have used this landing since before my time, People will create stories out of nothing. Walk faster."

The servant's guise was deliberate. People placed a value on a hard-working servant equivalent to that of a draybeast or a goodly plot of land; therefore as chattel I merited a protection I would not have if I were freewoman but unchaperoned. Further, I might be sold and resold again and again, thereby increasing my opportunities to travel and to learn. And, having been at this practice long, Rau had added certain refinements.

A chain of bronze and copper Kwengii coins, stitched into the hem of my skirt, were a valid medium of exchange Worldwide. My heavy amber earrings, which pierced midway up the curve of the ear, Zanti-style, could be bartered in a pinch. Trust Rau to detract from my Other ears by drawing attention to them. As to the plague-tattoo . . .

"A relative safeguard against rape," he had said, etching it into my wrist with berry juice. Its precise shape and color denoted one of the more virulent and deadly of the venereal plagues. "Though do not rely upon even this among the most desperate."

"Is one not to use the fending techniques?" I had inquired at the time.

"As to that," Rau had remarked dryly, picking himself up from the dust after I'd thrown him yet again—I was surprisingly deft, for all my ineptitude in most things, "defend where you can, but not at the risk of being seen to have superior strength. Better to submit than to burn as a witch."

Easy for him to say, I thought. Easier for any male to say than female to contemplate.

Rau seemed to have run out of tales. We traversed the wood in silence.

This, then, was crossover. I considered what lay before me, in contrast to what I had left behind. OtherWorld was ordered, safe, predictable, from birthing to schooling, from mate-bonding to the dignified crossover of death. We had even mastered the weather, which we controlled and tempered with the meteorological screens protecting our cities. For a thousand years we had been clean, warm, well-fed, universally literate, and in optimum health, peaceful, temperate, and prosperous. Had two years been sufficient preparation to thrust me into a world whose only predictables seemed to be dirt, disease, and the probability of untoward death? Rau glanced at me once as we found the road out of the wood.

"It is said the wood is haunted," he observed. "Admission of uncertainty is not failure. We can turn back."

"Not I," I replied with what I hoped passed for dignity. We came to a village.

It was no more than a clearing in the erstwhile haunted wood—a dirt road, a huddle of thatched huts, and some few market carts, some bright with paint and clearly on their way to better places, some old and weatherworn and lacking wheels as if they were never going anywhere. The reek and smudge of wood smoke from either edge of the clearing suggested further households, and there were a handful of folk upon the road to come haggle with the cart-keepers. Rau propelled me along with a firm grasp on my chain, heading for one of the wheeled carts.

The usual procedure for Monitors, unless they were assigned to fill a specific place, was to let the crossover take one where it would. Those trained in specific areas of political science or military history or economic theory might be assigned to a

68

particular region where some significant event was taking place.

Rau never placed his Monitors thus; it seemed to him too much like overt espionage. Preferable to let oneself be swept up in circumstance as a passive observer, interacting as little as possible with history, thereby not altering it beyond the inevitable change wrought by the presence of one more person. Hence courts and marketplaces, farms, villages and great cities were possibilities open to me, all with advantages, none with any so outstanding I was irresistibly drawn there.

To seek some tiny hamlet whose dialect was obscure and customs unknown to us, to live out a certain allotted time and return safely, possessed of a small, perfect study of a single culture, might be preferable to losing oneself in some great teeming mercantile city, garnering political gossip but ever on the peripheries, ever the outlander, prey to any who thought me peculiar, possibly to fall afoul of the law before I could report on what I had learned. Yet if the People continued seaward toward the Archipelago, which was of the greater value?

"If a ship bound straight for One Greater left the People's shores tomorrow, would you have the power to stop it?" Rau wanted to know.

He had been attempting to teach me the fingering of a Droghian lute, and stopped in what amounted to defeat, grateful for the distraction of my question. Others are possessed of perfect pitch and can master music theory almost instantly; nevertheless we had abandoned music among the negative passions and neither played, composed, nor listened. Too, in this skill as in all else, I was still Lingri, and fumble-fingered.

"I offer you no agenda," Rau told me. "Do what circumstance and your own judgment give you to do, and you will find your way."

Thus he had given me skills that would support me anywhere. Domestic skills that would please a merchant or a prosperous farmwife weary of feeding her own livestock and peeling her own vegetables. Linguistic and rudimentary musical skills and the conning of great numbers of ballads and sagas and singstories—my voice was adequate, if my fingers fumbled—that I might please some regional dignitary in need of a minnesinger or amanuensis to record his glorious exploits.

My studies also included a course in known sexual practices among the Fourteen Tribes, though this had only been by way of background. My plainness of appearance and the plague tattoo, which marked me as a carrier, purveyor of prolonged and painful death in exchange for a moment's pleasure, would hardly facilitate my employing this particular course of study in practical application. Yet I was prepared, should the need arise.

Rau's reputation in these parts went before him, and the tinker whose cart stood next-to-last on the road leading out of the village recognized him at once.

"Rau is it, old sod?" The tinker squinted small canny Lamorak eyes in a face that was mostly beard, then laughed and clapped my teacher on the back in a way that might daunt a lesser being. "Where've ye been keepin' o'yerself, and why is't ye never seem to look a day older time by time? S'truth but it's a soft life ye slavers lead for all yer protestations! And ye've come to the right man. Business has been good. What're ye offering this day?"

He seemed to expect no answers to any of his questions except the last, which was asked with those canny black eyes largely upon me, as if to undress me with them and contemplate my muscles, if nothing else beneath my garments, and their serviceability to him. I noted too the eyes of a female of about his age (whatever age that might be; I had yet to learn how People's lives could wear on them), doubtless his mate, watching me over the edge of a chased silver serving platter she was fineworking on a small deal table set up before the cart.

Rau feigned reluctance to extol my virtues, as if I were not of the fine quality he was accustomed to dealing in.

"I'll tell ye truth, Darvis-man," he said at last and after much prodding, lapsing easily into the local dialect, "she's the last of a good lot I've been placing adown the countryside, and being the last she's hardly the best. Strong and silent, as that goes. And a fair worker, too. But there's also this . . ."

He turned my wrist, manacles clashing, to show the tattoo. I feigned resistance, snatching my arm away as soon as he released it, hiding the mark as if it were a sore point on what little pride a servile might possess.

"Man who sold her to me claimed to be her father. Said he'd no idea where she'd caught the plague, but by the look of him a body could surmise, if ye see what I mean. The plague don't harm her any. She'll live and work as long as any wench. But she's the kiss of death to any what tamper with her."

Darvis laughed his gusty laugh and shrugged this off.

"It's naught to me. Even if the wife didn't provide for all I need, and she does that . . . " He winked and leered at the woman, who pretended not to hear, ducking her head with shy pride. ". . . she'd not let me out of her sight that long. And this one's too scrawny, for a fact."

With that he took a proprietary interest in feeling the muscles of my arms beneath my garments, and I stood passive, though stiffening slightly as if affronted. Such subtleties of attitude would determine if I could "pass" with Darvis; if so, I was safe among most People.

What I found uncanny in the encounter was the ease with which I, a nonTelepath, could read this man's unguarded thoughts. Were all People so easily read? Small wonder they would have reason to fear us.

Rau and Darvis had begun to bargain.

"She's worth more than that, Rau-man, s'truth!" Darvis protested Rau's initial price. "Do me no kindness out of old acquaintance. Or is she useless after all?"

"Well . . ." Rau shrugged, enjoying such banter with me as

its object. He did not meet my eyes. "As I say, a hard worker, and silent. But she's had no training in any craft, and I'd not vouch for her quickness at learning . . ."

He was playing his ironies overmuch for my taste, but there was nothing I could do about it but suffer them in silence.

"There's those who would want her for more than one purpose, but the plague-mark thwarts me there, so much so I'd almost thought of scratching it off her wrist, but then who'd not question the scar? To tell it plain, I'm weary of having to drag her about and feed her, and you'd do me the favor of taking her off my hands so I'm free to go back down the coast for my next lot. You can always resell her if she's not what ye'd wish."

So saying, he had planted the seed of my future, and led Darvis off to some serious haggling out of the earshot of females. I was left standing, still in my chains, within the eyes of Darvis's mate, who stopped her work to offer me cool water from a wooden cask and ask if I was hungry.

"Argetha am I," she informed me, spooning out cold millet porridge which might have been cooked days or weeks ago; I ate, not knowing how often my new master might choose to feed me. "Though I suppose ye'll call me 'mistress' after the custom."

"Yes, Mistress," I replied dutifully, trying it out on my tongue, though I'd called Rau "master" for as long as I'd worn the manacles. Others make poor actors, as Dweneth so often said, therefore we must rehearse long and constantly in order to convince ourselves, if not our audience, of the roles we play. The voice I used was hoarse and sounded frightened; that and the clanking of the chains at my every motion moved Argetha to a kind of rough pity.

"Oh, I do wish the menfolk back here to free ye of these 'orrible things!" she cried, shaking at the chains impatiently, her sunstained face transformed into a mass of wrinkles in her distress.

Close, I saw that she was scarcely five years my elder, though pockmarked and unwashed and missing half her teeth, worn down with a life constantly on the road, a demanding spouse and, I was to learn, the birthing of seven children, none of whom had lived. She was but an average female of her time and place.

Her moods changed frequently, like a child's, as did the focus of her attention. Now she was stroking my hair.

"How fine it is, and clean withal!" she marveled. "Were ye bad treated where ye came from?"

"No, Mistress," I said, hanging my head as if I could not bring myself to speak of it, and in truth I could not, having not yet mastered Rau's flexibility with truth. But Argetha took my reluctance to be painful memory, and let it pass.

"Well, ye'll not be treated bad here!" She patted my arm, where the sight of the tattoo and the sound of the manacles only irritated her afresh. "He'll not beat ye, my Darvis-man, and the plague-mark is not all to keep him away of ye, for he's that faithful to me. Though, truth . . ." Her voice took on an edge of sadness. ". . . I could sometimes wish him a wee bit less—faithful!"

She rose wearily from where we'd been sitting together on an old tree root, motioning me to stay and finish my porridge.

"One thing he will do is work ye hard." She smiled down at me, near-toothless, and the smile faded. "But I think ye'll be all right."

She went off to find the menfolk and demand the key to my chain. I would wear no iron as long as I was hers.

"Two things," Rau had advised me. "First, there is a fine line between compassion and pity. Cross it not."

"And the second—?"

"First master the first," was all he said.

Argetha's misery was no more nor less than any I was to encounter from that very first day, yet I could not Discipline my thoughts away from grandiose plans to free her from it. Laboring beside her, attempting unobtrusively to work the longer and more steadily, to take the heavier loads in carrying wood and water, for I was the younger and of the stronger species, I could not but envision a future in which she would know no more such drudgery, and could take from Other learning the one thing she yearned for most—a living, healthy child. Was it so much to ask?

My thoughts were similar toward every female in any village or farmyard we passed on the rutted, dusty, or rain-sodden roads, as our creaking, clanging cart announced our wares. They would raise their matted, weary heads briefly from their work, bent and ancient even in youth, to follow us with their indifferent stares. Whether they labored beneath the sky in field or kitchen garden or, as I would encounter them in the larger town and cities, as wan-faced carders and weavers and facture-slaves who never saw the light of day, mattered little. They would tax the staunchest Discipline.

As for the males, could they not be taught a freedom from the need to prove themselves in brute strength and sexual posturing, of the loud voice of war and the constant need to jostle to the top of whatever heap? I had less hope of any impact here, considering the relative worth of the female in this world so different from my own. Yet I considered Darvis, who cursed and bullied me beneath the eyes of his fellows because it was expected, but who daily inquired through Argetha—always through Argetha, lest he appear soft, to concern himself with the affairs of females—was I well fed? Had I no cloak for the cold season? Did I require any physick or remedy for the things that ailed the "weaker sex"? Was I content in my work and not over-used? These were not the inquiries of an owner concerned with the health of a draybeast, but the concern of a man possessed of some measure of caring beneath rough mien and manner. People also hid behind their masks, and this was Darvis's.

My days took their shape from the nature of Darvis's trade. He, Argetha, and I journeyed from village to hamlet to weeks-market along the winding roads, our way varied by expanses of flowering meadows, the occasional deep wood or scorched field punctuated by a tumbledown keep or shattered stockade to indicate the uncertainty of peace in these parts. Rare was the crossroads that did not sport a gallows, wheel, or gibbet whereon, frequently denied burial and left to predators, hung the broken remains of those who had transgressed one of many and often incomprehensible laws.

There were also the witch-pyres: circles of burnt brushwood, a charred stake, a pile of cracked and blistered bones, sometimes a surviving scrap of cloth (on one such stake a hank of luxuriously long auburn hair somehow spared the flames fluttered—pain-colored, disconsolate—on the dank and death-smelling breeze).

"On'y womenfolk is burnt for witches!" Argetha informed me with a warning glance.

The grating squawk of deathdaws was everywhere in this country, and any Other, empathic or not, would find it difficult to shield against the presence of death, the echo of death-shrieks in these places. I stared transfixed as our cart lumbered past.

"Turn yer head away!" Argetha would chide me. "Look away afore yer stopped and questioned! 'Tisn't proper to stare so!"

There were days of unending sun, blinding in their accretion, and days of unrelenting wind and rain and mud. My respect grew daily for any whose life lay always on the road.

Our cart was pulled by an old war*graax* whom Darvis had named Krex, acquired by dint of much scrimping, and my master's pride and joy. No creature this large was indigenous to the Archipelago, which would have lacked sufficient forage for their voracious appetites, and Others had never enslaved the creatures of this world either as food or pet or beast of burden. *Graaxen* were yet one more metaphor for the differences between us.

In its natural state the *graax* was a peaceful creature, its size and weight and natural armor plating protecting it from predators. People had long used the creatures as war machines, bedecking them in chains and bells and spikes and cymbals pierced through the *graax*'s natural armor. The pain and constant noise of these devices drove the *graaxen* into a frenzy, and struck terror in the hearts of enemies.

A *graax* thus enraged could charge through barriers of wood or stone or living flesh, could crush with its heavy hooves whatever it did not rend with its horns—one sprouting above the snout, a second under the lower jaw, both often honed to razor sharpness and gilded with gold or swordsteel. Whether mounted or pulling a blade-wheeled chariot, a war*graax* was terror incarnate.

Yet, with its horns filed down and its chains and bells removed, the creature reverted to its placid state, and could pull a cart or plow tirelessly and in the mildest humor. Darvis's Krex was a particularly companionable beast, and as it fell to me to feed and groom him, we soon reached an understanding. However well he came to know me, Krex could never resist nipping at the hands that fed him or backstepping, with a kind of *graax*ish chuckle, onto delicate Other feet. Doubtless it meant he liked me.

We traveled usually in company, as strength in numbers against brigands and for the companionship of our fellows, who kept up lively shouted conversations along the way. Darvis drove the cart while Argetha rode with their clutter of belongings in the back; the cooking pots and various wares they had wrought between them hung in clattering display along the frame and sides of the cart. I followed afoot, silent as was my place, known only as Darvis's Boundwoman, for though gossip carried my story and eyes followed my progress—especially the males', hoping to get a glimpse of the plague-mark—few cared to learn my name. This was as I would wish it. Invisible, I was free to listen and to learn.

If there were other Monitors among our company, they did not make themselves known to me. It was part of our training never to communicate except in dire emergency, and serviles did not speak unless spoken to.

We stayed in each village for as long as the trade would bear us, selling new pots to the more affluent, repairing old ones for the less. Argetha Fineworker was occasionally called upon by reputation to refurbish some local dignitary's preciousware, that he might have sufficient silver or even gold plate with which to impress his constituency at the next formal dinner, for there is a People's saying that "he must be great who sees his own face reflected in an hundred plate and spoons."

It was my lot to haul wood and water, to keep the forge hot whenever we tarried long enough for Darvis to work, to assist Argetha with the cooking and washing and mending. I was content. None of what was required of me violated any Discipline, and those who saw me daily accepted my guise without suspicion. And while Darvis was betimes called Once-Armorer, he no longer made war-tools, a fact as distressing to him as it was a relief to me.

"Time was, lass," he'd address me, sweating bare-chested over the forge while I worked the bellows and no one else was about to listen, "I was among the best. Mail and plate and spearhead, shield-bossing, dirk and sword-hilt did I, though never the blades. That good I wasn't, nor any sorcerer neither!"

There was such obvious pride in his recollection. It had not occurred to me that one could cherish the skill employed in the making of objects whose sole purpose was to kill. Yet I considered the loving detail which was customarily lavished upon shield and sword-hilt, armor and helm. Would that such energies were expended instead on nurturing, healing, and the quest for knowledge, I remember thinking. People would have no need of Others at all.

"Cheer thee, lass!" Darvis chided my silence one morning as we clanked and rattled out of yet one more dreary village. "We'll soon to Town and Marketfest!"

Few places had been as melancholy as this last place. The grain had succumbed to a fungus, and those who ate it were struck down by an enemy too small to see, too mysterious to fend against. Most of the ancients and children had died; the women were made barren. Proper storage could have prevented the plague, simple inoculation cured it. Yet it was so commonplace.

Many who survived had lost several fingers and could no longer grasp ordinary tools or cooking-things: Darvis was much in demand to alter what they had. He labored in a paroxysm of sweating, coin-gathering delight, too busy or too jaded to see the hollow-eyed, ravaged faces, hear the silence of a realm where there were no more children.

"She's sensitive, man, have a pity!" Argetha scolded, elbowing Darvis in the ribs and smiling bleakly at me. "Poor lass as can't have childer of her own for the plague—of course she feels from them as has namore! Have a pity, man, do!"

But even Argetha's mood was soon lightened at the prospect of Marketfest.

"I'll have me new clothes to wear!" she crowed. "And I'll save the old for you, Lingri-girl. Maypoles and dancing and feasting and cirques, and himself too drunk most of the time to bother of me . . ."

To this I could give no answer. Whatever complex web of caste or hierarchy or social acquiescence might rule a given portion of the World, why was it a given that the female must submit to copulation whenever the male demanded, regardless of what she might desire? To this day I do not understand it.

Trade caravans were a motley of language and ethos, the fellowship of the itinerant largely superceding intertribal prejudice. Hence dark-skinned Dyr and jewel-eared Melet from the Shadoward Isles, hairy Forest Lamorak like Darvis (who favored brides of freckled Windward Wertha stock like Argetha), silken-haired Zanti, veiled and tattooed Tawas from the Hill-past Wastes, met and traded and parted on the roads or traveled awhile in company, sharing food and drink and singstories wherever they camped for the night. Intermix couplings were not infrequent, and the resulting children were unusually appealing to the eye. Small wonder, though, that villagers, rooted to one spot and wedded to its customs, looked askance at tradefolk, and our own company was usually the only fellow-ship we knew.

Not that we trusted even our own. Few ventured the roads alone or after darkfall, for dangers real and conjured lurked behind every tree and in every mountain pass. And though we camped together and often ate from a common pot over a communal fire, fights and thievery were sufficiently frequent that every caravan had an official watchguard and, when the singing was over and the fire banked, most cart owners kept their own watch over the few goods we possessed.

(I employ the People's "we" here, a puzzling collective for a nonTelepathic species to employ, which usually translates as "we the majority." Hence, technically, though I partici-pated in the serving of that nightly communal meal and was permitted to sit beyond the circle about the fire with my fellow serviles and listen to the storysinging, at no time was I invited into the inner circle to sing as well. Serviles spoke when spoken to, and did not sing at all. There was no reason for this, beyond that expressed in a common People's aphor-ism: "There is none so low he does not glory to see someone below him.")

At the time I made my crossover, most People's literature was an oral tradition, in the form of epic poems and the so-named singstories. It had been part of Rau's wisdom that I commit to memory whatever singstories I could, assimilate additional dialects and lingual subgroups, and refine my own sing-technique toward a time when I should be called upon to use it.

"The People delight especially in witch-tales, many of which, whether coincidentally or from actual encounter, describe beings of our shape and powers," he would tell me. "Perhaps one may counteract these negative traditions by introducing more positive tales of our own."

"This does not constitute intervention?" I had asked quite seriously, aware of the power of story in semi-literate societies.

Rau had twinkled at me. "That will be for you to decide."

Darvis, as it happened, delighted in witch-tales, the more grotesque the better. Whenever it was his turn to sing, or even out of turn, he would seize the traditional singstick and roar his tales out at the top of his lungs and in his unique kind of limping doggerel:

> *Faeries, elves and sprites, my dears*
> *Do boggle in the night, my dears*
> *Steal a calf*
> *Rend it in half*
> *And drink the blood for spite, my dears*
>
> *Graaxen-ears have witch, my dears*
> *The which they'll twitch at yich, my dears*
> *Bed with yer wife*
> *Bring yer much strife*
> *And childer poxed with itch, my dears*
>
> *From vapors out the ground, my dears*
> *Or seas where mortals drowned, my dears*
> *They rise and teem*
> *Like poisoned steam*
> *And blight all farm and town, my dears . . .*

His voice would have tortured my Other ears were I *not* possessed of perfect pitch. He seemed to have a limitless store of verses, though he would get through less than six of them before the gathering shouted him down. As a storysinger, my master was an excellent maker of pots.

Whenever we had preciousware in keeping, Darvis kept the watch nightlong, for while he seemed to trust me, I would not be the first servile to serve him ill. When there were only ordinary wares to guard we divided the watch, he taking until midnight, I from then to daybreak. Roused from where I slept in a nest of rags beside Argetha (who had been reared in a one-bed family and could not bear to be alone) to watch the

80

stars and listen to sounds of breathing beasts and men, I came to know why she so cherished preciouswork, not only for its esthetic pleasure beneath her hands, but because guarding it kept Darvis away from her of a night.

"Och, man, no, not this night!" I would hear her nightly whispered pleas. "I'm that weary I—ow, all right then, give us a minute—ouch, gods, oh— !"

Her protests were lost in grunts and moans and a great heaving of the wagon against the wheel-chocks, and oftener than not I would hear her weeping after, while Darvis snored. I would have preferred neither to hear nor to witness, but while as servile I must keep the watch, so as Monitor I must learn everything the People had to teach me, including this.

When at last the night grew silent, or as nearly so as it could with snort and stamp of *graaxen* and draybeasts, the cries of wood-creatures and sleeping sounds from the encircled carts, I would compose my body and my thoughts, employ the Mnemonic Discipline, and record all I had learned that day. That done, I could compose my poetry, also stored in memory against such time as I might be free to write it down.

Other ears heard the music before any of my companions', before Marketfest ever came in sight. There were marshes and a wood between us and Town, and Darvis reckoned midnoon before we saw the outskirts. Yet the animals heard it too, for Krex pricked up his ears and began to dance sideways in his harness, mindful of what it had been like in his earlier career to march in time to pipe and gong and trump and tabor—

". . . pipe and gong and trump and tabor . . ." Gayat mimics me, reading over my shoulder; I have been so lost in the past I did not hear his Telepath-tread. "And what of concertina? Cannot have a 'fest without a squeezebox or two, can they?"

I blink at him. He is a faintly luminescent shadow against the rest of my darkness, clad in Telepath's white, a shade brighter than the page upon which I scratch. Doubtless he has disturbed me for some purpose. I wait him out.

"The lights are gone completely," he announces. "The Guard were here to dismantle the power plants and cart the vitals away, and they will punish swiftly if they find any private generators. Seventeen died in hospice when the life-supports gave out, and most of the remaining medicines have perished. I have brought tapers."

That is what he carries clutched against his thin chest. I watch him set one in the wall-niche and light it carefully, sparingly. Only windowless chambers such as mine dare this much light; on Three Greater and many of the Lessers, Others died for the light spilling under their privacy shutters, back when the power plants still ran and the Guard stalked the streets in random patrols, taking lives for a series of ever-changing infractions. A child might be arbitrarily shot for looking directly into the face of a Guard; the next day one might die for looking away. Elders are killed for the simple fact of being older than any People can live; newborns, nurtured in the hidden places, are sought out and snatched from the breast for merely being more physically whole than People's infants. The Guards' logic is illogic, their best weapon against a species which rules itself by Discipline and still perversely expects it from all intelligent species. I no longer ask Gayat for status reports on what happens beyond my chamber; he provides them anyway.

"The last of our original stock," he reports, indicating the candle. "We have learned to salvage most of the paraffin after burning, but there is nothing out of which to make the wicks." As I do not comment on this, his thought goads me before his words do. "Your gratitude is accepted, of course, spoken or no. Or are you so gifted you can write in the dark?"

"Dried and plaited seakress, dipped first in the hot wax and allowed to harden, will comprise an adequate wick," I reply calmly, my eyes upon the interrupted page now dancing painfully in the light of the flame. In my day even Telepaths had some respect for age. "As a last resort, braid twenty strands of a WiseOne's hair, but do not sacrifice the light for the sake of unskill.

"And, as you ask, indeed I can," I continue tightly, feeling my Discipline fray, my dry voice rise, "write in dark or light, in calm or chaos, on *graax*back, under seige, or in a moving boat, by mnemonic or onscreen, on parchment, tree bark, and occasionally my own flesh." I hold my breath, find some control. "Was there purpose to your coming here, beyond bringing the tapers?"

"We were not aware of such uses for seakress," Gayat said soberly, nonplussed. He who has never ventured offisland or, for all I know, beyond the microcosm of One Greater, still believes Others hold all useful knowledge. "Nor did anyone else suggest it. How did you know?"

The answer is so obvious even a Telepath should be able to understand it: the making of hand-dipped tapers has not been a needed skill in OtherWhere for five hundred years, while among People it is still sometimes all the difference between dark and light.

"I have heard of you," my young Telepath observes, refusing to acknowledge his own ignorance, "that in the end you are more People than Other, from having lived so long among them. 'Pipe and gong and trump and tabor.' So it would seem from your turn of phrase."

I have set aside my stylus, and with it my Discipline. Would that I had continued my brief study among Telepaths, that my sending skills might be sufficient to send this upstart son of a Telepath physically out of the room!

"What of it?" I demand. "What in my 'turn of phrase' troubles you so, that are not a poet and have no right to judge?"

"There is neither time nor taper to spare for this—this profligacy of detail!" Gayat gestures at what I have just written. "Musical instruments! Marketfests and the whims of *graaxen*! Our race is dying, and you write not of us but of those whose Marketfests will endure long after we are gone. Perhaps they will set aside a special one, a Day of Rejoicing when they've killed the last of us. Yet still you cherish them and their customs in your descriptions!"

As I have, as I will, until my last breath, though it be their hands that throttle it out of me. Though they strip the flesh from my body as they attempted once before, though they strip me down to bone and mind and throbbing heart, I will cherish them, Gayat-*la!* He knows nothing of my private thoughts. How can he understand?

"The Council has given me to tell you that providing you with tapers relegates whole families to darkness, yet you squander the light on Marketfests. Futility, this chronicle, in my opinion, when an accidental spatter of flame might end it . . ."

His white eyes flicker toward the flame and I wonder with some detachment if he will dare. His Discipline has been less than formally taught in these troubled times, and I know not whether his gifts include kinesis, or whether he will dare to use it here. To an extent I can understand his woe; he is so young, and has scarcely lived, and soon, to all appearances, his life will be ended. I grieve with him. But if his youthful zealousness should threaten one word of my chronicle . . .

I am sending with every atom of my being, and make no effort at control. Anger is not unDisciplined when one's lifework is at stake.

"Gayat-*la* Telepath," I address him formally and with great deliberation. "Given license, I would be out among Others giving aid to the ill and the hungry, offering whatever I possess in strength and time and energy. Had I the skills, I would aid the Telepathy in composing the eidetics where the Legend and the Histories are being stored. I would give my last drop of blood to save anOther life. But the Matriarchy has named me chronicler, and thus will I serve, in manner and style and content of my choosing. Neither WiseOne nor Telepath will dictate to me in this regard!"

My sending begins to take effect. Gayat rolls his eyes and clutches at his temples in sudden pain. Only when he has staggered back out of my space, all but out of the chamber, do I relent and retreat once more behind my mask. Let him retaliate; my defenses are down. I bow my head over my interrupted page. The Discipline requires twice as much chanting as before. Is this what we have come to, that at the last we turn upon each Other?

"I ask forgiveness!" Gayat gasps; doubtless pain is a new experience for him. I sense a new direction in his thought; he grows more luminescent with it. Perhaps if he could remain here I would have no need of tapers. "I am also sent to tell you that the children depart at moonset. The *bRi* gather already. If you wish to bid any farewell . . ."

He does not finish. Most of the youngest children, by their parents' decision, are to be smuggled across the sea this night, to waiting Zanti merchant ships. A small group among the Mystic Zanti have agreed to adopt and rear them as their own. The journey is fraught with dangers from the outset. It is not even known if the *bRi* can safely slip the children past the Guard, yet the attempt is to be made. It is our last hope.

The moment fills me with a vast unOther sorrow. "Am I needed to *bRi*-speak?"

Gayat shrugs. "WiseChior will be there."

"Chior is a better -speaker than I." From childhood WiseFrayin's son did everything better than I, except what I do here. I resume my stylus; too much time has already been lost. "Tell him he may bid the small ones farewell in my stead."

I have dismissed Gayat from my presence, whether he physically departs or not. I dare not consider the possible fates of these children, any more than I consider the fate of my own, though he is no longer a child.

My memories of him are largely ordinary ones, times we spent together when our mutual presence was all that transpired, all that mattered.

Too long ago, the morning sun found him at the end of the jetty on One Greater's shore, a *bRi*-calf nipping playfully at his ten-year-old's toes as he whistled and chattered with it. Joreth possessed a greater *bRi*-skill than I, who had taught him the speaking.

His laughter carried above the surf as the calf breached and sounded, soaking him. He had not been Other-reared, but bridged both worlds, and his laughter was a never-ending marvel to his unlaughing mother. So too his father's wildly curling hair, tangling down over his shoulders in the breeze. But ah, those shoulders—tanned and boy-wide, but so thin! Yet the healers had pronounced him fit.

He had passed the rigors of Survival Year, though more than a few WiseOnes had cautioned against his attempting it owing to his frail People's physique, and his father had resisted mightily, saying that this, of all his heritages, should not be tried upon him. But I had been as adamantly in favor of it, for the Purists were already on the rise among the People, disseminating their doctrine of Other-hate, and whatever my species-bridging child would face in the future, Survival would strengthen him.

For once my will prevailed. And Joreth had prevailed, for all the dire predictions. Now I had him in my care for a few days more before he returned to his father's world. I had let him sleep long and luxuriantly. I had plied him with whatever he wished to eat in whatever quantities, the better to restore the flesh lost from those growing bones in the rigors of Survival. Other though I am, I wanted to weep for looking at him, else drink him in with my eyes, who would soon be parted from me.

"Joreth," I said, and that softly. His ears were Other; he heard.

And turned, tickling the *bRi*-calf with one bare foot. I saw he was wearing his short breeches, the better to prepare for his return to a world that dictated such modesty even for swimming. Like all his garments, they had grown too small for him. The *bRi*-calf sounded once more, and my son laughed aloud, pushing the tangled hair out of his eyes, standing wide-legged on the jetty to contemplate me.

"I've given him a secret name, Mum!" he announced, tickling the *bRi* with his toes. "It makes us brothers, though he's the better swimmer. He's going to follow and visit me once

I've returned to Father. If his own mum will let him. She's as strict as you."

"It is against Other-custom to impose a name upon a creature whose comprehension of any temporal appellation is at best limited . . ." I stopped. My humorlessness had turned him from me more than once. And it was impossible to remain Other-stern in the face of Joreth's merriment.

"It's my own custom, and I'll abide by it!" The merriment held a trace of a scowl; Joreth had stubbornness from both his heritages. "Watch us race!"

He dove into the surf in pursuit of a goal no Other child would have contemplated. To swim with *bRi* for the sake of swimming was one thing; to impose the concept of competition, a race to be won, was alien to us still. Perhaps it was well, I thought, watching the streaming head bob up from the surf at last as Joreth bid his flippered companion farewell and strode ashore, that he returned to his father's world soon. Joreth's soul, like his father's, was impossible to Discipline.

It was then that he astonished me with his request.

"D'you think I could stay with you?" Breathless from the swim, he shook himself like a wildcur before flopping down onto the sand beside me. "Here—on the Archipelago? Father's too old to keep up with me; he's said as much. Could I?"

"Stay with me, or on the Archipelago?" I wondered, knowing he knew the difference; I was less often here than he was. "Is it because they mock you?"

He looked at me under his eyebrows. "They don't any longer." "They" were the full-blood People's children, his supposed peers and schoolmates, who tormented him for presuming to be what he was. "Father says I've become a two-fisted diplomat."

This troubled me. "Does it please you?"

"It's necessary, until they learn better," Joreth said with a wisdom beyond his years. Still looking at me under his eyebrows, with his you-wouldn't-dare-refuse-me look, "You haven't answered my question."

87

"Stay with me, or on the Archipelago?" I repeated. "I return to the mainland with you, to remain the longer. And you have been restive beneath Other ways before."

"Mayhap I'm growing up," he suggested, toying with some small stones, avoiding my eyes this time. "There are as many things in Father's world I can't abide either."

I knew without asking he would not tell me what these were. His eyes were upon me again.

"Where am I to live when I'm grown, Mum?"

"That will be for you to decide." I could no longer resist the urge to run my fingers through his tangled curls; he tolerated this as long as any male child might, then pulled away before I could learn what he was thinking. "Most intermixes spend their days in both worlds, as most full-Others now do. The choice will be yours, when you are grown."

"In both, or between both, Mum?"

I had no answer for him.

I will not think of Joreth now. I will put my mind on Marketfests. When Gayat finally leaves I extinguish the taper, which with its fellow I shall redistribute on the morrow—one to a family which has kept its children, one to a family which has not. In darkness, I write. Lingri has gifts even Gayat does not suspect.

> *There is a realm clept OtherWhere*
> *Where folk may dwell without a care*
> *Rules ElvenQueen with raven hair*
> *In OtherWhere.*
>
> *Who will be the first to trust?*
> *Who dare allow the sword to rust?*
> *Or hearts and minds abandon lust?*
> *Who does finds OtherWhere . . .*

(Fragment of a version of the epic poem *OtherWhere,* variously attributed to the anonymous oral traditions from the People's twelfth century. While the first verse, usually considered the Chorus, is common to all versions of the work, the second is apocryphal and appears in no version save this one, dating from about 1561 P.A.)

"On the Training of Telepaths"
(Author Unnamed; from *Documents of the
Thousand-Year:* Code20512516120819)

Telepaths will prove to be either our salvation or the end of us. It is simply unlikely, despite the most rigid Discipline, that such a power can always be contained, channeled, and utilized solely for the good. To begin, there is too much variation in opinion as to what constitutes 'the good.' Assuming this debate to be resolvable, if only temporally, there is still the matter of 'how far is too far.' Those who are Telepaths aver that we who are not cannot judge them, for their morality and their purpose operate on a plane unknowable by those who have not journeyed there.

Perhaps so. But as the Telepath's power impacts upon the nonTelepath, we can judge, we must *judge. Let them set themselves apart, let them journey where they will within their own enshielded enclaves, but when they walk among the rest of us, let them keep what they possess unto themselves unless and until we seek it.*

five

People needed little reason to hold a Marketfest. Rejoicing over a good harvest, consolation for a poor one, a way of staving off Windseason or welcoming the Thaw, it mattered not. This one marked the onset of Softseason. Seed had been sown, grazing flocks were in foal but not yet ready to deliver, and farmers could afford a day or two of idleness. Ten holydays intervened before the pieceworks and factures extended their hours into the lengthening daylight, and even the lowliest facture-slave earned a few days' respite before the harder work began.

Provincial warlords and governors welcomed Marketfest. It channeled the energies of the masses, made them forget for a time the misery of their lot and dreams of insurrection, meant a rapid depletion of consumer goods which would need to be produced in ever-increasing amounts for the next fest. To the Other mind it seemed exploitative, and a poor substitute for real economic evolution, but it was the norm in this time and place, and I must observe it at firsthand.

My master and mistress were as enthused as the dancing

Krex, for they stood to make sufficient coin to cover Darvis's drinking debts and still turn a profit. Argetha had a further joy to share with me:

"With child am I again," she confided all in girlish whispers and with sly glances toward her Darvis, her worn hands folded over her waist, where nothing showed as yet. "Since we've had ye, Lingri-girl, I think yer that much luck for me, for I do think I shall keep this one!"

I wondered. She was ashen pale beneath her freckles, chronically malnourished and edemic. Would this child survive where its siblings hadn't? Would Argetha? I murmured some vague congratulation, and did not trouble her happiness with my concerns.

Marketfest had no counterpart in my world, and I thought it only one more opportunity to learn. Had I known what awaited me amid torchlit processions and drunken weave-dances, it might have given me pause.

Description fails even the chronicler here, for what I saw and heard and smelled and felt transpiring upon the length of greensward of this dingy sprawl of Town could have been multiplied by as many eyes and ears and hands and tongues and noses as experienced it. Musicians and jugglers, mimes and swordplayers danced and tumbled through the narrow lanes between stalls containing every manner of goods that People's farms and factories could produce. Wine-and-spirit sellers and sex-sellers hawked their wares with equal abandon, and Other eyes scanned narrow, shadowed alleyways to glimpse many a figure sprawled upright against inn- or house-wall swallowing down great drafts of the first commodity while the second was offered—standing, clothed and furtive—to the body below.

It needed all my Discipline to give witness to the number of half-grown children of either sex earning their scrap of bread and nest of rags to sleep in from this shadow-skill. Yet a swallow of wine afterward could for a time numb their woe as they joined the general merrymaking between assignations. If their eyes shone with some febrile intensity in the torchlight, they took as much delight from the nightly fireworks as any inviolate child.

While my master and mistress did their seeing and tasting and dancing and purchasing, I was set to tend the wagon and wrestle with the nuances of coin-changing, which varied from one province to the next. It did not help that Others had not used specie since the Thousand-Year, nor that coin-clipping was common practice in some places and punishable by death a few miles down the road.

Between financial dilemmas, I had much opportunity to observe the passing flow, and to make a sale or three. I was as deferential as servile was meant to be. This seemed to invite the customers to commentary.

"Yer master gone off and left ye in charge, is he? Now there's a foolish man! What's to stop ye runnin' off wi' the coin, if not the merchandise?"

"If not my native honesty, master, then only that I'd be the more easily caught," I would reply, turning my wrist to allow the plague-mark to show. My use of the idiom had grown more natural, and with it my confidence in speaking it.

"Aye," the customer would leer, "and wouldn't I love to know how a wench as unspoilt came by *that*!"

"If the master's curiosity is worth the risk . . ." I would begin, and he would invariably back away as if my mere proximity would give him plague, or else his spouse would drag him away, with a murderous glance for me.

How peculiar it must be, I thought, to have every aspect of one's life so colored with sexual nuance. It was so different in my world.

Thus it transpired for the first two days of fest. I had just concluded the sale of a soup pot and some good ladles to a robust, toothless farmwife, when I became aware of what could only be telepathic sending. Here, in this place? I need not glance up from my coin-changing to know that somewhere in that milling crowd, Other eyes were upon me.

While Rau steadfastly refused to teach a Telepath, opinion

about this differed as with all else Other, and not all teachers were as circumspect. There were also the Espions, self-appointed messengers of change who slipped about in the People's part of the World with their own agendas. While Espions were not strictly forbidden to make crossover . . .

". . . nevertheless, the Matriarchy discourages it, until it be determined whether we do more harm than good," he finished for me, speaking in Plalan, a near-dead language considered by commoners to be a scholars' tongue, useful for legal documents but difficult to speak. Doubtless few here knew more than a word or two of it, yet it would not be deemed suspicious for outlanders to speak it. "Though some of us would be dead by the time that particular debate be settled, and will not wait that long."

I forced Discipline into my eyes before they met his white-irised ones. How dare he presume to read my thoughts in this place?

"Perhaps it is with good reason that the Matriarchy prefers its most controversial citizens to remain at home." I too spoke in Plalan, to convey that I understood him, and what he was.

"There is an opinion that any manner of crossover is by its very nature intervention," he countered. "If that were so, what are you doing here? Is there aught that is Other and not controversial?"

He had crossed the sward and was near enough to finger the merchandise hung from my master's cart, and as he did so I considered him. He was dressed as a Zanti beggar, all in tatters and with a blindman's bells about him, as a guise for his sclerose-seeming eyes, though he might have better gotten color-implants before he left the Archipelago. Or was he, as a blindman, better able to see?

"Does one who cannot see desire that I describe what wares my master offers?" I turned my tongue to Hraregh, the common tongue, to make it clear I would not play his game until I knew its rules. "Or shall I permit him to study them with his Other senses?"

"Better," he replied coldly, though acknowledging my

choice of tongue, "that the seeing heed what blindman sees that they do not."

"Truth, I confess I do not understand you, Stranger." My eyes and ears scanned the passing crowds to see if any took undue notice of us, or if my master was in the vicinity, to find me over-friendly to a Zanti beggar. "For, never having been blind, I know not what a blindman sees, except it be what lies behind his own eyes."

There. Let him know I was no Telepath. Let him seek elsewhere for accomplice in whatever he was up to. But he was nothing daunted.

"A troop of Kwengii, Lingri-one . . ." He had read my name before he had so much as made his presence known; Espions lacked the most basic respect for privacy. ". . . marches this way from the coast. They traverse the wood, ignoring the smaller villages and neither burning nor looting. They mean to save their energies for this Town."

"What is this to me? If you know who I am, you know what I am, and what my duty as Monitor forbids me . . ."

"Doubtless they will follow the usual pattern: to swagger in and allow themselves to be feasted and showered with presents and seemingly lulled, then to slaughter their hosts in their sleep. This much I know, though their own kind seem never to grasp it."

"And knowing this, what will you do? What is your intention, Stranger?"

"Gentle saboteurs," Loriel had named all Espions once over latemeal at Jeijinn's table, provoking an all-night debate, "but saboteurs nevertheless."

"Espions do only what their Discipline dictates to them," Jeijinn had replied, her voice as always sharper than it need be. "To turn the People's minds away from violence, in whatever way . . ."

"Is intervention. Sabotage," Loriel replied, winking at me.

Other children were never precluded from attendance at adult discussions, no matter how contentious. It was how we

94

ourselves learned to debate. Despite my youth, nothing stood between my curiosity and what promised to be a fascinating difference of opinion; I ate in silence and listened.

"They will be upon us soon, this second species, these 'People,' as they call themselves," Jeijinn pointed out. "So the Monitors observe. So reads your own report to the Council."

"Within approximately twenty years of yon Lingri's birth," Loriel agreed, pouring herself more tea unasked. "Already they possess the rudimentary skills to set sail and find us, but fortuitously either their gods or their domestic woes usually intervene. The Council has my report, complete with projections. What will you do?"

"As Councillors? What we always do!" WiseJeijinn's voice took on an added layer of irony. "We will debate. We may need twenty years and more to reach any manner of decision."

She dropped the irony for something bordering on apprehension.

"Nevertheless, they will come. We cannot stop them. And they are violent."

It was always the second half of the thought: The People will come, and they are violent. I would hear it from every Other's lips.

"So were we once, and not so very long ago," Loriel reminded her, seeming unperturbed. "When they see the alternatives to violence which we offer . . ."

"Mother, your skills are many, but sociology is not among them. Leave it, I ask you, to me and mine . . ."

"We are not native to this place!" Loriel presumed to raise her voice above anOther's characteristic soft tone; I understood now where Jeijinn had learned sharpness. "They are! If they choose to claim back from us what is rightfully theirs—"

"—which we have caused to flourish through our efforts and in our own way? No!" Jeijinn slashed the air with a negative gesture. "This I will debate you on, as will the Council, though it take twenty years or a lifetime!"

Thus armed, she carried the debate, and with it her espousal of Espions, to the Council. How often did my child's curiosity find me leaning over the gallery rail, listening to her harangue until she was hoarse?

"Whatever our origins, wherever we have come from, we are here now and can go nowhere else. We have the right to preserve what we are where we are!" Her strong voice, so strident at close quarters, resonated magnificently within the Council's flawless acoustics. "We have taken from no one, and we have made good what we have found. We desire nothing more than to retain what we have wrought. Tell me the species, reasoning or not, that has not the right to live! If we cannot do what harms no one and does both us and the People good . . ."

In truth, her argument went around and circled back on itself more than once, but it was never meant as persuasion, only filibuster, to convert the already converted. Yet even as a child I had wondered: How can she be so sure what is good for the People when she has never been among them? Now here I was among them, confronted with this very embodiment of what Jeijinn preached, and more uncertain than ever.

"What is your intention, Stranger?"

My tongue had slipped back to Plalans. Safer. My tone held an edge of challenge: How do you presume to seek me out, to pluck my name out of my unshielded mind without so much as offering me your own?

"Surely you do not require the assistance of one both female and servile in order to warn the local garrison?" I confess I goaded him; I wanted free of him and his unspecified plots. "The word of even a blindman, so long as he be male and free, carries more weight than any of mine."

" 'Warn the local garrison'?" Had his Discipline eroded in crossover, or had he always been this rude? "Warn the local garrison—how ingenuous!" he sneered at me. "I would hardly need you, if that were all I intended!"

I knew now what he would do. He would pervert his Telepath's Silence into a wave of such nameless, formless fear as might turn unshielded Kwengii minds away from their intended violence, or goad them on to more. He would not know until he tried it.

"The garrison is poorly armed, its soldiers as besotted with festing as the most foolish peasant!" His blind-seeming eyes had taken on a strange, febrile cast. "Useless! I had hoped to encounter in you a sending-skill to augment my own, but as I read you, you are no Telepath."

"Nor would I assist you if I were, who will not so much as offer me his name." I sounded overfastidious even to myself. But I would have his name, if only to hold him accountable should either of us survive what he intended.

"For what it matters, I am called Naven," he condescended. "Nor do I require your 'assistance,' Lingri-one. Only the assurance that you are powerless to interfere."

He had me there. With my limited skills, I could at best shield my own mind and some few nearest me. To attempt to inform on this Naven was worse than useless; my word would not be accepted by any authority. Further, inform as to what? How explain telepathy to People? My moments would be numbered from the instant I spoke to the time they bound me to the witch-pyre. I could only watch, and wait, and hope to hold the moment when it came.

Naven was gone in a jingle of blind-bells, blending into the crowd with a Telepath's alacrity. At the end of the sward, a great stir and commotion announced some new arrival. The Kwengii were upon us, their helms and breastplates gleaming in the sun. With them, in as motley a collection of wagons and beasts and unusual persons as I had heretofore seen, came Dweneth.

"They gave us a choice, the Kwengii did. Here we were with our rattledown carts and a four of weary plowbeasts apulling them, all innocent as sunshine on the road, when out of the wood they strut, marching smart in all their swords and splendarmor.

"We couldn't hide, we could hardly outrun them—my heart was in my mouth. Then their leader sashays up and starts to babble in his broken Hrar' that either we let them escort us into Town or they'll kill us outright. 'Harbor not with the one who kills' be damned. I'd like to know what you'd have done!"

How do I describe her? Only Other memory could presume to accuracy after eighty-two years and with all the overlay of event and happenstance between. Other memory is all that preserves what *was* within what is and might-have-been of Dweneth DainsDaughter, who was to become my dearest friend.

Start with her talent for wordsplicing, which I was later to adapt to my poetry. "Rattling" plus "broken-down" became "rattledown"; "splendid" plus "armor" became "splendarmor"—the variations were endless. This talent baffled me at first, trained as I was to anOther's precision with words, but I came in time to understand it as the product of a mind so agile it would absorb all that Other could teach it without ever losing that which made her People, bred in the bone and forever.

What I first saw was an impossible torrent of redgold, green-gold hair, gleaming brighter than Kwengii helms in sunlight, all tumbling in a bright confusion of ringlets down her back to her plump waist . . .

" 'Plump!' " I hear her shriek, though in truth her voice was lost to me ten years and seven days ago. "Oh, cruelty, you! Was I, even then?"

"I fail to understand your species' habitual overemphasis upon matters as trivial as physical appearance," I say Other-solemnly, though she knows I am teasing her; it is a talent she taught me. "Truly, 'plump.' Burgeoning. Alive, vibrant. Then as now. Genetic accident, nothing more. Why does it beset you so?"

She sighs, despairing of making me see.

"Not that beauty or the lack of it ever troubled you, old Stick! Forget to change your clothes or comb the mares'-nests out of your hair if someone doesn't chastise you. You could be so lovely if you tried!"

"And it was always you who did the chastising," I remind her.

98

"As it was you who told me I was lovely in spirit. 'What matters the wrapping if the inside be exquisite' is how I believe you expressed it. Was this untruth?"

"Never mind!" she chides me, shaking her head in bemusement. "Get you back to your description. From this distance it reads better than I remember it!"

Not plump, not truly. I write this only to tweak her memory, to reconjure that long-gone voice within my soul, brief warmth and small comfort in a World now both cold and comfortless. She was, in truth, built wider and more solid than ectomorphic Other, and called me Stick all our days—a two-bladed appellation, and only one of several—but it was more vitality than flesh that filled out her form. Vitality danced sparks in her amber eyes, glowed from flesh as tanned and freckle-spattered as Argetha's. But where my mistress was wan and drawn and sickly, this Dweneth burst with life. Awake she was all energy; asleep, insensate as a stone. She owned no middle ground.

Garbed in Players' spangled particolor, she rode into Town atop the most garish wagon I had ever seen. The legend painted on its side in high gilt letters for those few who could read proclaimed: "DainsTroupe: Farce, Cirque, and Tragedie: Come All!" And this redgold, greengold, spangled and particolored confection, waving and smiling and blowing kisses amid an entourage of diverse clowns and beasts and stalking tragedians soon had the crowd's undivided adulation.

"Come all, come all!" she cried, her voice high and lyric but no less able to carry over the heads of the throng. "Full-out Cirque in the tent at nightfall, storysinging at Sirdar'sInn after! Come all, come all!"

"Dwe-neth, Dwe-neth!" rose a chorus of male voices, for the troupe had played this Town before, and Dweneth was their favorite. She acknowledged the accolade with more smiles and blown kisses, though when one bold lad leapt onto the wagon to claim his kiss in person, she dispatched him with her hand in his face, shoving him back into the crowd and all but under the wheels, without a shred of remorse. The crowd roared.

99

"There's a girl!"

"Friendly, but no tart is DainsDaughter!"

"Dwe-neth, Dwe-neth!"

". . . no, nor bear-baiting, nor boxing, neither! Da won't allow it, and I can't abide such cruelty to animal nor People!"

The greengold hair was false, a fall of artificial ringlets pinned on beneath the redgold, which was all her own. I discovered this when, being sent by my mistress to fetch her Darvis out of the inn before he was too drunk to count the day's income as it slipped between his fingers, I heard and saw her through the half-drawn curtain of the tiring-room—her particolor exchanged for a deep red gown which offset her coloring, as she chatted with some unseen admirer behind the curtain. I watched as she removed the half-wig, shook it out, and stuffed it into her Players' trunk before joining those in the common room.

"Here!" she called to the innkeeper, sidling up beside me at the ale-table, where I had been attempting to wake my snoring, head-on-his-arms master without drawing undue attention. The Troupe's tent, where the Cirque was still going on, had been pitched at the far end of the green, and the spillover crowd had not yet arrived for the storysinging. "Let's have a cool one, luv, 'cause the roads was dusty coming here and my throat's got work yet this night!"

So saying, she turned her eyes on me, and did not look away. For the first time in crossover, I genuinely feared for my life.

"I'd take you for Zanti, if it weren't for your eyes," she said without preamble, looking me up and down. She had any number of voices, depending on whom she was addressing; her tone with me was more formal, more wary, than with the innkeeper. "What are you, then, or am I being rude?"

"No, mistress," I replied, hoping my lowly status would cool her interest before she asked further questions for which I might not have the answers. "But considering my origins, my ancestry might prove as much a mystery to me as it would to you."

Legat's Parallel or Liiki's Dilemma—it was certainly truth, but a precarious one.

"Well, but you must have come from somewhere!"

Darvis snored the louder; I wished he would wake, to extricate me from this.

"Indeed, mistress . . ." I groped. On the sward this midday she had promised storysinging. "If you like, say I come from *OtherWhere*."

It was an old lay, known in several tongues the world-wide, about an ElvenQueen and her mist-shrouded, mystical-mythical realm, dangerous to sing in some parts, endlessly welcomed in all its variations elsewhere. I was about to learn which was the case in Hraregh.

"I see," Dweneth nodded. The innkeeper brought her ale; she downed half of it while her mind ticked over with possibilities. "I took you for educated, and I wasn't wrong. Well you mention *OtherWhere* to a Player, who recognizes the joke, but 'ware who else you say it to."

Her amber eyes took in my ragged servile's garb and the plague-mark. She greeted the latter with a small intake of breath indicating—what? Horror, pity? A second glance and she was skeptical; her trade lay in disguises, and she was somehow not convinced. She set down the ale-mug and took a step closer; we were all but touching. By caste I should have stepped back, looked aside or down, but I did neither. That made all the difference.

"Well!" Dweneth said at last, breaking the stare to finish her ale and signal the innkeeper. "As your master there is not able to naysay it, will you drink with me?"

"I do thank you, mistress." This time I took a small step backward. "But I think it would be unwise."

"Your choice." She shrugged as if it made no difference to her, though she was clearly disappointed. She shook back her redgold hair, letting it catch the lamplight, as well as the eye of every male in the room except my slumbering Darvis. She feigned indifference to this as well, and continued to gratify her curiosity. "You speak remarkably well, for a servile. And you ken *OtherWhere*. Have you stories of your own to sing?"

"Perhaps, mistress." What better chance to fulfill Rau's charge, to infiltrate Othersong into a performance attended by half the population of a Town, compounded with trader-folk, Players, and a regiment of ubiquitous Kwengii? And, perhaps, a seeming Zanti blindman, who was not what he appeared. "Is there any thinking creature that has not?"

That earned me a thoughtful look. The moment held some strange, poised eternality.

"I never thought of it quite that way before . . ." Dweneth began. What might she have said more, had Darvis not raised himself up in mid-snore, to shake his great hairy head and squint at this redgold vision before him?

"Whuff!" he ventured muzzily, staring past me at the Player-maid. "Hullo! Are ye real, then, or faerie dreamgeld?"

"As real as any dream, my brave merchantman!" Dweneth flattered him smartly, letting his eyes rove over her as if she expected it. "Penny ha'penny for you and your ladywife lets you see and hear how real, do you come hear me sing at midnight. Bring yon sea-eyes for nothing, for serviles come free, if ye like!"

She spoke to him, but her eyes never left mine. What songs, she must have wondered, did this "thinking creature" have to sing?

I half-carried drunken Darvis back to the cart; he would be dead asleep by midnight. So much for my chance to sing. And what, meanwhile, of Naven?

"Mistress?" I had ventured when Argetha and I were alone with the cart that afternoon. "What know you of the Kwengii?"

Darvis had begun his drinking early, and most of the Town had gone to see the Cirque. Only bearded, horn-helmed figures swaggered the sward—waiting, assessing, planning, fingering merchandise and the occasional inviting bodice with impunity—and a blind beggar could be heard betimes in the distance, jingling his bells and pleading alms in a thick Zanti accent.

Werthan lands adjoined Kwengis on several borders; if any had experience of this nation of pirates it would be Argetha. She turned my question over in her mind and then dismissed it.

"They can be got 'round. Do they ask for all ye have, offer them a third and they'll take two-thirds and spare ye. Offer them the whole and they'll slay ye for insulting of 'em. That's all I know."

"Is it not said of them that they will take the two-thirds smiling, then slay you for the last third, smiling still?"

"It's said, but I've not seen it." Argetha patted my hand to indicate I had spent my allotment of questions. "Don't believe everything ye hear. D'ye think they could carry off a whole Town in those longboats?"

It was as far as her thinking went, and it seemed to be the Town's consensus, for I saw no alarm among the populace, no more than an edge of uneasiness as Kwengii filled the Town as if they never intended to leave it. Naven was right; there was nothing I could do. Except, perhaps, intervene in what he intended to do. Whatever that might be.

"Fret ye not, Lingri-girl," Argetha chided me, seeing the question still beset me. "Do you fetch me a brew from the inn, while I put my feet up till there's customers."

Darvis had forbidden her to attend the Cirque.

"But he can't object to storysinging," Argetha mused, eyeing him after I'd brought him back. He slumbered away his drink beneath the quilts and cooking pots, oblivious. "Yet now, here's the rub: do we wake him and bring him along with us, he'll insist to sing in that *graaxen's* voice until the Players shout him down, and there'll be heads broke. But if we was to let him have his sleep . . ."

There was nothing I desired more than to attend this singing, for where would most of the Town be gathered, and doubtless Naven with them? If I was to stop him, at least mitigate him, it would have to be there. But Darvis, even sleeping, stood in the way.

"We cannot leave him alone in this condition," I was constrained to point out. "What if someone plundered the wagon? Nor, mistress, can you attend the sing alone."

It was the right of tarts and Player-maids, but not of upright married women, to venture out after dark alone.

"I've thought that out as well." Argetha smiled her gap-toothed smile, beckoning to a shadow figure lingering in the nearer alley. "You, boy!"

He detached himself from deeper shadow to stand blinking in the torchlight. A sex-seller—smooth-cheeked, rheumy-eyed, snuffling, very young and dirty. Argetha flashed him the gleam of a half-coin, more than a night's work would earn him after he'd paid off his procurer or, if the procurer were a kinsman, the usual arrangement, more than he'd ever see at all.

He snatched it without a word, spiriting it away in some hidden pocket, and clambered into the wagon, keeping well clear of Darvis. A jagged, handwrought street dirk glinted in one dirty fist.

"That much coin again," Argetha promised him, "do I find nothing's missing when I get back."

She had Krex sniff the boy to recognize him, then tied the *graax* near enough to guard the wagon as well. We hurried along the cobbles toward Sirdar'sInn; the sing was just beginning.

Had I been alone, I would have kept to the back, to watch and wait upon my opportunity, but Argetha pushed and squirmed to the very front of the crowded common room, dragging me with her until we were actually inside the near-circle.

Circles are a universal among all the tribes of People, a concept very different from our own half-circle, which implies that we are part, as well as all, of the All. Wherever People gather they gather in circles, closing themselves and their hearthfires in, and strangers out. My nights among the traders had been spent always on the peripheries of such a fire-enclosing circle. In Sirdar'sInn the fire itself formed the final arc of the circle, enclosed in the inn's great stone hearth, which was itself shaped like a circle upended. It cast its heat and light upon those nearest, leaving the rest in dark.

Despite Argetha's prodding I was able to find some portion of that dark to shield me, concealing myself in the shadow cast by the arc of the hearth, to search the crowd for Naven's alien presence. Townsfolk and traders I recognized by their garb; those strange-garbed and exotic, with traces of cirque-makeup still clinging to their clean-shaved faces, I took to be Dweneth's fellow Players. Where would a Zanti blindman conceal himself in such a throng?

There were Kwengii here too, though not many—an armed pair flanking the inndoor, three or four more, ever changing, mingling among the crowd. They swaggered and smiled, hands on their sword-hilts, brushing closer than necessary to women whose menfolk feigned not to mind, their heavy gaunt-leted hands too near the fragile heads of children, their swords too near to suckling infants. Where were the rest—already taking over the Town? What was I to do?

Here at last was Naven, wending his way to the very front of the crowd, where Dweneth had just passed him the sing-stick.

She herself had been singing the end of *CoxComb*, a merry inconsequential lay I had learned from Rau, though this ver-sion contained certain bawdy ornaments, improvised with mime, that had the crowd aroar with delight. They were laugh-ing still as the stick passed to Naven, and did not feel the weight of circumstance fall upon them with this passing. The Zanti blindman seated himself against the backdrop of the roaring hearthfire, and began a dirge.

Dirge was all it could be called. He gave it neither name nor introduction, but simply sang a droning What-if tale of a

People done in by their own incaution, dead at the swords of smiling strangers. Babes dismembered, their mothers raped and killed—so it did go on.

The crowd grew ominously silent, for none of this was alien to any of them, who lived in violent times. They grew so still that the studied move of Kwengii hands to Kwengii swords all but screamed.

"No!" a single voice cried out, female-high and cutting across Naven's mournful drone—there never was a Telepath who could carry a tune—and Dweneth seized the singstick, shoving the Zanti blindman unceremoniously off-balance into the crowd, to break his spell as the People jeered in false relief.

"My friends, this simply will not do!" she chided them, as if the mood were their doing.

She waited while Naven was roughed and pummeled to the back of the room. She might have sung more of her happy, feckless tales, might have chosen any to sing from the suddenly giddy crowd. Instead her eyes found mine and she thrust the stick at me.

"What Zanti has done, let Zanti undo!" she cried, brazening for the crowd and the watchful Kwengii, whose swords slipped back to their scabbards for the present. "Spare us troubles past or yet to come! Sing us of *OtherWhere*, Sea-eyes, and make it quick!"

Why did she say that exactly? It was as if she knew my mind.

In servile's rags and not untrembling, I took my place before the fire. This was precisely the opportunity I sought. Why did it give me pause? In a voice that rasped and cracked until I taught it Discipline, I sang of OtherWhere.

I began with the standard version of the old tale all People's children knew, though I gave no name to the ElvenQueen whose island realm lay to the Shadoward of the Great Sea; for all I knew, it was Govin who ruled the Matriarchy these ten days. Then deftly—so I thought, for none made murmured protest at it—I began to interweave improvisations of my own.

A single verse introduced the Legend, couched in terms mythical rather than astrophysical, of the One who brought his children out of the Bowl of the Sky and left them alone upon the land. Two verses followed incorporating the Otherwars, and I let the Kwengii know that one at least knew what they intended here. Let them kill me for singing it, so my singing warned the People. But nothing happened. Still alive and breathing, I sang on.

A single verse sang of the Thousand-Year:

> *Who will be the first to trust?*
> *Who first to stay her hand from violence*
> *And so invite death?*
> *Who causes death lives with death*
> *While she who dies brings life . . .*

It is the very enigma upon which Other children cut their moral milk teeth, and as it had balked us for five hundred thousand years, I mentioned it only in passing to an audience unready yet to comprehend it. Was Naven listening? Before I gave over the themes of the Thousand-Year, I dared a variation: what principles are worth dying for? Are any worth killing for? Is any opinion worth the loss of a single life? If so, how many lives, up to and including the whole of a species? The crowd grew restive, baffled; I moved on.

The remainder was no more than travelogue, a nostalgia piece about the place where I was born, and which I had not realized until this moment that I longed to see again. For every verse I sang of comforts and technologies, I added one on order, tranquility, peace. I sang unaccompanied, and did not sit as was the custom, but stood to use the whole of my body as instrument, swaying to the rhythms as I sang.

Whatever the esthetic quality of my voice, I was poet-innate and Rau had been my teacher; neither my rhyme nor my meter could be faulted, and I seemed to have my audience's attention. I had not been this taken out of myself since Lerius and I became entangled in the Legend.

The People sat enraptured, Argetha among them, entranced to think her silent servile owned such a tongue. Was it my words which filled them with such longing for a world none of them had ever seen, or was it that world itself, by virtue of its very improbability? I need only add a verse or two, and I would be done.

Or might have been. At some point the guard by the door had retreated into the night, and only three Kwengii remained in the crowd, not an alarming number in a realm where no man traveled without at least a clasp-knife on his person. All might yet have been well, at least in the inn's vicinity, had not Naven begun his sending.

There was nothing I could have done, only finish my song and try to hold some portion of that mob with quavering and soon-drowned voice. My listeners slipped away from me, giving way from growing confusion to fear to mounting panic. The precise how and why remain unclear to me to this day.

Was it that Naven's sending was too imperfect to select among an entire Town and target only Kwengii? Or was it too powerful against these untrained minds, to send such abject terror into the warriors nearest him that they struck out blindly, foreseeing their own deaths and choosing the victims to accompany them into eternity?

The result was a sudden killing frenzy. My song stuttered to silence as blood-tempered Kwengii steel as silently parted Naven's head from his body, spewing Otherblood everywhere and starting the stampede.

Screams and sounds of carnage erupted from without as well as within the inn, and in the sudden press of bodies I could only search in vain for Argetha to try to save her. Finding the singstick still in my hand, uncertain of the custom in these parts and more concerned with the living, I flung it into the fire. O fool, Naven! Did ever a Telepath live who wasn't at least some part fool?

"That fool blindman!" Dweneth raged, forcing her way through the crowd and hysteria, shoving me along ahead of her. "Your mistress is outside. Through the kitchen yard, go!"

As she pushed she found some from the Cirque troupe, and took charge of them as well.

"Ho, Gause!" she called to a brawny Dyr tumbler, half a head taller than the tallest in the crowd, whom she stayed with one small hand on his bare muscled arm.

"Lady?" he breathed.

"To the tent, before they tear it down. Set the animals free, and salvage what else ye can. Father's to Refuge, I'm sure. Hie ye and follow—ho, Omila!"

This latter was a fragile, large-eyed tragedienne, about to be swept up by the mob; Dweneth and Gause pulled her to by main force.

"Find as many as you can. Tell them to Refuge before the gates are closed. And—Omila? Look to the animals . . . especially Hrill!"

"Aye, Lady!" the pair responded in unison, as brawny Gause hove Omila onto his shoulders and they plunged again through the crowd.

We found Argetha in the courtyard, shoeless and stunned, sitting dazed against the innwall, oblivious of the tumult and the crowd near to trampling her. Nearly every structure in Town was burning. Wisps of thatch flew loose from house roofs to singe our hair and clothing, and the ghastly light of flame was all there was to guide us through the dark.

"See to your mistress!" Dweneth shoved me a final time and was gone.

I helped Argetha to her feet; as soon as she saw who I was she clutched at me and began to scream.

"Darvis! Oh, my Darvis-man and all our goods—oh!"

Shrieking and wild-eyed, she dodged through the still-fleeing crowd toward the greensward and I followed.

The killing and looting seemed to have passed this way and gone. Things still burned and crashed, shadow figures loomed and scattered against the wall of flame. Darvis's cart was overturned and smouldering, whatever goods could be carried already gone, along with the street-child, instinctive survivor like all his kind.

Rearing and screaming, reliving ancient battles, Krex had been tethered too short to protect his master for, eyes skyward and staring wider than ever they did in life, brains spattering the cobbles, lay Darvis. Argetha shrieked and threw herself upon him, blind with grief and beyond reason.

She did not hear the straggling warrior clanking and creeping toward us, but Krex's ears and mine were as keen, and we heard him simultaneously. The old beast screamed and reared, his great hooves plowing the air as if to rend the Kwengii's skull, whereas I—

—could not anticipate Argetha quick enough, as she flung me aside and threw herself upon the Kwengii, shrieking:

"Namore, namore! Ye'll take namore of mine, ye murthering—"

He cut her down in mid-shriek and turned on me, slashing sideways to catch more bone than flesh on my upraised arm as I fended and brought his legs out from under him, toppling him hard on the cobbles. Between Krex's proximity and whatever demon seemed to possess me, the Kwengii suddenly had enough, and fled.

I tore a length of gipon-hem to staunch the blood, more concerned that its hue reveal my Otherness than that the wound be serious. Afar in the vicinity of the garrison the tocsin sounded; the Town was taken, the worst of the fighting over.

The garrison, given the choice of joining its conquerors or being slain to the last man, had no doubt yielded to the expediency of the former. Fires would burn themselves out, looters pick everything clean and withdraw, survivors emerge with the dawn to learn their fate. What would happen to them, much less to a clanless servile who at present had no master?

I had no time to ponder it. As I knelt beside my dead mistress, to compose her cold limbs and close those pale eyes at last in rest, a hard hand clamped itself over my mouth. Its companion twisted my good arm behind me, dragging me into the shadows. I could have fended, but would not, against an adversary I could not see. I made no move, and was taken.

"Brigand Kings and the Right of Three" (from *The Approved History of People*, revised ed. Volume I: *Before All That*, pages 466-67)

. . . lest these Others, who would prefer to take full credit for every new idea, forget: we too had our innovations, and the institution of the Brigand Kings was among them . . .

The idea came out of the plague years and the early kingdoms where, whenever rebellion was threatened, or too many felons filled the keeps of the city-states, the kings thereof, rather than begin a war or purge where splinter groups were many and the cost in lives and materiel might be too great, the offending masses were collected together and exiled to some tract of unclaimed land, whether mountain or marshland, there to live unmolested so long as they did not enter the cities again. The most renowned of these was begun in Droghia, and its best-known Brigand King was Brok DainSon.

These Brigand Kings were often far more powerful in their own small realms than the legitimate kings in theirs, not having to answer to parliaments or rule of law whenever they chose to divide spoils or sever heads or elsewise exercise their authority. But however savage they may have been, we must not forget that we owe them the establishment of the Right of Three.

This right stated simply that any freeman or -woman, condemned to death for whatever reason, had the right to ask of his accusers three questions, which must be answered truthfully and completely before the sentence could be carried out. While this began innocently enough, as a means of setting the record straight as to who had accused the condemned and why, the right was sometimes abused in later years to include filibusters or long-winded legal questions which might take months and a herd of lawyers to answer, if they were answerable at all. As a consequence, and with the arrival of Others, the Right of Three has fallen into disuse in all but the most backward of nations, and while it is true that capital crimes have also decreased in number and category, the romance of the Brigand Kings is sorely missed.

"Not a sound! Promise me?" I nodded and she released me, wiping the hand that had clasped my mouth fastidiously on her Players' pantaloons, as if either of us were the filthier under the circumstances. I know not what I looked like, but Dweneth was covered with soot.

"Well!" she breathed, surveying me and the surrounding carnage with hands on her hips and inordinate calm. "Couldn't have you shrieking and bringing some stray fighting man back down on us, could I?"

"Mistress, if you will, I am not in the habit of 'shrieking' under such circumstances as . . ."

She was not listening, but had gone to kneel beside my slain master and mistress. Strangely, Krex seemed not to mind, for the old *graax* had grown incredibly still, nuzzling her shoulder as if in sympathy. With no sign of revulsion, the Player-maid seemed to mourn these two she never knew, making some final religious gesture over their two bloodied forms before she turned to me.

"You could have run away."

"Where was I to go, mistress?"

She puzzled over that. "These are all that owned you?"

"Yes."

"No deed or written document to prove it, I suppose?"

"None I am aware of. Neither Darvis nor Argetha could read."

"You destroyed the singstick!" she accused me, on her feet once more. "You belong to me now. Can you ride?"

"Mistress, I have never had opportunity to ascertain . . ."

She had Krex by the traces—an uncanny feat, for the beast ordinarily shied from any but Darvis's touch—and, soothing him with words I did not recognize, stroked his nose and breathed into his nostrils until he stood beneath her hand as docile as a flock-beast. The traces bunched in one hand, she grasped his nearer ear and swung herself up onto his broad, armored back, her small slippered feet fitting expertly beneath the foreleg plates where *graax*-flesh is tenderest and the beast can be guided by those who know how. Obviously Dweneth was one such. Primly she stretched a hand down to me.

"Mistress, I know not—"

"Best you find out," she cut me off, and hauled me up behind her. I clasped her around the waist; it was a long way to the ground.

"Has the beast a name?"

"My master called him Krex."

Hearing my voice from this untoward position, he flicked his ears in amazement. Before he could begin to dance sideways and indulge his characteristic whimsy, Dweneth had him in control.

"Ho then, Krex, old son!" She prodded him gently with her heels beneath the foreplates to get him going. "Hie you— we're for Refuge!"

"As the beast has a name, I suppose you do as well," Dweneth called over her shoulder after we had passed brazen and un-hindered past a double pair of sentries, through a gate both locked and guarded and well into the forest, on nothing more

114

than her winning smile and a sergeant's memory of her performance the year before in the *Rose Allegory*. "What are you called, who sings so poignantly of *OtherWhere*?"

Poignantly? The word was hers, and puzzled me. I had sung in the only way I knew. Perhaps it was not the objective quality of my singing that she meant, but her People's receptivity to it.

"I am called Lingri," I replied, wondering how many more questions she had and how I was to answer her truthfully. "Mistress, if it is my place to ask . . . you might have fled the Town as soon as we parted at Sirdar'sInn. Was it only because of the singstick that you came back for me?"

I expected any response save the one I got. She seemed about to answer—I could feel her intake of breath—but suddenly could not speak. She shook her head wordlessly, hunched over the *graax's* withers, and began to shudder all over with weeping.

AnOther would not more willingly witness such uncontrolled passion than she would succumb to it. I leapt off Krex's back to stand in the road and turn my head away; were I a freewoman I would have fled outright into the wood. Krex and I, unlikely co-conspirators, listened to the susurration of leaves as the dawn gave way to sunlight, our heads bowed together until the storm had passed.

"Well, I must say you're a comfort!" My new mistress at last tossed her redgold hair up off her face, smeared tears and soot together with the backs of her hands and wiped her nose on the hem of her tunic, then slid down into the road to confront me. "Not that I don't always do that—wait until the crisis is well past before I go to pieces. But even a stranger has been known to offer a bit of solace!"

With that she threw her arms about me. Such a flood of unshielded emotion was enough to stagger me.

People's passions are ever easier to read than Others', and I was always cautious whom I touched; still their thoughts had formed a constant undertone through all my days in crossover. Darvis's mind had been simple, concerned with the here and now. Argetha's mind had been more fanciful, embroidered about with dreams of the future and her impending babe, but finally as pragmatic as her man's.

This Dweneth's thoughts were nothing like, but were such a chaos of terrored memories and present fears all tumbled together in such rapid succession that my own mind could not process them rapidly enough. I could only offer physical comfort, whatever value that might have and, awkwardly, put my arms about her as well.

"Scared you, did I?" she sniffled, recovered at last, feeling my awkwardness and pushing me aside. "My, you are a cold one! Not a tear for them that owned you, and even less for me. How does your arm?"

I had trusted the pain-Discipline to do its work and quite forgotten the sword wound. Last night in the light of a burning Town it might have passed inspection; I could not have her examining it in daylight.

"It is—healing, I thank you, mistress," I said quickly, clamping my better hand over the makeshift bandage to prevent her undoing it. "I shall tend it myself."

"Be that way!" she sniffed, leaping onto Krex's back once more, as graceful as a Player. "Up you get. The hysterics are over, I promise you. Or would you rather play the proper servant and walk the rest? We're not that far from my brother's camp."

I walked. Were Refuge and her brother's camp the same? Who might her brother be? As we left the main road to pick our way along a forest path, narrow and sunless, thick with fallen leaves, treacherous with low-hanging branches and hidden roots (not to mention Krex's huge feet which, his whimsy restored as he scented People's habitat up ahead, he could not resist setting down too close to mine), it occurred to me that she had not answered my question. Why had she come back for me?

"Because that singstick has been in my family since my grandmother's day!" she told me crossly, once we were safe in Refuge. "I was nine years old when I watched my mother, my sister, and two brothers killed, and it was all I saved. Fled with it across a countryside and I won't tell you what terrors, then one little Kwengii brawl and you panic and throw it into the fire!"

"Mistress, in some places it is the custom to destroy the stick rather than have it fall into a murderer's hands, that it might not have its powers turned to evil." It was all superstition, but if it were People's custom, I was bound to abide by it. "I ask forgiveness if in misunderstanding the custom hereabouts I—"

"Oh, shut up about it! The more I think of it the angrier I get. Best you not let me think of it!"

Not knowing how I was to do that, I retreated into silence, wondering what disposition she would make of me now we were in Refuge.

Refuge at first had seemed no larger than a raft upon a marsh, poled indolently by a ragged one-eyed scarecrow who peered at us closely with his surviving eye as he neared our shore. When he recognized Dweneth with a loud hallo the woods on the far shore behind him became suddenly alive with folk appearing from behind trees and underbrush to wave and stare and call out Dweneth's name. She for her part slid down from Krex, removed his harness, and slapped him on the rump to send him on his way.

"He's too big to row across, and *graaxen* are unwieldy swimmers. Let him forage the woods and go free, or hang about and we'll find work for him. He'll decide."

"Were ye followed, lass?" the boatman wanted to know, leaning on his pole as Dweneth lightly stepped aboard the raft and indicated I was to follow.

"Mercy for you, no, for all the racket ye made!" she scolded him, then realized she had grabbed me by my wounded arm. "I don't like your color, and I'll wager that bandage soaked through. You'll let me look at it once we're across."

It was the last thing I wanted.

"Doubt ye'll have the time," the boatman interjected, ignoring me until my presence be explained to him. "There's a babe due among the Brigandfolk, and Gridl's broke his arm again. Too, there's the usual collection of childer with bruises and gut-pains, old uns with the bone-ache, them with burns and grumbles . . ."

"No rest for the weary!" Dweneth sighed.

She had not set both feet on firm ground before she was surrounded by adults and children alike with hurts and ailments for her to tend. She examined and advised even as we walked, while I was gawked at but not spoken to, as I had been by the boatman. Refugers were on the outside of the law and trusted no one; only Dweneth's patronage had gotten me this far alive.

". . . yes, that's well, keep the poultice on it until the swelling goes down, then keep it clean but give it air. . . . It looks a bad break, truly; let me know when you're feeling brave and we'll rebreak and set it proper. . . . A purge of dinnet-leaves is what you want. Boil five to a pot, let it cool and give to him to drink, it should cure the flux . . ."

We found Gause the tumbler by his stature above the motley throng. He shouldered through to seize Dweneth in his rambunctious embrace.

"Safe?" she asked him searchingly, breathless from the crush and the importuning voices ("Dwe-neth, Dwe-neth!" these folk entreated her as had those in Town, though softer and more plaintive). "Cwala and the children, too?"

"All safe!" Gause assured her vigorously. "Stili got roughed and called some dirty names, but every person's safe. We lost the tent, though, and some of the animals, which puts your father in a *graax* of a mood, but your nasty Hrill survived unscathed. We've made you room in the best stilt-house."

He set Dweneth down on the steps of this most practical adaptation to the marshy ground, and she gently dismissed the crowd before she went inside.

"Tell the Brigandfolk I'll attend the birthing as soon as I've had to eat. For now I want a bath and peace. Mercy, you know I'm hardly going anywhere!"

118

*　　*　　*

It was while the bath was heating that I broached the subject of the singstick.

I had shed my servile's protocols almost at once, for such conventions, as I had observed, were not upheld in Refuge, and I had seen none indentured but myself in this ragtag company. Most who inhabited the stilt-houses and tree shelters on this cluster of marsh islands seemed escapees from some manner of oppression, living in careful contiguity with true felons and the ubiquitous Brigandfolk. Runaway slaves and dungeon dwellers, many with scars and brands and tattoos more telling than mine, intermingled with smugglers and Players and folk of no identifiable trade, and there was neither caste nor custom like what held sway in the world beyond this wood. Which is not to say there were no rules, but these I had to learn.

Dweneth's precious trunk had been salvaged, and she soon had its contents strewn about the stilt-house in search of clean garments for herself as well as something which might fit me. A small shaggy creature scurried constantly about her feet, yipping and tugging and being a general nuisance, as is the way with most lap-pets. This, as I learned to my detriment, was Hrill.

The creature immediately hated me, lunging at me from Dweneth's arms, growling and snapping his small vicious jaws. Dweneth held him tightly, slapping him on the nose to no avail.

"Odd, he usually loves everybody. Doubtless he senses how furious I am with you. I have no other explanation. Oh, *hush*, Hrill, really!"

She thrust him toward one of the children filling a great wooden tub with hot water. In the silence of their departure I dared mention the singstick, and was told not to let her think about it.

There were places where a singstick was treated like a living being, its destruction the equivalent of murder. What penalty would my new mistress exact?

119

"Here!" she snapped, still cross, tossing an extra skirt and gipon at me, having found the ones she wanted for herself. "Try those on for size. The skirt you can tie in at the waist, I suppose, but—no the blouse will flap like a tent, I can see that." She held it up to me, ruing my prominent collarbones. "You have been underfed, haven't you? Mayhap Omila's got something more your size . . ."

"Truth, mistress—" Irony could not make her angrier. "—I have always been this thin. It is no one's fault but my own. Forgive me!"

She began an angry retort, laughed a little instead. I held the borrowed garments carefully away from the dirt- and smoke-ruined things I wore.

"Further," I ventured, "if I were freewoman, I might suggest that there are matters better resolved before you take the trouble of clothing and feeding one who by your custom might deserve a different fate."

"You talk like a bloody barrister!" she snorted, hardly meaning it as a compliment, and sat on the lid of her Players' trunk to hear me out. "If I knew you only by your words, I'd swear you never were aught but freewoman, and of a higher station than I for that. Very well, as you'll not leave it alone: what's on your mind?"

"Were I freewoman—and, truth, I see no servile in this place—I would ask what you intend to do with me once you have me clothed and fed." I took a deep breath, steeled myself for what could get me killed. "I ask the Right of Three."

"So you fancy yourself on the verge of death?" Dweneth laughed again, but there was no humor in it. "You're nearer than you know! Fair enough. The Right of Three granted."

Again I gathered myself. "First, as I had destroyed the stick, you might at the least have left me to a Zanti's fate at Sirdar'sInn. Instead you saw to my escape. I can only assume you returned to seek me out after and exact some price of me. If so, finding my master dead, why did you not exact it?"

"Is that all one question?" Dweneth marveled. "What are the two that follow?"

120

"Say they are two parts to the same question," I suggested. Was it only that I had spoken so little these many months? Where did all these words come from? "The other is, why out of all the multitude in the inn you gave the stick to me?"

"Are you finished? Is that all?"

"Yes, mistress. You could have killed me back in Town, or left me to the Kwengii. That you went to such pains to retrieve me indicates you will not discard me now."

Had I said too much? Dweneth approached me nearer, as she had that first time at Sirdar'sInn, hands on her hips, frown lines etched between her fine arched brows.

"Something about you, so-named Lingri, is no more servile than I am the Rose of the *Allegory*. I don't expect you to tell me who you really are, or why you choose this guise—not now. But mark you: someday I shall also demand of you the Right of Three. For now, to answer you: I gave you the stick because of what you said of every thinking creature's having songs to sing. I wanted to hear yours. And as the uproar was begun by a Zanti tale, I thought to end it with a second. Whether you truly were Zanti or no, you looked the part, and the Kwengii would not quibble over fine points."

"And thereby I alone would either calm the disturbance or be its only victim."

She managed to look abashed. "Perhaps I had no right to decide the fate of chattel who was not mine. But I'd have recompensed your master smartly, if you'd happened to be killed."

Was this irony? She was a Player, harder to read than most. I chose to take her at her word.

"And the death of one, however undeserved, were preferable to the death of many. The attempt was most reasonable, if ineffective. I commend your reasoning."

"That barrister's tone again!" She could not make me out. "We're talking of your death, and I was only joking. Yet I do believe you mean it! And I'm not being totally honest with you either."

She peered out the doorflap to be certain no one lingered

to overhear, then sat again on her Players' trunk, and for the first time motioned me to sit as well. I chose the floor.

"Why didn't I take the stick from you when the riot started? If you tell a soul I'll cut your tongue out, but I wanted rid of the stick. Too many bad memories cling to it, my mother's death being only one of them. I've had a new one carved and named and waiting for me in Droghia, the next time we're on tour. But one can't rightly own a new one whilst the old one lives, and one can't destroy the old one out of hand if it was one's granddam's, do you see? Thus I needed a cat's-paw, and thus you served. I'd have offered your master a good price for you once I heard you sing. This way I got you for nothing, see?"

I both did and didn't. There was no true callousness in what she said; in a world where thinking beings were bought and sold, such a rationale was a given. But what made me so valuable to this mood-struck being, beyond the songs I sang? Her station was not such that she could readily keep a body-servant, nor did she seem to need one; the children of Refuge alone would clearly tend her every whim. Again, what did she want of me?

"Oh, besides the singing? Not what you're thinking, so set your mind at rest." For the briefest moment I wondered if it were part of the Players' art to read minds as well. "Though that's been said of me, by men who can't get what they want. I'll flirt because that's stock-in-trade, but I'll go no further. So you're safe. And not for what drudgery your master used you, either."

She had grasped my wrists to muse over my workworn hands and, once again, the plague-mark. Rau's invention had thus far earned me more attention than it had spared me.

"Pity!" Dweneth sighed, then released me, tested the water in the great steaming tub, shed her garments like a second skin, and climbed in.

"A fetish of mine, cleanliness," she said offhand, rubbing herself vigorously with the soapstone. "I've tried to introduce it to my people, for this silly notion I have that it prevents some sicknesses, though I know not why. Perhaps evil spirits dislike hot water? Most think me daft, of course. One more of DainsDaughter's affectations. Well, Barrister? Aren't you coming in?"

I will admit I was somewhat taken aback. In less formal circumstances Argetha and I had often shared the same mountain stream with the rest of the traderwomen, an experience in truth more chilling than cleansing, so modesty was not the issue. Where bathing in privacy and warm scented water was such a luxury, I knew it not unusual for several to share a bath, but always by rank and by turns, the lowest bathing last. One moment I was treated as property, to be bought or sold or dickered over, the next I was considered enough of an equal to share a bath. But these were People who often shared a roof if not a bed with livestock. It made sense to them.

I temporized as I might, retrieving the chain of coins from my skirt hem, tossing the bloodied bandage surreptitiously into the fire. Cautiously, I examined the wound. It was no longer bleeding, but the scar which formed was no color People would find sanguine.

"That looks infected!" Dweneth exclaimed, seizing my arm at the instant I stepped into the tub. "Why, how shy you are! How came you by the plague-mark, I do wonder, if you care so little to be touched?"

She clapped a hand over her mouth when she realized what she'd said. The particular plague Rau had "given" me was frequently congenital. The Player-maid's great amber eyes brimmed with tears.

"Your father, then, or your mother—? Oh you poor, dear child!"

"One more mouth to feed!" was how DainTroupe'sMaster greeted me, looking me over for further flaws of body, soul or temperament. "First the tent burned, our props and half

123

the beasts missing and all our number scattered, Stili drunk and his dresser beaten withal, Cwala gone preggers again, and now this! Belike the lass wants to kill her own father!"

"Oh, Da!" was all Dweneth said.

Her father was a squat, clean-shaven man, remarkably cheerless in view of his calling. But as his part of running the troupe was the management of incomes and expenditures and he rarely set foot in the ring, such disposition was perhaps understandable. The only person who could bring light to his eyes, for all his grumbling at or about her, was his dazzling daughter. Their reunion after the carnage of Town was loving and effusive, until dour Dain caught sight of me.

"I've heard it sings to bring the house down," he scowled, addressing Dweneth with his eyes on me. "How much does it eat?"

"*She* is called Lingri, and you'll treat her civilly, Da, thank you!" Dweneth scolded with her arms about his neck and her lips at his ear. Such open affection I found fascinating. We had not its like in my world, and I could not but wonder how Evere would react if so treated. "She's mine. I won her fair. Besides, she can do many things besides sing, can't you?"

She did not wait for me to answer and, truth, I knew not what "things" dour Dain might value.

"She can read and dance and tumble, can't you?" Again no pause for me to answer. "Gause can work her into his routine. Is Cwala really pregnant again?"

Dain grunted, fidgeting with his quill pen.

"It happens!" He looked me over once more. "Mayhap we can use her. Mayhap we've no choice, as we're stuck with feeding her or throwing her on Brok's mercy. Have you seen your brother yet?"

"My brother can wait!" Dweneth said too quickly, as if it were an old conversation, and a sore point between them.

Dain returned to his ledgers with something like despair. "Mayhap could yon Lingri do figures as well, I might believe in gods again!"

124

"If it please you, master," I ventured, far safer in what I was about to offer than in either dancing or tumbling, whatever this latter might be, "I can do some simple figuring, depending on the currency."

Dain glowered under his eyebrows and thrust the inky quill at me. "Show me!"

I did—laboriously and with much blotting and sufficient error to be convincing. Not that this was artifice. Lingri without a computer was neither gifted in sums nor skilled in the handling of quill pens. This one had belonged to some large marsh bird which had no doubt ended in a cooking pot; its lingering life-force fought my hand. But my columns tallied eventually and, were I to judge the quality of Dain's grunt, he was satisfied.

"We'll see!" he acquiesced. "Reading I have no use for, and almost anyone can sing, or thinks they can. But we need a new tumbler now my best's getting big of belly. She's not allowed back in the ring until she's weaned the babe, and that's more than a year. Childbearing ruins a tumbler's timing, I've always said. Are you virgin?"

"*Da!*" Dweneth objected, turning over my wrist. "It's hardly going to matter with this, unless you know a man who's more than part a fool!

"He only asks that of tumblers, on account of the timing, you see," she explained. "Anyway, Da, she's mine regardless. I'll feed her out of pocket if I have to."

"You may yet, my girl!" Dain grumped, though his eyes were smiling still. I wondered if there was anything Dweneth could ask of him and not receive. "You Lingri, as you look lithe enough, I'll take you for a tumbler and not yet one more of my daughter's strays and charities. How came you by the sword-wound?"

"Fighting off an armed Kwengii that killed her mistress, Da," Dweneth chimed in; I wondered how much of that she had witnessed. "She was most awfully brave!"

Dain grunted.

"See it heals before Gause starts you. After that, don't dis-

125

appoint me. As for you, my darling daughter, do you go speak to your brother or we're all out on our ear!"

"None enters Refuge without my brother Brok's permission," Dweneth explained. "Hence I must sup with him or he'll not allow Da and the troupe to stay. They've been at odds for years, my father and my last surviving brother—it's complicated."

"Am I to accompany you, mistress?"

"Brok has demanded it, but not yet. It's my pleasure to keep you from him as long as I can."

On that cryptic note she was gone, leaving me to fend for myself among Players and Brigandfolk. Only Gause welcomed me, motioning me toward a communal campfire where various joints were roasting. I demurred at these as well as a pot of eels, making do with what vegetables and grain porridge there was; Refugers harvested whatever the marsh had to offer. I endured their silent stares, who offered me no names though they knew mine.

Thereafter I ventured a brief walk about the camp, as far as my curiosity and Refugers' wariness would permit. Word had spread quickly that Dain employed me and I belonged to Dweneth, and as the first was much respected and the latter beloved, there were some gestures of welcome amid the watchfulness.

But the watchfulness remained. However occupied these folk were in the days that followed—in plucking fowl or beating washing upon the flat river rocks, in mending tents or making boats or nursing babes or scolding children—their eyes followed me everywhere. Never had I felt so Other.

I walked for as long as seemed judicious beneath those eyes and the suspicions behind them, then returned to the solitude of the stilt-house. Dweneth had promised to attend the birthing after she dined with Brok. I would have ample time and privacy to invoke the Mnemonic Discipline and store all I had learned these past days. So deep was I in the eidetic trance, I did not hear Dweneth until she was standing over me.

"What *are* you doing?" she demanded.

I lurched abruptly out of the trance and shuddered into equilibrium.

"I thought you'd be asleep ere now, or am I the only one who's crazy? A tumbler oughtn't to twist herself about like that, I'd think, or is it meant to keep you limber?"

"As to this matter of tumbling, mistress—"

"Or were you praying? I never thought to ask you your religion. Or is it taboo to ask that where you come from, wherever that might be?"

"Have you many more questions, mistress?" She was clearly overtired. "Shall I answer them all at once?"

She laughed, and collapsed on the floor beside me. "You're right. I'm dead on my feet and don't know enough to lie down. I beg your pardon!"

"How is the babe?"

"Practically delivered itself," she murmured. "They do, you know. Brigandfolk. Mother goes off in the wood and has it herself. It was only courtesy made them ask me to attend . . ."

She tipped herself over from sitting to lying and was fast asleep. Dutiful servile that I was, I found some quilts to cover her, listened to her breathing for some moments—how vulnerable these People were, after all!—and resumed my recording unobserved.

Did I wonder what transpired among Others while my world was no larger than a hut on a marsh isle in the middle of a wood? Curiosity was ever my species' undoing and I was not immune to it. Even now I wonder what transpires among the People of the wider World, now that my world is a room in a Citadel on an isle in the middle of the sea.

Then I wondered: What of Loriel? What new and controversial project had my grandmother embarked upon, plunging WiseOnes and the Matriarchy into turmoil, giving Govin and old Tagal further reason to snap at her heels? What of Jeijinn and the Council, as they weighed the reports of Monitors returned, waiting and pondering upon what was to come? Did she wonder where her errant offspring was at all? What of Evere my father, remote from it all, lost in his computer in the shadow of a tamed volcano? What of Rau? Was he alone on his tiny island, or had he a new Monitor already in training?

Wrapped in a quilt on the floor of the stilt-house, I slept.

Now I wonder: What of the Others trapped on the Mainland when the Guard first began their official forays? More than half our population were scattered about that vast continent, administering to the new world order both our species had designed. It has been years since any have been heard from. Are none of them alive? The Telepaths continue to scan the inscape of the mind for their voices and cannot hear them. Is this only distance, or is it death?

Again I wonder: What of Joreth, my son? I have not seen him since he was near-grown. Does he yet live, and in what manner? Living, is his young life one of constant watchfulness—in hiding, in exile, or in the freedom and privilege of being taken for one of the People, and a gifted one as well? Or if he has met death, was it easy? How much of it was my responsibility?

"You'd do this?"

The transcript I had brought lay between my once-husband's clenched hands on the tabletop; he would not touch it. His voice was ragged, his green eyes bloodshot. From grief or only drink? For all the years we'd joined and battled and rejoined again, I could not tell.

"You'd actually do *this*? The boy means so little to you? Or is this some final way to wreak your vengeance on me?"

"Husband . . ." I began, and could go no further.

Was the male of every species so short-sighted? I had risked the censure of two worlds in choosing this man, had presumed despite more recent rancor that he had once loved me. How could he so misinterpret what I did? Far more cutting words had passed between us in the past, but none quite so unjust.

"Do you think it has only to do with the three of us?" I

had not meant to raise my voice. "Open your eyes, man! The World is askew, and I will not sacrifice Joreth to its whims. I yield you full custody of our son; I know no better way. Is it such a crime, that might someday save his life? At least you are the better gifted at lying, that might save him."

"Betrayal!" He swept the transcript aside with the back of his musician's hand; its plastic casing caromed off the wall. He laid his head on his arms, voice muffled. "Hypocrisy! Talk of lying— ! What is it but a lie which says my son never had a mother?"

Doubtless you can choose him one from among the many women you've had in my absence, I thought but did not speak. Like most People, he was psi-null, and had never known my thoughts save when we were in the throes of mating.

"Betrayal!" he said again. "Betrayal of everything the generations have tried to achieve, from you above all—!"

"I will not play philosophy with my son's life!" I nearly shouted. "If declaring him half-Other causes his death, it becomes a gesture, meaningless and cruel. If he can live, under this you call a lie, it will be toward a better future. That is no empty gesture!"

It sounded so simple, spoken aloud, as indeed it was. As simple as lopping off a limb or cutting living flesh from one's own bones. Not complicated, only wrenching painful, to draw up this document now splayed in unswept corner, duly signed and authorized by the requisite authorities from both worlds, disavowing anOther's claim to Joreth's parentage, henceforward and in perpetuity. Surely his father could find him a safer foster mother, or leave him motherless. Joreth was fifteen— an adult, in OtherWhere. There was no explaining this to his father.

"Cold-blooded!" his boodshot eyes accused me. "Except when the rut is on you, you're every one of you so very cold!"

"Husband . . ." I began again. A mockery, this word, not true these many years.

"Cold and a hypocrite, who calls him still 'my son' and can't escape it!"

I retrieved the transcript from its unkempt corner, blew the dust from it, returned it to the tabletop.

"My error, then. For by this I have no son!"

Who was it, then, who lurked in shadow, hearing every word?

"Mum, *no!* Mum, wait! What is it? Is it me? What did I do? *Don't leave me!*"

But I must, and did, and never saw him more.

Did it work, this silly ruse, my only flimsy ploy against a World gone mad, a bureaucracy gone dangerous in its silliness, the ony lie I ever dared and got away with? Did it work, did Joreth pass as People, did it spare his life? Could I have done anything more, or less, or differently, beyond never birthing him at all? Still and again and for all the days remaining to me, I wonder. The wondering does not lessen the pain.

Lastly I wonder: What of Dweneth's legacy, of all she and I did together and separately throughout the wide World— all vanished, all undone?

Wrapped in darkness and the sound of my own breathing, I cannot sleep.

While I sojourned in Refuge, as it happened, Loriel had indeed begun her last and most controversial project: a city built entirely underwater, to satisfy both those who insisted that we leave the World to the People, and those who insisted we conceal ourselves from them.

She had submitted the plans to the Matriarchy in the year before my birth, and that esteemed body had at last wearied of this particular debate and granted her leave to proceed. Loriel knew that a city on the sea floor large enough to contain most of the population of One Greater alone would consume at least ten years in completion; she knew too from her own projections that the People would find us long before that.

Nevertheless, she began, taking up residence in a control sphere on the sea floor to supervise the work directly, spending as much time as age would permit in hands-on supervision.

Sheathed in a wetsuit, flippering about webfooted in the icy water amid the curious *bRi*, Loriel remained unchanged, except in parting with her floor-length silver hair, cropping it close to her Other ears, the better to shake the seawater out of it at day's end.

Jeijinn my mother, mindful of her daughter's presence on the mainland and of reports of newer violences on that far side of the Great Sea, grew conspicuously less vocal in her support of Espions and interventionism. One report before the Council was of particular concern. Coming out of Droghia, wealthiest of the seafaring nations, it told of its Droghiad or merchant-king who, armed with the assurance of his best scientists that the World was a sphere and not flat as was more widely held, was building a number of great deep-drafted ships, his eyes on the far horizon.

The great Debate, meanwhile, continued apace:

———

GOVIN: *Give us a hundred years more, and we can conceal ourselves and all our works from any unschooled eye, but we cannot do this in the time remaining to us. Give us leave to focus the powers of the Telepathy and we might drive these People back in fear and confusion without their ever seeing the source of their distress, only knowing that there are parts of this sea where they might not safely venture. But the Matriarchy is undecided, treating this as ancillary to the Great Debate, and addressing it not. Let those who will fend wait on the beaches in order to do so, but this the Council forbids outright. Perhaps the Debate is its own answer: those who are not prepared to put aside their own differences deserve annihilation.*

FRAYIN: *How can we be so certain their immediate reaction will be hostile? Surely the examples of their own extinct cultures indicate that they will not hesitate to take advantage of any race they deem weak or inferior, but there is no instance in their history of an encounter between an exploring race and one technologically superior—*

131

GOVIN: *—which, not incidentally, has no visible weapons.*

FRAYIN: *Granted. But do they need to know this? Can we not simply greet them, offer them the hospitality of our cities, and show them our way? Will they not forego the need for weaponry once they understand what else we offer?*

A THIRD VOICE: *And how much do we show them? How much give them? Shall we give them the atomic technology of the Five-Hundred Year? For while we survived its temptations, will they? And what of—*

JEIJINN: *(interjecting) Whatever we possess, either in technology or in the knowledge behind it, which might be used to harm themselves or Others, would be expunged from hardcopy and microstor and relegated to Eidetics. A rider to my proposal addresses this, and there are some twenty among the Telepathy who have volunteered to serve in mnemonic capacity.*

THIRD VOICE: *And if the People notice something's missing and demand it of us?*

FRAYIN: *We hope by then, Mother, that their conscience will have matured commensurate with their thirst for knowledge . . .*

(Transcript of an intercepted
InterPraesidium broadcast: "Interviews
with the People in Charge"
1643 P.A./T-Y1100/EspionCodeNet
cross-ref.)

SPECIAL GUEST: *. . . goes without saying that the disenfranchised in any nation are the new leader's best sort of fodder for fomenting of rebellions and overthrowing legitimate governments. Not only do these smallfry feed on dreams of glory and their own importance, but they can be tossed into the fray without objection if you only promise them some fancy title and a chance to get out* *of the swamps and foothills. When we were seeking for elite members to start up the Guard, we didn't have far to look for such prime bully boys, and we emptied the jails to fill up their legions at the same time.*

INTERVIEWER: *Is that how it was done?*

SPECIAL GUEST: *Yes, certainly. The worst of the lot we shipped off to the Archipelago and gave them pretty much of a free rein, so long as they were back in barracks at curfew. The Others were expecting bad, but not that bad. For the first night or two they did nothing but baby-bashing—just herding a bunch together at gunpoint and snatching the small ones right out of their mothers' arms, bashing their brains out and making the mothers clean up after. The boys loved it; it's almost as good as sex for them, I'm told. [Laughter] Amazing how stone-faced these Others can be even at something like that—further proving, as the psychpriests like to point out, that they aren't People, after all. Try that with any of our own and you'd have them howling and gouging your eyes out in spite of the rifles. Though it does take the fun out of it, not being able to get a rise out of them, and after the first nights they were careful to hide whatever babies were still alive.*

INTERVIEWER: *Not to change the subject, but doesn't the problem become what to do with these Guards once they're finished on the Archipelago? I'm told some sources say leave them the confiscated lands once they've eliminated the, um, problem. All the rotten eggs in one basket, so to speak. Then put a ring of patrol boats 'round the islands and you've got a first-class jail. Because how are you going to let them back into the mainstream after they've had that kind of power? Can't have them bashing heads on the Mainland.*

SPECIAL GUEST: *True, but then again, do we want to give them all that rich land and ready-built cities? Doesn't seem equitable somehow, when we've got all the droughts and crop failures to contend with over here, and the crappy highways and the bad air. Maybe we should leave them the Mainland instead, eh? I'll tell you off the record, there's a proposal right now before the Praesidium to get the neutron bombs on-line that much sooner and solve the whole island problem in a swoop—nonPersons and the Guard all at once. Then send in a sanitation troop to dump the bodies, and you've got all these perfect cities and the mines and compucenters empty and waiting for new citizenry. The only problem is a public relations one, really, in that practically every family has a delinquent son or no-good father in the Guard. How will we explain it to them? Nuclear accident, maybe, and some kind of compensation? It's sticky.*

INTERVIEWER: *Seems to me as long as they get the compensation . . .*
(Transmission lost.)

———

OtherLore: "The Color Days"
(from Histories: T-Y1020)

The Color Days were among the minor reforms initiated during the Year One of the Thousand-Year. Where once a certain color might be the sole emblem or 'property' of a given tribe and its flaunting by a rival tribe was sufficient to initiate years of inter-tribal war, the Elders declared all colors free of these totemic significances so that they might be used by all [cross-reference: Monopolies, Trade Agreements, Patent and Copyright Laws, Tribal Meldings].

From this evolved the tradition, still in use on Three Greater and many of the AgriIslands, of the Color Days, consisting of a ten-day cycle in which each day is marked by the wearing of a specified color. This specified color can be worn as a sleeve or scarf or badge upon the outer garments, or sometimes as the entire garment itself. While skirmishes and misunderstandings still occurred on some of the outislands as late as T-Y103 [see the "Orange and Green War" of that year], *in time the custom was adopted wholesale, and only recently abandoned on three of the four Greaters.*

The effect of so simple a gesture of solidarity was both salutary

134

and curious. The Psychology, following an extensive study, provided evidence that certain colors enhanced certain moods or dispositions, and certain in the Telepathy had been employing them as focus for generations. And though the custom is largely abandoned, certain associations are still made, almost innately, in respect to certain of the 'extra' colors, those recently discovered to be beyond People's normal visual spectrum, and yet perceived by Other senses.

seven

"What d'you think?" Lord Brok demanded of me. "Is there naught but demons to the Shadoward of the Great Sea? Is the Droghiad out of his mind?"

Gossip about the land that had exiled him, and doings elsewhere beyond the wood, reached Brok's cave with remarkable speed, by means of the tappers and bird-cryers. The unusual means of communication had not been reported by any previous Monitor, and I was most eager to learn their codes.

The tappers used hollow tree trunks to drum their coded messages across great distances, one to the next. The cryers used a language derived from birdsong to call from tree to tree. I had at first thought they were communing with the birds themselves, as we did with *bRi*.

"Of course not, silly!" Dweneth chided me as we harked to them throughout the camp, invisible in the trees. "Imagine trying to talk to a bird!

"We had a bird act once. I shall never forget the din. 'Squawk, squawk! Prettyboy, prettyboy!' Feathers and shit all over everything, and then they all died of some pox. Ugh!

Talk to birds, indeed! What ever would we find to say to them?

"Listen you . . ." she went on, a bandage half-rolled in her hand as she harked to the near calls and their faraway answers; I began to pick out a rudimentary musical language. "It's a code, to keep us current with events the World-wide, or at least as far as Droghia. How else would we know if there was danger approaching, or brushfires, or a plague atown? Brok and all the Refuge lords have spies from here to Droghia, and some as far as Lamora. It wonders me anyone who can read can at the same time be so ignorant!"

Reading had become a sensitive issue between us. Our second morning in Refuge, I saw Dweneth studying me as I combed out my hair and braided it back over my ears. Were the ears themselves the cause of her scowling, or was she simply lost in thought?

"I told Da you could read," she said slowly. "Was I much mistaken?"

She tossed what she'd had hidden in a fold of her skirt—a leatherbound, parchment-paged book, read up-to-down Hraregh fashion, though with right-to-left Plalan marginalia. A textbook seemed an odd possession for a Player-maid.

"*Can* you?" she demanded as I turned the pages of this curosity gingerly, uncertain of its durability. I had studied such antiquities kept in stasis in the Archives, but had never held one in my hands.

"In what languages, mistress?" I asked without thinking. The life-force of the creature whose hide had been used in the binding lingered, though the tome was a hundred years old; it stung my hands, distracting.

"Well, in Hraregh, for starters!" The full import of my question exasperated her. "Just how many can you? And how does a servile come so easily by what I've struggled for all my life? And for pity's sake, stop calling me mistress! It's an insult, coming from you!"

"Yes, m-my Lady," I tried, humbly. The day was not going well.

Deliberately I placed the book binding-down upon the fabric of my skirt to separate myself from it, allowing my fingers to touch only the pages. It was obvious from the thumb-worn margins that Dweneth had indeed struggled mightily to con what looked to be a simple peasants' apothecary, and in a single tongue. How dare I flaunt my knowledge against such struggle?

"I can read some Hraregh, Lady."

"Then tell me . . ." She seized the book, plumping down beside me, fluttering pages and tossing her redgold hair back from her face, running one finger down a dog-eared page, her tongue caught between her teeth in her fervor. ". . . what this word is and how it's pronounced and what it bloody well means!"

" 'Pharmacopoeia.' It means the whole of the cures and remedies one has in store. Ideally it means all drugs and curatives available in the known World—"

"—but in my case it falls to a handful of roots and herbs anyone could gather who took the trouble to learn, and precious little against serious illness!"

She scooped Hrill onto her lap to quiet him; the creature could not come near me without reacting with a ferocity ludicrous in something his size. Even with his mistress petting and soothing him, he felt compelled to growl and gnash his small teeth at me. I could not but wonder what he would do if Dweneth let him go.

"Refuge had a healer-woman once," she told me after I'd read a passage and she'd followed along with me, committing the whole to memory as a key for later reading, "but she was burnt for a witch and we've never found one to replace her. None wants the risk of fingers pointed and the stake when cures fail, as they're bound to. The skilled physicians live soft lives in the courts, so it falls to us flotsam to make do where we can.

"There are old ones who know spells and midwifery, but naught about washing their hands. Whenever I'm here, it somehow falls to me to fill the gap, as if I had some special magic. It's patience, that's all. Even on the road it's always

138

'Dweneth, I've cut my finger' or 'Dweneth, what's for an aching back?' Or a flux or a toothache, or what you will. Once it was 'Dweneth, the babe's bleeding from the ears and will not stop.' " She shuddered all over, and there were tears. "I lost that one and blamed myself, until I learned how the mother used to beat it!"

She wiped her eyes one-handed and Hrill lunged at me; she slapped his nose and thrust him out through the doorflap.

"What drives a mother to kill her babe, when I'd all but kill to have one?"

I thought of Argetha. "Are you . . . unable to, Lady?"

"Oh, I'm able, just not willing!" She slammed the book shut viciously. "If only it could be done without men . . . It's a long, long story, and frankly none of a servile's business. Read me more!"

I did so. Her interest was insatiable, her grasp quite thorough for someone largely self-taught.

"Were it possible for you to learn more formally of this physick, Lady, the better to minister to those that ask you?"

She laughed at that, bitterly. "And how am I to do that? Imagine a female presenting herself to the Collegium of Physicians to ask their admittance! Oh, they'd admit me, surely, though not for the learning of medicine, and what were left of me be suitable only for their cadaver pits. Or shall I be reborn a healer, my simple Lingri? Perhaps it's possible in *OtherWhere*. But here it's born a Player, die a Player, and though it's a better life than some, I wish I could do more!"

"She could have been a luminary," Gause informed me as he pondered on how to use my inexperience in his tumbling act. "One of those who play the great cities and are feted by kings and wed to princes, she's that good at her art, and beautiful besides. If what happened hadn't happened . . ."

"Gause, hush! You talk too much!"

This was the tragedienne Omila, who liked me no better than Hrill did, and would nearly as often bare her small teeth at me.

139

"It's not what she wants anyway!" Omila would sniff, dismissing it. "Dweneth wants to be a healer, the silly child!"

"You'll read with me every day," was Dweneth's instruction. She closed the book reluctantly, returned it to her Players' trunk. Sick and injured Refugers had been arriving for some time, to stand patient and silent outside the stilt-house, waiting for the only healer they knew. "You'll teach me. I've nearly twenty books—more than anyone, excepting Droghen in Droghia."

I thought of the millions of volumes in microstor on the Archipelago, and the inequities of circumstance.

"And you'll sing me more of *OtherWhere*," she added dryly, gathering her rudimentary cures and analgesics. "Mayhap include a verse or two on women who become physicians. And one on birds who talk. Somehow I'd believe them both from you."

"You never flinch nor blanch nor sicken, no matter how grievous the wound," she remarked as I helped her tend the sick. "Nor is there any clue in your face to tell the patient how grievous they're afflicted. How do you keep your face so still?"

"Say, Lady, that it is a mask," I suggested. "Much as what betimes a Player wears."

"But we're not playing now." She watched me sidelong as she swabbed a child's infected ear. Her own face bore a smile that few could see was forced. "Only your eyes move, and whatever they betray is beyond my interpretation. How do you do it?"

"I knew a wise man once . . ." I held the child's hands so that he would neither squirm nor intervene in the treatment. He stared transfixed at my Other face, his pain forgotten, and I could see that Dweneth made note of this as well. ". . . who studied to contain each of his passions, that they might not distress Others. I learned from him."

It was the closest description of a Disciplined Other I could give her. Would it serve?

140

"Where did you know this wise man?" She sent the child on his way, with *chu*leaf packed in his ear for antiseptic, a honey-sweet in his mouth, and a pat on the backside to dismiss him. "Or is this more of *OtherWhere*?"

"It's a long, long story, and frankly none of a mistress's business," I dared, and the murder in her eye suggested it were well I had said this in front of her people, where she dare not spoil her reputation by striking me. I changed the subject. "Why is Brok banished here? I thought him lord of this place."

"Your ears are bigger than I thought!" Dweneth seethed, still furious. "And Gause talks too much. So Brok is: chief thief among a nation of thieves. He was Droghen's chief of the exchequer once, but succumbed to sticky fingers.

"There is no caste in Droghia, you see . . ." An old one came to kiss her hand in gratitude for her prescription of fresh berry juice, which had cured his scurvy. Her smile was radiance itself this time. ". . . its being a nation of self-governing merchants. Droghen himself is but a butcher's son. Hence it was possible for my mother's firstborn—my mother having been Caretha, the Queen of Tragedie in her day; ask Omila—a Players' son with no talent at all for playing, to find himself a place there.

"When Droghen caught Brok with the coins between his fingers, he gave him a choice: a quick death, or take with him into exile the riffraff of every town in Droghia and somehow govern them here. So he does, if ruthlessly, and as long as they never set foot in Droghia, they are free to continue their larcenous pursuits as they please. Transgress once, and they find themselves caught between Brok and Droghen, squashed like insects."

So saying she slapped at such a creature on her neck; like any swamp, the place was rife with them. I felt its small life gasp and vanish.

"Remarkable," Dweneth went on, "but some actually become reformed here, for the swamp tolerates no slackers, and any trouble's dealt with swiftly and needing no court nor judges. Thus Droghen has all his rotten fruit in the one basket and Brok, as only I can live to say, is among the rottenest."

She slapped a second insect. "And, like rotten fruit, milord Brok draws flies. Why all the questions?"

By my count, I had asked but two. "Lord Brok has asked after me again," I explained, as insects lit on me as well, but left without biting; they had no taste for Otherblood.

"Damn! I knew he would. What did you say?"

"I replied to his messenger that, as I belonged to Lady Dweneth, and as you were not present at the time . . ."

"We'll ring him 'round the roses between us. Damn!" Slap! "He'll catch up with you eventually, Brok will, but relish the evasion while you can. And tell me why the bugs don't bite you?"

"Perhaps I am too bitter for their taste?"

"Lucky you!" Slap! "I'll not stay here for Baskseason, I swear! No matter that we have no tent, and Da can't make up his mind which way to go—I won't!"

Had the troupe not lost so much of its kit and menagerie in Town, we would be well away on a tour of the Windward countries by now, but dour Dain dared not venture out of Refuge with the Kwengii still about. None knew how long Brok would let us stay here. Dain's mood was darker every morning I came to do the books.

"You're daydreaming!" Dweneth chided me, drying her hands as the day's last "customer" departed. "Wash up and get you off to Gause. How's the arm?"

"Healing." I showed her; the scar was clean and already disappearing. "Though it avails me little in this matter of 'tumbling.'"

She rolled her eyes at me.

"I had to tell Da something! How was I to know you'd come in handy for the accounts? Besides, most of us hold a job or three beyond what we do in the ring or on the boards. Would you rather shovel *graax*shit?"

"I have done that before, Lady. At least there I knew what I was doing."

"Besides . . ." She did not answer me. "I've seen how you twist yourself about when you're praying. You're agile enough.

Tumbling's no more than a lot of jumping about and being thrown in the air. I did it myself before I did Comedie. It's Gause needs the true skill. Watch him and Cwala; you'll catch on."

So I did—watch, at least. The catching on took longer, and a considerable number of bruises.

"Your timing's strange, that's all," Gause assured me, or perhaps himself, pulling me out of the marsh-mud, which he'd deemed the softest place for a workout since his training mats had been lost with the tent. "I don't know where you learned your routines, but they are surely different! That backwards double-axel, now—it's suicide! Show me again."

Tumbing, as I had ascertained almost immediately, watching Gause and his partner Cwala—a more slender but no less muscular version of her spouse, beaded and braided where he was bald-shaved and tattooed—was no more complex nor arduous than the fitness routines mastered by Other children in infant school, differing only in the flourishes that made them look risky, and in the accompanying music. But if Others are innately graceful, I had never been among the more skilled or coordinated. With considerable surprise I discovered that among People my skills were deemed superior.

But, as Gause said, my timing was strange, and it took me much pondering to determine why.

I executed what he called a backward double-axel. It was no more than a back half-circle flip on each leg in turn, the whole of it ending where it had begun. One of the simpler movements I knew, and I was much out of practice. Yet Gause for all his experience could neither master it himself nor fit it into the rhythm of his routines. Alternatively, I could not match his timing whenever he seized me by the waist and tossed me upward, shouting instructions to me in mid-air, with the result that I consistently slipped through his hands or missed him altogether, ending again and again in noisome marsh-mud until Dweneth's borrowed tights and particolor were a uniform color the same as the mud I sat in. Gause must have thought me too weary to continue, but I was only thinking.

"Gause Tumbler," I addressed him formally, though from where I sat the formality must have been comical, "is the World round or flat?"

He laughed his great gusty laugh, looming over me, hands on his hips and shaven head thrown back at such an idiot's question.

"Why, flat, of course. What has that to do with anything?"

"But does not DyrCreed state that it is an arc?" So my studies with Rau had indicated.

"No, no, no, the *sky* is an arc, which the Great God holds between His two hands, thus." He demonstrated; acrobats think with their hands, as dancers with their feet. "The mud between is flat, as this you're sitting in, with the odd bump or pit here or there to signify mountain or valley. But, overall, flat. Besides, I repeat, Lingri-one, what has religion to do with what we're doing here?"

"The two are related," I assured him, pulling myself out of the mud. Cwala was pouting on a log nearby, resenting my presence because Dain meant me to replace her; when I tried to sit she made no room for me, but turned her back with a sniff of disapproval. "Tell me this, Gause-one: how come you this far Windward? For by your accent I surmise you are not only blood-of-Dyr, but born there."

Gause had liked me from the beginning, in part because I had Dweneth's patronage and he adored Dweneth, in part because Gause was the largest, strongest person he knew and, fearing no one, he was free to like everyone. He grinned at me.

"Why, so I was, and how sharp of you to notice! I came here overland with the caravans, working my way as a *'vek* driver over the Wastes because this lady here—" indicating Cwala "—was angry with me for violating the rites of which she was a priestess to pour my heart out to her in the temple, and I had to prove myself before she would take me to husband. Again, what has that to do—?"

"In your travels, did you ever chance to look from end to end of the caravan as it wound across the Wastes?"

Gause shrugged elaborately. "I suppose so."

"Then did you chance to notice . . ." I demonstrated with my hands as he had done. ". . . how the lead animals always disappeared *below* the horizon, rather than extending as far as eye could see?"

Again Gause laughed, sitting beside me on the log, squashing me over so that his sulking spouse would be forced to make room.

"No, I did not, and it's obvious you've never been to the Wastes, Lingri-one, for consider: the most of your travel is done by night, when you're limited to what you can see by moonlight, which is mostly the ass-end of the *guravek* in front of you, and heljacks aprowl and looking to pick off a weak man or beast, heljacks not being particular as to their choice of meat. In the day it is too hot to move, and that is when you sleep, or try to, your cloak drawn over your head for a tent, plagued alike by flies and shim-mirages, and too sunblind to see any horizon."

I should have thought of that before I asked him. "Nevertheless," I persisted, getting to my feet and centering, "could you imagine for a moment that the World might be round?"

Gause laughed. "Is this a play?" But Cwala's stony face grew animated, and she turned to me.

"In Dyr I was rites-priestess. I have drunk the vision drugs. I have seen whatof you speak."

"Then see it with me now, Cwala Tumbler," I invited, taking her hand to help her up.

She stood a head taller than I and formidable, no trace of pregnancy yet visible on her long-muscled form. Her three children I had seen in Refuge were strong and healthy like their parents; tumbling with its plentiful diet and strenuous exercise had its advantages.

I held Cwala's hands in mine to demonstrate. "Will you trust me?"

She nodded, closing her eyes, and I guided her by voice.

"First find your center, then seek the center of a round World and weave the two together." Cwala envisioned this, nodding again. "Never lose that weave no matter how you move. Now consider: a round world circles around itself and simultaneously around its sun, two different movements at two different speeds. One gives us the day, the second the year. Do you feel it?"

She did, and nodded, still clinging to my hands. Gause was shaking his head.

"Superstition!" I heard him mutter. "Women's spell-weaving!"

We women ignored him. "Now, however you move, Cwala-one, weave your movements according to these movements, moving round your center—so!"

I released her hands and flung myself into the axel. She hesitated but a moment before doing the same, her multiplicity of small braids flying, her long fingers and toes barely touching the ground before she sprang upward, flying past it. Finishing upright, she began to laugh gleefully.

"It's true, Gause! She's right—oh, try it!"

She and I began a series of interlocking axels around about a perplexed Gause, ending breathless in the mud, she hugging me and giggling, I lacking similar luxury, but no less pleased. Was physics ever before taught by an acrobat?

When we had caught our breath we seized on Gause, pulling him into our rhythms until he finally caught on, and the three of us used my round-world figures with his more traditional routines—though Gause swore by the Great God he never did believe in mine—until we had a performance to ring the World 'round.

Was it happiness I experienced in such moments? Certainly it was something I had never heretofore known—a sense of discovery and accomplishment at once, both shared with those who could appreciate it. As I know no better definition, let me state then that for the first time in my life, I was happy. How unlike—

Someone is tapping on my wall.

I have for some moments been meditating upon the last functional stylus remaining to me, and the prospect that I may soon be out of paper. The latter is not so critical as the former, as I may if needed reverse my alternating hand and write smaller between the existing lines, but if the last stylus runs dry—write with what? The drawing charcoals will not serve for such fine work, and there is nothing else suitable in the entire Citadel.

Yet, someone is tapping, in a pattern and code I recognize. The sound seems to emanate from the Sunward wall, which separates my chamber from the labyrinth of the Citadel, as if whoever is tapping knows it is my habit to face to Windward as I write, and the sound will reach my Sunward ear. Is this chance, has Gayat talked, or is the tapper someone who knows me well? I must not prognosticate, but listen.

Whoever it is uses the very tapper's code I once brought back from Refuge. Someone who knows me, then, and all my works. I translate:

LINGRI ONE COME AT ONCE GAYAT ILL FOOD CONSIGNMENT QUANDARY CITADEL LINGRI ONE AT ONCE SOLIAH

Soliah—the only Monitor my elder whom the People did not capture in the last forays. I had thought her dead. How did she get out, and what does she want of me? I acknowledge her message and begin one of my own:

SOLIAH ONE WELL RECEIVED I COME AT ONCE LINGRI.

The tap terminated, I consider. Though Soliah's message came as if from the far side of this very wall, I know she is deep within the Citadel, using its innate acoustics to send her message wholesale, since none but Gayat knows my precise location. This is deliberate. Those with a particular function, including the chronicler, are hidden throughout the City, that the Guard may not have the pleasure of torturing their where-abouts out of any Other. Soliah cannot come to me; therefore I must go to her.

What time is it—day or night? Dare I venture outdoors into the open ways, or must I wend the labyrinth? This subterranean way alters daily as buildings are razed or declared unsafe, and as a means to baffle the Guard. The message requested urgency. How was Gayat taken ill, and why summon me to deal with him, or are all the healers dead? Has my outspoken Telepath run afoul of some Guard who thinks to torture my whereabouts out of him? I am still considered a "ringleader," a special prize if caught. It was one reason why I have remained hidden from most Others, that none but Gayat may precisely know my whereabouts.

Was that the import of Soliah's message, that Gayat has been questioned about me? A Telepath can, under duress, bring her mind down to a point where it cannot be retrieved. And yet, the message contains Gayat and food consignments as if they were all of a piece.

Food consignment? A further mystery. Is this the same crisis which has made Gayat ill, or something else? I am overtired, my judgment skills gone shallow; this is the shadow-side of the fatigue Discipline. Food consignment, food consignment—I fix upon the words as if they were the entity themselves, unable to make sense of them. If the tappers' code had a failing, it was in its brevity. I must go to the source.

Since we have been driven back behind the Purists' cordon, our nourishment derives from several unreliable sources. The kelp-harvesters, their labors severely curtailed by patrols, nevertheless continue to risk their lives to bring us sustenance. But we can no longer process the kelp, and most cannot digest it raw. The agri-islands are long gone fallow, returned to marsh and meadow where they have not been sown with salt for spite. We can harvest nothing from the land.

The food we are "given" by the Guard derives from two sources—what they discard, and what is actually imported for our use. If they thought to taunt us with the abundance they throw away, we have once again disappointed them. We scavenge their trash pits without qualm; where children and elders are hungry, pride is a luxury, ill-afforded.

What supplies the nightflyers airlift in are not without their price. A response to pressure from those few People who will not see us starve, they have betimes been stolen outright by the Guard, who shoot us down as we venture to retrieve them where they drop. And there are subtler forms of sabotage, which an innocent like Gayat would know nothing of. I must go.

I stretch the kinks out of my spine, shake out my rumpled garments, adjust my eyes to the lesser darkness of the corridors, and feel my way along the walls. The labyrinth is broken now by open spaces I must cross, rubble-strewn quadrangles barren beneath mocking stars. Some of the Guard have been known to lurk here for days hoping to find secret entrances, or merely to murder any who dare cross. My night vision and my hearing are better than theirs still; a mouse could not sigh in this morass but I would hear it. I listen; the place is in fact as empty as it seems. Perhaps the Guard have killed the mice as well. I cross.

The first reentry I try has been sealed over; it does not open to my touch. There are two more I know about. The second of these is still accessible; I touch the proper place, and it whispers open only long enough for me to pass. As I hurry, my mind returns to the same thought: Has Gayat sacrificed himself for me? Ah, Gayat! Young and a fool, but not deserving this. As the passage closes behind me, I hurry.

It is nothing so noble, of course. The young fool has blundered into a consignment full of animal carcasses and, not knowing what they were, presumed to handle them and suffered an allergic reaction. Following convulsions, he has now lost consciousness. Soliah tells me all of this.

"Who gave him leave to open the parcels without scanning them?" I demand somewhat abruptly, kneeling beside him.

"Does anyone give a Telepath leave to do anything?" Soliah's patience is as thin as mine.

I call to him.

"Gayat!"

His body is rigid, his white eyes rolled up beneath their lids.

His hands look burned where he has touched the meat; he is more sensitive than I was at that age.

"Gayat-*la* Telepath, it is I, Lingri. Return!"

Voice alone does not work, and I do not know his soul-thread. A fellow Telepath would know precisely which stratum of the mind to probe to find and fetch him back. The surviving Telepaths cannot leave their Eidetics now, and I have neither their skill nor patience. I take the young face between my hands and slap it once. Gayat's body jerks. I slap again, harder; his eyes roll forward. He gags and shudders and sits up, hanging his head, ashamed. Behind us, Soliah sighs.

"Fool Telepath!" I chide him. "There might have been explosives within. Seven died in this manner on AgriSix. Where is your mind?"

He sits shakily, his head between his blistered hands, frightened of what he has done.

"So many are hungry, I could not wait! Why do they mock us so, to send us slaughtered creatures?"

"To evoke precisely the response they got from you," I reply pitilessly. "As if they are not capable of far more! Poor, innocent Telepath! Get some unguent for your hands, if there is any left, else evoke the Healing. And hereafter leave food consignments to those who know what they are doing!"

"Rather they let us starve . . ." he mutters down the passageways, innocence betrayed.

"So they may have," I murmur, looking to Soliah for some common sense. "Is there nothing here but meat?"

"Some moldy peas and weeviled grain. The kelp harvesters could not go out last night. Too many patrol boats."

I study her, who once was beautiful enough to infiltrate a Tawa harem and be the chosen one of its caliph. She sports the tattoos still, entwining her bare arms like blue-leaved vines—an affectation, perhaps, but one that she has earned. Her spine was broken under torture and the healers no longer have the instruments to realign it; she drags one leg and has the use of only one arm. Her face is striated with scars whose cause I can only guess at. But her eyes and mind are clear.

150

"Soliah . . ." I avert my eyes so she cannot read the pity in them. ". . . there are many who have no allergy to meat, especially among the intermixes . . ."

She nods, as pragmatic as I and also masking pity when I mention intermixes. She knows of Joreth.

" '. . . and take no animal life except to save your own,' " she recites. "Does it matter, I wonder, that the life was taken by someone else?"

"Not something the Elders needed to consider in their time. And if the Council does not hear of it, there will be no need of debate in our own time. As for the rest, boil the peas to kill the fungus, and cook the weevils with the grain for extra protein."

"My own thoughts precisely." Soliah reaches into one of the food parcels to give me something. "There were waterfowl, still feathered. I thought you might have need of these."

Wing quills, such as I have not used since Dain's day. Soliah's good hand is raw from plucking them. There are roots and barks that I can grind for ink. I cannot find words for my gratitude. How did she know?

"Return you to your chronicle." She deflects my gratitude, dragging a sack of grain into the measuring corner with her good arm. She will not see the pity in my eyes; it wounds her further. I return the way I have come.

Daily I repaired to Dain's tree-shelter to balance the books, and noted that his scowl tended to lighten somewhat at my arrival. Beleaguered as he was by first one then the next crisis among his high-strung troupe—

"—I find you strangely restful, Lingri-one. One of the few in Refuge I know won't trouble me further, but may actually take some of my troubles away."

That said, he would glance at my plague-mark, visible where I rested my wrists on the writing desk, and sigh ruefully.

"Not that you'd be aught but bones and trouble anyway!" he would grumble and be gone. Was it lust or only loneliness that made him sigh?

151

Pondering this, rubbing inkstains from my hands, I would change to tights and singlet out of my growing store of clothing—part Dweneth's, part Omila's, part castoffs from nearly every female in Refuge—and rehearse with Gause and Cwala. By afternoon Dweneth would be done with her patients and rehearsing the Comedie, which it was my duty to watch.

I say duty, for as I never laughed, what good was I as audience to the Comedie?

"You *are* hopeless!" Dweneth wheezed, weak from her own laughter, after I'd driven her co-star Stili off in a snit by observing his crudest antics without twitching an eyebrow. "And you're ruining me. I can't look at you without breaking, and Stili may never speak to me again. You don't even make a good straight-man! Well, Omila always needs spear-carriers. We'll serve you up for the Tragedie."

Hence daily did I play the role of Lingri Servile, hidden behind a mask of no People's creation. Hence nightly was I cast in the mercifully speechless role of Walk-ons and Sundries, treading the boards of the wheeled stage-wagon as if I knew what I was doing. Where there was Crowd called for, I was all of it, alternately shaking my fists in anger or wringing my hands with grief. Omila instructed me, and I was at least, she grudged, a good mimic. My masks and costumes were various, my functions multitudinous. I played the form of every passion, and never understood any of them.

Now I wend the ruined ways of my birthplace, mindful of Soliah's scarified face and broken form, and am impassive. It occurs to me that I see no one on my journey. Are we so weak we stay holed up in our assigned places, moving not without necessity? Or is our number so decimated that the ways are now empty again? I could have asked Soliah, could yet ask Gayat, how many Others there are left. I dare not. I must hold to my chronicle, and my impassivity. Having learned grief and anger, I can no longer act them out. This is irony.

"Who are you today?"

It delighted Dweneth so to have me ask, that thus I came

152

to know the whole of Shadoward Comedie, for she knew it all from memory. Each time she emerged from behind the curtain, clad in some gaudy confection I had not heretofore seen, she could not resist prompting me.

"Well, go ahead: ask me!"

And I would indulge her, together with my own curiosity, in asking: "Who are you today?"

"I am Rose of the *Allegory*," she would announce, parading the costume for me, or " 'Haughty' from the same piece," which she preferred as it was mostly mime and slapstick and included the wonderful dance at the end. Or, "Helie, Hgree's wayward daughter in the *Folly*," or any number more.

She played nothing but the broadest Comedie, a never-ending delight to the ragtag children out of Refuge who swarmed through the wood to follow us, their only source of entertainment. As new to this as the children, I was fascinated by the number of moral lessons that could be honey-coated and fed to an audience that elsewise would accept no teaching.

"And, truth, People do relish this manner of performance?" I would ask ingenuously. Dweneth would roll her eyes at me.

"Grown to adulthood in a box, you were! Of course they love it! Can't get enough. Shower us with presents and me with offers of marriage, always crying for more. But there are Players' troupes in Zanti, I know there are! How can you be so ignorant? Or, from the way you talk, shut up in some scholars' enclave from birth, and if so, how came you here? Well?"

"Right of Three, Lady? Or may I ask you as many questions?"

"Never mind!" It always shut her up at once.

"Gause says you got your start in tragedie. He says you knew the Windward Cycle by heart when you were but a child. He says you could have been a luminary, whatever that might be."

"Gause talks too much! Comedie's what People want. There's too much Tragedie in real life, and they deserve escape."

" 'Escape', Lady? Better a fleet-footed *graax* to ride and warn them of what really wants escaping."

Tappers and cryers were frantic with Kwengii-news from beyond the wood, and my thoughts tended toward what a single Other in a skimmer might accomplish, to warn an entire province of their coming in a single night. Silent and with running lights flashing, we could provide the Kwengii with an omen that would alter the course at least of local history. If to think the deed were as culpable as doing it, I was as guilty as Naven.

"Looks like you and I between us did damage enough at Sirdar'sInn." Dweneth sat downstage, swinging her legs idly. The ubiquitous clump of children, bored with such adult conversation, scattered into the wood, their random play under the watchful eyes of the tree-dwelling cryers. "Stop the wars all by ourselves, shall we? No, I think not. Only help the survivors stitch their lives back together when it's over, and forget."

"Escape and forget," I mused. "And what does the Comedienne, having helped these stitch their lives together, do when she wants to forget?"

Gause's words had made me curious. It wasn't only the death of her mother that made the face beneath the fixed Player's smile too often look as if it would rather be weeping.

"What do the folk in *OtherWhere* do?" she diverted me neatly. "You've never mentioned Players there. Nor music nor dancing nor sport nor games. Why not?"

The children's shrieking, running, chasing games echoed everywhere around us in the wood. Otherchildren practiced running to become fleet and strong; they never chased nor shrieked at all. Such predator's games were no longer part of our culture, nor were any of the things Dweneth mentioned. How was I to tell her?

"There are none such in *OtherWhere*."

"Sounds a boring place!" Dweneth sniffed. "What ever do its people do for fun?"

Fun? Should I tell her how Others spent what little leisure

we allowed ourselves? "Mathematics, Metaphysics, and the Moot" was how Loriel characterized it. All "fun" beyond mental games had been exorcised in the name of Discipline, and we had not felt its lack since the Thousand-Year. What manner of narrow, linear realm had we created?

"A gray, dull place, for all its wonders." Dweneth stared beyond the treetops, picturing it, no longer liking what she saw. "Don't sing it for me more, unless you give it color."

"Color, Lady?"

"Aye, color." She began to stalk about the stage, flaunting the day's berry-bright costume. "Tragedie's all stark blacks and whites and the shocking splash of blood. Comedie's pastels and gauds and sweetmeats. What's *OtherWhere*?"

I pondered. "A place where each day has a color of its own? Where folk show their unity one with the Other by all wearing some bright splash of the same color—blue one day and green the next, through all the spectrum and begun again . . ."

She could see this too, and liked it better. "Sing it me!"

"Do you spin this all yourself?"

"Not all, Lady. Most of it I learned from Others."

"And it all stays in your head?" She poked the firepot restlessly. "I'd worry I'd forget it."

"You don't forget your Comedies."

"But you can write; I've seen you. Why don't you write it down?"

"Because it is not all mine, Lady, but belongs to Others."

"Foolishness!"

We had had two days of tending croup among the children, but her restlessness was more than that. Even Hrill, yapping at her heels as she paced and stirred the firepot, could not cheer her this night. Brok had summoned her that morning and there'd been a terrible row, heard the length and breadth of Refuge either in person or by rumor. Refuger eyes continued to follow me everywhere, no longer merely suspicious, but quite hostile. Had the quarrel to do with me?

"Nor do you sing of heroes, or their deeds and friendships."

Only before the Thousand-Year had we had what she would define as heroes. I could not sing her that part, not yet.

"Again a colorless place, that has no heroes whose exploits bind them in eternal friendship, that each would give his life for, and transcending even the grave." Dweneth sighed. "Perhaps you're right. No point in writing it down. None but I would have the patience to hear it through!"

"Are heroes only male, Lady?" I wondered, finding the concept quite odd. "And do only men have friendships?"

Dweneth's laugh was humorless. "In songs and sagas, so they do. Women have babes or lovers, never friends. And in real life some of us have neither. Fellow Players aplenty— some like Gause who would die for me—but I am ever Dain'sDaughter, one of them yet apart. None truly calls me friend."

She stopped her pacing, turned on me.

"If you were freewoman, would you be my friend?"

No question could have surprised me more. My many masks were useless here; I must be Lingri-true. Typically, I sought for irony.

"I did not know I sang so well that you would free me for it."

"Don't *joke*!" Dweneth warned. "Do you answer me! It's important!"

"In *OtherWhere*, there are not friendships as such . . ." I temporized, more disquieted than I knew. How was I to be Monitor, all objective, if charged with this? "There is rather what we call the continuum, whereby one gives to anOther, who goes on to help a third who thereby—"

"Stop babbling and answer me!" she commanded. "*Will* you? I must know!"

More depended on this than she was telling me. I gathered myself.

"Like you, Lady, I have never had a friend. I do not know if I could be one."

"But if I freed you there'd be no barrier. You're better

156

learned than I at any rate!" The tone she used was pleading.

"Lady . . ." Again I temporized. "I am not learned in this matter of friendship, but this I know— " Where did this answer come from? "If you require me, I remain."

She stopped her pacing with relief. "I had hoped as much. Brok wants to buy you of me."

Was this what I had been tested for? "For what purpose?"

"Is that all you have to say?" She was incredulous. "No objection at all?"

"Does servile own the right to object?"

She gave me a sour look.

"You've set me straight often enough! But this is something deeper. Just like at Sirdar'sInn, when you accepted fate. Or when I found you still beside your dead master. 'Where was I to go, mistress?' quoth she, when any servile would have fled."

There were tears in her eyes; I would not have caused them if I had a choice.

" 'For what purpose?' Well, not the expected one. Brok knows of the mark you bear. Nor certainly to hear you sing, he'll tell you himself he has no truck with that. I think it's just to take from me, because it is his pleasure. As if he has not taken from me before, and everything I had!"

She also gathered herself, locking away whatever terror throbbed tangibly about her in this tiny place.

"But that's ancient history, and none of your business. For now he says he'll have you of me or the troupe must leave Refuge, Kwengii threat or—Where do you think you're going?"

I had gathered my few possessions while she spoke. "Does Brok desire me this night or on the morrow? If you will direct me to his cave . . ."

"He has not coin enough!" She almost screamed it; the silence of the camp beyond our walls grew silenter. "Or am I so poor a mistress that you wish to leave me?"

"Does servile own the right to wish?"

Was I overly perverse? Insufficient facts always invite danger. Some hidden agenda, some truth unspoken, made me cautious here.

"You do if I say you do! I'm asking you, what do you *wish* to do?"

I held my wrists out as if she bound them, a gesture learned of Omila and the Tragedie, and nothing of mine.

"I will not endanger the whole of troupe for my one life. I trust you will know what to do to prevent that."

She shook her head, dashed tears away.

"Just like Sirdar'sInn! Pity they don't feel the same for you, for more than one waylaid me to say I should be rid of you! What strange courage makes you give your life away?"

Courage? It was only practicality. I had no better answer.

"Go then! Let Brok see you for himself. Gratify his curiosity, but no more. He'll not have you of me, and no one hurt for it either. Mayhap women can be heroes after all!"

"What d'you think?" Brok demanded of me, wiping sauce off his chins and chewing steadily. "Is there naught but demons to the Shadoward of the Great Sea? Is the Droghiad out of his mind?"

"I am no seer, Lord, only a singer. And as I know not this Droghiad personally, I cannot vouch for his sanity or the lack of it."

The tappers and cryers had brought Brok the news from Droghia, that the very lord who had exiled him was drawing charts and building ships to take him across the sea.

"It's not mere curiosity," Lord Brok informed me, "but the sincere hope that Droghen sail himself over the edge of the World. The better to bring a new ruler to his land, and me my lost position back."

Why was he telling me this? Mine not to question such a bounty of information, but to make note of it for my report. Doubtless, living so far underground, Brok needed new audiences to attend him.

What manner of being would choose to dwell in such a

place? I had wondered as one of the Refuge children led me to the mouth of the near-hidden cave before whisking away into the underbrush. The long entrance hall, carved deep and dank and dripping into the nether depths of a natural limestone cavern, lit its entire length by smoking torches which someone must replenish, spoke of a lord who kept servants in a place where few had the means to more than feed themselves. What manner of petty tyrant was this?

Brok's audience hall was an entirely natural formation of towering stalagmites, in a hollow of which a fire roared, barely dispelling damp or darkness. The chill trickle of groundwater somewhere in that darkness punctuated our dialogue throughout.

Lord Brok himself sat, or rather lolled, on a throne of sorts carved out of the natural rock and softened with plump cushions; its curious design augmented the slightest whisper spoken anywhere in the chamber; it also accentuated Brok's unfortunate tendency to wheeze. Lord Brok was a desperately unhealthy man.

He gave the appearance of the gigantic, unformed pupa of some unimaginable insect. No amount of rich, brocaded garments could disguise the grotesquely bloated, deathly pale, completely hairless body even now replenishing itself from a long table heaped with every manner of food and drink. He could not, I thought, be more than thirty years, middle-aged by People's measure but, in this guise, ageless and ancient at once. There was no evidence of Dain's lineage in that fat-enfolded face, nor any kinship between this creature and Dweneth. What circumstance had shaped him thus?

"Where d'you come from?" was his first question, asked between swallows. He offered no preamble, nor so much as an invitation to be seated; in fact there was no furnishing here but what Brok was sitting on. He was not to offer me so much as a cool drink, while he continued throughout to gorge himself.

"From the protection of Darvis so-named Once-Armorer, my Lord." It was all I could do to hold my Discipline and answer rudeness with humility, as was my place. "At his death, to the ownership of Mistress Dweneth."

Let me not say that she found me free and did not pay for me; let Brok work for the information he sought. I watched his fat fingers wallow in a serving platter while his eyes never left mine, and his jaws continued working.

"And before that?" he burbled.

"Before Darvis, I belonged to a slave-dealer name Rau, my Lord."

Something dribbled down his chin into the embroidered collar below; he paid it no heed. "And before that—?"

"Before that, Lord, I suppose I had a parent or two like any Other."

Brok licked his fingers and roared, half choking.

"That's good!" he wheezed. "Woman with a past and none of my business, eh? My sister said you had spirit. Where'd you come by the plague-mark?"

"How many ways are there, my Lord?"

"Which is to say, also none of my business." His tiny eyes in his grotesque face narrowed at me. "You know I can have you killed for simple rudeness?"

"You are lord of this place; that much I know."

"Good!" He had actually stopped eating for a moment, and now made up for lost time. "What's this *graax*shit you sing about *OtherWhere*?"

"It is a lay like any other, Lord," I replied carefully. "There are at least as many songs as there are singers."

Brok swallowed. "Word around here is that you sing it as if you believe it, as if you thought it were the truth."

"Credit my mistress then," I suggested, glibly, "who has taught me all she knows of the Players' art."

"Where did you come from erst?" Brok persisted, his small eyes growing smaller still. "You could almost be a demon yourself; you look like nothing I've ever seen. Tell me what you know of *OtherWhere*."

"It is called *OtherWhere* for many reasons, Lord, one of them being that it is not here." Oh, glib! I thought.

"Well, leave it somewhere else, then! It makes People restless, and unhappy with their lot. I'll not have it sung in Refuge."

"You are lord of this place," I said again, not acquiescent precisely.

"As for you—my sister will not part with you; I know not why. As she likes men so little, mayhap you offer something, all sticks and bones as you are! Tell her I've withdrawn my offer. You and the troupe may stay until the Kwengii leave, then off with you. Only sing no more the while you're here!"

It was a small price to pay, I thought, thinking also that for all the People there were like Dweneth, Gause, and Cwala, there were also those like Brok.

———

"The Player-Maid's Request"
(from *Council Minutes*: InfoNetCompile4235145208: T-Y1020/1563 P.A.)

Being a Player is only being what you're not. Though that's not really it, is it? For how could you be it if it wasn't inside you to begin with? So in that sense, those of us who can play villains or tarts must have some inner villainy or tartishness with which to play them. The same for tragic characters—victims and weepers and the like. What I mean, I suppose, about being a Player, is that it consists in great measure of being what you can't be every day, or can't be in the caste you're born to, or in the time and place you're born in history. Does that make sense?

Why I'm telling you this is because if you don't understand this about us you call People, you don't understand us. Don't understand that we all want to be what we're not—bigger, smaller, older, younger, braver, richer, more sinful, or daring. Not like you. Your kind is so tranquil, so content to be what you are. Is it because you're better Players than we, to play the same role all the time? Or is it because you have medicine and telepathy and such wonderful

161

things in your heads, and have made such a wondrous place for yourselves that you don't share the restlessness that drives us?

I want to tell you to beware that restlessness. It's what People are all about, and it's going to cause you no end of problems. My own reaction when I first came here is a good example. Ambivalence—is that the word I want? Fear and longing all mixed in together—best expect that from any of my kind who stumble upon you. You'd be advised, if you were asking advice of the likes of me, to start training intermediaries, those to stand between two worlds and cope with that ambivalence. That's why I'm here today, to ask admittance to your hospice.

I want to be a healer. I am quick and I can learn, and I'm not shy about hard work. Let me do this, Mothers, and I swear to you: I'll stand between the two worlds for you for all the rest of my life.

eight

Somewhere on the road to Mantuu, under cover of night, a Tawa cloth caravan was relieved of two *guravek* and the saddlepacks of cloth-of-*garnah* they carried. The two *'vek*, stripped of packs and harness, caught up with the caravan by midday. The cloth-of-*garnah,* stitched by the Brigandwomen into a new Cirque tent, was their gift to Dweneth for her help in healing, and for officiating at the birth of the babe, who was destined to be chief.

Old Krex, who had never gone far from Refuge on his side of the stream, was discovered to have an affinity for Cirque as well as martial music, and with minimal training learned to prance about the ring with the best of them. Dweneth then coaxed him into the traces of the lead wagon, and the troupe left Refuge, bound for the Windward provinces and Droghia.

The Kwengii, who did not care for the warm season, had taken their longboats up the coast for home. In their wake, Scavengers—raggeder, dirtier incarnations of the Brigands, and with an unBrigandlike habit of stealing from the dying as well as the dead—roved the smouldering villages like so many carrion birds, equally dangerous if challenged. Behind them followed lungrot, pox, and plague. There were places, the tappers told us as we picked our way out of the wood, where grain ripened and rotted in fields overrun by weeds and vermin, for no one remained alive to harvest it. More than once on the road we passed children laboring in the fields, scarce tall enough to reach the harrow-handles, struggling mightily to harvest where their parents had sown the season before.

The gallows and gibbets at the crossroads were perversely more active than ever. It was a marvel that a People so enfeebled and bereft of numbers could still find criminals to hang and executioners to hang them, but there they swung, adding to the vermin, stench, and contagion, and the sadness of the land. As anOther, I could only grieve, and hold my Discipline.

But however weary, sick, or decimated, People still found time and energy for the Cirque, whose bright billowing tent drew them from the surrounding countryside no matter where we set it up. Dweneth was right: Ours was the only entertainment broad enough to divert them from the memory of recent horrors and, in a curious way, to help them mourn their dead.

"Look you, Devo," I would hear one toothless crone speak to her youngest child. "How the *graax* dances smart, and how the lady balances on him. Didn't your father love such sights?"

Or, "Pa, look, the jugglers. Didn't little Kimmin laugh to see them last time?"

Their faces shone in torchlight and for the moment they were happy, their fantasies made real in pasteboard and greasepaint. Who was I to criticize?

We never asked for payment in coin, knowing how little they had, but somehow they always found some manner of currency with which to recompense us. In one region, nuts or grain were the price of admission, mushrooms or eggs elsewhere. Dour Dain glowered over his ledgers and muttered to himself, snapping quill-pens in frustration.

"At least the beasts are fed, Da," Dweneth would soothe him, popping a roasted egg into his protesting mouth, "and

164

you know you've a fondness for fresh eggs. Cheer you; we've tightened our belts before!"

Farther inland, nearer the border with Mantuu, were lands the Kwengii had not touched, where life went on as always. Here we spent most of that tropical season the People call Bask, until the rains came.

Relentless, cold, unseasonal, they flattened crops and washed away homesteads, brought fevers, croup, and ague, struck fear and gloom into those who knew nothing of meteorology, only that "it weren't natural." Bad weather was always blamed on evil spirits, the impending end of the world, or someone else's sins.

In the observatory on One Greater, Chior, Frayin's son, had been apprenticed to old Tagal who, now that Loriel was away at work on Undersea, had consented to return to the halls of research. Chior's area of study at the time was global weather patterns. His scans predicted accurately not only the untoward rains, but flooding and tidal waves to follow in early Windseason.

Chior studied his maps and watched his monitors with mild interest—meteorology was not his primary area of study, only a sideline—safe and warm and dry in the observatory, while I, wrapped deep in a sodden cloak with my hair dripping down my neck, led a grumbling, stumbling, steaming Krex through mud as deep sometimes as both our knees. We had played out the country hereabouts, and the rain was too heavy to set up the tent. We must move on.

The cities on the Greaters had been weather-screened for fifty years. Too, the Archipelago lay largely in the temperate zones, and Others' experience of rain even on the Lessers was as a mild, pleasant drizzle, except in Stormseason. Only during the adolescent's Survival Year need Other live and work in such constant inclemency as was suddenly my daily fare.

Hence I was no more pleased than my companions to squish about in soggy garments, wet boots, and stringy, dripping

165

hair, unable to cook or wash or make a fire for warmth for days on end. Further, I was subliminally aware, as any Other would be, of the toll on animal life, of creatures drowning in their burrows and insects struck down on the wing, of the wail of plant-life protesting such assault, their voices not unlike the scent-cries of the sensitive *gli* and *kressha* in my world.

We had no coin for inns, assuming we could have found one standing that would take in Players. Nearing the Hraregh Hills we found one partly burned and empty, with only the swollen carcass of a milkbeast in the innyard to suggest what might have happened. We took the liberty of supping on whatever provisions remained unspoiled, and drank deeply of the landlord's ale while toasting ourselves about the luxury of a fire. That night, we sang.

"Ah, but that tale's nothing! Were you with us the time Clymena, Dowager of Plalas, kept us at court nearly a year-round? We'd taken on a firewalker—or so he said he was—from Tawa . . ."

Stili the Comedian's voice was loud with drink but most of the troupe were as merry, if only from the warmth. Members of the company were quick to cheer our way through mud and wet and devastation with tales of plays and mimes and galas, of courts and balls and extravaganzas, each regaling the rest with what adventures she or he had met with before joining this particular troupe. Though many of the tales were old and oft-repeated, they lost nothing of their lustre in yet one more telling. I listened to such tales in rain or sun or firelight, committed them to memory, and keep them still.

". . . never saw anyone run so fast as that firewalker once the draperies caught, and poor old Clymena, wide as a *graax,* huffing and squealing for her retinue in all that smoke and din—well, I never!"

"Buffoon!" was Omila's opinion. She liked few in the troupe or, so it seemed to me, in the World at large, save Dweneth,

166

on whom she doted. The Tragedienne was telling fortunes, and it was Dweneth's turn.

"The Dark-Visaged Knight," she announced, turning up a card from her five-sided pack, watching Dweneth with her huge luminous eyes, so often berimmed with tears, hence perfect for Tragedie. "In conjunction with the Wheel—" she indicated the card beside—"it warrants journey at the behest of a higher power. The Droghiad wants aught of you."

"The Droghiad ever wants aught of me, though it scarce has to do with journeys," Dweneth sniffed, drawing her shawl tighter about her against drafts through the innwalls, or something less tangible. We were moving on in the morning; it had at last stopped raining. "Besides, he's dark-visaged, but no knight. Are you certain?"

"Would you prefer to tell the cards yourself?" Omila inquired archly, feigning to sweep them from the table into her hand. "Or perhaps your cant-eared servile might."

Omila had been among those wanting rid of me in Refuge.

"You're only her pet!" She urgently whispered at me once we were on the road, her tiny pouting face with its great eyes all but lost in a cloud of pale frizzy hair some past lover had thought attractive. "No more to her than Hrill, whom she'd no more part with had Brok wanted him instead of you. Don't flatter yourself!"

"I would not know how to do so, Lady," I had responded mildly. Omila's hostility puzzled me; I had done nothing I knew of to warrant it. "I am her servile, nothing more. Where she dictates, I will go. What fault find you with that?"

Omila had looked at me under her plucked-to-invisibility eyebrows. "I don't like you. I never will. I'll work with you and eat with you and if necessary share a bed with you because Dweneth says I must. But expect no more."

Now, pouting, resentful of my very presence, she made to sweep her telling cards off the table, but Dweneth stayed her hand.

"Go on with your telling," she advised quietly. Gause and

Stili, who had drawn closer to our telling-threesome in the hope of witnessing what Stili snidely called a "cat fight," moved back to their own more mundane games of cards, somewhat disappointed. Omila sniffed and turned up the next card.

"The Broken Sword. That's danger," she said ominously. The next card: "Flowing Water. Also danger. Danger imminent and from natural causes." She noted Dweneth's alarmed look, let it linger before saying not unkindly: "Patience! Likely there's recourse further on."

She turned up three more cards in rapid succession.

I had tried to learn some pattern in her turning up of cards, some consistency in her telling of them, and had come to the conclusion that the whole was a subjective interpretation drawn out of intimate knowledge of her listeners and what they wanted to hear, or what she wished to tell them. Clever, but more amateur psychology than telepathy. I kept my opinion to myself.

"Do you believe what the cards tell?" I did ask Dweneth once when Omila was out of earshot. She had shrugged.

"I'll believe anything until it's proved false. Consider you: I even believe in *OtherWhere!*"

Then I knew Omila had her ear as well as mine, intending to plant skepticism there. As the three of us studied the cards, I also studied faces, to see how Omila would shape her telling to its listener.

"Lover and Masked Stranger, with the Scales between," she clucked at the last three cards, as if disapproving what her own hands had dealt. She looked at Dweneth solemnly. "It means you must choose between the Lover and the Stranger as the only way to avert what Sword and Water both portend. Unless you can find a better meaning . . ."

"Mayhap I'll have to!" Dweneth cried, sweeping to her feet and all but upending the table, fluttering the cards. "For as I have no Lover and know no Stranger, this makes no sense to me. I'm to bed!"

Dutiful servile, I was about to follow her, but found myself lingering in the liquid malevolence of Omila's eyes.

168

"Can you only tell the cards for those you know well?" I asked, my own stare as unblinking; let her know I understood her game.

"I'll tell you yours," Omila shrugged, indifferent, though something of Otherness must have slipped through my mask, to make her hands less than deft in gathering up the cards, "before your mistress summons you to bed."

I took the cards from her, familiarizing my fingertips with their awkward pentacle shape. The ritual required I shuffle the cards myself, thus determining my own fate, which the teller need only interpret. It would have been a simple matter to choose and memorize the arrangement of the cards—Other hands were quicker than People's eye—but as I could not as easily anticipate Omila's interpretation, I let the cards fall where they would, memorized them anyway, and handed them back to her.

She turned up the first card, known as the key, her eyes never leaving mine, never blinking in their malevolence. Behind her, two more pairs of eyes—Stili's and Gause's—also watched.

"Trillfish," she announced, giving the People's name for *bRi*. So inaccurate was the representation of this elegant creature, which had the flukes all wrong and seemed more fish than mammal, that I was distracted from what Omila was truly saying. "It means you are not what you seem."

She made it seem a challenge.

"Well, Lady, as I travel with Players, and am a tumbler one moment and tragedienne the next, the while I am also book-keeper, laundress, healer's assistant, reader, singer and chief-sweeper-of-*graax*-dung, this surprises me not. Does it you?"

Gause chortled behind her. Omila glared, turning up a second card and a third.

"Fire and Ice. Two extremes which can either mean a great test of courage, a choice avoided, or a means of death, depending upon who you truly are."

"I shall rely on you to tell me."

Stili found this amusing, but Gause gave me a warning

glance, seeming to suggest that all of Omila's powers were not in her telling of cards. There was one last card to turn.

It was meant to be the Sorceress, a powerful card for good. Instead Omila slipped her fingers through the deck so quickly only I saw, to find the one card she had all but imperceptibly nicked at one corner, the easier to find it, or avoid it, when she chose.

"Death," she said, throwing it down dramatically enough to make Stili gasp and clutch his heart, and Gause recoil, hissing. Omila swept all the cards back into her hand, gloating. "Best you take stock of your life and your possessions, for you have lost the one, and have little time to bestow the latter."

I removed my amber earrings, and the coin chain I'd taken to wearing about my neck in this trusted company, and held them out to her.

"Which will you have for the price of your telling?" I asked evenly. "So long as I can take it back if I prove you wrong."

It was Gause who cautioned me after she'd stalked off.

"Own you a knife, Lingri-too-truthful? Best you sleep with it in your hand. That one has ways to make her tellings true!"

She had no need to, once we reached the Hills.

Droghia was a lowland, easy to reach by sea, but by land it was ringed about with hills, and accessible only through the mountain passes. Some of these were toll roads held by the Droghiad's men, some by Brigands wanting bribery in coin or worse, some were still snowbound even this late in the year.

Dain and Stili had gone before us on one of the easier toll roads, to set up a schedule of performances in the villages ahead. But the till was low and paying the way for all our wagons out of the question, so Dweneth chose one of the rare free mountain passes, broad enough at its start, but narrowing as it climbed until it was no more than a footpath along a sheer cliff face, scarce wide enough for the wagons single-file, and promising death in the rain-swollen river below to any who misstepped.

The morning was over-warm, bright with sun and promise.

The rains which had dogged our progress seemed not to have been as severe this far. We might have waited a day or two, but we had a schedule to keep.

Nevertheless, we were cautious, leading the wagons afoot—one holding the draybeast's head, a second watching the wheels behind. Thus Dweneth led Krex while I followed, with Cwala behind me leading her beast and Gause minding their wheels. Their three children perched on the top of the wagon, leaning toward the cliffside to weight it more away from the river. Their small, sturdy legs kicked gleefully, and I could hear their giggling. On the great Cirque wagon, only Hrill sat kingly in the driver's seat, yapping idly at whatever took his fancy. No one paid him any heed.

". . . the whole of our revealed truth being got through the vision drugs . . ." Cwala was explaining DyrCreed as we walked. ". . . which, with the vision rites, do take their toll. Most priestesses die before they're twenty, ancient before their time. My luck Gause wooed me away, or I'd be long dead. But, ah, the visions! There is nothing like!"

Hallucinogens, I thought, and powerful ones, to have such an untoward effect. I must report this to our biochemists, and some later Monitor might obtain a sample. What extremes People would go to in search of a cosmology that Others already knew!

Cwala and I walked with our eyes on the road, not needing to see to whom we spoke. It was not uncommon for the female of either of our species to master the art of doing one thing while speaking of something else. But the two took all our concentration, and neither of us noticed Hrill.

His feeble attention caught by a flock of birds startled out of our path by our lumbering passage, he hurled himself mindlessly after them, remembering too late that he could not fly. He skittered to a stop at the very edge of the roadway, only to have it crumble from under his flailing paws. Helpless, he began to yelp, and Dweneth was suddenly after him.

She flung herself flat in the road and grabbed the creature's hind legs; I flung myself at her and grabbed what I could—a flailing ankle, a length of skirt tearing in my hand—as the entire place where we lay broke free of the cliff and began to slip, slowly but inexorably, over the precipice.

Krex remembered his war-training and halted the instant Dweneth's hand left his bridle. Feeling the wagon begin to back into the slide that claimed us, he pulled away forward until the road felt safe beneath his great feet. Cwala meanwhile had halted her wagon, shouting instructions to her spouse to back them out of danger. We three—Dweneth, Hrill and I— hung suspended over the river, the shelf crumbling beneath us, rocks and debris tumbling into the river far below.

"Don't move!" I shouted, attempting to better my grip. It was not to be. Any forward motion only made the shelf slip farther. How long could we pit mere muscle against gravity before the whole thing gave way?

"Move? Not bloody likely!" Dweneth spat at me, dirt in her mouth from Hrill's frantic struggles, breathless with fear. The unobstructed view from where she was was doubtless terrifying.

Hrill at last grew still, whimpering in his mistress's hands. Time hung suspended. The rumble of wheels behind me indicated that Krex had taken matters in charge. Bereft of rider in battle, he would have repaired to the nearest settlement, so now he would bring the wagon downslope to safety. We could hear Gause shouting the wagons behind him back, back! out of danger before he edged himself as near as he dared to us.

"Lingri-one! What can I do?"

"Naught here, Gause-one!" I cried, wishing we could use his tumbler's strength. "The shelf cannot support more weight. But if you could find a length of rope . . ."

"Done!"

While he was gone to get it, I decided. Time to use anOther's gifts, regardless of the risk.

"Lady? 'Between Lover and Stranger,' Omila said. I think it is now you must choose."

It was a ruse that had to work to conquer her fear. I heard her groan as the prophecy came clear. Truth, as she saw it,

172

she could claim unquestioning love from only one living creature. She would have to let Hrill go, and trust me to save her.

"Omila also—predicted your death!" she gasped. "No sense—both falling—for this idiot beast. Do you—let me go and—"

"Not bloody likely!" I echoed her, tightening my grip.

She would have laughed had she breath to do it. Instead I felt her steel herself as she began to speak to Hrill in that same soothing tongue she had once used with Krex, and let the creature go.

For once his instincts saved him, and he twisted about, flipped backward onto his mistress's outstretched arms, ran over her back and mine (with time to growl at me—ah, Hrill!), lightly leapt the growing chasm between us and the roadway, into Gause's rope-burdened, waiting arms.

With that I lifted Dweneth bodily away from the precipice and pulled us both to sit upright on the ledge. The feat surpassed anything that might be expected from a female of my size. I did not need to see Dweneth's eyes widen even as Gause's hands went limp with disbelief. Had I evidenced an ability to fly, neither could have been more surprised.

"How did you—? I must outweigh you by—well, never mind! Impossible—you could not—"

"Lady," I said, peering past her over the precipice. "We have not time for this."

We clutched at roots and clumps of grass as the ledge continued to slip.

"There is a shelf some distance below, just above the water. Can Gause get us the rope . . ."

He had already thrown us one end of the rope. "Let me pull you both—" he began, but pebbles and scree slid under him, and he could barely keep his feet.

"I won't have it!" Dweneth shouted, taking charge. The very sound seemed to affect the slippage, and we whispered after that. "Gause Tumbler, get your family to safety! Go round about to NearVillage and my father . . . you'll want bribe money . . ."

I tossed my coins and earrings to Gause; he tossed me the rest of the rope.

"Fly high!" he called ruefully—tumblers' good-luck—and took the wagons back down the way we'd come.

"At this rate we'll get to NearVillage before they do!" Dweneth grimaced, teeth chattering with fear; she had held the facade until her people were gone. "Assuming you can fly as well as lift more than your weight. Now what?"

"Now to the rock ledge," I replied calmly, securing the rope to a stunted tree growing out of the cliff below us.

"Rock ledge!" she snorted. "That was fantasy to keep Gause from dying with us—and I appreciate it; don't get me wrong. Prefer to die in dignity . . . no one to watch . . . let Omila gloat; I'll not be there to hear it—*oh!*"

She was far less calm than she feigned to be, her babbling near panic. Every pebble or clump of dirt that broke free and fell increased her terror. We could not cling here much longer.

"Climb onto my back, and at once, please."

"You're crazy!" she offered, wary of me and my recent display of strength. "Omila's prophecy—"

"Lady, I have no intention of indulging Omila's prophecies, not now or ever. Climb on my back—*at once!*"

I had never raised my voice before. The ledge slipped; she shrieked and clutched at me.

"Pulling me back from the edge before was a fluke . . . tumblers' strength . . . happens when People are scared . . . I do thank you, but it's only prolonged the end. Look you: I'm no longer in tumblers' condition, and I'm feared of heights . . . can't climb down, and you can't carry me. Unless you truly are a sorceress!"

"A chance you'll have to take," I said, prying her fingers from my throat and taking hold of the rope.

Succinctly: we arrived on the rock ledge in a scatter of loose scree, just as the shelf we'd been clinging to broke loose entirely and tumbled into the torrent below, drenching us. At least now I knew how cold the snow-fed river was. The tree I'd tied the rope to had gone as well, and so the rope. Our only recourse now was the river, frigid with snow-melt and swollen past its banks with recent rain, treacherous with floating branches and debris.

"In the dry season there's a footpath used by the Lamorak," Dweneth reported, catching her breath. "Droghen gives them leave to hunt here when it's too cold in their lands. There's a rope bridge, farther down, though it often washes away. I wonder shall we starve or die of cold before the waters recede?"

Her voice was calm enough, but she was trembling, not only from the wet.

"How far to the rope bridge, lady?" I kept my tone conversational. "And how well can you swim?"

"An afternoon's walk, and not at all," she answered as calmly, until she fully understood my question. She tried to scramble to her feet on the rock shelf, but succeeded only in bumping her head. "Oh, no you don't! Don't even think of it! In these parts it's death to set foot in running water. The Lamorak's water-god kills the transgressor, if his tribe's poisoned arrows don't!"

Lamorak, I knew, preferred sweathouses, when they bathed at all. At last I understood why. Easy to fear a malevolent water-god in a land of fast-running streams and hidden undertows.

"Besides which, I tell you, *I can't swim!*"

"No matter," I said, already tying up my skirts, my feet dangling over the edge, "for I can. Quite well, in fact. Well enough, barring Lamorak arrows, to bring us both to safety, if you can bring yourself to trust me."

The roar of the river was the only sound between us for what seemed a very long time. At last she shook her head, staring down at the torrent in wordless fear.

"Dweneth." I had never spoken her name before. " 'Who will be the first to trust?' "

She clenched her fists, squeezed her eyes shut against what lay below.

"You'll not convince me of this, not even with your

175

OtherWhere. Sing me that part whilst we wait here for death, but—"

"I'll sing it when we reach the bridge," I promised, threatened. "Else I'll never sing it more."

As in the best of her kind, Dweneth's curiosity conquered her fear. Clasping my outstretched hand, eyes closed, breathless, she jumped.

The water was not much colder than some sealanes I had swum with *bRi,* the current not that much more powerful. Dweneth struggled to the surface downstream from me, gasping, her redgold curls adraggle. I seized a passing tree limb for her to cling to, a second to float behind us and divert whatever flotsam might be hurtling past downstream. As promised, I sang all the way of *OtherWhere.*

Who will be the first to trust? Who lay aside the sword and offer the bare hand, perhaps to have it severed at the wrist? Who to offer the naked heart, only to have it pierced through? If no one risk this, how long can the whole endure? Who will be the first to trust? If the death of the one give life to the whole, is this not equitable?

If the Other strike thee, permit it. But pick thyself up from the dust and ask her: "Why?"

And if she offer no answer, but make to strike thee again, do not permit it, but do her no harm in thy prevention. Then ask her again: "Why?"

But if she offer an answer and her answer is reasonable, grant her the next act uninhibited, whether it be to strike thee yet again or to offer the hand of reconciliation. For reason is the one incontestable argument.

Dweneth had not told me that the river did not stay within the hills, but ran somewhat precipitously past the ruined rope bridge, to empty eventually into the Windward Sea. As soon

176

as the current was mild enough we waded ashore, to confront a new dilemma.

"Kwengii on the seaward bank, Lamorak on this side," Dweneth explained wearily as we pulled ourselves out of the river, all fear leached out of her. "The river marks the Hraregh/Droghian border, but Kwengii honor no borders and will stay as long as it suits them. Droghia and Lamora are at peace for the moment, hence we're better off this side of the river. Did we cross and climb yon hill, we'd see Kwengii sails aplenty."

"With respect, lady"—I was wringing out my heavy skirts, wishing for a fire—"I have seen sufficient Kwengii for this lifetime."

"You know nothing about it . . ." Dweneth murmured, standing like a stone. The sun was going down and it was cold; we were sorry, river-spewn flotsam, unsheltered on an open heath. I must get my mistress moving.

"The only Lamorak I ever knew was my former master, though he was not a hunter. What's your advice?"

She shook off some of her malaise. "We've a full day's backtrack to NearVillage—and that in daylight, not stumbling about in the dark. I have known Lamorak, but not this far Leeward. Odds they'll leave us be. We'll have to take our chances."

"Take our chances, Lady, and do—what?" I prompted, trying to be practical.

She began to walk aimlessly away from the river. Had I been to NearVillage before, I could have found my way now, even in the dark, but that smacked too much of sorcery, and we had had enough of that for one day. There was neither path nor track across this vast treeless plain, and what food there was was only roots and leaves and flowers, sufficient to sustain me, but hardly Dweneth. Wind and weather were the more immediate threat. Yet my mistress walked as if entranced, or beyond the ability to care. The sun slipped below the farthest hill. Dweneth walked; I followed, until she turned on me.

"I was prepared to die!" she shouted, her voice dangerous for having nowhere to go in this silence. "Fool enough to risk my neck for that idiot beast, I deserved no better! Now I've you to worry about. Why did you risk your life for mine?"

"Because I thought you worth as much as you thought Hrill?" I offered—glib, ironic. Perhaps anger could dispel her lethargy.

"I won't have your death on my conscience!" she raged against the spreading twilight. The night would be moonless, a small advantage. "I won't be responsible for that!"

"Lady, I am aware of nothing here which will cause my death." I scanned the ground, meanwhile, for anything edible. There were medicinal plants aplenty; had Dweneth brought her healer's pouch and a better mood she would have been delighted, but both were with the stage wagon, wherever Krex had ended with it. "Unless, of course, you continue to draw attention to us by shouting."

She stopped her meandering, dumbstruck. "You're right, I'm being quite hysterical." She pushed her wet, tangled hair back, collected her wits. "What shall we do?"

"What did you do when your mother was killed?"

The swirl and buffet of her past terrors assaulted me here as they had on the road to Refuge.

"I—hid—in the Forest of Gloom . . ." The words caused her a terrible struggle. ". . . burrowed under the leaves for warmth, and so they couldn't find me. I survived."

"Then surely what a child did there, two adults can do here." I turned away from her deliberately, walking toward the foothills.

"But there are no leaves here, no shelter . . ." she protested, trailing after me for once.

"There is shelter of a sort . . ." I dropped down into a small depression in the ground I had noticed that she had not, "if we are not overly fastidious."

The soil was moist and easy to scoop out with our hands; we piled it up around the depression to form a kind of burrow, primitive but functional. A like shelter had been mine to share with Chior during Survival Year. The philosopher's son had not masked his disdain at my digging, which he found inferior, and did calculus in his head to help him sleep at night. A tree root lodged between my shoulders no matter how I turned, I slept not at all. Further, Chior snored.

There was none to criticize my efforts now; Dweneth seemed instead quite awed by my stamina, as hers flagged with weariness and lack of sustenance. I tried to minimize my greater strength, but it was needed, and it had been a day for surprises.

We were covered with mud at the end of our endeavor, as we had been covered with soot when we left Town. Would we find some place to wash on the morrow, or must we draggle into NearVillage as if we were made of the soil itself?

I would not think of sonic showers and clean sheets, of the climate-controlled environment and creature comforts I had left behind in OtherWhere. There were places on this side as well that I had not yet seen—might never see, at the crawling pace at which I had traversed the land thus far—palaces and even workmen's huts built adjacent to hot springs, places where even People ate well and slept comfortably. This was no time for self-indulgence. I must remain alert, for Dweneth's sake. I could not dispel the feeling that we were being watched. What we needed most was silence, concealment, and warmth. Perhaps we could burrow into the very soil itself; Others often slept in the sand during Survival . . .

". . . except that this would prevent our effective escape from whatever might require our escaping it. Assuming escape were truly feasible in so exposed a landscape, unless our attacker were alone, in which event we could flee in opposite directions and one of us, at least, escape. However—"

"Oh, do shut up!" Dweneth said crossly, down in the burrow scooping out the last of it as I scanned the horizon, Other-eyed, one final time. "Or when we reach Droghia, if we do, I swear I'll sell you to the first wight who asks. Else I'll have your tongue cut out. I know them that can do it, too!

"Besides, I don't care! Better cold than dead. Once raped, twice careful, I suppose, though as a rule the Lamorak don't rape . . ." She caught my puzzled look even in this darkness, seemed surprised herself at her own sudden candor. There was mud on her nose. "Oh, yes—my great secret. Want to hear about it?"

"Only if you wish to tell it."

"Come down here, then, and stop gawping at me!"

Was I gawping? Gingerly I climbed down into the burrow. As she had on the road to Refuge, Dweneth "went to pieces" in my hands.

———————

"Ruminations on the Verge of Death"
(from *Journals of WiseFrayin Philosopher*,
uncoded/hardcopy only)

There exists, then, a cosmic continuum, about which we had only begun to learn before this apparently teleal phase of our existence. Of its possibly infinite facets, we had mastered two:

First aspect was the helpingsense, whereby the very nature of a Disciplined life suggests the logical assessment of need in the outer realm as relative to one's innate gifts. It is to offer help to that need, regardless of where it is encountered, then to move on. Conversely, where one has a need, that need will theoretically be met by anOther's gifts.

This begins with primeval simplicity, in the nurturing of a child, the teaching of an acolyte, the succoring of the weak or afflicted. But where we differ from the People is in not seeking equal recompense from the one served in 'repayment' for our service. By the very nature of continuum, one serves that the service may be passed on, not returned. To return deed for deed or service for service is to lock the mode into a closed, inclusionary system which, by definition, becomes also an exclusionary system. This is one definition of what People have called "friendship," and we cannot subscribe to it.

180

Rather, if the continuum is to be served, the one's needs are served, who then offers service to the next one's needs; she serves the next, who serves the next, until the whole of the species—or, as we had once hoped, the whole of the World—be interlinked in a seamless net of served and serving. In such an ideal realm, no need however aching would be unfulfillable, no trauma unhealable, no suffering unassuageable. This is, of course, only theory, and shall so remain, having never been given opportunity for true testing . . .

From first aspect derives second aspect. Primarily a Telepath's skill, it was hoped in time that all could master it, but it is this: once interlinked in continuum, one can hypothetically learn to read and recognize the soul-thread of any Other. Thus it would be possible, as some have mastered it, to reach into the inscape, locate any individual soul-thread, and cause it to resonate with one's own, thus linking oneself in non-intrusive communication with the Other. Telepaths have done this for generations. Yet, outside the mating bond, most Others continue to fear it. Why is this so? . . .

Had we had sufficient time to master second aspect, we might have prevented this present state of death. And, oh, what richness might have awaited us in that expanded inscape thus offered! But we shall never know. What further aspects of continuum might we have learned? There is no telling, not on this world. Yet surely there are life-forces elsewhere in this universe who continue to search and are that much more advanced than we. Our disexistence as a species will scarcely impact upon that search or that continuum, but while we were a part of it, it were joy!

nine

"**G**rown to adulthood in a box, that's you!" Dweneth accused me, not for the first time. "How else deny the obvious, that every man's born with a weapon every woman in some way fears, and some of us learn that fear far too soon?

"I told you how my mother died, and my brothers and a sister. I told you how I saved the singstick. Did you think it a tale with a happy ending because I lived to tell it?

"Da and Mother never got along; she was too fine and he too plain, as it seemed to my child's eyes. How they ever had the children they did, I'll never know, but until that night there were five of us: Rella and Conn between Brok and me, Mikon a babe at the breast. Mother wanted a tour of the Shadoward countries; Da was more concerned with finding Brok apprenticeship before he ate us entirely out of pocket. So Da stayed with Brok in Droghia, while Mother went off in a huff with the rest of us and the troupe to play the provinces near Gloom.

"We children were born to it, except for Brok. Players before we could stand. The three elder of us did Crowds and Choruses; the babe was the living sacrifice in *Kerilesh,* though he'd tend to giggle and spoil it. It was seeing him later, covered in real blood, that has me shun the Tragedie."

She took a deep shuddering breath before she could go on.

"We never heard the Kwengii, until they were upon us. What you saw at Sirdar'sInn was nothing. They slew all the males outright, including Conn, who was but eleven, and little Mikon, too. For male children, to their thinking, are only minature men who will grow to fight them later. They dragged Mother and Rella into one of the wagons and used them until dawn; I could hear Rella's screams the night long. Only when she at last grew still did I attempt to flee. I suppose they slit her throat. I never stopped to look.

"Somehow they didn't see me at first. My hair was cropped short for the Choruses then; perhaps they took me for a boy. I lay beside Conn's lifeless body most of the night, to make them think me already slain. I'd grabbed the singstick at the first, and had it hidden beneath me. If I'd only stayed still I might have been spared, but when I tried to run, they caught me."

At the very moment, I thought, that I was pulling weeds and chopping logic with old Tagal, fretting over no larger tragedy than a *gli*flower's distress. Curious, I thought, watching tears course down this gentle creature's face where she thought I could not see them in the dark, how this species with its many gods of good and evil enacted its greatest evils upon itself.

"There were—four of them—I think," Dweneth went on. My impulse was to touch her, hold her, as she had needed once before, but impulses were not Other. I remained, untouching presence, in my corner of the burrow. "Betimes—I did not count and—betimes—I no longer knew. Why they did not kill me—after—as they had Mother and Rella—I know not either . . . It was still dark, and they had not found the singstick. When I—awoke—the sky was lightening and I could find the stick. I crawled to it, and hid us both beneath the leaves until there was no longer sound of Kwengii."

Her eyes glowed febrile in the dark as she remembered.

"Somehow I must have gone back to the wagons to find clean clothes. Mine were—like me—all torn and bloodied." Her breath caught in her throat. She swallowed, forced herself to go on. "How I could think so clear, or get me past the bodies of those I'd known and loved I don't remember either. Found myself upon the road, barely able to walk. Slept in a ditch, which is where the farmwife found me. Brought me to the healerwoman, who knew the whereabouts of some Players. With them was Omila, who had toured with Mother. She got me back to Da in Droghia, and the rest . . ."

She dried her eyes on the backs of her hands and sniffled, her face twisted with loathing.

"The rest perhaps my living brother Brok can tell you better! There were games we'd played as children, games of his inventing. There's little privacy in Players' wagon—you know that—and Brok often spied on my parents, then tried his newfound knowledge first on Rella, then on me. Rella learned to run or fight him off, but I was neither strong nor quick enough. When we met again in Droghia I was, shall we say, no longer a child. Brok wanted the games to continue as before.

"The healerwoman had taught me much—to divert me from my sorrow, and because she saw that I was quick. She taught me cures and curses, and I cursed Brok with every curse I knew. His hair fell out and he grew bloated, except for the part of him he valued most. He never touched me more nor, for all I know, any woman after. Da never knew any of it. I think it would kill him, else he'd kill Brok."

She sobbed briefly, then sighed, her complex passions spent. It was hard for her to hate.

"I almost envy you your plague-mark . . ." I heard her murmur, hugging herself sleepily. "Never to know man at all is better, I think, than knowing him as I have . . .

"Odd, isn't it?" she mused from her corner, shivering betimes with the cold. "I do so love children, and it can't be all that bad to be a wife, else womankind would not so eagerly

184

pursue it. But I'm unbetrothable, in the strictest sense, being 'spoiled' as I am, and those men who would have me—there are many, as you may have noticed . . ."

The pride she took in this was interesting.

"I have," I concurred, having watched the looks and leers and more-than-suggestions, the clinging and pleading outside the tiring-room after a performance, as we'd traveled hamlet-to-town-to-village.

"Such men are nothing I can stomach. They belch and slobber and are too much brotherly . . ." I heard her yawn. "Tell me that in *OtherWhere* babes are born of wishing, and I shall journey there this night . . ."

"Not precisely," I said. No point in so much as hinting at Other bonding customs, as if she would believe me.

"Cold!" Dweneth murmured; we were huddled together for warmth. She dozed, though I had not the luxury, but something brought her bolt upright.

"Why can't I hear your heart beating?" She was wild-eyed, wrenched from sleep, irrational. "You have no heart!"

"Peace, of course I do!" It was too silent in this place, which sheltered neither bird nor night creature. She could hear her own heart thundering in her ears, but not the softer Other-tempo of mine. "You simply cannot hear it past your own. We are both overweary. Sleep!"

"I will not!" She shrank from me to the farthest corner of the burrow, and I wondered if she would flee. "Betimes what I cannot see waking comes clear to me in sleep. Weary I may be, but not so weary that I cannot see it is no ordinary being who carries me down a cliffside without effort—"

"Not exactly 'without effort'; you are not light of weight—"

"—swims like a trillfish while instructing one who cannot swim, who knows the whole of *OtherWhere,* and who has no heart! If you are demon, sorceress or ElvenQueen, I will know it now!"

"Were I any of these, would I let you live?"

She was not to be diverted.

"Truth!" she demanded. "I will know the truth!"

"As you wish, *but keep your voice down!*" I was more certain than ever that we were not alone upon this steppe. She muttered some obscenity; once again we whispered. "You said you'd one day ask the Right of Three. Is it now?"

"Are we that near death?" Her voice shook. "Truth, who knows? The Right of Three, then, if you like."

"And nevermore again?" I held my hand palm-upward, as I'd seen the children do in Refuge. "Three answers and we're even? Swear!"

"Melodrama!" She brushed my palm with hers, no easy thing in her present fear of me. "Even. I swear."

"Then ask your three."

She sat up straighter against the night sky, cleared her throat. I wished she would be still.

"I demand to know what manner of creature has your strength and secrets," she began grandly, ever the Player-maid. "One: what are you? Two: where come you from? Three: why are you here, and what do you want of me?"

"Asked truth, answer truth."

The voice was Rau's. Easy for him to say. Perhaps with sunlight she would think she dreamed it.

"One: I am of that race your People call variously elves, demons, witches or simply Evil Ones, though I assure you we were never evil, only misperceived. Some few facts of our existence, though much fancified, weave themselves through your lays of *Faerie* and *OtherWhere,* suggesting that perhaps some of our kind have passed this way before, in less than careful guise."

She was deadly still now—perchance, I hoped, asleep. But no. I heard her stirring, impatient for the rest.

"Two: I am of that place which I have styled to you as OtherWhere, which with all the newer verses I have added is less tale than truth. Three: I have been sent to observe of your world, before it too abruptly meets with mine. And four, though you have not asked—" The snort of a *guravek* punctuated what I was about to say. " —we are not alone."

Dweneth heard it too. They were mild, skittish creatures,

except in rut or when startled. This might be a stray from a wild herd traversing the plain in search of forage. Other eyes could discern its shaggy, antlered form against the stars, its head down in our burrow, its soft, snuffling nose a hairs-breadth from our heads. Was it alone, or had it brought company?

"Don't move, don't speak! Come up out of there!"

We were hauled bodily out of our hiding place and an arrow—poison-tipped?—touched my throat, discouraging resistance. Dweneth, I could see against the starlight, was likewise held.

The voice that ordered us was Lamorak-accented, weather-roughened, but decidedly female. It belonged to a slight, hooded figure clad like its larger fellows in cured *'vek*-hide. Someone lit a torch.

"No sound nor struggle or we'll tie and gag you!" The small figure peered at us beneath its face-concealing hood. "Goddess, you're a filthy lot! Come along of us, and no tricks!"

There were seven of them, all armed. Shoved forward with their arrows at our backs, we had little choice. Glancing sideways at Dweneth, I expected fear. Instead she struggled with a secret smile.

"Renna!" she addressed the hooded form. "You stinking, *'vek*-bred bitch!"

The slight one threw back her hood and laughed a great hoarse laugh.

"The same to you, I'm sure! As the saying goes, never try playing to a Player!" In spite of the mud, she began hugging and pounding Dweneth by turns. "Put up your bows, lads; we're found out!"

There were seven *guravek* for seven riders. Dweneth shared Renna's. I walked.

"Permit us to better understand . . ." WiseJeijinn would address me, once I had concluded this portion of my debriefing before the Matriarchy.

She had leaned forward intently from the Chair, her head

187

tilted to one side the better to hear—my handsome mother's characteristic pose when listening to that which she would prefer not.

"Are we to understand that your traverse of a portion of the ShadoWindward Quadrant for the greater part of a year netted this much: close daily association with two females, both of marginal livelihood and neither part of any mainstream or conventional mode of family-bonding? You traveled a certain distance, much of that in wilderness or between minor settlements, garnered some stale court-gossip out of Droghia—the only major metropolis you visited—and incidentalia regarding forest communications and as well of music, an art which we have long abandoned, and with good reason? Are we to assume that this is the sum of your report?"

"It is an adequate synopsis, WiseJeijinn Matriarch," I replied, addressing my mother formally, as was expected under the circumstances, "provided that one add the obvious conclusion: that I am returned whole, to give my report in person."

When would I learn not to be glib in my mother's presence, particularly in so public a forum? The unobtrusive rustle of garments in the gallery was the only sound in the Council chamber, where a hundred eyes watched me, as they watched Jeijinn, to confirm her objectivity and her Discipline in this particular debriefing. It was expected that she would be more stringent with me than with a Monitor not her offspring; nevertheless I could not, it seemed, resist what Dweneth would call "queering it."

"Prior Monitors have brought us more extensive, detailed information, with often far less expenditure of time," Jeijinn said tersely, itemizing their reports upon the tips of her fingers as if she had them displayed before her, rather than committed to memory. "Else they have remained in crossover for however many years were necessary to submit a complete report. I gave you Heged's 'Evolution of Weaponry in Tawa and Kelibesh,' WiseMari's 'Religions of Zanti.' Your own teacher Rau's monograph on torture and penal systems in the Shadoward principalities. Soliah's 'Extended Family and Polygamy,' 'Sailships and Navigational Algorithms for a Hundred Years' . . ."

"Predominantly scientific reports compiled predominantly by scientists," I presumed to interrupt. However I resisted, my mother's sheer presence brought out my innate stubbornness. "Further, as these areas were already reported upon in broad, I saw no reason, given time restraints, to add trivial and possibly redundant detail. I had a somewhat different purpose in mind."

"Which was?" Jeijinn prompted.

"An attempt to understand and thereby explain, from a study of these two 'marginal' females—in a society which, so unlike our own, largely views most females as 'marginal'—the world they lived in, and their People's heart."

Again the subtle shift of limbs in the gallery above me, the subliminal hum of the infonets recording every word and nuance, to be transmitted to every commscreen on the islands. Among the eyes that watched me, two were Rau's, and twinkling.

Jeijinn had exhaused her allotment of questions. A new voice asserted itself.

"Tell us, if you would, Lingri Monitor," WiseGovin began in his most reasonable tone, "the circumstances surrounding your breach of the Alimentary Discipline . . ."

The first time was not from necessity but from ignorance, and from the pragmatic wisdom that when in Lamora, one does as the Lamorak. Though more than eighty years have passed, I tell the event still with no little shame.

But

    even I

       must

          on occasion

           sleep

The stimulant hisses against my neck, and Gayat's fingers are at the reach centers of my face, initiating a probe. First mentally, then physically, I shake him off. I know not how long I have slept, fallen face-forward on my writing desk, my unkempt hair flung about, mouth open no doubt and drooling on the page. My hand is so cramped about the last, now empty, stylus that I can no longer distinguish where one ends and the second begins. Gayat intuits my problem and pries my fingers loose. My mask is locked firmly in place; he will not as well intuit my shame.

"Shall I fetch a healer?" He sounds concerned.

"Have healers so little to do?" I massage the numb hand with the functional one; I must remember to alternate hands as well as script when I write again. "Or is sleep now forbidden us as well?"

"Normal sleep is still permitted," Gayat replies. "But what overcame you here . . ."

If I can evoke sympathy in a Telepath, I am a sorry sight.

"And you, Gayat-*la?*" I counter. "Are you sufficiently recovered from your—?"

"Fit," it is in my mind to say; why soften it to "illness"? Let him read it as he will; either way he does not answer me.

"Tell me, Gayat Telepath, what do you do when you are not tending me? Are you engaged in the Eidetics, or is there else to keep you occupied?"

He does not answer that either. I surrender.

"What brings you this time?"

"The Guard have gone," he tells me.

The Guard have gone. A simple statement, four words in duration, signifying untold permutations. Where have they gone, and why? Have they decided we no longer bear watching at the expense of so much weaponry and manpower, that we can be contained in our exile by the patrol boats and the nightflyers? Has it only been mutiny or disaffection among a Guard too long stationed too far from home with too little to entertain them, now that we will no longer permit them to bash our infants' brains out on the waysides? Has there been a change in command at the Praesidium level, which has decided to abandon us to survive as we will? Might the Guard have been removed before the ultimate weaponry is moved in?

Neither Gayat nor I presume to speak any of this aloud, though the son of a Telepath can read my thoughts, and he refuses analysis. All he knows is that the gatherers and the kelp harvesters were able to work a full day unmolested, and the seabaths are working again.

"And as we have the freedom, however brief or spurious, to both eat and bathe . . ."

"And as you thought I might be in need of both . . ."

"Precisely," he says flatly; irony is wasted on Telepaths. "I will tidy the place while you are gone."

If he does he will discover that I have not used his dear-bought tapers. More importantly, I will permit no one near my chronicle in my absence.

"You will do no such thing," I caution him, "unless you wish to be the first recipient of anOther's violence since the Thousand-Year! Touch nothing! You cannot conceive of what I do here. Come with me or I shall not go."

He acquiesces, reluctantly I think, presuming to take my arm and lead me up the corridors. Again I shake him off. Do I look so helpless? But the violence of sunlight after so long in darkness staggers me, and the nictitating membranes shut over my eyes involuntarily. I must steady myself against the archway until they have receded.

"What is the color today?" I ask, to have something to say. Eyes still shut, I feel my way along, my hand running along familiar facades and garden walls.

"Gray today. You slept through green."

This brings me to a halt. Only in direst illness have I ever slept the sun around. Though I am scarce a hundred years, theoretically in my prime, I have never felt so old.

"Never, Gayat-*la*, never!" I sigh, letting him take my arm this time. "Perhaps the Matriarchy needs a newer chronicler."

My free hand strikes empty air where there should be a dwelling. I totter and Gayat steadies me.

"Don't open your eyes," he cautions, but too late. I must

see. What I see is irreducible rubble—too familiar in the People's world, but until recently unknown in ours.

"What was here? Was this not Frayin's house?"

"It was. Razed by nightflyers two nights ago, along with the entire suburbs, and more selective targets."

"And I slept through that?" It explains why no one found me; all but Lingri were engaged in something else. "How many dead?"

"Don't ask me that."

" 'Selective targets,' then. Meaning what?"

"Meaning the Guard were seeking WiseChior primarily and, unable to find him, sought out Frayin, then destroyed her house!" my Telepath blurts, exasperated that I must have a catalogue of each aspect of destruction. "The bombing may have saved the children . . ."

"Sought out" Frayin? To interrogate and, earning no answers, then what? Gayat's wording is too careful.

". . . too many Guard engaged elsewhere, and none to notice the small ones smuggled offisland."

"What of the children?" At the least he can answer me this much.

"No word yet," he replies, tight-lipped. It could mean they are safe on their way to Zanti, or any number of alternatives.

"And Frayin—?" I don't expect an answer. "At least tell me—"

"I can tell you nothing!" Gayat answers shrilly.

We have almost reached the end of the old city wall and the open strand where as many Others as can have gathered. Gayat will no longer speak at all. Either Gayat does not know Frayin's fate, or has been instructed not to tell me.

"I refuse to be led to the baths like an invalid. Go now, and not back to my chamber, either!"

I gather my dignity, as badly slept-in as my person, about me as I cross the strand alone, my aching eyes now aided by a sudden gathering of clouds. It will soon be Stormseason.

Others pass me coming and going, but I speak to no one, as is my right, for anOther in her own land is still free to carry her privacy with her, wrapped about her like a cloak, when she must think undisturbed in public places. Discreetly I search out Frayin among those gathered, scarcely expecting to find her. Nor will I inquire of those of every age and station (except the very young—gone, all gone, and who knows to what fate?) if any know of her or have seen her. What answers I earn might prove less bearable than this present uncertainty.

I choose not to acknowledge the sidelong glances of those who step aside in my presence, knowing who or rather what I am.

"Way for the chronicler," I hear their soft whispers. "Way for the chronicler, whose time is more freighted than ours."

"Way for the chronicler, that she may not be inconvenienced."

I am not supposed to hear. What do these masks barely conceal—concern, pity? Resentment, however atavistic, of my "preferred" status? Or only curiosity, greatest of Other gifts and profoundest of our flaws, who could never leave anything alone, but must examine it to its most minute degree, whether it be a subatomic particle or a People's heart? I take my place in the queue with everyone else, waiting as anOther waits—silently, patiently, and with my thoughts elsewhere.

The baths are a recent reincarnation of an ancient concept, reconstructed on the ancient sites after the Guard dismantled our hydrology plants for no clear reason beyond an attempt to harass and demoralize. Our obsession with hygiene amuses them. But the Guard are gone, though their patrol boats can still be seen betimes on the horizon. What is their game? Pondering, I complete my ablutions and choose to swim, out past the breakwater into the open sea, as pure and unencumbered as when first I swam into the realm of air-breathers at my birth.

"What a marvelous idea!" Dweneth exclaimed, the first time she witnessed anOther birth.

How long had we brought our offspring into life this way? Possibly since that primeval time when we first observed how *bRi* birth their calves. We have refined the custom, bringing the water to the parturient female rather than her to the sea. The water is purified, heated to body temperature, and the female floats tranquilly in a specially constructed tank, in the company of spouse and healer, that the child may make its transition easily, floating from that first womb to the womb of the larger World. It is a fact that Other children, thus gentled into life, are well and whole and never cry at birth.

Or so it was. The last Other children were born in exile and duress, and Other children are born no more.

Dweneth introduced Other birthing practices among her People, abolishing along the way their many unsanitary, superstition-ridden customs. Children born under her methods were healthier and more balanced than any the People had ever known. Others lived in the hope that a new generation of People born without pain or fear would unlearn violence, and for a time this was so.

Now I cannot but wonder if Dweneth's practices continue or if, like so much she brought between the worlds, it too has been abandoned.

I am indeed grown old before my time, I realize, as my long, steady stroke carries me beyond the breakers, down the coast to what remains of Loriel's Undersea, for every random thought I think is so encrusted with long-past associations that I cannot shake it free, any more than a single individual through however much labor could free my grandmother's last, best dream of the ravages of age and entropy.

Succinctly: I swim as naked as I was born, and if any of the Guard should encounter me and take offense, so be it. In my experience, no amount of clothing, nor consideration of age from infancy to antiquity has ever dissuaded rapist from his goal. Once raped, twice careful? For all else that was done to me, that fate I never suffered, though what I have witnessed in my hundred years has made me no less careful. Nevertheless, if the inoffensive flash of this dry husk through cold seawater inflame any to violence, again: so be it. Let my presence serve to deflect that violence from some more susceptible target. There is not much more that can be done to me. Besides, they will have to catch me first, and there never were People who could outswim Lingri.

Having found my destination, I plunge deep below the surface, beyond the play of sunlight, to what once was the entrance of Undersea. It is vast, though barely visible beneath multifold crustings of coral and tangles of kelp and debris, obscuring its Other-wrought form beneath the inevitability of their decay. Fish flicker by, indifferent, scattering as I approach.

Here were to have been the living quarters, there the workplaces, ringed about the outside. There the gardens and the meditation chambers, beyond the solar plant and waste recycling, and areas whose intended function Lingri never-scientist can now, swimming among them, only surmise. They are indistinguishable one from the next beneath their layers of corruption. I remember what was where only because Loriel once brought me here to show me—proud in her quiet, Other way, of what mind and hands had wrought.

"What do you think?" she had asked me softly; we two alone in the control sphere, her arm freely about my shoulder as there were none to witness. Equally, her thoughts were open to me. Something about my absence in crossover had visited my grandmother with intimations of mortality, of mutability, of that which needed to be touched with hands in order to interweave it that much more permanently with the soul. If she were not Loriel, I might have called her frightened—for me, as for us all.

"Grandmother, it is— " I sought a word of both truth and accuracy, and chose one of Dweneth's, "exquisite. Wellwrought. An optimum balance of form with usefulness, and esthetically pleasing as well. Would that I could be among its denizens!"

Loriel squeezed my shoulder silently, then let me go. Her eyes were closed, but still I saw the fleeting pain slipped irretrievably through her mask.

"The World has different plans for you!" she barely whispered, bringing the control sphere to the surface.

Undersea was in time abandoned, left unfinished, and I never saw it more from that day to this.

Sunlight breaks through clouds above to tease at what remains—sparkling, bejeweling. Loriel's dream is beautiful even in decay. What would she think if she could see it?

I swim beyond the Old Gate, to avoid not only Gayat but the necessity of returning past what once was Frayin's house. AnOther on the beach provides a mantle for my nakedness, and several more share their meager food. We do not speak, but watch silently out to sea, as if to see the patrol boats now out of visual range but no doubt reading us on infrared. It is as if we would infer from their invisibility what the masters of those boats intend next.

My hair uncombed and damp with seawater, I return alone to my solitary room to find it undisturbed. I sit, sharpen one of the quill pens, and attempt to explain, as I once did for Govin Councillor, how I first violated the Alimentary Discipline more than eighty years ago.

Having hauled me out of the burrow, Renna gave me only a passing glance in torchlight.

"Your servant?" she asked Dweneth.

"My—yes!" that personage replied, on the verge, perhaps, of saying "friend." But friends did not answer the Right of Three with fabrications out of *OtherWhere,* and it was I, after all, who had first demurred at friendship. We were, as she would say, even.

"Nice you can afford one, but I hope you got her cheap!" Renna remarked, examining me closer when we got to her camp of hair-tents, where blazing campfires exaggerated my alien strangeness. I met those near-black eyes in the high-boned face with my own unblinking gaze. Let her kill me for making her look away first, or else draw her conclusions and leave me in peace.

"She's an odd one!" the huntress remarked, talking past me to Dweneth, as if I had neither speech nor thought of my own. She had indeed had to look away first, but laughed it off, as she laughed further when I refused to change my muddy garb for the tanned hides everyone here wore. "Where'd you find her?"

"Among a nation of liars!" Dweneth snapped, slipping into a tunic and leggings like those Renna wore. In spite of her high coloring she immediately became the part she played; she could have been as much of Lamora as her hostess. "How did you know to find me?"

Renna did not answer at first, still studying me with mockery in her eyes, rubbing idly at a bluish pigment worked deep into her chilblained fingers. Lamorak artists and artisans favored blue pigments. Had Renna talents beyond hunting and sarcasm?

"I read the future, not the present!" she said at last, ignoring me to warm herself at the fire. "We were hunting *grebbok* in the wood by NearVillage when Gause and the rest straggled in. I'd gone to chat up your Da when Cwala stopped me with the whole goddessawful tale of you going over a cliff and drowning. Your Da's whole, by the bye, though frantic at your missing, so we said we'd backtrack ye, if only to fish the bodies out of the river. We watched ye and—this—drag ashore. Never expected ye'd get this far downriver."

"You watched us all that time, digging the burrow and everything, and never let us know?" Dweneth's head nearly brushed the tent-top as she stood, hands on her hips and furious.

Renna squatted by the fire and laughed. Leader of hunters, queen of all she surveyed, she could be irreverent.

"Ye're here now, aren't ye? It made me entertainment. Whatever else she is, yon strange one's strong. How did ye get this far downriver?"

"Sorcery!" Dweneth glowered at me. "Is there food? We've none since daybreak."

Renna fetched what I thought to be an ale or wineskin from a saddlepack.

"Starters," she announced, passing it first to Dweneth, who drank deeply. Renna drank as well, then passed the skin to me.

The touch of the skin itself was unpleasant enough, but less pleasant was the knowledge that I was being tested. There was no tribe in this region, I knew, which imbibed of blood. Whatever else I might not be able to drink did not occur to me until I swallowed.

"W-what is it?" I managed to croak before my throat constricted almost completely.

"What else but fermented *'vek*'s-milk?" Renna snorted. My discomfort amused her. "Living in these parts and you've never—? La, Dwen, this is an odd one!"

"Don't mock her!" Dweneth mumbled sleepily. She might, but no one else.

Renna sidled closer to me as I ceased to choke and regained my equilibrium. The unwashed and *'vek*-greased stench of her and her hides was enough to nauseate me anew.

"All our livelihood be from the *guravek*," she explained as if to a child. "She gives and we accept, whether meat or hides or hair for tents, dung for fuel and urine to clear the skin and keep away the biting-bugs. Bone we use for tools and antlers for art and telling futures." She dug an antler-flute out of the saddlepack, carved and painted with the same blue that was on her hands. "Look you . . ."

She produced a second bit of antler and a shoulderbone from a bag decorated with curious symbols; these pieces were fire-blackened and elaborate with heat-cracks.

"We offer them to the goddess through the intercession of fire, and she reaches down her finger to draw the future upon

198

them. The patterns tell us what is to be." She fingered a crack on the shoulderbone, scowling. "Goddess, you *are* here! Small wonder I did not know what this meant afore."

She shook her head so that her silk-black hair shone in the firelight, then shoved the artifacts back into their pouch.

"As to the milk, as toddlings we suckle beside the calves, so the 'vek becomes our spirit-mother and we her childer. When we are grown we drink the milk fermented to celebrate a hunt or the return of friends; it makes us one with the 'vek. Thereby we are all of the same herd, and will even welcome strays like you. Goddess knows your ears be more like 'vek's than People's. Drink up!"

She laughed again when I refused, handing the skin back to her. Mockery was to be her way with me; I accepted this and did not rise to it and she soon left me alone. Once the spasm left my throat and I could swallow again, I made do with some roots and dried chokeberries, while the rest supped on 'vek and *grebbok* flesh and wondered how I survived.

That was the first, though not the last, occasion upon which I tasted of the forbiddens and suffered the consequences after. The first time was ignorance, the rest necessity.

WiseGovin, as I recall, questioned me minutely about the incident; to this day I am uncertain why.

"And the tents were actually woven from the hair of the creatures?" he persisted. "How is this done, precisely?"

"The hair is cut without harming the *guravek*," I explained. "When it grows back, it is cut again. Thus the finished hair-tent is not a forbidden, but emits only a mild tingling, to indicate that its origins were once with a living creature."

The explanation did not succeed in convincing Govin that my crossover had not corrupted me entirely.

Govin was among the rare nonTelepaths who never left the Archipelago, and among the first to die here when the People drove us back. He was never to master either subtlety or the value of silence, and the Guard's attention was drawn to him immediately. Perhaps he provoked them deliberately—to voice his final disdain, or to draw their wrath away from Others. I do not know. His death was prolonged and particularly excruciating—meant, one supposes, as an example to the rest of us. But an example of what? To this day People fail to understand that anOther cannot be made to fear death, regardless of its means.

Having taken time from my chronicle to swim and, inadvertently, to sleep, I do not take up it again immediately upon my return. Something diverts me for the present: the need to know Frayin's fate. This is not time wasted, but time conserved. Impossible to know whether time or materials will fail me first; as I conserve the first I squander the second, and conversely. Yet, if none will tell me gentle Frayin's fate, I will discover it myself.

When no Other could live without a commscreen at her elbow, a moment's inquiry through the 'nets would provide me with the status of anyone on the Archipelago. Other deaths would be mine on a 'net as well. We were spoiled in that respect, and all but forgot what it was like to live before or without such amenities. When the system was dismantled there was a not inconsiderable amount of turmoil in our heretofore ordered lives. The majority of us had become too dependent upon *things,* to the detriment of the inscape.

Communication now consists solely of what Other can whisper to Other in passing, or tap upon a wall. For those few who know how to access it, there is the continuum.

Ordinarily, this is a Telepath's Discipline, though I have had reason in the past to master some of it. Much disused, it will have to serve me now. Composing my body into the meditative posture, composing my mind to the degree I can, I reach.

Every Other has a soul-thread, a unique internal voice that is her own. Frayin's was once well known to me; if I reach far enough now I can recall its resonance. If she lives and is nearby, I will find her. I reach.

And encounter nothing. Either my skills have atrophied for lack of use, or gentle Frayin is indeed dead.

Shall I grieve this individual tragedy when so many of us have died, are dying? It is at least a sorrow, for though her life was longer than most and gave much to the continuum she so eloquently preached, it should not have ended in this way.

"Your kind live *two hundred years!*"

I can still hear the incredulous squeak in Dweneth's voice. That Frayin lived to one hundred and fifty would have sufficed for Dweneth; it is half again what any of her People can hope for with all the medical advances we have helped them to. Yet the perspective does not assuage. Taking years from our lives will not add them to the People's. If Frayin is dead, I must mourn—for her, and for the agency that killed her.

Ask then: if Other possesses this ability to reach anOther on the continuum, why have I not sought to learn if Dweneth still lives, or Joreth? To answer the first while preserving my privacy: I cannot. To answer the second, Joreth is an intermix and untrained. While I knew his inner voice at birth, time and distance weaken reception, and what he resonated as a child will alter in the adult. Further, I know not where, in the People's world or beyond it, to search for him. Not only my room is windowless.

Joreth asked me: "Why won't you let me be trained?"

It was to be our last time together on the Archipelago; I knew this but he did not. Long had I weighed what I must do. Keep him here in Others' care, while I as always roved the larger World, no longer able to do good, for the Purists had rendered that impossible, but occasionally mitigating evil? Leave my near-grown son, then? Surely I could not take him on my peripatetic way, as I was more often than not in hiding and under threat of death.

I had already begun the process which would deny my parentage, consign him forever to his father. Call me coward for not telling Joreth this directly, but he would not have understood. Adolescent eager, he continued to embrace my world with a dabbler's fervor. I had always hoped he would take from his Other heritage what he found of value, and graft it onto the People in him to shape a new form out of both. Too late now, and dangerous. The less he took from Others now, the safer for him. Yet again, he asked me.

"Mum? Are you listening? Why can't I? WiseLerius says he will teach me, at least for the first levels."

Trust Lerius, I thought with no little bitterness, to deny what transpires beyond his enclave, to cling to the old ways though the sky be falling! Not with my son, he wouldn't!

"He was skeptical at first, Father's being psi-null," Joreth went on, self-absorbed, unable to read my carefully masked thoughts, "but he says I test high, for an Intermix. I'm no Telepath, Lerius says, but he could bring me up into the continuum. Why won't you?"

By next year he would be sixteen, adult in either world, and would not need my permission. By next year the Purists would likely hold the entire World in thrall. But Joreth was no different from any People's child, in seeing world events only as they affected him. And with the grace of adolescence, he thought himself invincible.

"If you were to be trained, even at first levels, the skill could be used against you." I tried to keep my words gentle, but the reality they spoke of made them harsh. "Do you know what is done to Telepaths who are caught in the People's world?"

Joreth's mouth tightened and he shrugged. He read the infonets but, again, he was invincible.

"It wouldn't happen to me. It would make me stronger. This way, with no skill, my mind could more easily be ripped apart." A tremor passed over his gangling frame. Not entirely invincible, then. "Besides, they'd never catch me. Never even suspect me. Look at me—do I look Other?"

"You will not be trained," I repeated. "I refuse permission."

"Next year I won't need your permission!" His tone was less defiant than pragmatic; he was this much Other.

"We shall see," I said, and Joreth was not trained.

As to death by violence and what it was meant to teach us, it is interesting to note that only in his long and painful death did WiseGovin finally keep his silence.

———

"On the Disposition of Women" (based upon a dialogue between the WiseOnes of the Four Greaters and representatives of the faculties of Sego and Tolay in Plalas of the People: Infonet-CrossRef#231513514/T-Y1043/1586 P.A.)

. . . it would never have occurred to us, having from ancient times judged each individual as an individual and according to her gifts, that the majority of People should consider the female of the species to be inherently inferior. This was made quite clear to us by the refusal of many leaders even to speak to any of our Matriarchs unless they were male. When we questioned the scholars of Sego and Tolay specifically, two eminent universities which do not under any circumstances admit women (to our knowledge only the universities of Gentii and Droghia do so, and those accepted are usually the offspring of professionals in medicine or law, or those whose parents contribute generously to the university fund), they were astonished that we could not see the "obvious" differences.

"They are so much smaller than men," one pointed out. "Surely their intelligence must be the smaller, for their brains do weigh less." When asked where in the brain the factors determining intelligence might lie, this personage regaled us for some time on the "science" of phrenology, and thereafter changed the subject. When a second scholar was asked, he offered as evidence the "natural"

203

physical weakness of a creature which must spend the greater portion of its life in child-bearing, and cited statistics on deaths from traumatic labor and puerperal fever, and the fact that a woman who bore an average of thirteen children could not hope to live past her thirtieth birthday, whereas the average male could anticipate a lifespan of thirty-five or even forty!

While most of the assemblage of scholars would admit exceptions to the rule in such regional variations as the artist/huntresses of Lamora and the rites-priestesses of Dyr, they remained adamant in their certainty that the female is constitutionally and intellectually inferior to the male.

Having traveled freely throughout the Archipelago at our invitation, some few of these scholars did on occasion reconsider, for everywhere they saw women working coequally with men and, in certain skills, surpassing them. They decried, however, the nomenclature of the female principle, whereby we address our Councillors as 'Matriarchs' regardless of gender, and where when we speak of a generic 'one' we invariably say 'she' instead of 'he.' When we presumed to broach the topic of Changers, the People's scholars were unanimously horrified, and asked that we 'speak no more of these things.'

(Note: There has been divided opinion about the wisdom of mentioning Changers from the first, recalling to mind how some People had reacted with shock and disbelief, if not outright disgust, when informed as to the nature of our biologically imperative bonding customs, despite the fact that in certain regions of their own world such customs might well be considered within the norm. To our knowledge, however, with the exception of some Zanti mystics, whose Changers are only spiritual (in that they lack the medical expertise to effect the physical changes, no People possessed a concept of change for any but physical transexual purposes.)

Therefore few, however educated, could overcome their prejudices in this regard. It behooved us to recall that as recently as five

204

centuries ago Changers were still considered by some of our own to be bizarre. How could we expect People, who considered anything female to be in an incomplete or lesser state of being (if not something abhorrent and innately evil, as many of the religions preach), to comprehend that a male, once he had produced offspring, might desire to embrace the female principle in body as well as in spirit? Of all ethnological sticking-points after religion itself, this was perhaps the most insoluable.

Consequently, a Lamorak tribe might have a queen and even a goddess principle, and the priestesses of Dyr might eschew childbearing and all intercourse with men in order to commune with higher powers, but the majority of women of the People would find difficulty in obtaining equality with men however many and varied their societies.

ten

"**P**ity the rains held ye," Renna told Dweneth. We were a-road again, having met up with the troupe at last in Near-Village, amid much celebration. "Ye might have got to Droghia in time to see the ships launched."

"Oh, have they already?" Dweneth was truly dismayed; my own thoughts were less disquieted, but for Other reasons. "Why do I always miss the good parts? Did you see them go out, Ren?"

"Droghen threw me out of town!" that personage grumbled. " 'Bad luck are women around ships,' says he—and hence that much worse am I. Methought it was more he wanted me out of his bed. Besides, the moon said hunting, and ye can't argue the moon."

"*You* couldn't," Dweneth sniffed. "I'd have stayed."

In truth, Renna seldom stayed anywhere for long, garnering gossip on '*vek* back from Llellaar to Mantuu. She made her way by hunting or selling her artifacts, or else by Lamorak magic and telling futures. None could hold her, not even the string of lovers or the babe or three she had weaned and left in the care of kin, a tradition among the huntress-queens of her tribe. Dweneth envied Renna her freedom more than anything.

"So they're already launched?" They were still talking of ships; I listened.

"You know Droghen," Renna said. "He'd hardly wait for anything once it were proper Bask and the currents right. He had me do a future for him ere I left. I told him wondrous exploits, of course, and so he gave me leave to paint the figurehead on the *Foremost*."

" 'Gave you'?" Dweneth was not a little envious. "More like you pestered him out of it!"

Renna laughed her raucous laugh. "Can Droghen refuse me anything?"

"Nor any wench he beds with!" Dweneth retorted. "How I can see you reading futures amid the dirty sheets, with all his extra ladies 'round about! Someday you'll all want him at once, and then 'ware his damaged heart!"

"Then sober Thrasim gets the First Seat, and no more frolics after," Renna grimaced. "No tickling Thrasim. Goddess knows I've tried. I wonder if it's men he likes, or no one at all?"

Sex to Renna, I had learned, perforce overhearing in the thin-walled tents at night as she took her pick of her fellow hunters, was no more than an itch to be scratched. An animal urge, like hunger, and no thinking about it after. So also, it would seem, with this Droghen.

"Jealous, Dwen? Droghen gave you chance enough!"

"And I had sense enough! Who treated him for the private-rot last time he tried to hide it from his physician? Take care, Renna mine, you don't bring more away from him than memories!"

As Dweneth was still vexed with me, and Renna bored with mocking one who could not be goaded into anger, I was being thoroughly ignored. Such random sexual couplings were unknown in OtherWhere, much less post-coital discussion. Fascinated, I listened. Betimes the talk turned to greater matters.

". . . war again in Mantuu—two wars, for a fact," Renna said. "More of the holy war against what's left of Plalas, then border skirmishes as well against the Melet, who will not stay on their islands since the drought. Ye'd think Mantuu'd have had enough after three years of famine, but their gods blame that on Plalas, and thus war. They'd rather a fight than food or sex, I think. La, fools! At least their fleet's too busy chasing Melet outriggers to give Droghen competition cross-sea. Less good news out of Kelibesh."

"What do you know of Kelibesh?" Dweneth scoffed. "You've never been that far!"

"Tawa caravans have," Renna replied. "And as they pay well for *grebbok* pelts, I bought me some *garnah* for a fest-gown, and the gossip came for free."

"You in cloth-of-*garnah*? You'll take up bathing next!" Dweneth marveled.

"Mock me and ye'll have no further news," Renna said airily, her near-black eyes scanning the trees above for game.

"Forgive me, do," Dweneth pleaded exaggeratedly, "and go on with your telling!"

It mattered little to her, gossip from places she'd never been; she listened to have something to do as Krex lumbered along and she perched on the wagon seat attempting to reshape whatever fingernails had survived our night of digging. I, contrarily, was all Other ears.

"Kelibesh— ?" Dweneth prompted.

Renna continued to pout, drawing her shortbow up off her thigh suddenly and sighting on a smallfowl in a nearby clump of trees. The uneven bump of *guravek* hooves notwithstanding, she caught the bird in midair as we passed beneath the tree, pulling the arrow before the poison spoiled the meat. I felt the small soul shriek and die.

"Dinner!" she grinned, stuffing the dead thing in a saddle-bag. It cheered her out of her pout. "Kelibesh, la! They've ships enough and slaves enough, and for once their borders are quiet. The Caliph's sworn to meet Droghen in mid-sea and sink his fleet, says rumor, else slip by him and sail the long way 'round up Droghia Harbor in triumph. The Tawa say, and Droghen's spies confirm it, that Kelibesh launched ten ships last Bask, but none returned. Still, it put a fever up Droghen's ass to get his three launched the faster. You could still smell the pitch in the planking, they were that new when I saw them. Oh, aye, they'll be well away by now!"

"Damn!" Dweneth sighed. "I would have liked to see them go!"

I pondered in silence the juxtaposition of Droghian ships with Kelibek slave galleys, both vying to see who could round the World first, when neither was entirely certain the World was roundable. Given equal opportunity, which would reach the Archipelago first?

For his doctoral thesis, read in his eighteenth year as was customary, Chior, Frayin's son, had completed a study on the statistical probability of any known tribe of People, unaware that we or our islands existed, actually arriving on our shores. Obliged by complex interfamilial protocol to attend Chior's orals, I had sat in sufferance of his theory that, factoring in wind direction, prevailing currents, cartographical errata and seasonal meteorological variants, the People would miss our islands, insignificant as they were in the expanse of the Great Sea, entirely.

How reassuring it must be, I recall thinking at the time, to be as certain as Chior, who had never been off-island, had never seen any People's map, and had not considered as significant the difference between the poorly nourished crew of a slave gallery and that of a Mantuul or Droghian sailship, whose sailors were freemen with a profit-share! Even before crossover, I had never possessed Chior's certainty, and now, on the road to Droghia, I was more filled with doubt than ever. Nor was I entirely indifferent to the fate of the crews of the ten vanished Kelibek ships, no doubt becalmed and dead of thirst. Would I rather they had made land among us?

The Kelibek had been the first to develop firearms, and prided themselves on their superior fighting ability. Whom they did not subjugate by slavery or marriage-rape they must needs kill. How many weaponless Others might they slaughter on the outislands before their munitions ran out?

Droghia was known as a nation of merchants and seafarers, inventors of much of the machinery used worldwide, of time-pieces and navigational devices of great accuracy. They were known to be peaceful, at least under this-Droghen, unless attacked. Yet finding us neither in need of their trade goods, nor desirous of exporting raw materials, nor eager to embrace any of their several missionary religions, what disposition might they make of us?

Would Kelibesh's frank lust for conquest be more or less damaging to us than Droghia's slower but no less relentless desire for control? How much did Monitors elsewhere in the World know of the two nations' progress, and with what haste would they hie themselves back to the Archipelago with what they knew? Or did it all depend on me? At the rate I was going, I might never emerge from the Droghian foothills, while already three ships had been launched.

Droghia was a land cleaner than most, with a vast network of canals to bring folk and their goods from inland to the sea and back, a land where refuse was burned or buried rather than left in open pits or teeming gutters, a land where many were literate, a land of seeming order and prosperity. Rare were plagues here, rarer poverty or destitution, absent the castes and hierarchies that fostered such blights elsewhere. If Others had to choose a People with which to first negotiate, Droghia might prove the optimum choice.

Among their observable flaws, Droghians were overly fastidious, and obsessed with equating beauty with virtuousness. If they were also tight-fisted and greatly profit-wise, this came of their having wrested a living from a grudging land and a hostile sea, and would not be overcome within a generation. Droghia was, however, noted as a haven for artists and musicians, though only those who had passed the arbiter of the

Droghiad's personal taste, and his Greathouse often hosted Dain'sTroupe or its like.

Droghia also sported neither gallows nor gibbet at its crossroads.

It was, however, the first place I was to encounter firearms. Our Monitors had previously reported them only in Kelibesh and parts of Tawa. Costly, cumbersome things, they were imported from beyond the Hillpast Wastes to gradually replace lance and mace and crossbow, though never the sword, still considered a "gentleman's weapon," whatever that might be.

Finally, Droghians were born to water, restless ashore. They lived and died beside or upon the sea, wove it into the state religion, dipped their newborns in its frigid waters at birth, and those males who did not cry were promised a commission in the Droghiad's fleet at manhood.

Thus this harbor—visible from every vantage of the city as our gaudy wagons negotiated the switchbacks of the Guardian Hills and lumbered along the seawall—replete with its hundreds of tall masts, thicker than trees, was not replete enough for me, who wished their number still augmented by the three that rumor had already launched before our coming here.

"Have you ever been on sea voyage?"

It was the first Dweneth had spoken to me since Renna found us on the steppe. She had halted Krex to rest him midway down the final rise overlooking the city, which was in part below sea-level, reclaimed and held by an intricate arrangement of dikes and sealocks.

"I was born beside the sea, Lady," I replied, my eyes upon the lesser sea of mast and sail arrayed at our feet.

Dweneth narrowed her eyes at me. "That's not what I asked you!"

"As you don't believe me anyway," I ventured, clucking at Krex to get him moving down the slope, "it's all the answer I can give you."

Renna shouted down whatever reply she might have made,

standing upright on her *'vek*'s bare back to point over the forest of masts.

"Dwen, look! They've not gone after all. There's the *Foremost* taller than the rest, the *Yeoman* and the *Venture* either side of her!"

She urged the *'vek* to a gallop, headlong to the Greathouse to find out why.

"The Filaret read the auguries Holyday last and said they boded ill. Odds he was lying for to keep me off-balance, but it spread among the sailors and I thought it wiser to wait a second telling . . ."

The Droghiad's voice was rich and mellow and carried above the pallid dinner music as far as the kitchens, whence I'd been relegated. The troupe's extra mouths required greater service of the house staff, and Dweneth had volunteered me for kitchen duty—somewhat vengefully, I thought. The newly consecrated singstick, which never left her hand, reminded her of old grievances to add to the new. Between conveying huge serving platters, most containing some ever-more-elaborate preparation of animal flesh, my hands numb from constant tingling, and trying not to trip nor spill, I kept my ears open.

". . . one last time before Windseason when the current's right. Won't risk ship nor sailor once there's ice and fog and sleet, though I'm told it's milder the farther out to sea . . ."

He was wise and well-informed, this Droghiad, if ill-favored by most People's standards, being bandy-legged though no rider, his broad-shouldered body seeming too heavy for his spindly legs to carry him. Too, his visage was dark as Omila had read it in the cards, and beetle-browed besides, as well as scarred with some vestige of long-ago pox. Yet his manner was easy and confident as befitted one who knew himself a natural leader, and his voice was among the pleasantest I ever heard among the People.

Droghen's conversation dominated the high table, but there were lesser dialogues wafting about as well. Renna, for one, eschewed the table, flirting behind a pillar with a fair-haired, ascetic-looking man who was dressed in Droghen's livery but with the mien of a priest.

". . . and Thrasim the mild does ever what his master bids!" Renna mocked, though this one named Thrasim seemed no more disturbed by it than anOther. "You've a background in the sciences. Do you really believe his maps and charts, or is he leading you all to your doom?"

"Do I believe his charts? Not entirely. But he's my lord; I follow. Besides, who else will keep him out of trouble if not me?"

Troupers alternately eavesdropped on the royal conversation and shared with Droghen's entourage what morsels of gossip were prised from them. Stili was drunk and drowsing over his soup, so the rest could be overheard. Around and under conversation wafted this pallid chamber music. It puzzled me. Was this the music Droghia was celebrated for? Computer-generated Other synthsound held more feeling.

". . . depart as soon as the High Holyday festivities are done. You'll stay to see me launched, fair Dweneth, will you not?"

"Only if the troupe is staying," my mistress demurred, seated at Droghen's right hand at the High Table, wearing her green-gold curls, which glistened in the light of a thousand tin-backed tapers, and a gown too lowcut to go unremarked. Who was she playing this night? "You'll have to work that out with Da."

At the farther end of the Low Table, all but out of hearing of such pithy conversation, dour Dain was in a darker mood than usual. Whenever I came near to serve him he only grunted and waved me off, more concerned with lip-reading what transpired between the ruler of this place and his headstrong daughter.

"You're not needed till the games and serious drinking starts," the head cook sniffed at me. "Get ye out from underfoot. A breath of air, mayhap, a chance to see the big city. Only avoid the docks and be back afore the curfew."

Such freedom being unheard of anywhere else in the People's world, I took advantage of it to repair straight down-harbor to the docks. If in my lack of expertise I could not find the three ships I sought, I might at least locate some *bRi.*

Unable to distinguish one mast from the next, plagued as twilight deepened by idling sailors offering me varieties of assistance I did not require, I had also to avoid certain of the narrower alleys where packs of wildcurs—larger, fiercer versions of Hrill and with no greater love for the scent of Other—were wont to lurk. Nor could I, short of appropriating a boat or drawing undue attention to my swimming prowess, find a way to get outharbor to where the *bRi,* wiser than I, stayed well clear of this place and its inhabitants. I returned to the Greathouse.

Placards at waysides and on the many bridges spanning the canals advertised various wares and cures and ships wanting crews, and I was soon lost in perusing them. Returning at last along the clean-swept cobbles, I became aware of soft carcophonies wafting down from the upper casements of the townhouses I passed, as if this prosperous and surprisingly literate populace frequently passed its evenings with music. Perhaps this was the true music of Droghia; its effect upon my Other ears was as varied as the music itself, and I barely heard the curfew.

"Are ye daft or only childish?" the head cook chided me as, breathless and no doubt wild-eyed, I ducked through the rear court as the last bell sounded. "Gone meandering with the fog due in—get yourself lost good, you will. I never!"

She went on at some length—not the first elder to so chastise me nor, as it turned out, the last—but as I washed my hands before serving dessert, she was somewhat mollified.

"I'm told you read in several languages." Droghen cleared his study's tabletop to unroll the charts he'd brought. "How good are you at geography?"

"Passing fair, milord Droghiad," I answered, putting careful distance between us. The man's all-but-insatiable sexual heat had been evident even as I passed him things at table; I had no desire to get nearer. "At least as much as woman dare aspire to."

His fierce eyes darted up from his precious charts.

"This is not Tawa or Kelibesh!" he said irritably. "In my country woman can know as much as man and often more."

This much was true. Few rivaled Droghia in making learning available to any regardless of gender or class, though what a female was to do with her hard-won education was as severely limited as elsewhere. Droghen liked clever women about him, provided they did not prove too clever.

Droghen Droghiad d'Droghia—"person impersonating the People," as it rendered in his language—had sent for me in order to flaunt his charts before a newcomer, and also to gratify his curiosity about me. Renna, nudging Dweneth in the ribs as I went, was certain she knew what awaited me; Dweneth only watched me anxiously. Droghen knew about my plague-mark and, apparently, did not care. I had learned this our second night here.

It was the troupe's performance night. Well-fed and no longer road-weary, we were to give back to Droghia for what it had given us. The grand salle of the Greathouse, larger than any tent Dain'sTroupe had ever owned, was filled to capacity with any who could spare the time from their weighing and measuring, buying and selling, to attend at the Droghiad's pleasure. Our arrival had occasioned a flurry of cleaning and polishing and festooning what was already, Droghian-wise, better scrubbed than any place this side of the Greaters.

The troupe gave all we had that night. The menagerie beasts were quicker, fiercer, more agile than ever; even Hrill jumped his hoops with alacrity and none of his usual coy missteps, lapping up the applause like new milk. Omila's tears were never more copious; Stili and Dweneth reduced the throng to help-lessness with their slapstick. Cwala, growing child-great though she was, threw herself into this farewell performance; she, Gause, the children, and I did turns and tumbles to spin a world around, ending in a pyramid of flourishing torches which I for once did not catch on the ends of my flying hair.

Flushed and breathless, we took our formal bows—down on one knee, bow from the waist, arms extended with a subtle flourish at the wrists, quite elegant—before the First Seat. Raising my head, I found Droghen's cold hawk's eyes piercing mine. Standing beside him, his pale lieutenant Thrasim, as much his master's opposite in looks as temperament, whispered something in his nearer ear. Renna, an ale-cup in her hand and one leg flung over the arm of the Second Seat hunter-fashion, was as usual laughing at me.

I met Droghen's gaze with my own eyes hooded—let none presume to read me where I did not wish to be read—then I turned my wrist deliberately, to display the mark. A strange smile flickered over Droghen's lips, from which I read "No matter!"

"It's his heart," Dweneth informed me after while we changed; something about Droghen's look had made her choose to warn me. "He dismissed his own physician for telling him outright he's less than a year to live, but he can't escape the truth. It's a born thing, something his own father died of before the age this-Droghen is now."

"T'short, he'd rather chance the plague and die in the throes with his cock kept warm, than list to his own heart's ticking, awaiting it to burst!" Renna said importantly. She above all should know. "No plague can spare ye this time, Miss Priss!"

Dweneth silenced her with a shove.

"It's made him feverish driven," she said to me sincerely. "Makes him snatch at pleasures wherever he can. I don't know what he sees in you, but it's my mistake for telling him how clever you are, and nothing I can do about it. Droghen is Droghen, and Droghen is Droghiad. Whatever you do, be careful!"

Could she have interceded for me? I would not have had her do so if she could. If no worse fate than sexual coercion awaited me on this crossover, I was better off than most, and what information I might gather for the sake of the many on the

216

Archipelago was worth whatever happened to me. If the Droghiad wanted me, for whatever reasons, I was on my own.

We began with geography.

I studied his charts, and not lightly. The fate of Otherworld might hang on what was outlined there. They gave Droghia as the center of the known World—a not-unexpected conceit—and were not inaccurate in depicting the coasts thereabouts, though they lost definition on the Sunward coasts, where neither Llellaar, Gleris, nor Kelibek would knowingly permit foreign cartographers to tread. But beyond the better-traveled waters of the Great Sea, Droghen's maps erred radically.

Where our scattered Archipelago lay, Droghen's cartographers had postulated an entire continent, nearly as large as the mainland containing the Fourteen Tribes. Navigating on so false an assumption, Droghen would likely find nothing but open sea, and pass OtherWhere by entirely.

Yet I could not but wonder how accurate were the charts the Kelibek threw.

"When I was a child . . ." he began, his open palm coming to rest on the small of my back—fever-hot, obtrusive.

Only my strongest Discipline prevented my pulling away. No Other readily tolerates touch unsolicited, particularly not one such as this. Droghen's will was rife with fevers and appetites and desires unfulfilled, crying out in his first name, before he became Droghen. I would not have had such knowledge of him, and strove to block his thoughts from mine.

". . . I used to mock my teachers when they went on about goblins and monsters over the edge of the sea. Frights and terrors to keep us close to shore and dependent on religion! These things I never believed, and it got me in no end of trouble. I might be a butcher's son still, were it not for natural ability and a Holyday's good augury. The World was given to us to explore it, and I shall!"

As his spirit strove to explore the World, so his hand persisted in exploring me, journeying ever downward. He drew his body closer as well, so that I could feel his fever through

217

his clothes, the while I pretended indifference, held tight to my Discipline, and guardedly studied his maps.

The light backward flick of an Other wrist could easily discourage his activity, could in fact propel him toward the farther wall, but he was Droghen in Droghia, and I was but a servile. My conduct would impact upon my mistress as surely as Droghen would impact upon that wall. I endured.

"Curious, my Lord"— I still had my composure —"if I may venture an opinion . . ."

" 'When in Droghia, all are Droghians,' " he quoted. I believe he believed it, despite the sweating hand now working its way into my nether cleft as his second seized my breast and none too gently; he pressed himself against me, his hot breath clamoring in my Other ear, as with no less violence his desires clamored in my mind.

"Then by my understanding"— I had withdrawn into my innermost self, removed from what my body must endure; it was an ancient technique—"you have merely exchanged an older uncertainty for a newer one. Unless there be those who have seen this continent so limned upon your charts and returned to tell of it."

"My continent is here!"

He freed my breast to tap his temple, the while his first hand continued its explorations and his voice, too loud at this range, thundered in my ear.

"I need no handful of its soil to prove it. All my scientists but one agree—and he is Thrasim, hence inviolate—that if the World is round, it must have as much land on its far side as it does on its near, else the whole would tip over to the heavier side, and we being upon it would have to cling to a land suddenly over our heads, to keep from falling off!"

He laughed, as I did not but took the opportunity to brush the nearer corner of his precious chart so that it rolled in on itself; as he lunged to save it I whirled about to put the table between us in a move to make Gause proud.

"This is not Tawa or Kelibesh, my Lord," I reminded him

somewhat heatedly across table and chart, "and to my knowledge, though my lot be servile, I am not to be used in such
wise as you desire. If it is truth that in Droghia all are Droghians, then what my plague-mark and your own heart cannot
fend against, my own will should. Are these only high words,
Droghen-born-Gerim, or has a servile truly the right to refuse
you?"

My brazenness startled him less than the use of his name.
Would he think me a spy, to have such knowledge? But
Droghen laughed again.

"Dweneth has more confidence in you than is evident," he
said, "for you did not learn my name of Renna."

"No, Lord, not of Renna."

"Then tell me, which has your greater concern—my health
or your virtue?"

"The two are concomitant, Lord, for how am I to claim
virtue if you should die in my arms?"

The sheer impertinence made him scowl, but at last he re-
rolled his charts and clasped his hands behind his back.

"You're entirely too clever for anyone's good, and nothing
cures ardor faster than a clever woman. Come you both inside!" he called into the antechamber, and Dweneth and Renna
tumbled undignified into the room, as if they had been listening at the door. Droghen gestured from Dweneth to me. "Fear
not, your minion's intact, though how you manage her's beyond me. Have her groomed to sing for the Holydays; she's
clearly wasted in the kitchens."

Dweneth well knew the difference between Droghen's suggestion and Droghen's command, which was how she and I
and a pouch of his coin soon found ourselves among the stalls
on market day, in search of a barber and some cloth merchants.
For once we were free of Renna, whom Droghen had com-
missioned to paint a mural to decorate the smaller audience
salle leading off the grand salle, in celebration of this-
Droghen's feats, and the impending voyage. We found the

huntress-queen mixing pigments and grumbling, though she clearly enjoyed the work. Dweneth could not leave her without a final admonition.

"There are ways to pleasure him, Renna mine, that need not endanger his heart. If he dies before he names a successor, you know what Brok and the rest will do, and what then becomes of the peace in these parts."

"As if it had to do with me!" Renna actually blushed, daubing colors on her palette to avoid the issue. What was visible on the wall thus far was an outline of the inevitable sea, and what promised by their rough sketched shapes to be ships or *bRi* or both. "And spare me the lecture—at least what I know's through practice, not out of books!"

"Mayhap if you'd ever learned to read . . ." Dweneth dodged the color-laden palette knife aimed at her head and sailed grandly out of the salle.

"Something's wrong!" she said suddenly as we crossed the outer courtyard heading for the commons. She shivered and hugged herself in the midmorning heat. "Droghen's ships are not meant to sail. I feel it!"

"Have you learned to tell the future like Renna?" I wondered. "Or have you been reading Omila's cards?"

We passed through the main arch into the gathering market throng, and I was aware that I was being stared at, as I had not been since Refuge. It could not be only my appearance, for Droghia was the most cosmopolitan of cities, with all the nations save Kelibesh represented in all their ethnic splendor.

"I feel it, that's all!" She shivered, then shook the mood off, her small feet skipping lightly on the quayside. "Maybe it's just that I'm on the rag and it makes me morbid. One more month squandered!"

With that she stopped stock-still. Passersby bumped, jostled, parted and moved around us. Dweneth stared open-mouthed at me.

"Nearly five months we've been together, and you haven't bled once. I wonder why?"

Ah, Lingri apt-named Inept, who had fully intended in that

220

past five months to offer some evidence of "normal" menstrual function but had somehow never managed it! Other females are estrually dormant until the onset of the mating cycle in our thirty-fifth year, yet a few drops of blood from a newly-slaughtered animal, had I steeled myself to acquire it, might have sufficed as proof for my fellow travelers, who owned little privacy for any bodily function. I had some explaining to do, aloud on a teeming Droghian street, and quickly.

"I know not why, lady, but I have not bled since my master Darvis owned me"— that much was truth enough —"and had intended to ask you for some manner of physick to remedy it. But as I cannot bear children, at any rate"— not for at least fifteen years, at any rate —"I thought myself better free of what women sometimes call 'the curse.' "

"Mayhap," Dweneth acknowledged doubtfully, as her healer's mind turned over what she knew of causes and cures. "I doubt it's a turn of the plague, considering how you came by that. Mayhap it's only that you're so thin; I've heard that happens sometimes . . ."

Clearly she was not satisfied with her own explanation.

"You are the healer, lady, not I," I reminded her.

"Aye," she said as we moved on, though not without her occasional sidelong glance added to the stares of those about us. Witch-pyres burned in my mind, even in Droghia.

And, even in Droghia, the simplest rituals can prove hazardous.

Droghen boasted his own personal hairdresser—to prevent assassination attempts, one supposed, or at least the importuning of petitioners bearing sharp objects. The populace at large had its grooming needs served by a choice of barbers in the market square. Hair-cutting and shaving, manicuring, and even simple dentistry were performed in open-air stalls under the curious eyes of passersby.

Dweneth and I underwent the barbering ritual together, where I hoped her burnished curls and merry public personality would detract attention from my plainer person. So it did until, her hair dressed and she still chatting with Mirko the barber about the troupe's latest performances, she stepped down from his chair to let the apprentice tend her fingernails, and I took her place. Mirko had no sooner unbraided my waist-length mane and swept it back behind my ears when—

"God's merciful sea!" he cried, recoiling, his shears skimming entirely too near my nearer ear. Drawn by his outcry, some in the crowd edged closer to learn the source of the commotion, and Mirko's cry was repeated by more than one. All eyes were upon me, and I knew why.

"Condemned by physical appearance, make no attempt at explanation . . ."

Rau's voice in my ears, telling me something I had decided even as I had decided I must be a Monitor.

"A difference so apparent as ears or webtoes or hue of blood cannot be explained away; the attempt debases Discipline, and leads to greater determination among one's accusers. If death be the consequence of silence, let it be death in silence, and with dignity."

"What is it? What's amiss?"

Dweneth spun around in her chair, yanking her hand out of the hapless apprentice's half-painted. As soon as she faced in my direction, she knew as well as I what the trouble was.

She had seen the shape of my ears often enough, and I had caught her staring, though she said nothing. What did she think? And why, when she questioned everything else about me she found strange, had she never questioned this? My life hung on the answers.

"The Filaret's sermon, the Filaret's sermon!" susurrated through the staring crowd, as jaws went slack and fingers pointed, and some felt unconsciously of their own round ears for reassurance.

Dweneth was on her feet at once, hands on her hips, eyes blazing. No slapstick Comedie this nor maudlin Tragedie, but the makings of high drama.

"What nonsense is this?" she demanded imperiously. "What whisperers these, who have not the courage to speak forward what frights them? Who here knows me? Ho, Gleth! For I

222

see you in the crowd—come forward, man! And thee, Mirko!" She turned to the barber, accusing. "Who am I? Speak!"

"Dweneth Dain'sDaughter," he muttered abashedly.

"Louder, man, so all can hear it!"

"Dweneth Dain'sDaughter!" he repeated, knowing that a word from her in Droghen's ear could have his shop shut up indefinitely while the constabulary combed the place for vermin or illicit games of dicing after curfew, or unswept clippings that could be used in witchcraft. "Favored of the Droghiad and beloved Player-maid!"

"Aye!" Dweneth nodded grandly, still playing her role, beloved and gifted Player-maid. "And who is this but my servant Lingri—tumbler and storysinger, nothing more. What, then, is amiss?"

"Her ears, marm!" shrilled a crone's voice from the multitude, which grew in size as rumor swept the marketplace. "Lookit her ears!"

Dweneth swallowed, and I saw her struggle with her role, for my ears, along with these many months of half-truths, troubled her as much as they did the crowd. And yet, even as she could mock me and Renna could not, so she could doubt me, but protect me fiercely from anyone else who dared.

"Are all your ears the same?" she demanded, sweeping her own hair back. "For while I'm told I've a pair of lovely matched cockleshells—or so a recent beau did flatter me—in truth, I do see many a jug-handle and cauliflower hereabout. Is it a sin to be born ugly?"

There was laughter from the crowd, but it sounded nervous and only half-convinced.

"But the Filaret's sermon . . ." the one named Gleth cried again, pushed forward by the crowd to explain, twisting his seaman's cap convulsively between cracked, dirty hands.

"The Filaret gave a sermon, Seaday last," he began all in a breath. "About the evil ones that lie awaiting over th'edge of the Great Sea should Lor'Droghen venture past th'horizon. Some, says he, was already abroad here in Droghia, to buzz words in sailors' ears and lure 'em to sign aboard the Droghiad's three. Day after he give the sermon, near all the sailors already signed did ask off the *Venture,* and as many off the *Yeoman* and the *Foremost,* too, no matter it cost them ten days' wage. None more has signed aboard since."

Droghen had said as much at dinner. But what Greathouse insiders saw as political manuevering by the head of the state religion, commoners saw as demons' work. Small wonder the three had not sailed. Prodded by the crowd, Gleth found wind to finish his tale.

"The Filaret also told what the evil ones look like, so's we'd beware of 'em!" the wretch cried, his breath coming in great sobs at his sudden newfound prominence. "Some, says he, has serpents' tongues, and some have hoofs or tail. Some has horns agrown out their brows, or hawk's claws for hands, or pricked ears!"

"Hence him you knew as neighbor afore Seaday is suddenly a stranger for the bumps on his brow that might be horns agrowing!" Dweneth sneered. Her voice resonated off the near seawall, carrying over the crowd. "Who among ye have I treated for chilblains or the bone ache, that make your hands look more like claws?" Furtive shiftings and murmurings in the crowd answered this without words. "Who among ye has the clubfoot or a gimp but is no demon? Answer me!"

She let their shame linger upon them for a moment.

"I pray you all, look closely at this Lingri-one. She's no great beauty, that I'll grant, but see you any horn or claw?"

She gestured to me to hold my hands out before me—palm down, palm up. I did. The crowd murmured further. Dweneth went on.

"Show us your tongue, my girl, for a certainty." I did so, mindful of my dignity. "And have ye hooves? Let's see!"

Thankful I did not favor the maternal webfoot line, I let my bare feet show demurely beneath my skirt hem, wondering how much further display Dweneth would have me make to prove her point.

"As to tails—" she began wickedly, provoking lurid interest

from the males "—yon Lingri's natural shyness forbids I offer proof. Ye'll have to take my word that none exists!"

The laughter this time was freer, easier. Well played! I thought, but wryly.

"As for those ears . . ." Dweneth faltered, and at last I understood her temporizing. She was no more certain here than was the crowd. Yet she leaned toward me and in her best stage-whisper asked: "Did I not tell you it would fool them?"

Before I could think what to answer, she drew the crowd in for the finale.

"As for the ears," she cried, "credit DainTrouper, who taught his daughter everything he knows by way of makeup and illusion, for these elfin ears are but an appliance, crafted of wax and swine-skin and tested here, for no purpose but to draw your attention to our coming sing. How many here know *Faerie*?"

There was murmured recognition of the ever-popular lay which Darvis used to butcher in his singing, but which existed whole and unadulterated in precious gilt-edged vellum in Dweneth's treasure-trunk.

"Well, then!" she cried, triumphant. "Watch you the posts and hark the criers, for *Faerie*'s to be Lingri's next sing, wherein she plays both ElvenQueen and Demon and all the parts between. A clever gimmick, was't not? Even Mirko here was gulled! Look you, man. See you not the seams where they're stuck onto the natural ear?"

"Aye," said the barber with great conviction, peering close. He would see whatever Dweneth instructed him to see, just so it saved his shop from the constabulary.

My hair remained uncut that day, but then so did my throat.

"Act normal!" Dweneth breathed, as we deliberately lingered in the market to show we had nothing to fear.

Her expert haggling wrung the price of three gowns out of Droghen's purse, the first new clothes I'd had since crossover, with enough left over for a pair of amber earrings not unlike

225

those I'd given Gause in the hills. We then perused the book-stalls, where I helped her choose what would best further her education; mudslides and rivers and Droghen-fests notwith-standing, I had read with her nightly as I could. Stares and whispers followed us around the market square and along the quays, but so did Dweneth's brilliant explanation, and more than one knowing wight sidled near enough, rancid-breathed, to assure a skeptical comrade:

"Aye, she's right! Look where the seams show, then!"

"You might have spared me the japery and gone straight to the ears, Lady!" I presumed. "I'm useless at Comedie—you've said as much!"

"It saved your life, didn't it?" my mistress countered smartly. "There's all the thanks I get. And wonderful advertising for when you next sing. I'll make a star of you yet!"

We dined from pastry carts and hot vegetable stalls until a rising cold fog drove us upharbor and back to the Greathouse. That night an unprecedented storm—unexpected in Droghia, though Chior tracked it from One Greater, and I read it from a *bRi*-pod I could barely see beyond the breakwater from where I stood on my chamber's parapet—set the harbor boiling, over-topping the seawalls, flooding cellars and cobbled streets, and foundering any number of boats. Greatest of these was Droghen's *Foremost,* whose mainmast snapped in the gale-force winds, swinging wild to strike the *Venture*'s forecastle, shearing it clean off to break up and float out to sea. The Filaret gloated in his basilica, and I must confess I too experienced some relief. For the moment, at least, Droghen wasn't going anywhere.

———

"Interview with a Sergeant of the Purist Police" (*Records of the Office of the People's Praesi-dium,* 1638–1641 P.A. Source Un-known)

Well, all right, admitted using the mutts was crude, but it got results. After the to-do when we found out our records had been got into and tapeworms destroyed half the Place-of-Birth files, we had to resort to something, didn't we? The People cutting our orders was getting restless, and there was that bloke up there on the vid nightly haranguing about how we had to "rip the Eternal Other out of our hearts before it turned us all to women"—well!

It was legend that the wildcurs didn't like 'em, could sniff 'em out at a great distance and set up a howl, and there'd been a row about the number of stray mutts roving the alleys and biting innocent children anyways, so it was two birds with one stone, see? We'd round up the cur-packs, pen 'em and feed 'em a good sniff of Other and a good regimentation in hunting 'em out; it was tighter than the army, it was!

As it had been my idea from the start, so to speak, they give me the best of the pack. Ripper was his name—ah, there was a mutt! Keenest nose in the unit. Could sniff out anOther trail three days old. I think he just hated the stink of vegetables, is all. And when we'd corner one—! It was my treat to him, see, to let old Ripper off the chain if he'd gone to all the trouble of running one down. I'll admit I had to hold him back a bit after we began bringing in more dead than alive, but me and the mutt got to an understanding. I'd let him rip in a bit, say on an arm or a set of balls—tits if it was female, Ripper had a particular thing for tits—then I'd blow the whistle and holler 'Hold!' and he'd be good about it. Oh, how he loved the taste of that tinny blood of theirs! He was a good mutt, Ripper was. Loved him like a son.

Problems with it? Well, it was too slow, for one thing, and not what you'd call efficient. You'd collect only one at a time and give the rest a chance to get away, and the cost in man- and mutt-power was horrendous. You'd be amazed how fast some of 'em can run, especially the young ones. Got a natural athletic ability, I'm told. And good at hiding or splitting two ways, once they'd learned what we were about. Or there'd be the old ones who'd just give

227

themselves up, getting in our way to buy time for the young ones, and that was no fun. Too, there was a row from some of the honest citizens about "brutality." So we had to think of something else then, didn't we?

I'd made sergeant at about this time, for all the grand work me and Ripper had been about, and there was a new captain assigned to our unit. "Too young," thinks I, and "don't know the territory," but me and the men give him the benefit of the doubt. Didn't he come up with the most brilliant idea of all!

"Music," he says. Naturally we all looked at him like he was daft. But he'd had some college before the service, see, and used to play one of them electronic flugelhorns that was popular at the time and, well, the rest was on vid for weeks, it was so brilliant. Worked so well it was tried from Dyr to Kwengiis and back. You must have heard of it; you'd have had to be not of this World to miss it.

———

"On Music"
(Author Unknown; from *Documents of the Thousand-Year*; Code 13211993

Perhaps never has so much passion been expended by Other against Other as upon this subject of music. Of all the outward manifestations of passion upon which we have finally agreed we must surrender, this has proved the most taxing. Music has ever been a creative form most precious to us. Nevertheless, we must hereafter forego it, for it appears to possess a power over us, little understood, which can evoke any of the passions, without warning, in the most elsewise Disciplined individuals.

We have freed ourselves of anger, lust, and violence; we must also forfeit the so-named "positive" passions we have known as well, that our transformation into Discipline may be complete.

228

"Not All Weapons Are Made of Steel"
(Essay by WiseRavaine Healer *Xeno-PsychNet*, T-Y1038, encoded)

A ten-year study by the psychoacousticians of Three Greater has finally concluded that the Other nervous system is peculiarly attuned to certain auditory stimuli which evoke untoward physiological as well as psychological symptoms. Depending upon range, duration, and configuration of notes, as well as the instrument or combination of instruments upon which these notes are played, these symptoms can range from extremes of lethargy to those of excitability, from extrovert lachrymosity to an introspection so deep as to resemble trance states.

Instances in our past when this only partly understood phenomenon was used to destroy—as the massacre of Agri-7—are replete. It has been suggested that as long as auditory stimuli are kept to the "safe" ranges which, for example, are used in subliminals for work-output stimulation, such art forms as the People's many musics may be experimented with, and the recent intermingling of our two species has in many instances rendered this academic. However, monitoring under such haphazard circumstances is difficult, and it is disquieting to contemplate how music might by some unscrupulous individuals be once more used against us.

"Overheard in a Tavern Near the Praesidium"
(from *IntelGather:*
EYES ONLY!!!)

The official story goes somewhat differently, but we're alone, aren't we? If I thought there was a wire I'd be a lot more close-mouthed, believe me, but this is how it went . . .

229

I'd been to university; I think I mentioned that. Nothing to be ashamed of, as I fully intended using whatever I learned for the sake of the Party and the State. And it's true some of my professors were Others. So I always let it out to the press that it was one of them, betraying her own, who let me in on what turned out to be our best weapon against them, but the fact is it was just some old drunk being loud in a pub we used to frequent near the campus. Gods know how he stumbled on it, but I bought him a drink or two and talked the information out of him, then threatened to have his tongue officially cut out if he ever spread it further.

The secret is something as simple as this: their hearing works differently from ours. I'm serious! Sure, everybody knows their ears are a different shape, but it's the internal arrangement that's important. Something about their auditory nerves, I think they're called. When we hear music, we just hear the notes as they're played, all on the one level, see? But they hear extra levels, ranges that are above, below and—beside, I guess you'd say—what we hear. Added dimensions. And the effect it has sometimes makes them crazy. Some of them cry, some have like epileptic fits, some just go roll-eyed unconscious on you. Depends on the instruments and the notes you choose, because not everything works.

What we'd do is this: we'd send a sound truck through a street, a village, even a forest sometimes. Through trial and error we'd learned what tunes got them most upset. You know that old Lamorak drinking song with all the stomping and the dirty words in it? The one they've made over into a Party Patriots' song? Play that on an organ or a string orchestra and they'll all come crawling out of the woodwork.

At first they'd flush out as easy as you please, helpless with weeping or the fits, and we'd round them up. Later they caught on, and only a handful would come into the streets, to cover for the rest. But we got wise and cordoned off whole blocks then, keeping the music on nice and loud while we took in hundreds of them. The ones with the strongest symptoms were kept for the experimentation *labs. As far as I know they're all dead now; this was five years ago, remember, and constant exposure to that kind of torture, even for them . . .*

Yes, I suppose the real credit goes to that old drunk in the pub, but the People have chosen to heap their praise on me for the deed, so why not? I've got interviews and speeches lined up into next year, and I'm thinking of running for office next term. Always glad to do my duty for the Party, of course.

eleven

"The Filaret says if God meant for man to sail beyond the horizon He'd have given him flukes like a trillfish!"

Renna's gods were not those of Droghia, but when in Droghia . . . She had been to that morning's sermon, the Seaday after the storm. Now she was back at her mural, paint on her nose, brushes stuck at angles in her silk-black hair, full of opinions.

I had also attended the sermon, concealed behind a pillar in the massive basilica, for infidel was not welcome here, and I was supposed to have been attending to my lady's wardrobe in the Greathouse laundry. But I was curious to witness the rituals of this thing called religion firsthand, and finished the washing that much quicker upon my return. I had seen and heard this Filaret; he reminded me uncannily of Govin.

"In regard to *bR*—trillfish—" I never could accustom my tongue to this unfortunate misnomer for my elegant fellow swimmers "—your depiction is most inaccurate."

"An expert!" Renna gawped at me from her scaffold. "What school of art have you studied with?"

"None, lady," I admitted, "but when did you last see trillfish close?"

"Only once. A dead one, gutshot by a cannon-spear. It stank," Renna said flatly, swinging down to her worktrestle, where she found a book in the clutter, fluttered through it, pointing. "But Axon's *Animalia* has pictures."

"Which are as inaccurate as yours." A glance told me. I found a charcoal in the mess and cleared a space on the trestle-top to sketch right there. "Look you: the flukes angle this way, in a logical extension of the body, not twisted awry as Axon has them. And the mane begins here, not so far backward on the skull, and follows the spine to midback. And, being a mammal, it has not gills but a blowhole, thus."

"An expert!" Renna repeated, skeptical, but her artist's eye knew I was right, if not how or why. She studied my rough sketch for a moment before climbing the scaffold to daub out her previous rendition and sketch over it.

"Why does the Filaret seem to oppose that very need for exploration which would seem to be innate to all People, but especially to Droghians?" I wondered aloud, watching Renna work.

"Because he is head not only of the religion, but of the opposition party trying to unseat this-Droghen at the next Assemblage," Renna reported matter-of-factly, as if it had nothing to do with her or her art, or her relationship with Droghen.

"Can that be done? I thought to be Droghiad was to be Droghiad for life?"

"Everyone knows of Droghen's heart, for all he's tried to hide it." Renna had already limned one credible *bRi*, and began a second. "By rights he should have named a successor long since, but that, says Droghen, is like casting his own shadow over himself. Hence the Filaret is determined to prove him incompetent, that he might name his own successor.

"If I were the Filaret"— she started the outline of a third *bRi* —"I'd simply wait for Droghen to sail over the edge of the World. Instead he gives his sermons, which only make

Droghen the stubborner to sail. Maybe that's what the Filaret intends. Not that it's anything I understand!"

"It's all that keeps me alive!" Droghen said of his obsession not only to rebuild his ships, but to be aboard the *Foremost* when she sailed.

He had shouted himself into near-apoplexy when told what had happened to his ships, had thrown on a leathern cloak to rush out into the wind and hail and see the damage for himself.

"No worse than any storm at sea!" he had roared against the wind, "and I have weathered plenty!"

That his heart survived the night only fired it anew.

"Now the color's all wrong!" Renna lamented, shaking me out of my thoughts, stepping back on the scaffold. "I don't suppose an expert could help me there?"

"Color varies with diving depth and water temperature," I supplied without thinking. How would she think I came by such exact knowledge? "Deep green when they dive in cold currents, iridescent green-to-gold near the surface. It's how we know the water temperature, by observing them—"

"Who's 'we'?"

"—lastly, pure gold when they sun themselves in shallows." I would not answer her. "Think you of the colors struck in Dweneth's false hair by candlelight."

The artist's eye required no more. "Right!" she said, and I left her spattering happily away. I had a more challenging task before me.

Clearly as Windseason gave way to Freeze, my fate was bound to Dweneth's and the troupe, and I was not to venture out of Droghia. But then, neither could the Droghiad. Soon both the harbor and the canals would be blocked with ice and all the roads impassable. Nor could I be held responsible for what might transpire in Kelibesh. And Droghen had plans for the troupe.

"My people shall have entertainments as long as nights are

234

cold and cheerless!" he announced, currying Dain's favor, whose eyes fairly gleamed with the wealth he foresaw. "My house's hospitality for all your troupe the Freeze-long, and payment beside, provided you change the repertory at least every ten days, for nothing bores like repetition."

Dain signed the agreement without thinking, and counted coin in his sleep. Signed, too, without consulting Dweneth, who was furious, for choosing the new program fell to her.

"Change the rep every ten days for a Freeze-long? Easy for him to say! There isn't enough in the whole of theater to entertain on that kind of schedule!"

She had gathered us together for consultation.

"Gause and I can vary readily enough," Cwala spoke up at once, as if hoping everyone would forget her temporary retirement. "Change of costume and altering the set-ups will fool the unpracticed eye. He'll never know it's the same routine reguised, and no one grows tired of tumblers!"

"Good enough!" Dweneth nodded to me to write it down in my clear hand, but with her eye on Cwala's burgeoning belly. "But do you let Gause and Lingri and the children do it; you're past where it's safe to—no, now, argue not! Do you tend the costuming and choreography, but keep you out of the set-ups. Who's next? Omila?"

"I have the whole of the *Garavayne*, here." Omila tapped her temple in imitation of Droghen, whom she found a tragic figure. "It's being a nonagy and bloody withal, few have the stomach to hear it through. But if I draw it out over nine separate performances . . ."

"Have you tears enough?" Dweneth tweaked her, and Omila smiled wanly while all but me laughed. "Done, then! Write it down!"

I did.

"Stili and I shall have to scrounge out some of those fusty old pantos that haven't been done since my grandmother's day," Dweneth mused. "What's left? You, Lingri, will have the *Faerie*. How much is there of *OtherWhere?*"

We had neither of us mentioned it since the night of the river. Was she giving credence to my version, or simply in need of new material, whether she believed it or no?

"As much as is needed, Lady," I began, thinking of an entire nation of seafaring Droghians to sing it to, but her thought of a sudden flew elsewhere.

"Musicians! We must have more musicians, and new music! Not the few of us who can play the usual rote, nor Droghen's sickly orchester. Here we are in the city that's known for the instruments; surely one of us could scrounge out them who can play 'em!"

She was looking pointedly at me. I had made mention of the mysterious strains of melody that had followed me along the quays my first night here. Thus it fell to me, who knew nothing of their arts, to find the troupe musicians.

The first I found was a street gittern-player, whose acquaintance was to lead me in such labyrinthine directions that I have not emerged from them to this day. He began by wishing me to the seagod's hell, and ended by being my guide there. Along the way he taught me never to accept any People by their visible face, but to seek as well what lay behind it.

In disparaging the flimsiness of my Monitor's report, Jeijinn could not know that I brought far more out of Droghia than court gossip, for much of what I learned has remained in confidence until now. There were stories I could not tell without invading privacies, until now. For now everyone I ever knew in Droghia is long dead, except too-long-lived Lingri.

The gittern-player was Redrec Elder, the greatest musician I ever knew.

I heard him before I saw him, in melodies so poignant, evoked from so simple an instrument, that they transfixed me, tugged at my Discipline, would have drawn me to him even had I not been sent by Dweneth. I recall turning my eyes and ears upward, as if to find this musical magician in one of the townhouses all about me. It did not occur to me to seek him in the streets, for yet one more thing which Droghia appeared to lack, along with castes and dirt and gallows and disease, was beggars, either of the simply suppliant or the performing variety. Further, it was threatening snow, and few citizens were voluntarily about. Yet here on the quayside cobbles, familiar from many a village square, were the tin cup, the wooden placard begging alms, the gaggle of onlookers surrounding a figure hunched tenderly over an instrument as battered and weatherworn as its master, though, like its master, somehow resplendent in its shabbiness, and in perfect tune.

That he was blind was apparent the moment his scruffy, bearded face beneath its slouch hat tipped skyward as if in search of the chord-change then selected. That the blindness was not organic in nature was apparent from the hard, hideous scar tissue surrounding his slitted, ulcerous eyes. Blinding with a hot basin was a form of punishment too readily enacted upon prisoners guilty of nothing more than witnessing what their captors deemed unwitnessable; this much I knew from Rau, who had seen it done. The ordeal was second only to having one's tongue cut out for the same crime of being in the wrong place at the wrong time—a fate whose precipice I had skirted daily since crossover—and I wondered if this fate, too, had befallen the musician. But Redrec had tongue enough, and voice enough, as I was soon to learn.

But blind, then, though in every respect else seeming a strong-shouldered, comely being of middle years by People's reckoning, and more than sufficiently talented even to my uneducated ears, to enthrall the merchants of Droghia nightly in performance hall. Strong, supple, long-nailed hands, in fingerless gauntlets against the cold, plucked and coaxed such variety and subtlety from a mere twelve strings as seemed incomprehensible. Why then, in Droghen's heavily patroned city, was this gifted person playing on the streets?

When he shifted the gittern slightly, I knew why. A pair of short, stout crutches leaned side by side against the canal wall, companions to his stunted legs which, in Droghia, were sufficient reason to be barred from public performance. Beauty and wholeness were the mark of the seagod's favor, their absence in any degree the mark of one's own sin or that of one's parents. In Droghia's cruel nomenclature, this gifted being would be designated halfman for the child's legs which finished his adult's body, unable to support it of themselves. He could not appear in any place where the merchant-elite congregated for amusement, lest his deformity offend their refined sensibilities.

Hence he played for passers in the street, who doubtless appreciated his music as well as the wealthier in their estate houses lining the quays. Betimes a head or two would appear in the upper windows, listening, then a scatter of coins would shower down, which those on the cobbles below gathered carefully to place in the musician's cup. More than one pair of eyes brimmed with tears, his music was so beautiful.

For myself, I was lost in the listening, so rapt I neglected to move on when the rest did. Awakening as if from trance, I realized the musician had long since stilled his strings with one strong hand, and it had begun to snow.

It did not snow on our more temperate islands, and I had eagerly anticipated my first encounter with this phenomenon. Yet here I sat insensate while it sprinkled, then tumbled about me, clinging to hair and clothes and eyebrows while I, lost in some realm reeling with the colors of the music I had heard, felt nothing.

I slipped down from the wall where I'd been sitting, legs dangling as Dweneth would, intending to creep away. How was I to trouble one so gifted with my flimsy quest? But he sensed my presence, and called out.

"Come here to me!" His voice was as harsh as his music was sweet. "Know you you smell like saltgrass?"

I knew no adequate response to that, hence made none, but drew nearer, wondering if he could see me at all.

"Not you exactly, but your form, and with the left eye only," he answered as if I'd spoken. He sniffed the air like a wildcur as I approached, and I could not but wonder if his response to the scent of Other would be similar. Doubtless in a moment he would growl and I must flee. "Bathe regularly, do you? Live in a rich man's house?"

"At present," I replied, adding quickly, "in a servant's capacity," surmising how little he would find to cherish in those who lived in rich men's houses under grander circumstances. "Do you compose the pieces you play?"

"Every one of them." A twisted grin replaced surprise on his hairy, damaged face. "An intelligent question, from a servant. Are you generous as well?"

I was, from Droghen's largesse, lent me by Dweneth to seek out new musicians. The clink of coin in cup altered this musician's mood.

"Fine. Now off with you! I play no more today."

As he did not reach for his crutches, it was clear he intended to stay. So did I.

"Are you as deaf as I am blind?" he roared. "I said go away!"

"The quayside's free to any who walk there, until the sun goes down," I replied boldly, for he seemed to prefer harsh words to sweet. "So says the law in Droghia."

" 'The law in Droghia'," he sneered, and there was pain in his voice as he slung the gittern over one shoulder, spirited placard, cup, and coins into a cobbler's pocket in his shabby tunic and groped for his crutches, having forgotten where he'd left them in the joy of making music.

I reached the crutches to him; he snatched them, swung abruptly to his feet, and was off.

"Am I wrong," I called after him, not willing to let him get away, "about the law in Droghia?"

It stopped him, though he did not turn around.

"Not *wrong!*" he bellowed, his voice echoing from the house facades. "Only innocent. Ignorant!

"The law in Droghia covers all the niceties—who's to plant flowers along the canals, who's to scrub the cobbles every morn. Fair taxes—aye, none fairer, for those that can afford to pay 'em, and I'm not one of 'em—and sumptuary laws to prevent us rousing our neighbor's covetousness. And, aye,

239

you're free to linger here till curfew so long as you're not soliciting, but as to *law* . . ."

He stopped himself, pivoted on one crutch, cocked his head at me.

"Speak you again!" he barked.

"What shall I say?" I asked, taking a few steps closer.

"Anything. Can you sing? Know you poetry?"

" 'There is a realm clept OtherWhere . . .' " I began.

"Enough! Your voice is beautiful, d'you know that? Are you beautiful as well?"

"No," I answered truthfully. It tickled him tremendously; he all but fell off his crutches with laughing.

"Good!" he roared. "For, plainly, neither am I. But if you can stand the sight and stink of me for the sake of a music lesson—and mayhap a lesson in more than music . . ."

He beckoned me nearer with one crutch and we began to walk together, I knew not where. He stopped; I stopped as well. Though he was half again my breadth, his great shaggy head reached not past my elbow.

"That *is* why you lingered?" he asked, tilting his blind eyes up at me. "To hear my music and learn more of it and me?"

"In part. There were Other reasons."

"Never mind 'other reasons,' " he said, taking off again, stumping along to great purpose so that only my longest stride could pace him. We were in a part of the city I did not know, the older part, built on solid land, before the canals were made. The streets here were winding, dirtier, the houses narrower, crookeder, their upper storeys nearly touching above our heads, shutting out the sky and swirling snow. "Saving food and sex—not always in that order—there are no 'other reasons' but music."

"Food, sex, and music," I mused. "Not justice?" I was rewarded again with his arrested step and uptilted shadow-gaze. "For only gross injustice could have given you such eyes."

He swung his nearer crutch to strike me; I side-stepped out of the way. He swung again, harder, nearly unbalancing himself, then stopped, panting, shifting the gittern more securely over his shoulder and resuming his stride.

"Better we speak of 'other reasons' than of 'justice,' whatever that might be!" he warned. "I know not, for it never fell to me—neither at birth nor after, as you can see from either end of me you choose."

"But what rests between is music," I said.

"And you think that makes all the difference?" The musician's voice was bitter. The snow fell harder, some few flakes reaching us through the dark warrens, blown on icy winds neither of us heeded. "You're like a child," he said wonderingly. "Why is that?"

I could no more answer that than anything else he'd asked me. "Am I, master? In what way?"

"I am no one's master, only Redrec," he corrected me, though his gruff voice and his manner had gone strangely gentle. "Have you a name as well?"

"I am called Lingri."

" 'Lingri.' Your very name is music. Perhaps it explains your passion."

Passion? For Other to accuse anOther of passion would have been a grave insult; to my knowledge such accusation had not been made in public since the Thousand-Year. I caught my breath and remembered where in the World I was. People prided themselves on their passions; the musician's words were meant as compliment. What truth did he surmise of me, and how?

"A blind man learns to see with his remaining senses," Redrec was saying, and I was reminded uneasily of Naven. "I knew your presence because I could *feel* you listening to my music— not with your ears only, but with your skin, your lungs, your heart. Few ever learn to do that, and most of them are children. We grow old, we grow hard, and that passion within us grows blunted, then begins to die. It has not died in you. Why is that?"

"Perhaps . . ." Carefully I sought some half-truth, seeming-

241

truth. Whole truth would have no meaning here. ". . . perhaps because I heard not music when I *was* a child, so that now I cannot but hear it *as* a child?"

"Have they no music where you come from?" I thought he meant to pity me.

"Not since long before my birth," I began, but could not go beyond it. Redrec's sad face twisted sadder.

"Was it a plague, that made your people deaf? Or some sorrow so great they lost the desire to sing and play?" he cried. I could not answer him. He shook his great head.

"How fortunate and ironic at once, then, that you were spared, and have such a natural ear! And you come to this land which once fair rollicked with music of all kinds, but now serves only the weak gruel Droghen tolerates! One of the gods' little jokes, I suppose, like the nomads' child I've heard tell of, who paints murals in the Greathouse and beds with Gerim, *'vek*-grease in her hair and all! Grown to womanhood in a tent, her gifts are for plaster and silk sheets—a joke!"

This blind man used more of his senses than most, it would seem, if from his exile in these sunless streets he knew both Droghen's house and name.

We had turned onto one of the narrowest of the narrow streets, and Redrec pointed one crutch to indicate a downward flight of steps leading to a pothouse in a cellar. Here the musician was apparently well-known, for the smattering of patrons hailed him warmly, and the wizened landlord served him at the table nearest the hearth, cut low to the floor and with a niche to set his crutches, which was apparently reserved solely for the use of the halfman.

"Will you drink with me, Lingri-one?" When I demurred, he motioned me to sit at the low table regardless. "Then keep me company, at least. And tell me what, beyond my music, makes you follow a halfman and stranger into the most dangerous part of Droghen's city?"

Dangerous? I had seen the shadow-figures lurking in dim passages and lightless doorways, their shadow eyes upon us as we passed, but had thought them merely furtive, hardly dangerous. There was some aura about Redrec, as if these shadows watched over him, that none might harm one so already harmed as he.

"An errand for my mistress," I explained.

"Either a mighty errand or a mighty mistress, that allows you to look unblinking into this face," he mused as the landlord guided his hand to the ale-mug, and he drank. "You can look at this man-wrought face without loathing. Why is that?"

I have only to look at the face, not live behind it, I thought but did not speak. Redrec's strong hand reached suddenly toward my face, to trace its lineaments and learn some truth thereby.

"You're plain enough," he observed frankly, "though not hideous, which sometimes explains an odd compassion. And your eyes *do* see?"

"Yes."

"Then tell me what they see when they look at me."

"A gifted musician," I replied; if I were plain, let me speak plain.

"And that's all?" His voice held wonderment, and he drank again. "If this be the servant, who must the mistress be?"

"She is Dweneth Dain'sDaughter," I began, but he wiped his lip and banged the ale-mug on the table, nodding.

"The Cirque-troupe! Aye, I know it. And you . . ."

His face contorted beneath its scars, became a grimace as his huge voice grew deadly, hissing soft.

"You were going to ask me to play for them."

Was he more amazed than furious? What blunder had I made?

"You or any you might know, master," I hastened to explain. "My knowledge of music being so inadequate— "

"You obviously knew not who I once was!" he roared, and all the pothouse grew still, to listen. "Redrec plays not for Cirque, nor *for* anything! My music is music, pure and of itself. Perhaps you are not as gifted as I thought, to understand not that!"

He shut me out then, leaning his low chair back, and took

243

up his gittern from beside the hearth to play some gentle refrain of far less flamboyance but no less beauty than what he'd played at quayside. Those in the room listened comfortably, as if they heard this often. What little light came through the sunken windows now faded and was gone; if curfew rang this far incity, I had not heard it here underground, and could not have returned to the Greathouse before dark at any rate. Should Redrec send me away, where was I to go?

He froze suddenly in mid-chord, tilting the chair forward with a bang and glowering at me.

"Dain'sTroupe plays for Droghen."

"We are at present under his patronage," I concurred reluctantly, hearing loathing in his voice at the mention of the name.

"And you would have me play for Droghen." He shook his great head, musing, incredulous. He set the gittern back beside the hearth as if he feared smashing it in his building rage, slammed the table with one great hand, and roared to all and sundry: "She would have me play for Droghen! She would have *me* play for *Droghen!*"

He spat on the floor, not entirely missing my feet.

"When Droghen gives me back my eyes, I will!"

"There are two versions of the story," Dweneth would tell me when I finally returned to the Greathouse. "One is that Redrec denounced Droghen-Gerim before the Assemblage, the second is that they merely quarreled over the same woman. The Halfman's quite a womanizer, for all his unfortunate appearance . . ."

She was furious with me, not only for my untoward disappearance, but because Hrill had somehow eluded her attention to fall into a canal and drown. Though I had as little to do with the creature as possible, this was somehow deemed my fault. For my part, I experienced no remorse. What I had witnessed in my absence left me little compassion for the likes of Hrill.

"Redrec was once court composer—you didn't know that,

did you?" Dweneth went on, making up her face for that night's activities, an edge to her voice; the amber eyes she daubed with gaudy colors were already red with tears. "He was considered so gifted most forgot he was a halfman. The scrolls in Droghen's library are full of his compositions, though none are played nowadays, because of the rift between them. He even led the orchestra in this-Droghen's predecessor's day. Didn't know that either, did you?"

She threw down her rouge-brush unused, absently fluffed up her false hair, tried smoothing her feathery eyebrows with a moistened little finger, finally lost her temper.

"I can't do this tonight, I simply can't!" she raged, then sighed, then gathered herself, ever the player. "Well, to keep my mind off my own troubles—Droghen-Gerim has a temper; you've seen that. It was worse in his youth, Thrasim tells me, and he *has* the power of command. Also, not being an artist, he doesn't understand how artists work around the rules. I suppose it's true, what he did to Redrec, but who's to say if he deserved it?"

" 'Deserved it,' lady?" My own shattered Discipline had rendered me speechless thus far. "Tell me who 'deserves' to lose his eyes, much less his livelihood— "

"It was before my time!" Dweneth half-shouted. Discussion closed. I was only her servile, after all. "Well before my time. Redrec's old by now, older than Droghen—near forty, if he's still alive . . ."

"This," Redrec cried, his already overlarge voice augmented by the dimensions of the crumbling arena surrounding us, "*this* is the legacy of your Droghen-Gerim. This is the shadow side of the land of fair taxes, these are the dregs of the cleanest city in the known World! See with your heart what I cannot see with my eyes, then speak to me of Droghen!"

We were outside in the moonlight, in a place accessible only through the bowels of the Droghiad's city, where there was neither curfew nor the Droghiad's law. I doubt Droghen knew this place existed, much less the souls who inhabited it.

245

"Yet these souls will weigh on his when he comes to die," Redrec declared, "and drag it down to Hell!"

Hell had been his constant theme since he'd learned my place in Droghen's house.

"When Droghen gives me back my eyes, I'll play for him!" he'd bellowed, spitting at my feet and struggling with his crutches. "Till then, you and all who cleave to him may go with him to Hell!"

Giving his gittern into the landlord's care, pivoting wildly on his crutches, he beckoned me.

"Come here to me! Send you to Hell, will I? I'll personally escort you!"

With that he vanished down a flight of stone steps spiraling down to more stone steps, his crutches flying at speeds that would have been unsafe for an ordinary man afoot. Were I not Other, I might have fled in the opposite direction, which to this day I believe he expected me to do—risking curfew and the dark and the crooked streets rather than accompany him to what he named Hell.

But Other knows no Hell but what is wrought upon this world. I went with him.

At the bottom of the steps lay a dim, damp wine cellar, row upon row of dusty cobwebbed casks, rat droppings (furtive scrabblings and the gleam of vermin eyes in corners). Redrec came to a halt before a seeping wall of seeming unseamed stone; only Other eyes could discern the worn places on the floor where a thousand thousand footsteps had passed. The musician worked some hidden mechanism, and the wall opened before us.

Through sewers into caves and catacombs I followed him, until it seemed we had traversed the whole of the Old City underground. More than once we doubled back, to baffle me so that I would not find this place again. Redrec did not know of Othersense.

I knew precisely where we were, though I could not but marvel at the blindman whose footsteps, as in the wine cellar, must have passed this way a thousand thousand times before.

When at last we emerged into the crumbling stone arena, ancient enough by my reckoning to have been used for sport or Cirque or bloodier pastime when Droghia had been part of the Plalan Ascendancy centuries before, the moon was at its zenith. It shone upon a gathering of ghosts. Two adults and four haunted children gathered about Redrec and he brought them forward that I might see.

"Once a butcher's son, always a butcher's son," he sneered of Droghen. "Only this one butchers his fellow man. Look you . . ."

"There in the cold and dark they came forward, lady, and he showed me . . ."

I must have sounded breathless, for Dweneth actually stopped her primping and paid me heed.

"The one without hands had also been a musician. His crime was composing limericks in mockery of this-Droghen, his punishment to have his hands severed at the wrists that he might write no more. 'In Droghia all are Droghians?' Is this what it means?

"The female they call only the Mad One. She'd been arrested for coin-clipping, not a serious crime, but Droghen took a fancy to her, in a way you and I know something about, and when she refused him he had her locked in with some of his troops, who'd been drinking that night. Perhaps you, lady, can better surmise what happened than can I. Now she neither sees nor hears, but rocks herself and laughs to keep from screaming. Betimes, says Redrec, they must tie her to prevent her pulling out her hair in handfuls. As to the children . . ."

Dweneth's face was pained enough to make me pause; she was ever drawn to and repulsed by any tale of rape or suffering children. Her paints and powders forgotten, she sat very still and stared at me.

"I've never seen you like this, Lingri Stoneface. I do believe you're angry. Tell me of the children," she added softly.

"Four of them, lady, brothers and sisters, so deformed in

the year the pox came that the elder two lack ears and fingers and the younger ones have spines so twisted they cannot walk. There was also a babe who died, as did the mother, Redrec says, their only crime being that they were spouse and offspring of one of the cutpurses who fled with Brok."

Dweneth grew soberer still. "Droghen's reign, it's said, is merciful. He does not kill. How many die in places where there is no cure for pox?"

" 'But we have medicine enough in Droghia'!" I reminded her, quoting the very speech Droghen had made to open the Holydays. "To allow those to die who could have been spared is tantamount to murder. What says *OtherWhere* of those who kill?"

" 'Harbor not with the one who kills, but make of her non-person . . .' " Dweneth said vaguely, dreamily, forgetting the rest. She turned her hands up in a shrug. "That's OtherWhere, not real. Deny all those who've killed in *this* world? We'd none of us speak to any of us."

"You have not killed, lady, nor have I."

"Not you," she agreed. "But I have put my curse on Brok. That he has not yet died of it does not keep me from wishing it. You're living in your box again, Lingri-one! Come out and face reality!"

I know not how I came to be on my knees at her feet; it was a gesture out of Omila's tragedies and nothing of mine. But I was adamant.

"Lady, I can no longer harbor in this-Droghen's house. Sell me, I beseech you. Send me elsewhere, anywhere, and take what profit you can thereby, but I cannot, I *will* not—"

"Get up and stop this at once!" She was on her feet, her hand upraised to strike me, only to stop herself at the last instant, but no less furious. "How dare you come to me with all this now? I've spent the night wringing my hands, frantic to know where the bloody hell you were . . ."

Or thinking more on Hrill than me, I thought but did not say.

". . . dare you dictate what I'm to do with you, when I should have sold you at the first opportunity, after the lies you've told me? You lied to me under Right of Three—I don't know of anyone who's done that and not suffered for it! How do you know this Redrec's not a liar, and these flotsam got their grievances elsewhere to blame on Droghen? Or does it take a liar to know a liar? Get up, I say!"

I would not move; let it embarrass her, who had no truck with melodrama save she wrote the script.

"When we were lost upon the plain, and I told you my tale of rape and rape again"— she stalked me, fire in her eyes —"what did I earn but cold, listening silence, distance in place of comfort, and finally lies? Where I sought friendship, I received denial. Yet the tales of strangers make you weep. Worse, you slovenly, unkempt wench, you hadn't the courtesy to wash the tear-tracks from your dirty face when you did return! Out past curfew and into the next day, and me frantic with worry . . ."

Or else too occupied with Holyday feasting, and then the loss of Hrill, to even notice my absence until I was called upon to sing. She was dramatizing, and we both knew it. She took a deep breath, calmed down, sighed.

"She neither laughs nor so much as smiles," she said suddenly, touching my face almost as Redrec had, "nor have I ever before this seen her angry or distraught. Yet she can weep, and weep prodigiously, for what anyone else would take in stride." She knelt beside me. "What *is* to be done with you, Lingri-one?"

"Let the decision be yours, lady." I found my feet, collected as much Discipline as I owned; the touch on my face had reminded me too much of Redrec, of the night and the music, "so long as it be not under Droghen-Gerim's aegis."

She was on her feet as well. "That's not for you to dictate—"

"—only to request—"

"—and be denied! I won't hear one more word of this,

249

except you tell me what—beyond the sight of blind and handless beggars, which I hardly think new to you—has made you act this way?"

"It must have been the music," I said suddenly, realizing it myself for the first time.

"Ah!" This she could understand. "Tell me."

How else explain that I held my mask and Discipline against a night's display of horrors, as Redrec and his ghost-brigade, the adults carrying the younger children, led me deeper into the Old City, to underground hovels and the skeletons of near-fallen buildings where lived further wraiths of this-Droghen's making, only to dissolve in weeping later? Not until Redrec had completed my Tour of Hell, as he called it, and he and his nameless, handless companion together greeted the dawn with ghostly music wrought out of the Hydraulus—

"The Hydraulus!" Dweneth exclaimed. "It's said on foggy nights its ghost-notes can be heard from the heart of the Old City, but I'd always thought that legend. It's said to be a thousand years old, if it exists at all. Yet you've seen it, heard it played? Oh, tell me!"

Tell her? Somehow recreate that scene for any who had not been there to see and hear with every cell what I experienced? I was not poet enough then; I doubt I am now. Nevertheless:

Picture the Hydraulus, indeed a thousand years old in its original construction, though its many moving, clacking, wheezing, squealing parts were many times reserviced and replaced, enthroned deep beneath the ancient arena with its Plalan grotesques carved upon its walls and colonnades, its mechanism powered by the very subterranean river which fed the oldest canals, so that its hundredfold pipes, rising to the cavernous ceiling, waited only the impetus of hands and feet on keys and pedals to fill a city with its sound.

Picture Redrec Halfman standing on the massive bench where an ordinary man would sit, his powerful arms leaning all the weight of his upper body on the fist-wide keys to wrest their voices from them, his hands flying and pounding, coaxing and punishing every tone a man-wrought instrument was capable of from this ancient device. Beneath his bench the handless one, his seeing eyes closed as if to seek chords engraved upon his eyelids, plied the footpedals in such perfect harmony with what the halfman played that their melody emerged unflawed and seamless.

Picture the wraiths as they foregather from the catacombs, bearing tapers to light the organ chamber and cast harsh relief upon the many faces of misery that they bear. Picture them rapt and listening, or humming low and pleasingly in tune with a music that soothes and comforts, leaches poisons from their souls, and seems to greet the dawn light peering hesitantly through time-wrought crevices in man-wrought walls, as if to inquire if its presence be welcome in these ceremonies.

Picture lastly a solitary Other, her every neural fiber a-vibrate with such passion as strips away all mask and Discipline, leaving only empathy and the taste of tears.

It was Redrec who tasted them as, his final crescendo echoing to infinity, the Hydraulus wheezing wearily into silence amid the departing shuffle of wraith-feet down the tunnels, he bid farewell to the handless one and only then seemed to remember me.

"Still with us, Lingri-one?" he addressed the vaulted ceiling in his great rasping voice, sniffing the air as if uncertain where he'd left me.

"Barely, Redrec Musician."

I sat curled near-fetal in the shadows of this cornerless chamber, shaking off the mnemonic trance, which I had engaged so that not one moment of this night would escape my remembering. I heard rather than saw him slide down from the high bench and crutch-scrabble toward me, for at that moment not only he was blind.

"Smells like saltgrass, tastes like saltgrass," he remarked, touching my face and tasting tears. "Have we broken your heart, Lingri-one? Why is that?

"The Tale of Droghen's Conscience"
(Anonymous, a partial lay attributed to
the Musicians of Droghia: ?1562 P.A.)

Then-Droghen seemed a godly man
Enlightened of enlightened land
But secrets dark lay 'neath his hand
Until he found a Conscience.

The feasters gathered in the salle
The Holydays to 'joy withal
And hear some singing, that were all,
Expected not this Conscience.

Her voice was fair, her face was not
Her simple words ne'er be forgot
For singing Droghiad to change the lot
Of those named by his Conscience.

She started singing sweet enough
But soon her words turned cruel and rough
To sadden with the suffering stuff
Wrought by Droghen lacking Conscience.

An outcry went the tables 'round:
"Oh, still this suffering so profound!
Or demand of Droghen he step down
And answer to his Conscience!"

"How could you take a man his eyes?
A man his livelihood besides?
How leave unmothered babes to die
Unless you had no Conscience?"

He started up in angry throes:
"My heart's not strong to answer those

252

Who, newcome here, dare flaunt my woes
In calling them my Conscience!"

Why did she not die on the spot?
For singing accusations hot?
Subscribe it to remorse she got
In pricking Droghen's Conscience.

First he knelt and then he wept
'Fore all assembled and Filaret.
Vows he made and likewise kept
In keeping with his Conscience . . .

(fragment 37–48 lost)

That Conscience never had a Name:
"Say only I am without fame
And serve my part to save the flame,
For Droghen e'er had Conscience."

twelve

Never in my hundred years have I experienced such shame.

"It serves you, Your Recalcitrance!" Gayat Telepath chides me, not a little smugly. I ignore him. The alternative would be most unDisciplined, and I have already been that.

The concept of shame, as anOther understands it, has nothing to do with external censure. No one can visit shame upon me but myself. It was shame in all its shades and nuances—a final soul-sickness at the wantonness and violence we enacted before the Thousand-Year—that drove us to our Discipline. In that sense it is a positive passion, but this makes it no less painful.

Thus I have shamed myself with a poet's wantonness: an inability, ever, to be brief, to get to the point, to say what must be said and no more, when time is running out and our remaining lives hang so precariously. I hug my shame to me like a wayward child, wallow in it, for Gayat is correct: it serves me. I have been unDisciplined.

The Matriarchy, it seems, is displeased with the lack of progress in my chronicle. It deals too much with People, I am told, and scarcely at all with us.

". . . a picaresque tale of long-ago events in then-Droghia . . ." is the Matriarch Jisra's assessment of my work thus far, her words all but replicating my mother's so long ago.

Jeijinn is long dead, as are Evere and Loriel and every Matriarch who sat in Council on the day I returned from crossover to give my report. Frayin, too, I have finally learned, is no more, her charred and battered body recovered from the rubble of a house that was once among the most welcoming places in One Greater. A part of me recites the mourning chant even as I give the rest of my attention to the Matriarchs.

This is a privy council meeting, barely a quorum, and the Matriarchs now scanning my chronicle are unknown to me. Many are outislanders, most are young enough to be my daughters. Most especially I know not this Matriarch Jisra at all.

". . . as if such tales do not abound in the World and will not continue to do so long after we are gone," she concludes, handing the chronicle to a second Matriarch, who concurs. "Nostalgia pieces for an age we raised these People from, who have now ceased to maim and kill their own for the pleasure they derive from killing us. We asked of you that you write of Others, and from our point of view— "

"You asked of me," I dare correct her, my hand upraised, "to write of Others and their interaction with the People, from the perspective of my own life and experience. If you required concision only, it is there for you in the chronicle's earliest pages:

" 'I am about to tell you a tale of two species . . .' " I begin from memory, and follow through to the end of my synopsis. "In essence, there it is. Discard the rest and free me to measure grain or dive for kelp or minister to children. But if I am to tell what I know, I must tell it *as* I know it. If the Matriarchy desires this not, why have you chosen me? I am neither scientist nor historian, but poet, and can only be mirror and microcosm

255

of what I myself have witnessed. Why was I provided with time and place and resource to record the whole of my experience if the Council wanted less? If what I write is unacceptable, Mothers, I pray you take it from me and give it to anOther, but do not presume to censor it as it flows from my pen!"

My voice sounds querulous even to my own ears. There is a quiet, murmured confabulation about the Chair, which gives me leisure to observe how starved and draggled we all are—how desperate and hungry both in body and in soul. And there is still no word of the children who went with the Zanti. Yet I presume to quibble over the disposition of a chronicle no one will ever read. Futility.

"It is not our intention to censor you, WiseLingri," Jisra Matriarch says at last; her young hands tremble on the arms of the Chair until she conceals them in her sleeves, "only to request that you proceed apace. BRi-rumor yields reports of armed maneuvers on several coasts of the mainland, and our numbers here decrease alarmingly. We honestly know not how much time remains to us. If your chronicle has you still in Droghia—"

" —then the People will reach our shores for the last time before they reach them for the first," I finish, to spare her this bitter paradox. "Gentles, Mothers, forgive me. Hereafter I shall endeavor, for once in my life, to be succinct."

Succinctly, then, this much transpired in Droghia before my leaving it:

A song was sung in the grand salle of the Greathouse on the holiest of the Holydays. Simultaneously Redrec and his ghost-brigade emerged in legion from their catacombs to stand in mute testament in Droghen's courtyard, that his crimes might speak for themselves. Droghen performed a public penance, reparations were made, and somehow the singer emerged with her life.

A Discipline bred out of the Thousand-Year dictates: "Harbor not with the one who kills." The duty of the Monitor was clear: "Intervene not in the People's way, no matter its direction." I had already violated this more than once. A Discipline more ancient than either of these gave birth to the concept of the Balance Mechanism so dear to my teacher Rau: "Be as balance, reconcile the irreconcilable, no matter that it cost your life."

I weighed the more recent against the ancient, and the ancient won.

Why did I not approach Droghen in private? Say that I had the example of Redrec's wraiths to teach me Droghian justice. Say also that Dweneth had taught me the value of playing to the largest audience possible.

There was no larger audience in Droghia than the host gathered in the grand salle that night, for the Filaret was there with his monks and entourage, and all the governing Assemblage, and every gossip in the city. In a lesser nation I might have lost my head by the second verse, but Droghen let me live, and oh, the consequences!

In fairness, he was a leader above all. He knew the temper of the times and how best to hold his People's hearts. My first verse brought him out of the First Seat and halfway across the salle toward my throat. Only Thrasim saved me, with his cool voice of reason in Droghen's ear, his iron grip upon Droghen's arm. I continued with my singing. Midway Droghen collapsed to his knees in tears. The guests sat spellbound.

Measure the value of a leader's public display of weeping for past misdeeds; I cannot. How genuine was it? I know that not either. But it had the desired effect.

Following a public flogging before the massive doors of the basilica at dawn of the religious new year—to the delight of the Filaret, though it ruined his opposition party's prospects—Droghen made what amends he could to all whom he had wronged. The adults he restored to their former places, with recompense for their sufferings and a lifetime's care by his own physician. The children he took to live in the Greathouse as his wards, "that their sufferings might be constantly before my eyes, to prevent my causing suffering ever again." Droghen

257

was an excellent speech-writer. He appointed Redrec as the children's tutor, and made him court composer once again. As for me . . .

"As for *you*—!" Droghen lay on his stomach, wincing as his raw back came under Dweneth's ministering fingers. He glowered at me. "*You* are an instigator!"

"As you say, my Lord, though I had hoped only to serve as arbitrator, to bring you and Redrec Musician to where you had been from the first."

"Well, you've—ouch—done far more than—*ow!* Dwen, Godamercy, have done!"

"I'll have done when I *am* done," she scolded, pushing him back down on the table to dab more unguent on his welted, lash-cut back. "Hold still! Or would you rather the physician and his leeches again?"

Droghen cursed mightily. "As if I had blood enough left for leeching after the Filaret's novices were done with me! I know not if they're pious, but they're certainly strong of arm!"

"And no more than you deserve!" was Dweneth's opinion, offered without sympathy; she too had seen the wraiths waiting in the courtyard, and had spent some time with the children since. "Though how your heart held out through this— !" She clucked her tongue, swabbed blood, dabbed unguent. "Hold still!"

Droghen lay with his chin on his folded arms, still glowering. His back would take a week to heal, and he would not sleep well for twice that.

"God knows what witcheries you used on the halfman," he muttered when Dweneth had done, easing himself painfully to his feet with neither her assistance nor mine, "but you managed to unbend his stiff neck and bring him out of his lair. Now I only wonder what witcheries you've worked on me. Sung into conscience by a storysinger—that's too new for my taste!"

The charge of witchcraft did not trouble me; if I had not

burned thus far I never would. But I had perhaps overstayed my welcome. My crossover must end, but how?

The obvious answer lay at anchor in the harbor, their damage finally repaired, their three masts tall in that forest of sail-trees, canvas spanking-new in the thin late-Freeze sun. Indeed, but how?

I learned the harbor drill in a single afternoon. Little good it did me.

"Females is bad luck 'board ship," one cagey, grizzled salt informed me. When I asked him why he only grunted. "They's just bad luck, is all!"

Pondering alternatives, I wandered beyond the city walls to the open strand, unPeopled on so blustery a day, and would have turned back before curfew, except that in the distance I heard *bRi*-cry.

Only Other ears could have discerned it above the howl of wind, or known it signaled distress. Far down the strand there was a rock jetty; the sound arose from there. Heedless of long skirts and People's propriety and the risks to female alone upon a beach, I ran toward it.

The *bRi* was entangled in a fishing net and cut severely; foundering in the shallows, she had beached herself and was prepared to die. Perhaps I could refloat her to join her kin; at least I could free her of the indignity of the net and lingering death. I was cutting the cords with a rock shard, for I carried no knife, *bRi*-speaking to keep the creature calm, when the curfew sounded. Late again. No matter. So deep was I already in Droghen's disfavor, this was a minor sin in my vast store. Against the wind, I did not hear the voices until those they belonged to were upon me.

"What's the wench doin' out here by its lonesome?" the first mused aloud to his three companions.

"Why, it's jabbering to that trillfish, obvious," the second said. "Faith, Grij, how can ye be so stupid?"

"Must be cold," was Grij's opinion. "Think we could warm it up a bit?"

259

"Dunno," the third one said. "It's funny-looking. Don't know if I could."

"G'on, you could with anything!" the fourth said, jabbing him.

I had moved away from the *bRi* by now, weighing my options. I had done all I could for her, and she was dead. I could easily outrun any of this foursome, skirts and all, could for that matter outswim them as well. Or fend against them if they touched me. If I were in OtherWhere.

"It looks familiar, Grij," the third was saying. "Seen it somewheres afore, has we?"

"We had indeed, Kepar me lad!" Grij answered. "It's Droghen's Conscience!"

It was the name all Droghia had come to know me by, yet one more reason why I soon must leave.

"Wonder what he'd pay t'have her back, Grij, d'ye suppose? If she was to get lost comin' home fra the beach, say?"

Grij rubbed his stubbled chin and thought. "Belike he'd sooner rid of her and namore asingin' ter him!"

Before I could offer any opinion of my own, I was in their custody.

Grij and his threesome belonged to a faction of city-bred Brigands not unallied with Brok of Refuge, who had eluded Droghen's constabulary for years. Informed of my capture, Droghen feigned indifference to having me returned—though I wonder, was he feigning?—and only the intercession of Dweneth Broksibling and a concerted search by Redrec's wraiths brought Lingri Inept out of the catacombs unscathed yet again.

"It's getting to be a bore, you know!" Dweneth threw at me, weaponless by prior agreement with the Brigands, who had turned their attention elsewhere while she undid my bonds with her teeth where fingers failed. Redrec listened down the tunnels lest any Brigand return too soon, his upraised crutch the only weapon he required.

I rubbed circulation back into bruised wrists and attempted to stand after being too long bound in one position. She steadied me when I tottered, and I read an anxiety far deeper than that of mistress for a servant. "What is, lady?"

"Saving your life. And for all the thanks I get. You owe me one!"

I held out one numb hand, childwise, to seal the bargain. Redrec had begun to growl.

"Time and place, ladies, time and place! This is neither!"

The incident served to remind Droghen all too forcefully that, even with the Filaret in his camp, he dare not sail without securing the fealty of every faction in his city. Still he balked at naming a successor, but he did name Redrec Regent in his absence. The musician was tickled.

Scrubbed and shaved and decked in his best court finery, including a pair of pretty gilded crutches and child-size dancing slippers on his tiny feet, he was a wonder to behold, though his long, deep-lined face would always bear a melancholy cast, and nothing could make beautiful those ruined eyes. Still, he was Redrec, and irrepressible.

"From undercity Trollking to Droghiad's Regent in one blow!" he roared, kicking his child's feet in delight. "Lingri-one, you are good luck for me!"

Lastly, Droghen arranged with DainTrouper to let his talented daughter sail with him on the *Foremost,* to sing and play and tend the sailors' hurts, and as well as faith hostage, to ensure that Brok would remain in Refuge. Dour Dain was consoled with great amounts of coin—poor recompense, he grumbled, for possibly losing his only daughter over the edge of the World. As if he could have dissuaded that headstrong individual, once she tasted salt air and adventure.

I had seen Droghen's newest charts and realized that the course he contemplated would bring his ships nearer the Archipelago than any People's ship had come before. Would Dweneth arrive in OtherWhere before I did? I must somehow find my own way aboard one of those ships.

261

* * *

"I am your servile, Lady. I go with you."

"Not this time you don't!" she sniffed. "Droghen's bought you from me outright."

He was the only one in the realm who could buy what or whom he wanted, or seize what was denied him. Public repentence or no, Droghen was still Droghen.

"Perhaps you should have freed me back in Refuge," I suggested, "or sold me while you could."

"Oh, shut up about it! It's more than I can bear, any of it! Da and the troupe off to Leeward as soon as the canals are clear, Renna and me for the ships, and you to stay behind. That's that!"

"Why Renna?" I asked, though Dweneth's glance said I knew as well as she.

"For the obvious reason, though she'd as lief stay as you would go. She's terrified of water, as any can tell by the reek of her. But Droghen doesn't seem to mind; I swear he's no sense of smell. Also, he wants her by to tell his future as we sail blithely over the edge of the World."

There were tears in her eyes—from frustration, at having Droghen succeed where Brok had failed? From fear, perhaps, of actually sailing over the edge? Or, was it possible, sorrow at having to leave me behind?

"If it's any consolation, Lady—" Was I out of my mind? I modified my thought mid-sentence. "—perhaps Droghen's charts are not entirely inaccurate after all."

"I told you to shut up about it! It's done, and nothing I can do about it!"

She hugged me then, quickly, fiercely, and I would have returned the gesture had she not then shoved me away. Why was this simple mode of touch so strangely comforting?

"Mayhap I'm better going over the edge of the World. Always going over the edge of something, it seems, and no Lingri to catch me this time. Well, it'll be quick at least!"

"And what becomes of me, Lady? Am I to go with the troupe?"

262

She pushed her tangled hair back from her face, a gathering gesture.

"Droghen bids you stay here in Redrec's care. To learn less harrowing songs for his return, says he."

Droghen, too, knew irony. But here in his city and near the *bRi,* I could teach him greater irony still. I bided my time.

The troupe's farewells were nothing if not tearful. Only Omila and I wept not, the tragedienne to save her tears for stock in trade, I because my mask forbade them. But poor Gause was nearly overcome.

". . . for if you fall off the edge of the World, we shall not meet again until the Great God bring us all to Paradise!" he sobbed into Dweneth's neck as she tried futilely to comfort him.

I embraced Cwala and she embraced me—a tumblers' silent farewell—and the babe between us leapt exuberantly. I read good health and a safe delivery, and wished I were free to tell her so. But Cwala had drunk of the vision-drugs; she had her own truth.

"None does the books as well as you!" Dain grumped expansively, his way of bidding me farewell.

As the Cirque wagons were loaded laboriously onto the barges that would bring them up the canals to Leeward, I found Krex for the last time, stroked his wrinkled hide in silence, earned the mischief in his small canny eyes as he tried one final time to stomp upon my feet. My eyes followed the barges until they were past the city locks and out of sight; my mind followed them long thereafter.

There was to be a gala on the eve of sailing, with music and feasting until dawn. Renna's mural, its colors still drying, was to be unveiled to great praise; in time the beauty and realism of her trillfish would be lauded as far as her ancestral village in Lamora. None grew so drunk that night that their eyes were not drawn again and again to the harbor, and the three ships waiting there.

*   *   *

". . . and only Lingri stays behind." Redrec's now-familiar fingers traced my face once more. "Want to go with them, do you? Why is that?"

He taught me every stringed instrument he knew—gittern and harp and crowd and lute—taught me composition and music theory and even, great honor and great risk to Discipline at once, to play the Hydraulus. In exchange I sat at his feet and listened to his tales, permitting him to touch my face whenever he desired. It was not only because he was blind, but because he knew that I was Other, and accepted it.

"Not concern for the mistress who's no longer your mistress," he mused; his fingers traced my ear and I permitted it. "You're Droghen's now, as much as the like of you or me can ever be anyone's chattel. But some Other reason has you looking ever out to sea. Why is that?"

"Do you tell futures as well as Renna?" I tweaked him; he quickly pulled his hand away.

"Bite your tongue—that's sorcery! Renna's permitted because she's Lamorak and tameless, but I've seen what's done to sorcerers elsewhere than here.

"Once on a time when I was young and callow and still had my eyes, I chanced to be in the train of then-Droghen, who was off to quell some uproar among the border lords near Gleris. We rode smack into some row within the castle-keep of one of 'em. Seems there'd been a local rebellion—taxes too high and a few ricks burned in protest, retribution taken in so many wives and daughters raped, and then a general uprising. The local lord had put it down and was about to execute the seven ringleaders, tenant farmers all, from a toothless ancient to a beardless boy. He preferred the wheel, did this lord. Liked his victims to die slowly and in pieces. He was tying up the young one when we rode in with the sunset.

"You never heard such wailing! Enough to send a stone's ears jangling, much less a musician's. Nothing I could do but listen to the women keening, and see could I work it into a dirge or something later, though I did find nerve to whisper to then-Droghen: 'What if you interfere, Lord?'

"Which he might well have, its being the custom there-abouts for the host to grant a guest as important as a Droghiad that sort of favor. He was a good man, then-Droghen, not that this one isn't, now we've got him straightened out . . ."

He smiled, traced my ear again, his fingers coming to rest just at the tip. I sat at his feet and listened, as transfixed as by the Hydraulus, only this time I did not weep.

"He might have spoken, then-Droghen, only he never got the chance. The crowd parts suddenly for this middling man to come to the fore—an outlander, from the look of him, for although his clothes were local, there was something uncanny about his lineaments that—well. He had this voice with all manner of resonance to it—a singer's voice, I remember thinking, as I did when you first spoke.

" 'Milord!' he calls to the border lord, though with then-Droghen in the corner of his eye as well. 'I'm man enough for these seven. Do you let them go, and I'll outlast your wheel for seven days!'

"It was insane, what he proposed to do! What man would willingly make such an offer? But so he did, and the border lord was so intrigued he took him up on it. The peasants took their new-freed kin and scattered like leaves. The stranger stepped himself up to the wheel.

"He lasted those seven days and never uttered a sound, though the staunchest man will cry out on the wheel, if only from thirst or despair. The lord kept his word and freed him, set him loose in the wood to die. So he might have, I suppose, though to this day I think he had some inner strength that would have saved him. I followed him."

"That was most brave," I interjected.

"Brave!" Redrec snorted. "Only curious. I had to know how he'd done it—survived a wheel's torments for seven days and nights with neither food nor water and never cried out once. When I asked he only smiled faintly and showed me his wrists where the chains had cut through almost to the bone.

" 'It's because I am not People, don't you know?' says he. And mayhap it was only the twilight, or mayhap his blood really was a different hue. But the poor folk came and nursed him, fed him and built him a fire, and we all of us watched over him while he slept. When he was awake I'd play the lute, and after we would talk. Seven days following the seven days, he was as whole as a newborn, and took the forest path without my learning anything of who he was or why he'd made the choice he had."

"You never learned more of him?"

"Only that his name was Rau, but what's a name without a point of origin? Yet ever since—" Redrec's fingers traced my ear once again. "—I've wondered if there wasn't some secret race of elvenfolk at work to better this old world like Rau. Wherever I find his like, I offer what I can."

Intervene not in the way of any People, indeed, I thought. Teacher mine, wait until I get home!

"And pray you, Master Redrec, what has this to do with me?" I asked, though I knew quite well.

"When first I heard your voice, that snowy day upon the quay, I thought me, 'There's anOther, just like Rau.' You smelled of saltgrass, so did he. And when I touched your face, I knew."

"Was it offering what you can that cost you your eyes?" I could not resist asking; he cuffed my Other ear.

"Brazen wench!" he roared, delighted. "A thousand scales on lute and rebec both before the gala. Go to!"

I would have practiced as many scales and more, until his ears were as weary as my fingers, but after half an afternoon he relented.

"Want you shipboard bad enough? Then do you forego the gala altogether—let them miss you; it will serve them—and this is what you'll do . . ."

I am told the gala was the greatest ever performed in Droghia, that Dweneth was extraordinary and Renna so drunk with praise for her mural that she had to retire early. Even the Filaret, moved to tears by the sheer incandescence of Redrec's newly composed Celebration for Full Orchestra, embraced Droghen before the multitude (Droghen trying not to wince for his sore back), promised to look after things in his absence, and bade them all "Fair journey!"

For myself, I took Redrec's advice and was present, though not in my usual form, when the *Foremost*, the *Yeoman*, and the *Venture* sailed out of harbor to the sound of cheering from the crowds packed on the quays, and wove their way through the melting ice, bound for OtherWhere. I had begun with the musician wishing me to hell, and ended with his fondest benison. As to how Redrec Elder became grandsire to my only son, that is a tale too long in the telling, and I shall not tell it here.

The Matriarchy is correct. To examine each of these threads in detail is to leave me yet in Droghia, and there is no time for that. Tales of what the People now refer to as their Middle Age abound in their own writing, now that the era is long past in the wake of our technology. A sun-celled skimmer can refute the flatworlders' creed in slightly more than a day, offering its passenger vistas of mountain and desert and ocean all at once, not that these topographical wonders remain unchanged since that not-so-distant Middle Age. In fairness to their ingenuity, the People have wrought almost as much havoc upon themselves as upon us.

They took our technology, freely given, and perverted it to greed and expediency. Where we used only sun- and water-fueled vehicles, painstakingly crafted with as little waste as possible from the metals we harvested and forged in our mountain isles, they sought a faster, cheaper way. When we offered them robotics to free their mine slaves, they instead combined the two to double output, and People died in mines in greater numbers than before. Facture slaves once relegated to weaving and handcraft were now set to making cogs and gears and levers. Where they once succumbed to white-lung from the clothiers' crafts, they now die of different airborne deaths.

Today the deserts gasp beneath layers of hydrocarbons. Plains and valleys heave beneath twisted, rusting discards and irreducible refuse. Whose responsibility is this? When first our species met, we Others produced virtually no environmental pollutants; neither, except for the inevitable wood and peat and coal smoke, did the People. Our technology freed them from dependency on fossil fuels, simultaneously providing them with the knowledge to create the more virulent poisons we had eschewed. Blame our knowledge or their naïveté or merely "the way things are." Whose fault?

I can no more document each irreversible step whereby we both have come to where we are than I can record every event which kept me a Freeze-long in Droghia. Of the time I determined to read the whole of Droghen's vast—for its time and place—library, only to find Dweneth had arrived before me on an identical mission and with far less skill but as great determination, I shall not write. Of the long discourses she and I shared in that same library as we learned together, I shall not write. Of the magic of learning music at Redrec's feet as he all unbeknownst inculcated in anOther what had been lost for a thousand years, I shall not write. Of Dweneth's fury when, unable to find me at the gala, she assumed I had refused to see her off, I shall not write. There is not paper enough in the World, much less the Citadel, to encompass all these things.

Succinctly, then: I departed Droghia aboard a ship named *Venture*—my hair cropped, and wearing the guise of a sailor.

"Now, you're the manner of man," Dweneth eyed me not a little lasciviously and with a sigh, "that I could easily grow to like!"

I did not stay the stirring-stick, but added more linens to the cauldron aboil amidships on this calm and smooth-swelled day. The makeshift laundry was Dweneth's doing, and the only way to control vermin among sailors who spent their lives on water but were loath to immerse themselves in water for such cowards' sport as bathing. Having discovered my identity scarcely two days from shore, she had put me in charge of the cauldron, the better to keep me under her eye and safe from certain sailors' pastimes for, in my male garb, as she was quick to point out:

"You're all the more attractive, for a plain female betimes

makes a pretty boy, as any player can tell you. Nor do some of these need to know which sex you are in order to use you. The younger lads are always susceptible on a long voyage."

So I had observed, sleepless and watchful amid furtive scufflings belowdecks. I had even found it necessary, my Other strength more proportionate to my new male guise, to strong-arm one persistent foul-breathed miscreant who tried to initiate me in my hammock the very first night. His hand-dirk wrested from him, his bruises evident to his crewmates, he thereafter left me alone. But the story spread across the distance between ships, to reach Dweneth's ears on the *Foremost* and make her curious. Borrowing Droghen's dinghy, she had crossed between the *Foremost* and the *Venture* as they sailed in close formation, and was at first horrified, then delighted, to see me.

"I won't ask why. I'll flatter myself it's that you couldn't bear to part with your generous former mistress. But I will ask how. How *ever* did you pass the recruiters—not only as male, but as an experienced sailor?"

"Hardly experienced, Lady, for as you yourself point out, I make a pretty boy, and as the recruiter thought me no more than sixteen years, I did not disabuse him. He wondered aloud if I might be a runaway, but as I proved strong and had all my teeth, he was less than fastidious."

"Droghen will kill you if he finds out. Or feed you to the trillfish."

Thus shortening my journey, I thought, having seen a familiar fluke or two already in our wake, and knowing they were following me. The *bRi* I'd helped to die had pod-kin who would honor me, spreading the tale seawide until, being *bRi* and easily distracted, their attention caught on something else. Perhaps before then I could find some heading toward the Greaters.

It was not to be. For fifty days we sailed, and no *bRi* came close enough, nor could I swim to them. It seemed I must let my crossover take me, and not try to act upon it. So be it.

On fair days when the swells were even and the wind drove

us easily before it, I worked my passage in so many leagues of laundry, boiled and hung flapping from the gantlines to dry. On days of squall or chilling fog I trimmed sails, worked rigging, and bailed the holds with the best of them, earning a reputation as "a strong lad, for all he's so scrawny." The crew came grudgingly to respect me for my work, despite my excessive modesty of person and peculiar eating habits. I worked, I recorded, I stocked the corners of my mind with poetry, and had ample time to contemplate anew Rau's theory of the unlikely candidate.

Few Monitors had spent as little time in crossover as I, and none with such mixed results. Nor had any ever returned under escort of three People's ships, for if Droghen stayed his present course, he would make land not only on the Archipelago, but at the very foot of the Citadel of One Greater, as handily as if I personally had steered him there.

Not that we need be the first ashore. Dispatches had been arriving at the Greathouse up to the day of our departure, filled with reports of launchings elsewhere. Spies in Kelibesh reported four more ships set sail to follow the ten that were lost before. If they trusted themselves to the prevailing currents, they would arrive within visual range of the Sector Five Lessers in under thirty days. If there were no mist and their eyes were keen enough, the Kelibek could rove unhindered among a hundred small, sparsely populated aits and atolls, slave-hunting or merely slaughtering.

Mantuu, despite its wars or possibly because of them, was also building ships, and Melet outriggers full of desperate refugees had also taken to the waves, seeking any landfall to spare them further drought and war. Even the Kwengii, long content to hug the coasts for plunder, had been turning their rapacious eyes seaward.

Loriel's report to the Council in the year of my birth had estimated twenty years before the People's arrival. She had erred by a matter of days. The time was now. And Droghia, with me in its train, would likely be the first ashore. All I had to do was nothing.

"They seem drawn to you," Dweneth observed as we watched the *bRi* from the *Foremost*'s aft rail one calm night. The frolicsome shapes and streaming manes made shimmering magic of moon-spangled waters. They swam ever closer, their seeming-smiling faces turned upward, one liquid eye on either side of their great domed heads forever watching us. "Odd! It's not as if you feed them."

Other never did so, for to disturb the creatures' instinctive feeding patterns would have been to render them dependent upon us. *bRi* must follow their own way, no more nor less than Others or People. Yet lately *bRi* in ever-increasing numbers had taken to following the wake of whichever ship I chanced to be on, crowding closer whenever I appeared too near the rails.

"Pretty creatures!" Dweneth mused. "And what variety of melodies they sing! It's almost as if they were trying to talk."

Her trained ear caught a repetition of phrases, and a smile spread slowly over her face.

"Listen you: they *are* talking. And it's your attention they want, Lingri-one. What do you suppose it means?"

"Perhaps they chide us because we do not feed them," I suggested, caught between truth and half-truth. I knew exactly what they were saying: it was a warning-cry, demanding an answer I could not give until I was alone. At that time I would also extend a warning, about the dangers of letting the sailors feed them. But not now.

"Pity you couldn't be at the sing last night." Dweneth changed the subject. "Not that you could sing with that voice. How do you deepen it so? It's almost as rich as Droghen's, and no player's trick that I know."

"Perhaps a musician's trick?" I suggested. Or anOther trick. Best change the subject again. "Besides, awkward enough it may be to be known thoughout the ships as 'Dweneth's favorite lad,' but I like not the thought of coming too near Droghen or the future-reading Renna in this guise."

"Droghen wouldn't know you. Nor would Renna, for that

matter, though she might try coming on to you even under Droghen's nose. She's always had a thing for pretty boys—"

"Lady, if you do not mind . . ."

"All right. I only meant the guise was perfect. It's got you this far unmolested, though still I understand not why you're here." She yawned; it had been a long day. "Peace, I'm to bed!"

Neither the helmsman nor the watch could see me for the shadows. I slipped over the side and clambered down the ratlines until I could touch the waves.

"*bRi*-friend," I trilled softly to a lead-female slipping her flukes silkenly through the water at my feet. Let any who chanced to overhear me think I was foolishly mimicking her sounds, as the crew sometimes did. "I bring warning, *bRi*-friend."

"I too," she answered, looming, raising her long snout above the surf to assure me of her seriousness. "I too. ssStorm!"

Some minor electromagnetic disturbance had been prickling at my Othersense since sunset; not until the *bRi* gave it name did I recognize it. No minor squall this, but a full-blown hurricane cut across our heading; as the *bRi* spoke further I could see it—unavoidable even if we abruptly changed course, and possibly violent enough to founder even Droghian ships.

"Gratitude, *bRi*-Mother, gratitude! And this-one's warning . . ."

She tilted her great doomed head so that her further eye now contemplated me, amusing posture for a more leisurely time.

"ssSpeak," she trilled, I thought with a touch of skepticism. What could I warn her of, puny airswimmer, that she in her sea-wisdom did not already know? "Speak. . . . I hear."

"I too warn of storm," I began; she nodded her head in amusement at the thought.

"What storm airswimmer knows that *bRi* does not?"

"Storm of airswimmer-making. Beware the airswimmer who feeds that it might later feed . . ." Ships' crews would throw the *bRi* galley offal, teasing them to leap and retrieve the choicer morsels, then hunt them later to supplement ships' rations.

The *bRi* weighed this against what she knew of my species, and of what she did not know of this third species, which swam the waves in moving islands and, like any airswimmer, behaved inexplicably. Takes an airswimmer to know an air-swimmer? Conferring with her pod-kin, the lead-female at last acknowledged my warning.

"I hear . . ." she said, and I watched the pod disperse ahead of the coming storm.

———

"Flotsam"
(from *Histories,* as compiled by Lingri Monitor and Others T-Y1021/1564 P.A./ Code612151918113)

For the first five hundred thousand years, we were nearer the stars than the World. Looking out toward any horizon, we saw only our islands and the sea; looking up from any vantage, we saw an infinite population of stars. Moon and sun and stars were better known to us than any solid land. We might have fancied ourselves the only thinking beings in the World, were it not for flotsam and the bRi.

From before the Thousand-Year, the tides had brought us puzzling refuse beyond the expected backwash of driftwood, kelp, and mollusk shells. Analysis of this compilation of broken spars and shattered planking, lengths of rope and sail canvas, as well as amphoras and crates containing goods and artifacts unknown to us, of bilge-ventings and worse, gave us to know that someone else lay beyond the horizon, and an inkling of what sort.

Why did we never build sailing vessels? Why, when we did build skimmers, did we never take them beyond our Archipelago? Some have argued that it was a fear of those very beings beyond the horizon, but this is doubtful. Perhaps it was only that we were content where we were and saw no reason to venture further. Content, perhaps, but no less curious about what lay beyond. For this, we inquired of the ever-communicative bRi.

Few had mastered the nuances of the sea-beings' complex tongues this soon; it was also difficult to comprehend a meaning without time-sense, existing always in an eternal present. Further, bRi *made no distinction between one airswimmer species and anOther, until we asked one scarred one which species it was that hunted hers. Thereafter we began to get answers, if disquieting ones. At about that same time, the first bodies of shipwrecked sailors began to drift onto our shores.*

Were we perhaps overzealous in our analysis of these sea-spawn sacrifices? Certainly we treated these dead with no less reverence than our own, committing them to the cremation rite and the requisite period of mourning after we had dissected their persons and scrutinized their possessions. We are aware now that some might view these acts as desecration, but we never intended them thus.

The bodies were given over to the healers, whose first examinations revealed a species more different from ours than was at first supposed. Scans revealed organs of similar, but not identical, function, situated often in differing thoracic quadrants, as the heart being where the liver should be, and so forth. Chemanalysis revealed differing blood compositions, as well as significant cardiac and renal variations. Dissection revealed disparate bifurcate brain function, and a gut filled with partially digested animal flesh.

Chemical and sociohistorical analysis of burns on some of the bodies indicated that these had drowned as the result of sea-battles and of ships forcibly boarded, burned, and sunk. There were also flogging scars both old and recent on nearly every corpse. What this suggested as government among the mainland species as a whole could only be surmised. It was, as more than one WiseOne suggested,

274

rather like trying to judge a volcano from having access to it only during eruption.

The scientists examined every boot and belt buckle, every surviving coin and pocket tool and amulet, every scrap of fabric and item of decoration to determine its precise composition and function. From this we were able to learn in small what political analysis could not learn in large and, on the practical plane, to replicate those items which had use for us. In the instance of items made of animal products such as leather, fur, or silk, nonorganic replicates were substituted, which we have utilized as synths ever since. Therefore, in a sense, the People's cultures and technologies contributed to ours, however inadvertently, long before ours did to theirs.

thirteen

Better, I thought ruefully, clambering back up the *Foremost*'s side to watch the iridescent creatures depart, that the *bRi* had told me nothing, for however skilled anOther, one alone could do little under my guise and circumstances to save three ships. Had I dared raise the alarm, against a fair breeze, a starlit sky, and my own inexperience as a sailor, I would at best be disbelieved, at worst suspected of lunacy if not again of sorcery. What was I to do?

What I did was collide head-on with Renna. It was yet some hours before dawn, and as I was off watch I was about to retire to my hammock, to lose myself in whatever sleepless meditations might yet provide an answer to impending disaster, when I came up against a barefoot, blanket-wrapped form, muzzy with sleep, who cursed me in ripe Lamorak.

"Mind your gangling limbs, stupid boy! Go you and wake Lord Droghen; I've a future that wants telling."

I remembered to keep my voice low. "Aye, mistress."

Curious how one who could barely see her own feet upon the boards could peer into the future, I nevertheless did as I was bidden, coming in as close contact with the Droghiad as I had since we'd set sail.

I thought he eyed me oddly, but Renna's futuring soon absorbed his full attention, and I slipped out as I had come, leaving them closeted alone. Droghen emerged like a whirlwind moments later, and the order was passed from ship to ship: Batten down! Prepare for storm!

Of the time that followed—of a dawn announced briefly by a sickly greenish sun quickly extinguished in scudding blue-black cloud, of driving rain so fierce it pounded the skull and forced the eyelids shut, of wind that, though Renna's forewarning gave us time to furl the mainsails, still drove us helpless round about before it in whirling, plunging, plummeting chaos, of bare straining masts heeled over until the toptrees dipped below waves a ship-size and more, of decks wave-crashed and tilted perpendicular, and of the woeful creatures lashed to them and clinging, cursing or praying according to their preference—I shall write but briefly. Others do not subscribe to miracle, but what else kept three flimsy ships in sight of their fellows through all of that? For all of a day and most of the following night did we contend with that wind, though few but anOther and the elder sailors could distinguish night from day inside that howl and crash and dark.

Somewhere about midnight we limped into the eye of the storm, with the awful knowledge that we had come only half-way, and had as much to endure on the farther side. Droghen had the ships brought as close about as they could be in this relative calm, the better to shout orders between them. He then had himself lashed to the *Foremost*'s helm, while Thrasim did the same on the *Venture*. Seeing the *Yeoman* short-handed, I leapt the distance intent on taking her wheel, and found myself in contention with the strongest man aboard her.

"Yer on'y a lad, a stripling!" he spat, mindful to do so to leeward. When I wrested the helm from him on sheer strength, his eyes widened with fear and he yielded to me.

Let me work my Other sorcery one last time. Without my intervention, most certainly the ships would be lost. Even with my Othersense to guide us through the storm, there was no guarantee of safety, yet I must try. Intervene not with the People's way? Let this be my Gleran border village, Rau, I thought. I cannot lose these ships, though I save them only to bring them to Other shores. Dweneth is here, I owe her one, and I cannot lose her now.

"Where do you think you're going? *What do you think you're doing?*" she shrieked across from the *Foremost* above the rising wind; the two ships' sides were scarce an arm's length apart, though the swells brought them towering and plummeting in turn. Dweneth's small hands clutched toward me, unreaching, helpless. "Droghen's mad, and dead soon, by the look of him . . ."

I could see him, white-faced and grim, at one with the wheel of his flagship, and I wondered if his heart would stand it. The *Foremost* swung about then, running athwart the *Yeoman*, and Dweneth's voice was swallowed in the wind.

"—never lose you—cannot bear it—never—!"

Gone. I could see her straining against the rail, hands outstretched, rain on her face like tears, lips still crying out soundless as one of the sailors, her wild curls whipping in his face, pried her loose and dragged her back.

Let Droghen's heart hold out. Let me focus mind and Otherstrength on this wheel, to bring the *Yeoman* straight into the wind. Let Droghen and Thrasim understand my actions and do likewise.

Wind shrieked, waves rose, rain torrented. The *Yeoman* leapt beneath me like a living thing, yawing into the wind. Of a sudden, there were *bRi*.

Never to my knowledge were *bRi* seen in storm; their absence in itself was enough to presage violent weather. Yet they had followed us, they explained, singing it to me, who alone could understand:

". . . returned, saving-one!" they trilled, their chorus loud enough even with the wind. ". . . returned to save one who saves . . ."

I had only tried to free one of their dying number on a

278

Droghian beach, yet they would risk this number to save me. I must think.

Others never had messiahs, but People's lore was rife with them, and it needed very little to create one out of nothing. If causing the beasts of the sea to rise up and lead her and hers out of darkness into light were all that qualified a messiah, I was fast in danger of becoming one. Nothing to be done for it; I fused my will with the *Yeoman* and hung on.

Dweneth's perspective at that moment was perhaps clearer than mine.

"We saw them crowding in the water, leaping higher than the bulwarks, throwing themselves into the air, dancing like things possessed. It was like the miracles in the holytracts— seas parting, creatures speaking to man, saints speaking in tongues. And the center of it all was obviously you! You answered them; we heard you!

"You know how superstitious sailors are. They were gape-mouthed at the spectacle. Wherever they were, however vital what they were doing, they stopped and stood transfixed. I couldn't have said, though, if they'd have sainted you on the spot or thrown you overboard for a witch. You solved the problem for them, of course.

"Not graceful at all; Gause would have been embarrassed for you. If it was meant to look accidental, you can forget that, too. Clumsy it was, and deliberate. Can you blame me if I screamed?"

Scream she did indeed—long enough and loud enough with her players' lungs to be heard above a storm and throughout the ships:

"LINGRIII!!"

Small matter the revelation now. I had leapt overboard with the sole intent of having the *bRi* carry me off and gone. Let it seem a miracle, let it seem that I had drowned. No matter, as long as I was no longer a part of what the ships did next. Dweneth! I thought, calling her by name: Forgive me. Surfacing as far astern as I could hold my breath, I began to swim away from the *Yeoman* with determined strokes, *bRi* surrounding me. Those on the ships could no longer see me, and the sky was clearing.

Orders were shouted, rigging climbed and sails manned. The three ships came about and headed toward where the sea was calmest. As the winds died, the rains tapered and ceased, and skies opened to a limpid predawn blue, I clung between an escort-*bRi* and one of the younger females, caught in the *Venture*'s wake and forgotten in the flurry of activity aboard. As my Othersense cleared of the storm's impulse-chatter I knew precisely where we were: less than a league beyond One Greater's sensor net, and less than a day from its shores.

The storm would have had little impact upon the Greaters through their weather shields, and sensors would soon detect the alien presence on One Greater's horizon. I, meanwhile, had not escaped in time, but was dredged out of a glass-smooth sea by some of the *Foremost*'s crew, overseen by a flushed and panting Droghen. As if Dweneth's outcry had not been enough, my cropped and dripping hair slicked back from my elven ears, and the thin linen shirt clinging too close with wet to any longer guise me as a lad, made no question of my identity.

"I should have let the Brigands roast you!" Droghen thundered, his eyes drawn to my breasts in spite of himself; they did not hold his attention long. "What in the name of all the Hells are you doing aboard my ships?!"

Explanations were due and overdue, and I might yet have had the distinction of being burned as a witch on the borders of my own country, save for the clearing horizon and the keen eye of the watch, whose cry at once diminished the importance of anything else:

"Land ho!"

"I was right!" Droghen triumphed, clutching the forward rail white-knuckled as if to urge the ship faster. "There's land, it *is* round—I *knew!* Ho, watch! What see you?"

"A island, sir. Naught else!"

Only One Greater would be visible this soon. But not the

full panorama of all four Greaters, the hundred Lessers, and all the Agris and Industrials between would satisfy a Droghiad seeking an entire continent.

"Only an island?" He was crestfallen, skeptical, impatient, and desperately out of breath. "Perhaps it's an outlyer. Foretaste of what's to come. Look sharp, watch! Report as soon's you see the rest!"

Meanwhile the wind died altogether. We lay becalmed, tantalizingly near this elusive shore, and there was damage to assess and repair. Droghen worked off his impatience, barking orders until he was hoarse, supporting himself with a hand on Thrasim's shoulder until his lieutenant took command from him. Droghen hauled me bodily to his cabin.

"Out!" he roared at Renna and Dweneth both, gathered agog and wanting to hear everything first hand. "You—!" he charged Renna with a shove. "Tell me a future that knows what lies on yonder island, friend or foe, or empty withal. Go to!"

"My head still aches from the last telling!" the huntress-queen pouted, digging in her heels. "Besides, I want to watch. Will you burn her first, or cut her head off? Or blind her like her scruffy musician friend?"

"Out!" Droghen closed the door on her, rounding on Dweneth.

"How much did you know about—" A jerk of the thumb at me. "—this?"

"Nothing," I began, as she simultaneously said "Everything," with a warning glance at me to hold my tongue if I wanted to keep it. She crossed to Droghen and began helping him unlace his sodden shirt.

"Da gave her in charge to look after me before he left for Leeward, no matter that she officially belongs to you," she explained glibly; she was never so smooth as when she lied outright. "Can you damn her for old loyalties? Or, for that matter—" She gave him a long-eyed, winsome look. "—for the small fact that she and her trillfish may have saved your ships?"

281

"It's that I'm wondering about!" Droghen said narrowly, waving Dweneth off, rummaging out a dry shirt from the press.

We were all a sorry, draggled lot, no one of us more or less sodden for having remained above or belowdecks or thrown ourselves overboard. The Droghiad had the luxury of changing; Dweneth and I must stay and drip on the floor. Droghen sat heavily on his little-slept-in bunk, breathing hard; Dweneth was by him again, feeling his brow and pulse and fussing with her healers' herbs.

"Sorcery!" Droghen said to me. My shirt was drying, my small breasts less prominent; he sighed. "She draws the critters like a very theurgist, 'saves' my ships by offering herself as living sacrifice, she's stronger than my strongest man, able to pass unmolested among an hundred horny sailors—"

"Lord Droghen," Dweneth bullied, fussed, "your heart!"

"I want some explanations!"

Just then Thrasim stuck his head in. "Your pardon, sire— you wanted damage reports?"

Nonplussed, Droghen blinked at him. "So I did. How bad?"

"Yeoman's took a lot of water; she'll founder if we don't bail first, and that's a day or two . . ."

He gave his report calmly, regardless whatever situation he found himself thrust into. Bland-looking, bland-seeming Thrasim, a man deemed lacking in color by all in Droghia save Droghen, never lost his calm. But for his coloring, he might have been anOther.

". . . *Foremost*'s mainsail's ruint. We've spare jibs can be stitched together to replace 'er, but that's wanting time as well. And *Venture*'s maintree's split dangerous-looking. Her pilot says band her and hope the winds is gentler going back, but I'd liefer find a stand of timber on yon isle and see can we replace her."

"We stay, then!" Droghen announced, not entirely disappointed; the sight of One Greater intrigued him, no matter what it might contain. "Make do where you can, Thrasim-one, and we'll see about that tree."

He returned his lieutenant's parting salute, gagged down some of the herbal brew Dweneth had concocted to calm him, let her do up the fasteners on his shirt while he studied me anew.

"Explanations!" the Lord of Droghia barked.

"Doubtless she's plenty, but is now the time?" Dweneth interjected, attempting to press the half-drunk sedative on him again, but he waved it and her aside. "Were I Droghiad, I'd less concern with this nonsense and more to see what's on yon island . . ."

I saw her hands were shaking, and she was staring hard at me. Her eyes had dilated until they were all center, and grew wider every time she glanced from Droghen back to me. It was as if she'd never seen me before, or never in this light. And why defend from Droghen what confounded all her own attempts at comprehension? Her tone was the same near-wheedling she used betimes to win her father, and as effective. But why dispel Droghen's doubts as her own increased? And how would her doubts encompass an entire island populated with my like?

"Who'll go with Thrasim to fetch the tree, I wonder?" she chattered on, addressing Droghen, but with her eyes on me. "There's some of us dying to set foot on land after all this time asea . . ."

"Get you gone!" Droghen roared, dismissing us both, worn down equally by my silence and her chatter, which was precisely how Dweneth intended it.

Dragging me no less forcefully by the wrist than Droghen had, she secreted me away from the eyes of sailors in the cabin she shared with Renna.

"Get you dressed!" she ordered breathlessly. "And then you can explain to me!"

I suppose I might have, this near One Greater, but I was not to have the opportunity. Dweneth was still rinsing the brine out of her tangled hair, I choosing what garments between hers and Renna's might garb me more honestly than as a sailor, when we heard mild Thrasim for the first time lose his calm.

"Sire, oh sire, 'tis a city on the isle! A city wondrous-like and strange!"

We had begun to drift upon the tide, near enough for the lineaments of the Citadel to take shape in the rising sun, for the spidery gleam of telfer rails and the sparkle of faceted glass and metal to catch the morning light. The most naïve eye could see this was no organic thing.

"A city!" Droghen mused, quite dazzled; it was the last thing he'd expected. "I'd thought perhaps some primitives, if People at all . . ."

His voice cracked, and he clutched his breast to still his thundering heart. Dweneth's hand touched his arm but he paid no heed, addressing Thrasim over his shoulder, unable to tear his eyes from the city. "Ready my small boat. Yourself, four oarsmen, and an armed guard—"

"—and your personal physician," Dweneth insisted, at his elbow with no intention of being dislodged.

"And me!" Renna piped up, insinuating her way through the sailors to cling to her Droghiad. "You'll not leave me here with this drooling lot!"

The crew, staring off the bows as the alien city grew more shapes and wonders momentarily, whispered and gestured fearfully among themselves. Only Thrasim found his lord's distress with clinging females quietly amusing. Droghen threw up his hands in despair.

"Women!"

His eye caught mine. I was decked in Dweneth's skirts and particolor, and for once seemed passing feminine.

"You too, I suppose?"

"Better to have all your troubles in the same boat, my Lord."

Droghen climbed laboriously down into the boat, and offered a hand up to me. Skirts and all, I swung aboard as gracefully as any seasoned sailor. Mild Thrasim laughed outright.

"The old salts are right!" Droghen growled. "Bad luck, every one of you!"

"Oh!" Dweneth said simply, as each stroke of the oars brought us nearer the spires of the Citadel, and the city's true size and shape and Otherness became apparent. "Oh!"

Possibly she never forgave me for those moments of intermingled terror and delight. But that was for later. For the moment my most urgent concern was with what manner of landing Droghen's small boat would make, for my Other eyes could see what no one else in the boat or aboard the ships could yet distinguish: a single line of Others standing far up the strand where the rocks began, all but one with the rock in their hooded, sand-colored robes, waiting. Foremost among them, irony of ironies, was my mother Jeijinn.

The Matriarch of the Matriarchy changed every hundred days, and this was Jeijinn's time. She it was who would embody all that was Other in this our first contact with the People—first to speak, first to welcome, first to die if that were called for. Little did she realize the role her errant offspring would play in that first encounter.

The oarsmen rowed in uneasy silence, the creak of their oars and the slap of waves, the occasional cry of a seabird the only sounds. Halfway between his ships and shore, Droghen quietly addressed his crew.

"Cities, lads, are not built by magic, but by People. Until we know what manner of People and how armed, we take no action. The ships will fire the big guns o'er our heads if we should fall; there's comfort in that. Arms at ready, stay alert, but act not without direct order from me. Histories will be sung of us long after this moment has passed. Let's give them something proud to sing about!"

The Others on the shore, ten of them, stood motionless until the small boat ground onto the sand at the tideline. Slowly they detached themselves from the rock line and became visible—only ten, a number fewer than we in the boat, unthreatening—striding slowly and with measured pace, cowled and barefoot, hands naked at their sides to show them weaponless. Whispered prayers and curses from those in the boat accompanied this unexpected movement.

"What are they, then?"

"Why on'y ten?"

"Aye, where's the rest of 'em?"

"Can't tell me they've come unarmed!"

"It's an ambush, I says! What's behind them rocks?"

"Steady, lads, steady!" Thrasim said, his famous calm recovered now that he really understood this to be a city. The tension in the boat was palpable—a miasma in the air, poisonous.

Only I knew what would happen next, at least among the Others. Stopping ten paces from the boat, they would lower their cowls to expose their faces, and Jeijinn would stand forward in order to speak. But would that simple orchestrated gesture of hand to cowl trigger some unbearable terror among the sailors, and end in death?

"My Lord," I addressed Droghen's broad back softly, though with the slightest Other-resonance in my voice, "if I may . . ."

"Not *now!*" He rounded on me fiercely, but with one eye on the shore. "This is not domestic quarrel for your meddling! Hold your tongue or I shall by God—"

Simultaneously he raised his voice, the ten Others stopped at the tenth pace, but Jeijinn did not step forward. Seeing Droghen the leader, she would wait until this minor difference with one of his crew be resolved, and she had his full attention.

Did any on the shore know who it was who caused the uproar? Sitting behind Droghen, I could not be seen from shore, but were there Telepath among the ten, surely she could read me. By his height I was certain that one of the ten was Lerius.

Droghen, meanwhile, was still shouting, whatever tension he could not direct at these cryptic creatures who seemed to have risen from the very sand directed instead at me.

". . . cut it out and throw you to them!"

"Saving my tongue, Lord, that is precisely what I was about to suggest."

Not a one in the boat did not gawp at me.

"If their intent be hostile," I spoke rapidly, struggling to hold the moment, "were it not best to lose the least crew-member in discovering this? My mistress has schooled me in mime. Let me try to show them that we come in peace. They can see I am but female and unarmed. As I now belong to you, Lord, grant me this."

"If you belonged to me you would not be here!" Droghen seethed, weighing what he saw of me now with the "lad" come to tell him of Renna's vision, and the "messiah" who spoke with *bRi*.

"No—no!" Dweneth murmured, trying to climb over the oarsmen to clutch at either Droghen or me. Neither of us paid her any heed, locked in our own private struggle.

"It's one way to be rid of you . . ." Droghen began, thinking he threatened me.

"Gerim—sire." Thrasim stood, balancing, astern. "If not him—her—" He could not accustom himself to my most recent guise, perhaps considered it as suspect as the rest. "—then me. Not the first time, Lord, my life for yours."

"Not this time—*no!*" Droghen said to that. The boat ground onto the strand, knocking Dweneth back, and giving me my last chance.

"Say this, Lord: that it's my own folly if I fail, but your praise I'll sing if I succeed."

His vanity prevailed.

"Go then, damn you!" he roared above the sound of waves.

As I stood ankle-deep in the surf, Dweneth was suddenly beside me. I was not surprised.

" 'Who will be the first to trust?' " quoth she, then dropped the players' pose and shrugged, diffident and scared. "Lost you once already today. Can't do it twice. Easier to die with you than to watch you die."

None had ever said this to me before. Something tugged at my mind, my heart; I had not time to analyze it. Dweneth

287

took my hand and nodded up the beach, where Jeijinn had begun to walk once more. We waded forward. All eyes in the boat returned to the ten on the shore.

No word was spoken. None was needed. A slight breeze, ever capricious this near the sea, tugged at cowls already lowering, blew back my hair as well as Jeijinn's and the Others. Within the context of my own, Dweneth knew me at last for what I was.

"S'truth!" Droghen cried behind me. " 'Tis the ElvenQueen herself!"

Lord Droghen Droghiad, scrambling out of the boat with his eyes fixed on my mother Jeijinn, chose that moment to collapse face forward in the sand.

Praise Thrasim for signaling the ships to hold their fire when they saw their Droghiad fall. Under the drawn weapons of the boat crew, Other hands raised Droghen up and gently bore him toward a skimmer judiciously hidden beyond the rocks. Before it reached the healers' hospice he would be on full life-support, his vital signs cross-matched with everything our science knew of People's physiology. Cryolaser surgery would give Droghen a stronger heart than he had had from birth. Thus did Other diplomacy make itself known in deed where words had not had time.

"Lord Thrasim, he will not be harmed," I hastily assured the agitated lieutenant as the motor-hum of the unseen skimmer further unnerved his crew. "Our physicians will care for him. I will return to the *Foremost* as faith-hostage."

"No need!" called one of the ten who had not gone with the skimmer, his accent in any of the People's tongues better than mine ever was. Rau came forward with his hands outheld and crossed at the wrists.

"Thrasim is your name? I am called Rau. A lesser personage than your Droghiad, but of more value as a faith-hostage than this Lingri. I will return with you."

Whatever his game, I could not read it, only the familiar twinkle in his eye. Poor hapless Thrasim, seeing in this bearded, stocky, twinkling figure something more familiar than the rest of these stone-faced, beach-borne wraiths, made his decision.

"Weapons down!" he told his restive crew. "You can see they're unarmed. And will you shoot at women? At ease, and stay you in the boat until further orders!"

He saw that Rau still held out his hands for rope or manacle and refused the gesture.

"I'd rather, milord Rau, you take me where you've brought Lord Droghen. For I see no weapons trained o'er your walls, nor any on your persons. That being, though I know not who or what you are, I'll trust you."

He went with Rau.

Jeijinn, her thunder stolen by the males of two species, was to make no speech of welcome. She did gesture that fruit and grain and fresh water be brought to those in the boat, who refused to partake until they saw Lerius taste from each of the receptacles he carried. The sailors took a little water, but no more. Thereafter followed silence, sounds of surf and seabirds.

What strange tableau did we present against that brightening morning? Six nervous sailors dared not leave their boat; six robed Others remained after those who went with Droghen. Between these two stood Dweneth, Renna and I.

Renna had somehow scrambled after Dweneth once Thrasim was gone, stood in her shadow stiff with fear, her laughing mockery failing her. I detached myself from the tableau to present my companions to the Matriarch.

"Mother," I began.

Her lightning glance took in my short-cropped hair, my patchwork wondrous garb, my callused hands extended either side to these two People. Did any of this surprise her? Could Jeijinn be surprised? By her mask, none would know it. She spoke before I could draw further breath.

"Prodigious and prodigal both!" she breathed in Othertongue, then turned from me to the huntress and, in flawless Droghian, asked, "And thee are called—?"

"Renna, marm!" she tittered helplessly, caught somewhere between laughter and fear. Say that her distinction was to be the first to laugh on Other shores since the Thousand-Year.

I half expected Dweneth to hiss at her, poke her, remind her of the decorum she as player-maid would have sustained no matter what. But Dweneth had fallen to her knees in the sand, and made about herself the same religious gesture she had made over the dead Darvis and Argetha—a warding-gesture, fending off evil or the unknown.

"Lady, what—?"

"Angels!" she murmured, finding a voice smaller than any I knew she possessed. "God's angels come to dwell with simple, sinful man. One sent to guard me, save my life, serve me when I should have served you . . ."

She could speak no further, and even Renna whimpered into silence, retreating to the boat with the sailors. Better the danger she knew than the one she didn't know.

"Lady, Dweneth . . ." Her name again, the speaking of it tugging in my mind. What was this? "Do not kneel to us, for we are only . . ."

No words. I extended my hands to raise her from her knees; she shrank back as if from serpents. I felt the tug again, and felt her distress as if it were my own.

A soul-thread? Their like were not uncommon among Telepaths and in some marriage bonds, but only Otherthread could bind with Otherthread, to my knowledge. The possibility of a soul-thread between Other and People had never been considered, for People's minds were deemed too different. Yet, what else could this sensation be? Did Dweneth feel it too?

Caring not what appearance I made, mindful of both Jeijinn and Renna watching me as if I were at the very least witless, if not dangerous, I dropped my mask and knelt beside my lady. I would not rise until she did.

"Never angels, lady. Never anything superior or fearsome, only different." I sought for words and somehow found them. "Beings, like yourself—corporeal, mortal, fallible, possessed as much as you of heart and mind and hope. Different only

290

in such matters as your inborn healer's curiosity would find fascinating in time. Fear neither me nor any of my kind. I am only Lingri, as you have known me, nothing more."

"No, not as I have known you!" she murmured, shaking her head, teeth chattering with fear. Had my presence brought her else, since she had known me? "Could not be as I have known you, and be one with what I see here . . ."

What did her mind's eye see, beyond what simplicity presented itself here on this shore? What was she able to surmise from a city glimpsed beyond a seawall, the presence of six beings—unarmed, unadorned, and far less exotic than many from her world—that could evoke such fear? Or was it indeed her own experience of the soul-thread that she meant?

Indeed. Curious!

It had been long since I had been among Telepaths, to feel that once-familiar warmth within my mind. Nor had any of my experiences with the mind-dwelling ones, from Lerius to Naven, proved aught but untoward. Now Lerius again. How long had he, seeming absorbed in offering food and drink to the newcomers, been reading me, and possibly Dweneth as well? Had he any concept, insular island-dweller, of the dangers? I had been too long in crossover, and forgotten how to shield. I as quickly remembered.

Read only me! I sent him, not expecting he would listen. He did not. Simultaneously I tried to block his egress into Dweneth's mind, without success. A muddle—I was never very good at this.

Lerius stood between us suddenly, looming over us as we knelt there, in all his wraithish height, apex of a triangle never before limned upon this World. I followed Dweneth's gaze the length of that robed figure to the white-eyed face and heard, as she did:

What is she to you?

And, as she did, both heard and spoke the answer:

That which it is easier to die for than to live without.

"Frayin's Continuum brought into question," Lerius spoke aloud, addressing me, but with his eyes on Dweneth's, persuading her to rise where I could not. "Or else a dimension added. Curious!"

The City needed no telepathy to know the ships were out there; their sails were visible from nearly every vantage, and their import was clear. The infonets were humming even as I was brought before the Council, all windblown and salt-rimed as I was, to give my report. Visicomm would broadcast my every word throughout the Archipelago. Lingri Inept's unexpected appearance caused as great a buzz in the gallery as did the presence of People in our midst.

And the debate which had begun in the year of my birth continued apace.

"This is the Council governing my kind," I had whispered to Dweneth as we stepped from the skimmer into the long hall of the Citadel; WiseGovin's sonorous voice reached us even there.

Other wisdom had seen to it that the windowports of the skimmers bringing People into the City were carefully screened, hence Dweneth and Renna, as Thrasim before them, had seen as little of the city as possible between the seawall and the interior of an edifice no larger and, in some respects less impressive, than the Greathouse in Droghia. My two companions took in the stark lineaments of our architecture, the angular quietude of our faces, and said nothing.

"I must give a report on what I have learned in my stay among your People. You and Renna may observe from the gallery if you wish—" A glance at Jeijinn confirmed this; let us begin with honesty. "—or a place will be found for you to rest, if you are fatigued."

"We'll stay!" Dweneth declared at once, elbowing Renna, who squeaked some manner of assent; the huntress-queen, who could tame the wildest *guravek*, had been motion-sick in the skimmer. "I want to watch, to listen. But are you sure it is permitted? Why, even in Droghia a commoner can't—"

"Remember you your *OtherWhere*," I said, pleased that she seemed to have regained her equilibrium. I indicated the rows of Others on the Council floor and in the gallery above, from small children to elders and all between. Doubtless she had never seen so many children so still and so attentive, and the presence of so many of us briefly unsettled her again.

"OtherWhere!" She grimaced. "Oh, aye. We'll stay," she repeated determinedly, dragging Renna with her by the sleeve.

I moved downward toward the floor, aware that Lerius followed, wanting words with me where I wanted none with him. Jeijinn had already assumed the Chair, the signal for Govin to table the debate; that which had not been resolved in twenty years could yield to more pressing matters.

Lerius stood between me and the Chair.

" 'That which it is easier to die for than to live without.' Curious. Do you hold her soul-thread even now?"

He could have plucked that answer from my mind. Did he expect gratitude for his circumspection? He had not spoken to me since our encounter with Old Ones; why speak to me now?

I studied him. The years had wrought him as they did most Telepaths, etching him like relentless wind against the hardest stone; he was more wraith than ever. Rare was the Telepath who lived the full Other lifespan. Their minds so subsumed their bodies that they often abandoned food and sleep, and burned away more quickly. Lerius was but fifty years and seemed twice that, but the choice was his. No pity from me, nor gratitude. If he had not deigned to speak to me since I was an unkempt child, I would not satisfy him now.

Yet was his interest more in me than in Dweneth? I saw her eyes upon him from the gallery, and knew he was aware. Yet if I sought to touch the soul-thread here, he would know. I gathered myself to my full height, not nearly his, but dignified.

"What soul-threads I hold, WiseLerius, are my concern. As for Telepaths, one who is not might question why they presume to go where Monitor would fear to tread!"

Thus I warned him to mind his own mind and, all unprepared, I took my place before the Chair, and began my report.

*   *   *

293

" '. . . it is not given to us to judge those who have evolved differently from us,' " I concluded, the Eidetic Discipline serving me for once. " 'Possessed of our gifts, our longevity and freedom from disease, our certain knowledge of the All, might not the People have evolved as we did, if not more optimally?' "

The wisdom was not mine, but Mayel's of the Eight-Hundred-Year, one of the few early Monitors who survived to tell of what she had encountered beyond the sea. Mayel's wisdom had not altered, only the need for its practical application.

I had satisfactorily answered Jeijinn's questions, and Govin's and Rau's.

"—and will answer as many as the Council chooses to put to me. But an infinite number of questions will not alter the fact that there are for the first time in our midst, drawn here as much by a curiosity not unlike ours as by storm and circumstance, four People as diverse as can be conceived in so small a sample. Gentles, I ask that you place less emphasis upon what I, Lingri, may or may not have done in crossover than upon what these People have achieved.

"In hospice lies a ruler, as brilliant as he is flawed. With his damaged heart now made whole and his fears of death diminished, he may perhaps the better turn more to brilliance than to flaw, and learn governance from us."

Let Droghen curse me for so merciless a description; I would remind him of the hands that had tried to seduce anOther, and had blinded a musician.

"In our midst is one both mariner and scientist, by his People's lights . . ." Mild Thrasim, leaning on his elbows beside Rau in the gallery, was at once pleased and abashed as Rau translated for him. Had I been speaking so long, that Droghen's surgery was done and his lieutenant felt assured in leaving his side? ". . . who with no more than lodestone and simple astrolabe can traverse the World's seas and safely return home. Lacking Othersense, which of our WiseOnes would fare as well?

"I give you also an artist," I went on, seeking Renna in the gallery, squashed in between Dweneth and Thrasim to avoid entirely Other-presence, "known also as the huntress-queen. Skilled in survival her lifelong, leader among her People, she limns in paint and wood and tapestry such wonders as we once practiced, but have lost to geometric functionalism and atrophy—"

Renna leaned toward Thrasim, who passed Rau's translation on to her; I heard her squeak, incredulous.

"—our world is the more colorless for want of her like.

"Lastly, Gentles, I give you the one who trusts." My eyes sought Dweneth in the lesser light of the gallery. Trust a little further! I thought to her along the soul-thread. "She has suffered much, but has transcended fear and suffering to embrace that of her People, for while her hands heal their bodies, her voice and wit as often heal their souls.

"Many like them have I encountered in my travels," I concluded, mindful of how Redrec would complete my catalogue were he here. "Out of the depths of their poverty, disease, and pain, the People have produced these. While we, in our freedom from these things, produce a single work—a *debate,* which has not been resolved in twenty years!"

My irony was heavy-handed, Loriel-irony, meant to shock, unsettle and outrage. Against the murmur I found Mayel to quote once more:

" 'To remain a part implies involution, and condemns us to homogeneity and sameness. Is this compatible either with our curiosity or our Discipline? While we possess our own diversity—for we are as diverse as the number of us who live—still the reach outward beyond what we are remains compelling.'

"Gentles," I finished, knowing from WiseGovin's glower what price I would pay for my glibness, "the time for debate is past. The People are here. Those of you who know me know I am no mathematician. Consider what irony makes me instrumental in offering you a whole that is greater than the sum of its parts!"

"What Is This Thousand-Year?"
(being a Dialogue between WiseJeijinn
Matriarch and Droghen Droghiad
d'Droghia, He of the People: T-Y1020/
Code4181578514)

JEIJINN: *Put simply, it was the year we ceased to struggle against our own nature. The year we began the learning of the Inscape.*

DROGHEN: *S'truth, lady, you'll have to put that to me in words a simple man can understand.*

JEIJINN: *Thee are no simple man, Droghen-Gerim, but as you wish: Consider whether in your experience you have ever witnessed creatures of the same species fight to the death for no cause of survival, but for the sake of the struggle itself?*

DROGHEN: *Aye, I've watched it oft among battlecocks, that betimes get so drunk wi'bloodscent they can't be separated, not even by grown and armored men, but hurl and slash with claw and spur until naught remains but pulp and feathers. There's that.*

JEIJINN: *And never among your own?*

DROGHEN: *Well . . .*

JEIJINN: *As with Others, before the Thousand-Year.*

DROGHEN: *(skeptical) Your kind? Your peaceable, delicate-mannered, woman-run race? How long ago was this?*

JEIJINN: *Why think you it is called the Thousand-Year?*

DROGHEN: *I'd not believe it, not even i'you told me how 'twas done.*

JEIJINN: *When a species matures to the point where it must surrender what reprehensible characteristics it relishes most, that is what I speak of.*

DROGHEN: *For instance?*

JEIJINN: *Pride, jealousy, greed, hate-thy-neighbor, the right to do violence at the least offense. All negative passions be repressed, and violence becomes a fog upon the landscape, quickly dissipated.*

DROGHEN: All *passions?*

JEIJINN: *Indeed. The positive as well. For too overt expression of these is as fraught with danger as the negative. And with them music, poetry, art, whatever might incite our innate lust for argument, which was the only outlet we retained, by naming it debate.*

DROGHEN: *But what of lust itself? At the risk of being indelicate . . .*

JEIJINN: *(eyeing him) Less of a difficulty, it would seem, for us than for you.*

DROGHEN: *(to change the subject) And all that in a thousand years? Impossible!*

JEIJINN: *Truly? Then how explain what it is you see about you?*

DROGHEN: *At any rate, impossible for my kind. Not in a thousand years, or in an hundred thousand.*

JEIJINN: *Far sooner than that, Droghen Droghiad, if they are to interact with us.*

fourteen

"**B**ut where are your waste-pits? Your armaments and almshouses? Your gaols, your churches?" Droghen asked again and again. To each inquiry Jeijinn gave the same reply: "We have none."

"Impossible!"

Recovered sufficiently within a day of surgery to tool about in a motivchair whose mechanism, true Droghian, he mastered almost immediately, the butcher's son was beside himself with the realm he had "discovered." Yet, being Droghen, he could not but suspect that a land so fair did not, like his own, possess a shadow-side.

"Neither serviles nor facture-slaves? How does the work get done? Neither palsy, plague, nor leprosy, none deformed or crippled? You've hidden them away, to impress us simple folk. And while I truly am impressed, yet I don't believe."

To which WiseJeijinn would incline her head with something like bemusement and reply:

"Believe or not as you choose, Lord Droghen. But if, as you or any of your party observe our land and ways, you

298

encounter anything which contradicts what has been told you here, I trust you will inform me of it."

Droghen, for his part, could not seem to wrest his eyes from the face of the ElvenQueen.

"This is your *mother?*" he had whispered aside to me, unaware of the range of Other ears. "She is the ElvenQueen incarnate! Scarce old enough to be your sister, I'd believe, and a beauty beside. She must have been a child when you were born!"

That information I left for Jeijinn to supply. For Droghen, partly out of curiosity, but more to have reason to memorize that face, asked the Matriarch a plenitude of questions.

"How is't . . . so far . . . from Droghia . . . you speak . . . our language?" he had managed, emerging from the sleep-drug following surgery, realizing that only Droghian had been spoken in his presence. Jeijinn had explained in brief the tradition of using Monitors, including one Lingri, and how over the years People's languages had been mastered.

"The configuration of your ships' sails was recognized from previous Monitors' reports," she told him. "The populace of the Citadel was then scanned for those who knew your tongue, and of the ten who met you on the beach, nine were at least passing fluent. The tenth, being a Telepath, required no additional knowledge."

"What in . . . Hell's . . . tele-path?" Droghen had muttered, scowling, the drug affecting him more strongly than it would anOther.

"Not unlike a future-teller, milord," I supplied briefly, an adequate half-truth for the time and his condition.

". . . think of everything . . ." Droghen muttered, content, with that, to sleep.

His sailors were less than content.

Thrasim had sent the small boat back to the *Foremost,* where repairs continued apace, and under Rau's direction had the three ships brought to anchor closer in, that their crews might come ashore and sample OtherWhere. But beyond the work crew needed to cut and dress the tree for the *Venture*'s mast, they refused.

Learning that we had neither pothouses nor gambling pits nor brothels to serve their immediate needs and, worse, that we were a nation seemingly dominated by women, and those of a kind they had not envisioned in their worst nightmares—educated, aloof, self-sufficient, strong—the sailors dared not venture from the strand. Most returned to the ships, except the boat crew needed to ferry Thrasim back and forth—the brave lieutenant did not yet trust a skimmer over water—who camped sullenly at the landing, subsisting on their own poor rations when they learned we ate no meat, grumbling and pining for home. None but Thrasim seemed to grasp the freedom of our way or our visitors' freedom to share it with us, and even Thrasim had his doubts.

"No curfew? No sentry nor picket 'round your Greathouse nor anywhere?" Thrasim's incredulity was an echo of his lord's. "Not even locks upon your house-doors or your treasuries? Best I keep my lads outside the city or they'd rob and rape ye blind!"

"A less simple matter than you might suppose, Thrasim-one," I'd heard Rau say, leading him out of the gallery.

Once I'd completed my report, I intended to have a word with Rau, regarding a castle-keep, some peasants, and a wheel, but my teacher was gone by the time the Council was through with me, off with Thrasim in search of a mast-tree, and on a skimmer tour of the Agris and Industrials, the better to help the lieutenant convince his lord that there were no lands here save our islands.

Thrasim had stood by Droghen throughout surgery, his hand upon his pistol-butt, though he relinquished the weapon thereafter when persuaded we had none. He had witnessed the carnage of field hospitals in time of war, and could scarce believe his lord's heart so readily repaired "with but a bit of snow and a pair of ruby lights!" as he described the cryolaser procedure which mended Droghen's damaged arteries with less loss of blood than People might require to lance a boil.

"Any race that can accomplish that," Thrasim marveled, seeing Droghen sit up and take food that same day, "has my full trust and 'legiance."

Rau had Thrasim in his care, and the hospice would manage Droghen. Jeijinn was to relieve me of both Renna and Dweneth. It happened rather quickly.

It was standard procedure for the returning Monitor to report herself to the hospice, for crossover took its toll on even the strongest of us. What surprised me was the immediacy of the summons, hand-delivered in the corridors outside the Council, when I'd already been on my way.

"A moment . . ." I began, when it was clear the messenger intended to escort me—this too was strange—for I felt compelled to speak with Dweneth first.

But whatever I might have said died in my throat when she shied anew at the sight of me, and Renna stood suddenly between us. Having trailed after Dweneth thus far like some disconsolate lap-pet, she had found her huntress's courage.

"How soon before you have us killed?" She pulled at my sleeve, snarling, unaware how voices carried here.

"Why should we wish to do that?" I wondered, the messenger in one corner of my eye, Dweneth out of reach.

"It's certain ye can't give us the run of your magical kingdom and then leave us go home to tell it!" The huntress's teeth were bared, and more pointed than I remembered. "Ye'll either lock us away in the dungeons ye claim ye haven't got, or kill us."

Others passed, their eyes averted at this breach of privacy in so public a place.

"Likely kill us, for it's cheaper!" Renna had her hand at her skinning knife, in case. She had seen what magic Lerius had performed upon the beach, and would hold her own against this devil's race, or die trying. Renna was reckless, but no coward.

"I only want to know is it quick. Not for me, mind—I grew up on pain; it's natural for me—but Dwen's suffered enough. You feigned to be her friend once. If this Jeijinn's truly your mother and queen of this place, you can get us an easy death!"

Still Dweneth said nothing. I touched the soul-thread with my mind, to set it resonating. Had she set Renna to test me? I could learn nothing.

"Other has not killed since the Thousand-Year," I began, "nor is Jeijinn queen . . ."

Renna would not hear this, but stuck her fingers in her ears, spitting Lamorak curses at me and howling as her tribesmen did to stampede 'vek herds over a cliff for hunting, unseemly in this place. It brought Jeijinn from the privy chambers.

Her very presence, soft-stepped, imperious ElvenQueen, reduced Renna to a whimper, though her irony was for me.

"What trust the Monitor evokes from those in her care!" Her hand was on Renna's shoulder, comforting. Where had she learned that gesture? "Is it customary, where you've come from, to keep a hospice messenger waiting?"

"Lie still!" the healer chided me, her eyes upon the scanner readout above my head, where I could see it also, though not appreciate its nuances as she did. "The one in question is an artist?"

Everyone on One Greater, it seemed, had heard of Renna's tantrum. I nodded and the scanners twittered nervously.

"Xenopsych is of the opinion that providing her with materials with which to practice her craft might ameliorate her disorientation and soften her present mood," the healer suggested. "Naturally, Xenopsych will want to examine her as well, if she will permit it. Do you concur?"

"It is out of my hands now, healer," I replied. Renna was now Jeijinn's problem. Between tests and scans and examinations, I too had been reading the infonets.

"It is said she was seen killing birds in WiseJeijinn's garden!" The healer's voice indicated she was scandalized, though her mask showed nothing. "Culture shock is to be expected, but hardly overt violence!"

"She was probably hungry," I offered. "It is the way where she comes from."

"She was quoted as saying she 'grew up on pain.' " The healer watched me for once instead of her scanners. "What does this mean precisely?"

"Renna has hardly confided such intimacies to me. However the Lamorak are not noted for gentleness in rearing offspring. It is a matter for Xenopsych, not me."

Let the healer raise her eyebrows at my overt impatience. No matter. I desperately wanted free of healers and their machinery, that I might enter my report into the files and have done. I had been away for more than a year; there were matters wanting my attention. Too, I must learn what disposition had been made of Dweneth, and must speak with her—soon, before Telepaths and xenopsychologists began their meddling.

"Xenopsych will look into all these matters," the healer assured me, with no intention of letting me go. "Lie still!"

She was silent for longer than I thought she should be, intent upon her scanners. I thought I recognized some borderline readouts, but nothing that would threaten life.

"Dietary!" the healer announced, diverting my attention from the scanners. "Malnutritional index at Y-level. Vitamin deficiencies in the P-through-L range. Marginal chronic fatigue indicators affecting metabolic and transcoordinal functions. And your gums were bleeding! Reprehensible!"

Dweneth would be enthralled by this! I thought, watching an entire field of data scroll through the diagnostics within seconds. Or would she? Dweneth had followed Jeijinn like a child, without so much as a backward glance for me, and while all eyes in the city seemed to be on Renna, there was no report on Dweneth. She remained closeted in Jeijinn's visitors' suite, neither reaching out, nor allowing Others to reach in.

The healer began shutting off various neural contacts, indicating that this phase of the examination was nearly complete. I tried to lie as still as possible; even so something set up an irritating chatter in the machinery.

"Your immune system appears relatively intact." The healer's drone was almost as irritating as her machinery. "No noticeable impact of People's viral strains, and the allergen response seems to have had no lasting impact. That is the good news. However, the dietary impact will require substantial compensatory treatment, and there is evidence of anemia. How you could have let your condition deteriorate so, over so brief a period . . ."

This healer was young, not much my elder. Had she never examined a returned Monitor before? If she had seen a fraction of what I had these many months! In not seeing it, of course, she would misconstrue the most basic essence of the People, as would most of my kind. I made a note for my report. The healer was still nattering.

". . . kindly tell me: what have you been eating?"

"Rather ask what I have not been eating," I replied wearily, itemizing some of the dietary dilemmas I had confronted, including fifty days at sea subsisting largely on hardtack and brined cabbage. My attempt to escape the mediscanner at this juncture was short-lived; the healer's expression persuaded me to curtail the attempt. I sighed, the readouts twittered. "Healer, the standard diet among all but the wealthiest People results in any number of deficiency diseases, notably scurvy, rickets, beriberi. As to the wealthy, their worst foe is food poisoning, for while they have foodstuffs in quantity, they lack the means to preserve them, hence—"

"There is one thing further you should know." She adjusted the last of the neural scanners, hesitated. "Certain readings indicate a discrepancy in age differential incompatible with actual chronology. You were born on 7 TasEth T-Y1000, were you not?"

"—in the sixth hour, at the thirty-fourth minute, plus or minus a second or two." I had at last been questioned out of patience and swung the diag table upright, stepping off it adamantly. Scanners quawked; I ignored them. Let the healer see to them.

"And how long, precisely, were you in crossover?" She ignored the racket as well, relentless.

"One year, two months, and an odd number of days." I began to dress. The healer waited. "As you wish: seventeen days. Sixteen point three-five, if you count the partial day upon the beach. I can calculate the minutes and seconds, if you like, though I am uncertain at what precise moment my foot touched Other soil, much less whether my crossover officially ended at that moment or when WiseJeijinn chose to acknowledge my presence there—"

"Unnecessary," the healer said tersely. "Leave the travel cloak. You are to remain here. Curious!"

The scanners, lacking anything to scan, finally shut down of themselves. I followed the healer, quickstep, to her cubicle in Consults.

"Remain here? For what purpose?" I must have sounded breathless. "Are not your examinations concluded? And what is so 'curious' that you cannot share it with its subject?"

"Its subject," the healer motioned me to sit, "has been too long among the People and has grown irreverent! Its subject has been too long among the People in all respects."

"Healer, if you will . . ." She had me concerned now. Dweneth, the soul-thread—these thoughts came to me unbidden. There was something ominous here that had not only to do with my health.

I saw the healer gather herself, leaning toward me within the limits of her Discipline, an indication of the gravity of her concern.

"Scan indicates a discrepancy of 1.923 days for every day you have spent in crossover. Succinctly, you are aging almost twice as fast as you should be, and there is neither indication of causative factor nor of whether this can be halted or reversed."

"Perhaps it is a function of the malnutrition?" I asked lightly, refusing to accept the import of her words. Had I just heard my lifespan reduced by half? "Surely I am not the only Monitor to experience this?"

"This particular test is new. However, longterm observation of previous Monitors has indicated no such conspicuous reduction in lifespan."

"Curious indeed," I acknowledged, but somehow it seemed not to affect me. If crossover had taught me nothing else, it had at least emphasized the fragility of this temporal existence. "But among the People, forty is considered a good age. Among them I should live to be an ancient, even at half a lifespan."

"I think you do not fully appreciate the ramifications—" The commscreen at the healer's elbow signaled; she put it on Hold. "There must be further tests."

"Is that the only reason I am being kept here?"

"It is my reason." She read the message, then turned to me. "For the rest you must inquire of the Council and the Telepathy."

"The Telepathy? What has the Telepathy to do with—"

"Message for you." She deactivated the comm. "Jeijinn Matriarch awaits you in the visitors' wing."

"You have but a single duty, and that is to file your report." Trust Jeijinn not to clutter her visitations with inquiries about my health or what the healers may have found. "Surely you can do that from the facilities here?"

"My obligation to Others," I presumed to correct her. "What of my People?"

The use of the proprietary gave Jeijinn a moment's pause.

"They are being cared for. Droghen has been released from hospice; he is with Rau and Thrasim on tour. Geography, largely, as well as science and technology, as much as these can understand."

"And Dweneth and Renna?"

"This Renna . . . " Jeijinn went so far as to sit down, something she rarely did in my presence lest it indicate weakness. Her characteristic aloofness seemed somewhat frayed at the edges. "Her behavior is most unmanageable. One does not expect Discipline, but some veneer of decorum, at least. It is all I can do to exert my presence in restraining her."

The image that conjured was a most intriguing one. There was little my mother could not manage with mere presence. I wondered if it was only the birds.

"What has she done exactly?"

Jeijinn sighed.

"Efforts were made to show her the simplest functions—how to work the food-synther, the disposers, the baths. She responded by shouting at these devices as if they were animate, in a language whose words I did not know but whose tone and import were self-evident."

My mother paused, as if uncertain how to go on. I had never known WiseJeijinn to be at a loss for words before.

"She will eat nothing we provide, not even freshly prepared where she can see it. She defecates in the garden. She cannot pass through any door without kicking it, accusing it of 'harboring demons' in that it opens of itself. Finally, she refuses to harbor under any Other roof. She has taken my best coverlets out over the casements to construct a manner of Survival encampment out of branches in the garden, and has cut down the *hreeda* for kindling. And what the 'nets report about the birds is true. Lizards as well. She is remarkably swift with that knife, though she laments the loss of her 'shortbow,' whatever that might be."

"It was washed overboard in the storm," I replied vaguely. This was so very trivial; Renna was simply being Renna. "Let Dweneth speak to her, or give her into Droghen's care, now he's well." I timed my next question carefully. How much did Jeijinn know of Lerius's intervention on the beach? "Mother? What of Dweneth?"

"There is to be a plenary Council session day after next." I might not have spoken. "You will attend."

"For what purpose?" I would play the game, for the moment.

"One assumes your report will be completed by then?"

"Barring further healers' intervention, it should be."

"Then Council will have a new assignment for you, relative to those you have brought among us."

It was in my thoughts to suggest that I had hardly brought the ships here singlehanded. Then again, had I not? I, too, could sigh.

"Give to the Council that I shall attend. Why am I being kept a prisoner here?"

Jeijinn raised her eyebrows. "You who have been among People dare speak of 'prisons'? This is a matter you must take up with the Council—"

"—and the Telepathy," I finished for her. "And as you are of the Council, and Matriarch at present, I ask you: why?"

"I am but one voice in Council, Lingri-*la*. Do not presume upon my authority or my patience." Jeijinn was on her feet. "There are matters I am not free to tell you, but the Council shall."

"When I report to the plenary session and not before. Now answer what you can, Jeijinn Matriarch: what of Dweneth?"

When had I learned imperiousness? I had certainly had role-model in Jeijinn, though even her mask could not hide that I surprised her. She did not answer.

"The 'nets mention her not at all, Mother, beyond that she is in your care. I tried the commlink to your visitors' suite; you've cut it off—"

"Only because it frightened her!" Jeijinn answered sharply. "As much of what we take for granted does. You above all should understand the trauma 'your' People are experiencing, and give her time—"

"She is accustomed to me, Mother. She will not fear me; I can explain. And there is something further you should know—"

Jeijinn raised a hand to silence me.

"Does it occur to you—" Her voice was deadly cold. "—that what she is 'accustomed to' does not exist? For how long has she seen you dressed in her manner of garb, mimicking her ways and manners, speaking her tongues, and thought you one of her own? Does it not occur to you that what she now perceives you to be, in context, is more alien than any of us?"

It had not occurred to me at all. "Has she said as much to you?"

"She says nothing to me." It seemed to trouble Jeijinn. "She eats what is brought her, sleeps where she is bidden, and is most gracious in her gratitude. For the rest, she merely sits

308

and stares out over the garden where this Renna makes her camp, and will not even speak to her, as the latter refuses to come indoors and Dweneth will not go out . . ." I dared not speak. Rare was it that my mother spoke as mother, not as Matriarch. Too, it was short-lived; I could see it in her eyes. "Tell me nothing further. I know what else you wish me to know, as does the whole of OtherWhere. Lerius—"

"Lerius!" I repeated bitterly. "That explains it! The Council and the Telepathy'! Have Others lost their privacy since I've been on crossover, or does that Discipline no longer apply to Lingri? All the Archipelago knows my soul-thread joins a People's. Only Dweneth, who most deserves to know, cannot be told."

"How would you tell her?" Jeijinn wondered. "The encounter with Lerius almost frightened her to death. He has told me—"

"Speak not to me of Lerius!" My voice was sharper than Jeijinn's ever was. "Meddling, impertinent—as all his kind, breaking Disciplines in the name of Telepathy, which we humbler nonTelepaths cannot presume to understand. Let me go to her, explain to her. Any explanation is preferable to fear. By what right—"

"Fear!" Jeijinn echoed me. "What know you, Lingri-*la*, of fear? Indeed, your Dweneth fears, but so do we all!"

This puzzled me.

"But what is everyone so afraid of?" I asked, and then it came to me. "I see. If the soul-link is possible with People as well as Other, then as Lerius suggests it either refutes Othercontinuum or adds an untoward dimension, in which case we can no longer hold ourselves superior to People—and we do!" I said, to curtail Jeijinn's objection. "Despite Mayel's wisdom of the Eight-Hundred-Year, it comforts us to think they will never achieve what we have, even given our advantages. Having no Other weapons but those of mind, and learning that People can access our minds as well, we become helpless before them."

"Simplistic, but essentially correct," Jeijinn acknowledged. "Hence the Telepathy's concern. While one soul-thread is not a danger in itself—and I find this Dweneth mild and altruistic in her nature, hence no threat—but the possible ramifications, should all People prove thus accessible . . ." She seemed lost in that thought for a moment, then gathered herself. "You and she must be kept apart for the present, before you can confirm the link, until the Telepathy determine how and why it was joined to begin with."

"And once again I become the subject of experimentation!" I refused this with a gesture. "Oh, no! I am no malleable child, and it is not Loriel and her scientists who wish to poke and probe me this time—no! This is my privacy, and I refuse!"

"It is also your species' safety!" Not even in her most fervid speech before the Council had I seen Jeijinn so intense. "It is thought this soul-thread might presage some unexpected dimension in future interactions with People—to whom, it seems now with this-Droghen's arrival"— at least, I thought, she wasn't blaming me —"we are irrevocably committed. I should not be telling you any of this."

"I do appreciate that, Mother." Still, I could not resist a twist of irony. "Interesting, this fear, from the Matriarch who once fostered the cause of Espions."

"Once—no longer!" Jeijinn said testily, her fervor spent. "Even before you gave report of Naven, I had altered my opinion. Enough. You will do as you are instructed. There is more at stake here than you know."

Or you, Mother, I thought. But she seemed to have dismissed me from her thought. I watched her do something else I had never seen before. She began to pace.

"Prodigious, from any perspective! Even Govin succumbs to it! He takes it upon himself to watch over those on the beach. He stands upon the seawall, projecting disapprobation as only Govin can, and they have responded, as I understand People will. To wit, they have pelted him with spoiled fruit and called him names."

Would that I were in the World at large; I might have laughed. I could not, of course, do so within the confines of my city and my Discipline, but I found the image no less pleasurable.

"Govin should mind his own business," I suggested. "My condolences, WiseJeijinn, for the burden thrust upon you. Perhaps if one were to put Govin and Renna in the same room and close the door . . ."

"Trivia!" Jeijinn's voice and gesture emphasized. "Oh—and to show that life endures no matter what, also a trivial matter, though from no trivial person: WiseFrayin wishes to speak with you, in the matter of her son. Chior wishes to offer a bonding-suit."

I could still be surprised by some things, then.

"Chior, a bonding-suit—trivial? Say rather, Mother, this too is prodigious. Why Chior, why me, and why so soon? We each have fifteen years or more before . . ."

Or did I, I wondered, in light of what the healer had just told me?

"Mother, in all seriousness, how am I expected to respond? I had hoped I would be spared this until biology made it necessary."

"This is not up to me!" Jeijinn said tautly, preparing to take her leave. The fate of worlds might rest on her shoulders, yet her offspring beset her with trivia. "I only insist you do not disgrace your family before Frayin's house. Make what decision you will, but conduct yourself properly in this much, at least. Have you not been the instrument of sufficient havoc already?"

Speak to Frayin? Indeed I would, but not now.

"Yield twenty megaunits ascribed LingriMonitor . . ." the hospice's borrowed commlink droned at me as soon as I'd logged on. "Encoding follows . . ."

"Affirmative," I answered automatically, but then: "Twenty units? Why so much?"

"Unspecified," was all the computer would tell me. Like Renna, I was strongly tempted to kick it. What bureaucratic dictate had deemed my lowly report worth so much microstor?

Or was I being "softened up," as Dweneth might say, for something else?

The actual composition of my report took little time. I who usually exulted in the flow of words from mind to fingertips found the process somehow flat and savorless. How many times did Dweneth's name appear in my report, how often did my mind return to Dweneth? What was she doing, what thinking, alone in her room in Jeijinn's house? To what extent would I permit the Council and the Telepathy to dictate to our lives? Their probes and inquiries would only serve to confuse and frighten Dweneth. How long would I permit them to keep us apart?

I kept a channel open to the infonets, scrolling them down one side of my screen as I completed my report. The 'nets reported an influx of Monitors from everywhere on the Archipelago to One Greater. Every Monitor not currently on crossover was required to attend the plenary session, as I was. Curious indeed.

Until then, of course, the Councillors could pursue their usual debate. I followed WiseGovin's latest discourse, while the cursor blinked maddeningly where I'd left off my report:

. . . music, this Lingri-one has offered, as a proof of their great intellect. But do not bRi *make music—some of it more complex than our research can begin to fathom? This does not prove their sapience. The question then becomes: have these People souls?*

Had he taken the time, I wondered, to wipe the fruit pulp from his face and clothing or, being Govin, had he worn it with him to the Council as evidence?

" 'And having made the crossover, she can never return the same . . .' " came a voice behind me.

"Grandmother!"

Accustomed to the heavy tread of People, I had not heard her, and seeing her for the first without the familiar cascade of silver hair was a shock, not easily masked. Was it only the seeming fragility of the long skull beneath the close-cropped hair, the naked openness of that taut-fleshed face, the ears grown longer fluted with increasing age, that made her seem so old? She was past one hundred ninety years. My conscious mind accepted that. Yet I had seen People one-quarter that age reduced to toothless decrepitude. Loriel was right; I would never be the same.

"You seem not yourself," my grandmother suggested.

"Perhaps I wish I weren't. Chior, of all Others, wishes to bond with me."

"Nonsense!" Loriel dismissed it. "He is in no wise your compatible. And does the suddenness of the suit not strike you as odd?"

I considered. Chior had been my childhood nemesis, besting me in *bRi*-speaking, in academics, in Survival training—besting me, with a kind of calculated perversity, in a society which never fostered competition for its own sake. What new perversity would have him choose as bondmate one so obviously his inferior?

He would have had to research carefully to be certain our mating cycles were compatible. He would have had to file his suit while I was still half a world away, with no guarantee of return. Unless he had done so even as Droghen's men were rowing us ashore.

"Of course it's odd, Grandmother. But how can I explain why? Everything strikes me as odd. I no longer know what is truth and what perspective."

"And thus begins wisdom." Loriel's irony was undiminished. She fingered my hair, as close-cropped as her own. "Is this some Worldly fashion, or have we set a trend, you and I? What stories you must have to tell! Circus and music and art! Storysinging and tumbling as well—whatever this latter might be. You must show me."

She had not been present in the gallery when I went before the Council, had been away at work on Undersea. Or had she? Undersea would no longer be needed as a place of concealment from a People already among us. Was it to be abandoned altogether?

313

"So the Council deems," Loriel answered my unasked question. " 'Expenditures outweigh utility,' I am told. Further, if, as it seems, it is decided that we are to share everything we know with People, I should have to spend my remaining days underwater, showing them how it's done. Grow gills and live on seaweed—not a pleasant prospect! But oh, how Tagal would have gloated! You did not know my old shadow-side has made a crossover of his own?"

I did not. He had certainly been of an age. Now I should never know if he and Loriel had once been lovers. Or had I just been told?

"I grieve with you, Loriel-*al*. And for you as well.

"As to Undersea," I continued, when the silence had gone on too long, "truth, Grandmother, if I could in conscience have diverted Droghen's ships elsewhere—"

"For the sake of Loriel's Folly? Which is what it has been second-named. Ah, Lingri! Worry not. Doubtless I shall find some new controversy with which to fill the time remaining to me. But consider: while you may have put me out of work, have you not also excessed every Monitor as well?"

So I had, though it had not occurred to me until now. Every Other Monitor was being recalled because of me. The burden was a heavy one.

"I heard what happened on the landing," Loriel said. "Lerius were perhaps better advised to keep his thoughts to himself. Telepaths! Did he do much harm?"

It was more than Discipline could answer. I could drop my mask, I could be bitter: this was Loriel.

"Scientific method, so my grandmother taught me, dictates that conclusions cannot be drawn in an absence of facts. I am merely the control in an experiment of Others' making. Being blind, I have no facts. Except perhaps the random element of a bonding-suit from a most unlikely source! Properly the soul-thread lies in the realm of Telepaths and sometimes bondmates, but once again Lingri breaks the rules. Did Lerius do much damage? I can only draw conclusions from the degree of effort that is being made to confine me, and to divert me. Confine me the Telepathy may do, but divert me with the likes of Chior? Not likely!"

Forgotten as we talked, the commscreen beeped at me. It too had its Disciplines, which dictated that a blinking cursor, too long unattended, must voice protest. The sound mocked my seeming dignity. I logged off, impatiently, and once again wanted to kick the thing. All this time Loriel said nothing, letting her silence speak for her. Did I see mourning in her eyes? Not for Tagal—that was past—but for me? I struggled for control.

"I am here, Dweneth is there, the soul-thread exists but can neither be explained to her nor answered to until tests and more tests determine if this single gentle being comprise a threat to what is Other! Ask Lerius how much harm he has done; I am only one-half of his victim!"

Loriel closed her eyes and sighed. When she opened them again, her mask was impenetrable even to me. She was Loriel, and practical.

"What do you want me to do?"

It was exactly what I had hoped she would ask.

"Dweneth must have the soul-thread explained to her, and not by Telepaths. There is also much psychic damage from her past . . ."

"The healers' domain," Loriel nodded. "I will see to it. And what else?"

"Someone she can trust, to talk to her where I cannot . . . "

"Someone elder, and possessed of great wisdom and sub-tlety," Loriel added ironically, on her way out the door. "I will see to it."

Scans and more scans, tests and more tests, until it seemed I had not organ nor tissue remaining inviolate from the healers' samplers, probes and scanners. At least I garnered one piece of useful information.

"As you describe the condition of the eyes and the manner in which the injury was inflicted upon them, we could not restore true sight. However, an experimental microprosthesis might serve to yield electroimpulse feedback which the brain could interpret as visual imaging. Other brain could, at any rate." The healer motioned me away from the scanners. "I know not of these People."

"Certainly your examination of Droghen has yielded sufficient data regarding optic similarities," I suggested.

"If cultural exchange is in fact to be initiated, as the 'nets suggest, perhaps you could bring this musician to us. We will then do what we can."

Cultural exchange, so soon? Would it be possible? The thought elated me, despite the morrow's Council session, where I must learn what Cirque hoops I must leap to prove my Discipline as anOther. Meanwhile tests and more tests, and no apparent way to stop me from aging at twice the normal rate.

With nightfall, six of Droghen's sailors—restless, homesick, and beset with who knew what fears as those they'd left aboard ship reported sightings of skimmers and stranger things from the mainmast watch—crept out of their beach encampment into the city, bent on mayhem. Several dwellings were broken into, some shops looted, a child's hand slammed in a too-quickly opened door. Jeijinn sent for Droghen and Thrasim at once. Rau was there as well.

"All foreseeable precautions were taken, WiseJeijinn," Rau explained. "Ordinarily the men would have remained where they were bidden, but the strain apparently proved too great. This could not have been readily anticipated."

"Nevertheless, it has happened." Jeijinn was mystified. "Is this characteristic of your kind, Lord Droghen? Do they act this way against their own? And, pray, what 'precautions,' precisely, were taken?"

In fairness, she was less imperious than she might have been. Woken from the deepest sleep, her silver-streaked hair tumbled about her shoulders, she seemed to her visitors more puzzled than imposing. Yet Thrasim's distress was palpable; he blamed himself.

"I thought the ring would hold them! It always has afore!" He knelt pale and sweating before his lord and the Elven-Queen, expecting no mercy from Droghen, but at least comprehension. "I should never have left them unattended, lord, even at your orders! It must be that they broke the ring!"

Droghen knew what he meant at once, but Jeijinn had to have it explained.

"I told them, lady, that the walls of your city were a sacred ring, ensorcelled by your ancient gods, and those who crossed it without leave were courting certain death." Thrasim wrung his hands. "Methought 'twould hold them; it always has afore. They believe such things where they come from, as I once did. We are so backward, after all, compared to ye, and it is all my fault!"

"Or your lord's, for taking you on the grand tour and forgetting!" Droghen grumbled magnanimously. He was more embarrassed than distressed.

"It was our error as much as yours, Thrasim-one," Jeijinn said, not ungently, raising him to his feet. The poor man's distress taxed her dearly. "We secure no possessions with bolts or locks, as your men quickly observed. Nor have we reason to expect violence from each Other. Truth, we should have anticipated these possibilities with regard to—your kind and your ways. As to how I am to reconcile this with those among the Matriarchs who do not want you here to begin with . . ."

Jeijinn gathered herself.

"The incident amounts to some minor thievery and a rape attempt, though as your men have learned, 'even our women' can defend, and my own healer will see to your man's dislocated shoulder. His was the most severe injury, and there was no more serious consequence. But something of value might have been damaged, and a child was hurt. There can be no repetition of these acts."

"There will not be," Droghen promised. "Thrasim?"

"Milord?" Droghen's word was law. "I myself shall wield the cat. What number each?"

"Twenty each, save for the would-be rapist." The Droghiad

considered his audience, and how the women in his part of the world loathed this particular breed of miscreant. "For him, fifty."

"Fifty of what?" Jeijinn demanded; the concept of flogging was not written in her philosophy. Once more it fell to Thrasim to explain. "Absolutely not! I forbid it!"

"Wise Jeijinn—" This from Rau. "—their ships, their law."

"But our city. I forbid!"

"Have you the right?"

She had not and she knew it. Reluctantly she gave Thrasim leave to go; he as reluctantly gathered himself to leave. The task ahead was a most abhorrent one.

"And for me, milord? What number?" Droghen made to protest, but Thrasim insisted. "It was as much my doing."

Droghen shook his head vehemently, his usual roar a whisper.

"Only as many as you would as well give me, brave Thrasim—one!"

I, of course, knew none of this; Rau was to tell me later. Lingri Inept, having taken a somewhat precipitous and unsanctioned leave from hospice, passed a grim-visaged Thrasim on the path from Jeijinn's house and, respecting his privacy, did not speak. The house itself was oddly full of light.

"What are you doing here?!"

What strange tableau yielded my mother and Rau together at the casement looking over the city's roofs to the sea, perhaps the very casement Jeijinn had watched through yestermorning when the 'nets announced the sighting of three sails. Beyond the two disparate forms—Jeijinn so tall and thin, my teacher quite the opposite—I could see the ships themselves, all unnaturally aglow with the watch lanterns, and I knew what this signified. Every People's ship carried its cats and triangles, though Droghen seldom needed them on his tight-run voyages. What prompted that need now?

My own purpose momentarily diverted, I watched transfixed as Jeijinn's body shuddered with each blow she could neither see nor hear from this distance, but could feel within from those suffering those blows aboard the ships. My mother, that most rare Other of all, an Empath? I had not known. It explained a great many things.

"Jeijinn Matriarch," I said at last, insistent even in the face of her suffering. "I have come to speak with Dweneth."

Could Lingri be implacable? So Rau would describe me. I only knew I would not leave until my will was granted. More than my life depended on it. Jeijinn seemed not to hear me.

"Such pain!" she cried, shuddering anew. "Why must they— *deliberately*—inflict such pain upon their own? Had I known it would mean this . . ."

Rau glanced at me to keep my silence, but I was implacable.

"Somewhat different when experienced in flesh than when heard or read from Monitors' reports," I suggested dryly. "What did you think we witnessed, Mother, who make crossover? I can tell you of such things—or Rau can, having experienced them firsthand . . ."

Let him think on that! I thought, relishing the surprise that flickered through his mask.

"Mother. I will speak with Dweneth. Now."

She shuddered again. I could almost pity her.

"You cannot. I cannot let you," she answered weakly, still watching out that window. "Neither you nor I have the right to go against the dictate of the Council and the Telepathy—"

"I have the right to avert a poor attempt to bond me before a prior link can be solidified!" I declared. "I claim the right of the soul-thread and all its untoward predecessors—though none so untoward, I grant you, as that between Other and People. I will act upon that right, Jeijinn Matriarch, the Council and the Telepathy notwithstanding."

She recovered herself then, stood between me and the privacy door of the visitors' suite. There was blood on her wrist, from a blow struck on the ships.

"Have you thought of what you do?"

"Mother, I have thought of nothing else."

319

She made a last negative gesture, staggered beneath the pain of a fresh blow. Rau came to her and took her by the shoulders, to support her.

"Let me fetch the healer," he began; Jeijinn dismissed him as well.

"I scarcely know you, Lingri-*la!*" she whispered painfully.

"Nor I you, Jeijinn-*al*." I touched the welling blood to wipe it away, found the new-formed welt beneath. My cold, aloof mother, an Empath. The World was askew.

"Go!" Jeijinn charged me; she would not be seen to be weak. "But know what it is you do!"

"I accept the responsibility."

I had not felt this detached from my own being since the day Lerius and I had spoken for the Old Ones. The door to the visitors' suite seemed to open of itself.

"Dweneth . . ." I began.

———

"Bonding Customs"
(from *Histories,* as compiled by Lingri Monitor and Others and presented to Droghen-Gerim, He of the People: T-Y-1021/Code2151449147)

Two inescapable factors govern Otherbonding, differentiating it from any of the People's many and diverse customs. Primary is the innate mating "cycle," which results in the occurrence of the mating drive once every seven to ten years. This inborn cycle governs all major bodily functions, and when it first occurs can neither be altered nor repressed; it must be answered, or the result is death.

Put simply: bondmates must be chosen from among those whose cycle is compatible with one's own. In ancient times, childhood betrothal was the norm but, with the advent of compuscan, compatibility factors can be more readily determined, and this custom has fallen out of use. Factors such as similarity of profession and compatibility of temperament are also included in compuscan, though these are not always deemed essential to the choice of bondmate. The primary concern is to match cycle with cycle, so that life may be preserved and, if so desired, procreated.

While Others may appear physically mature at about the same biological age as People do, the cycle remains dormant usually until the thirty-sixth year of life, and thereafter recurs only on the innate schedule. Fertility occurs only at the midpoint of a given cycle, though frequency of mating intercourse in the time between cycles is a matter of personal choice, and is protected under the privacies.

As to the matter of mind-links and soul-threads, these are at once less predictable and less readily controlled than mating cycles. The desired choice is the mind-link as established between bondmates. The Telepathy, of course, has its own parameters for multiple interlink, but among nonTelepaths mind-links are discouraged before the age of bonding. Thereafter, whether a link be established with the bondmate or not, one is free to choose links elsewhere, though many never seek a link, with its added dimensions and responsibilities, at all.

The second factor governing Otherbonding is that of ethnological and geographical necessity. Every Other is bound to replicate herself in a single offspring—no more, no less. Ethnological, because the species must continue; geographical owing to the absolute boundaries of the Archipelago which, until now, has been the only place upon this World where Other might safely live. Recent historical events may alter these factors, but this is unknown at present.

Hence, customarily, a first-bonded pair usually produces two offspring in two separate cycles, though there are exceptions [see below]. Consequently, Other population has not varied more than .019% since the Thousand-Year. Having produced their two requisite offspring, a typical bonded pair will biorepress fertilty for every cycle thereafter. Normal sterility usually ensues shortly after the hundredth year.

321

Those who for their own reasons cannot or will not procreate may "foster" the child of a bonded pair who wish to produce a third or even a fourth offspring. (Cross Reference: Law) Any bonding which is broken before the requisite two offspring are born obligates one party of that bond to replicate in a later bonding, or foster the child of anOther. Two further exceptions include the Telepathy, and the Changers.

Because of the need to preserve the Telepathic strain, Telepaths almost exclusively bond with Telepaths, or with nonTelepaths who carry the Telepath gene. As to Changers, much of their custom is bound by the privacies, though it may be said here that most Changers undergo the Change after they have replicated, knowing that the Change will render them sterile thereafter.

Once a given mating cycle has been fulfilled, the bond may endure for life or be broken by mutual agreement at any time, though most bondpairs with dependent offspring choose to remain together until those offspring are autonomous. Any number of rebonding permutations is feasible during a two-hundred year lifespan, though it is fact that the majority of Others bond for life.

fifteen

The lights in the visitors' suite burned dimly; my voice brought them up full. Did no one in the city sleep this night? Somehow I knew I would find her sitting tentatively in the plainest chair—set in the center of the room, as if that were the safest place—watchful. Even Renna had abandoned her to cleave to Droghen; the remnants of her sullen campfire, Jeijinn's smoke-ruined coverlets, the ruin of the shrubbery, were evident in the garden. Dweneth stood and turned her back to me.

"Dweneth . . ." I said again, and not in Othervoice. Her own voice was smaller than it had been on the beach.

"Can you also do what—he—does?"

"Lerius," I clarified. How difficult he had made this!

"Lerius, then. *Can* you?"

"If you are asking am I Telepath—no. It is thought that at one time all Others were Telepaths, that we could communicate our thoughts merely by touching each Other's cranial nerves. Whether this ability was lost in the need to spare our minds the depredations of the wars before the Thousand-Year, or through genetic selection in a time-before-time—"

"Do you realize that whenever you don't want to answer me you end by talking too much?" Her eyes blazed when she turned on me. "I don't understand what that means! I don't understand any of this, and well you know it! You're only showing me how clever you are, how much superior to me and mine—"

"Lady—"

"OtherWhere was meant as fantasy—a play, a dream. A thing I wished for because I knew it could not be. Now to find myself unwilling plunged into the midst of it, and with betrayal for a friend—!"

"It has been difficult, I know. You could be reunited with Droghen. Perhaps he or Thrasim could make your way here easier—"

"Oh, men!" She shook her curls back in disdain, restored almost to the Dweneth I had known on the far side of the World—mocking, in control. "Men see only surface things. Gears and gadgets and gizmos that fly or ride or facture things without motive from man or beast to work them. Thrasim was here, all full of what they saw. Conveniences, toys. Men see not the heartmatters, the things that joy or terrify. Except, perhaps, a man like your Telepath. I have never known his like in my World . . ."

"Perhaps I could help you address some of these heartmatters . . ."

"You!" She laughed, but it was bitter. "You are one of *them!* How do I know that anything you say is truth, after the lies you've told me?" She stood gripping the flimsy chair with it between us, as if that much could shield her from whatever monstrosity she thought me. Jeijinn was correct; I was more alien to her than any Other. "You are one of them! But one of what? What *are* you?"

"Our Legend states that we were brought out of the sky in a time-before-time . . ."

My voice took on the timbre and cadences of singing and she accepted it, ceased to clench her fists and stare at me.

"What it suggests, so far as we can understand it, is that there are worlds beyond this world, and we were brought here from one of them, by a race so far superior to us that they could easily traverse the distance between the stars. Whether this race still exists, much less the race from which we take our roots, we do not know."

She shivered and I stopped, saw her sit precipitously as if her legs could no longer hold her. Omila should be here, I thought with some Other-perverse corner of my mind, to learn how truly to play drama.

"I've heard talk of such things," Dweneth whispered, her voice and her being very far away. "Scholars who spent the Freeze in Droghen's house regaled him with such tales. The Zanti and their astral charts, ancient Plalan helioscopes for scanning the heavens and constructing calendars. As unreal to me as OtherWhere, until now. Hard enough to think of those points of light as harboring worlds—it makes one feel so small—but to think of those worlds Peopled, then to find some of their number in our World . . ."

"No stranger perhaps than *Faerie*," I suggested, "with its beings bred out of the vapors of your own World, and yet so very different."

A new thought had occurred to her; I felt it jangle on the soul-thread. She studied the floor tiles; to meet the eyes of this lying, alien thing just now might well destroy her.

"And so you were sent to spy on us—"

"Not 'spy' precisely—"

"—to worm into our lives and ape our manners and note down everything we say and do. Everything! How we speak and how we sing, how love and fuck and shit and kill . . ."

Was she wrong in anything but degree? Had not the debate raged over just such issues for more than twenty years?

". . . then lure us here, for what? To display us as examples before your Council? To exhibit us like menagerie-beasts—

325

some amusing and clever but obviously inferior form of life? To steal us back to your alien world, I wonder? And then do what with us?"

"What lured you here?" I gave my voice Other-resonance; let it quell her hysteria. "I? Or Droghen's obsession and your own need for adventure? Am I and mine at fault for merely being here, or for your finding an adventure greater than you imagined? Believe me that the majority of my kind would rather you never found us, to camp upon our shores with your weapons and your waste-pits!

"Had you found some race less evolved, more vulnerable than your own, what disposition would your kind make of them?" I warmed to my subject, let my voice enfold the room. "Consider what Mantuu wreaks in Melet, or Kelibesh upon its neighbors, or what destroyed both Gleris and the Plalans. Consider that my best guise in your world was as a bond-woman, chattel, saleable at will. It is not we who are the keepers of menagerie-beasts!"

Where did I find the words, who was usually less than articulate? From whatever source the gift, let me make use of it before it fled me. I must convince this one above all.

"Instead of a primitive, malleable race, or empty isles awaiting your despoilment, you found us. Do you still think the danger unilateral? Why *did* we begin to watch and study and monitor as soon as we were able to traverse the distance, when for the centuries before we were content to remain upon our islands—self-contained, separate, following our way? How many more of you are there than we? What harm has befallen you thus far, or have we not saved Droghen's life? What harm would your kind have done us, had not wise Thrasim intervened?"

"So I grant you!" Dweneth admitted, loud and grudgingly. She had not seen me this wroth since the Hydraulus. "Your people—Others—whatever get you be, have yet to harm us, I will give you that. Unless you count this poking about unasked in People's minds . . ."

"There is an explanation, if you will—"

"First study the enemy, look for weakness—that makes sense enough."

"We no longer have that word in our lexicon—'enemy.' "

"But *you*! Pretense and mockery withal! 'Mistress this' and 'Lady that,' when all the while you took your careful notes and sneered at me—"

"Never 'sneered,' lady—"

"Don't call me that—it mocks me still! There is no honor in what you did!"

"No more than in a players' profession," I argued. "How many characters were you in a given day—Rose and Haughty and Helie or, worse, cloying Dain'sDaughter who flirts but won't commit—Dweneth ever-winsome, so long as it gets her what she wants, the player-maid decked in masks and curls and falsehoods, afraid to dare her one true self, which is Dweneth Healer, or ought to be? No matter the circumstance, I was never more nor less than Lingri. Only my play was one you did not know, a play not yet written, or written on the larger World."

"Very pretty!" she pouted. "Was that this moment's impromptu, or have you been rehearsing it?"

Rau had warned me of this from the first.

"They will come, have no doubt of it. Assuming the first arrive peacefully, the danger is as great to both sides. You know how ours will respond, but consider the People. Recall the mourning rites you have studied: grief, anger, denial—all these they will suffer upon encountering us in context. Whether they are able to transcend to acceptance is a function of how we then respond."

My gratitude, teacher! I thought ironically; this helps me not at all! How was I to "respond"—with softness, pity, unmeasured understanding? Or with the one thing I sensed Dweneth would relish as much as Other craved debate, which was a head-on, night-long fight?

* * *

". . . saved your life, and more than once. Gave you shelter, food, clothing from my own back. When you wore it to your Council they gawked as if you were some slimy, sea-spat thing."

" 'Gave' me all this, lady, and exacted neither labor nor service in return?" My irony was acid. "Nor did I pluck you off that cliff-face; it must have been someone else. For that, at least, I'd say we're even."

"Befriended you, trusted you, poured out my soul to you. Pitied you as well, for this . . ."

She touched me, tentative, turned my wrist to find the plague-mark. I'd had it lasered clean in hospice.

"You never had plague!" she accused me through angry tears. "Never suffered anything, here on your pretty islands among your pretty, perfect people. How could I have thought you were anything like me? Everything I thought you were was falsehood. You *lied* to me!"

"Not lied, precisely. Say rather I answered you truth, half-truth and truth unspoken, and on occasion I exagger—"

She struck me, hard. I did not flinch. She struck again; again I did not move. A third time she raised her hand, but stopped in horror as if she could no more comprehend how she, ordinarily so gentle, could act thus, than that I could be unmoved by it. Only then did she feel the latent sting upon her own cheek, and brought her hand there. So it would be, as long as there was soul-thread.

Her eyes widened in recognition, horror.

"I—I'm sorry. Is this why? Why I hear voices in my head, ever since— Or, voice, really. Only one. Yours. Why?"

"It is called a soul-thread."

"What is it?" Still with horror. "What does it mean?"

"It means our minds, our souls, if you will, have met upon some common ground and, for the moment, interwoven. Our Telepaths—Lerius and his kind—form soul-threads frequently. As sometimes do bonded couples. More rarely, those who step outside the Continuum to presume, as I have, to personal friendships . . ." I saw that I was losing her. "It means our minds touch, yours and mine, at certain significant points. What we do with it thereafter is by mutual agreement. Often in a nonTelepath, as I am, the link is slow in forming and does not immediately manifest itself. I think this one may have begun as long ago as Sirdar'sInn. Do you recall?"

She did.

"But why? There's nothing like it in my world, except maybe Cwala's rites-priestesses, and she seldom talked of them."

"There is also no prior record of such between Other and People."

She pondered that. "Meaning we're the first?"

"So it would seem."

"Maybe there are similarities after all," she suggested slowly. Her posture had relaxed; she seemed less frightened of me. "I really know so little about you, Lingri-one. The you-in-truth, I mean. It's hardly fair. Tell me?"

I did, though it took a night-long. I laid my life out for her examination, holding nothing back, from Lingri Inept who failed her skillscans and, frothing at the mouth, disrupted ten WiseOnes with her speaking for the Old Ones, to Lingri Monitor who, in performing the simple task of gathering information for her own, now found herself caught between two worlds, never to be at ease in either.

"So you're as much a misfit in your world as I in mine," Dweneth said at last. We had ended on the terrace overlooking Jeijinn's walled garden; the dawn spun colors in her breeze-blown hair. "That much makes sense so far. It's a wonder they didn't try to bond you with this Lerius as soon as you were grown. To see if you could speak that way again. Did nothing further ever happen?"

"No," I said, thinking that the effort to bond us might have been made, had my cycle not been a seven to Lerius's ten. "It seems Others were given that single opportunity, through whatever conjunction of mind and circumstance, to gaze upon their ancient past. Never again."

"And so you remain a mystery to yourselves, as much as People." Dweneth mused, contemplating her small hands where they lay in her lap, as weary as the rest of her. Had she slept at all since she had come here? The soul-thread told me no. Could she feel it resonating, as I did? She was looking at me now.

"There is so much that I must learn," she said solemnly. "Can this—soul-thread—be broken—and then joined again?"

"Is that what you wish?"

"I don't know." She yawned and stretched. "I'll need to think."

"There will be Others, the Telepathy for one, who will attempt to break it for us. Or examine it into oblivion. It is not quite Disciplined, you see— "

"You mean it's like a sex-thing?" She came alert, horrified anew. "What you said about bondmates—I guess I wasn't listening. But I know what's done to same-sexers in my world. Stili had a friend once, journeying through Werthaland . . ." Her body stiffened with the story. ". . . they dressed him as a woman, tied him to a stake and cut off his—" She shook the image out of her head. "You don't mean they would do the like to us?"

I reached my hand out. How to touch and offer comfort, not further fear? I was so unskilled at these things, still.

"Souls have no gender." I left the touch unfinished. How was I to explain without blundering into the privacies, or confusing her further? "Else they have all genders; we are not certain. It is not that, not something thought to be a sin. It is that there are customs, Disciplines, decorums. Ways of doing things, in a certain order. Others are obsessed with order, as you soon shall learn. We may not have locks upon our doors, but we have them on our Disciplines. It is most complicated."

"As I begin to see." She yawned prodigiously this time, her head lolled back against the terrace wall. "I haven't slept . . . it's all so strange . . . and you were, most of all . . . too, this thing ajouncing in my head . . ."

"I shall attempt to control the resonance at my end." At least she had not said she wanted it severed. "I go before the Council tomorrow; the Matriarchy has some duty for me whose nature I have not been told. If someone were to be with you in my place . . ." I must phrase this carefully. ". . . an elder and a WiseOne to show you our world, answer all your questions—would you welcome her?"

She yawned again: I walked her to the sleeping room. "Not a Telepath?"

"No, not a Telepath."

She touched my shoulder vaguely, shrugged. " 'Who will be the first to trust'?" she asked, and slept.

Doubtless no Monitor ever knew how many of us there actually were at any given time; it would not have occurred to us to ask. Entering the Citadel barely on time—let it not be said that Lingri Inept had altered overmuch—I counted seventy present in the Council. How many more were still at large, impossible to recall from their many guises a Worldwide? The floor was replete, the gallery crowded, and all eyes were upon me. I squeezed between Rau and a pale, grim-visaged Thrasim in the gallery until I should be called. Below me sat Droghen, beside Jeijinn at the Chair.

Govin was reader that day. How the words must have stuck in his throat!

"It is therefore decided: We cannot but let these People go, free to return to their own realm. We can, however, choose in what manner they depart our shores, how long it will take them to return to their world, and under what conditions they may freely return to ours."

This would take some time. Breaking protocol, I leaned past Thrasim toward Rau.

"I will speak with you, teacher mine."

"Indeed?" His attention never left the proceedings on the floor. "Shall I surmise the subject?"

"Say it concerns a castle-keep, some peasants, and a wheel. Also a musician, who told me all the rest."

331

My teacher's mask was for once impenetrable. "You have encountered Redrec?"

"I have. Should that surprise you, in that his countrymen accompanied me here?" Thrasim had begun to master Othertongue; he followed as much of our sidewise dialogue as he might. "The years have not dealt kindly with him."

"Though well enough that he confided my tale to you," Rau mused. "I must say I'm impressed with your ability to inquire. Now, doubtless you will accuse me of unDiscipline, of intervening in the People's way, of failing to practice what I preach?"

"Of something like."

We spoke in whispers, but Other ears are sensitive. We earned more than one sidelong glance, which said simply: Monitors!

"Have you already formed your opinion," Rau asked me, "or will you countenance an explanation?"

Below, Govin droned on.

"You have read my monograph on torture." Rau's lips barely moved. "Was I to presume to accurately report upon a phenomenon I had not researched at first hand?"

I almost had an answer, but Govin's voice waylaid me.

". . . therefore our intention to compile a history of our race, rendered in all the known People's tongues, and printed in the form of ancient bound books, that it might be distributed, read, and comprehended by all who can read throughout the larger World. When the People have come to know us, they will it is hoped the less fear us, and some manner of concordance can begin."

There was a sea-swell of murmur from no few of the Monitors, who knew the likelihood of any People's blithely accepting something as strange as we no matter in what form presented.

" 'Research,' " I repeated Rau's word. "You will have neglected to mention to me that you have the gift of self-healing."

"As your mother neglected to mention she was an Empath. Has not even a teacher the right to some privacy?"

332

The murmur had died down, and Govin was still speaking. I heard him say the Matriarchy had at last set aside its decades-long debate and reached a conclusion. Wondrous strange; I could not believe my ears. Anything was possible.

"All Monitors here present thereby charged," Govin concluded, "to combine your gifts and findings into this all-encompassing *History*, whose final amanuensis be Lingri. Its completion be your first priority, before these ships can sail. So ends and begins it. Lingri Monitor, how do you reply?"

I rose to my feet in the gallery. Let Govin and the Council accept what I had to say from there; I would not descend.

"I accept the duty and responsibility," I heard my own voice, "but on one condition!"

The murmur rose again, incredulous. None had ever set conditions upon a Council's assignment. But Lingri Inept was also, still, Lingri Implacable.

"Hear me!" Had any ever shouted in Council either? Let *that* reverberate throughout the Citadel! "I will do what has been given me, freely and unstintingly, but only insofar as I am free to do so. Leave me my privacy, and do not attempt to hold me in any one place. And neither the Council nor the Telepathy shall dictate to me or mine!"

Let the infonets digest that as they might.

First I was released from hospice, a microscanner affixed to the flesh just above my navel, to take readings no matter where I was or why. So much for privacy.

"The aging process seems to have stabilized," the healer grudged me, refusing to acknowledge the reasons. "Nevertheless, there is no guarantee it will not resume. We require readings for ten days more, and then there will be further tests." She made the final adjustment on the scanner and indicated I might dress, though she did not dismiss me yet. "There were messages left for you, while you were enroute from Council."

"Messages?"

"One from WiseLoriel, who bids me inform you she has

taken your charge in hand, whatever that might mean." She banked her curiosity, though it cost her. "The second I understand not at all. What, may one inquire, is a 'loose cannon'?"

"This message was from Rau."

"Yes, how did you know?"

I did not trouble to enlighten her.

The compilation of the *History* took less time than might have been expected. From a central locus in the Archives—which I had once needed special permission to enter—I was able to interact both personally and onscreen with the Others of the Monitory. Those seventy in turn interfaced with any number of experts on custom, law, and the sciences, with linguists and xenopsychologists and teachers, and rare was the Other anywhere in the Archipelago who was not in some wise involved in some aspect of the final project. Perhaps never since the Thousand-Year had Others managed to put aside their differences for a single goal. Perhaps never will Others do so again.

Drawing upon the stamina my father Evere had always evidenced in work-mode, I labored the days and nights around, scarcely able to tell them apart. Whenever a given aspect of the *History* did not require me, I walked. Striding the corridors of the Citadel, the undergrounds and the ways, I was beset with voices—wafting out of doorways, rooms and corridors, through the very walls. How much did I truly overhear, how much was told me after? Back to hospice for more tests, I would hear Renna:

". . . first thing I remember is a mountain cave. Them as is too poor to own a herd and hence a decent tent makes do there. I think 'twas that my Da had broke taboo, and we were outsiders for some seasons. The caves is damp, and most childer die of ague or lung-rot before they're half-grown. I had four brothren, I think, and mayhap four sisters, but only I survived. How we'd fight like heljacks for what food there was, and how our Da would beat us . . ."

Jeijinn, in a cubicle elsewhere, under treatment for some residual scarring in the wake of the sailors' flogging:

"Certainly her recent demeanor disquiets me, healer. But has it not been documented that Monitors new-returned are frequently disoriented? The aging, you assure me, has ceased. What more? This new project occupies her overmuch; when it is done these matters will be dealt with. The Telepathy requires of her . . ."

Droghen, a loose cannon in his own right, striding the ways in search of new wonders with Thrasim at his side, thinking himself safe in speaking his own tongue:

"For I do tell you, Thrasim-one, as you know my heart, that could I have this ElvenQueen, I'd never want for more. To somewise persuade her to be my queen in Droghia . . ."

Thrasim only laughed.

Lastly, deep in my work deep in the Archives, did I not hear Dweneth's voice?

"But it looks like silk!"

Her voice reached me despite the aural dampers, found me wherever I was. Beyond the stacks and screens and carrels I could see her, bright and solid beside Loriel's ethereality, fingering Loriel's sleeve in wonderment. Loriel, as I could see, was enjoying this tremendously.

"If it isn't, what's it made of? It's really quite exquisite."

"And it possesses all attributes save one, that it is not derived from the life and labor of a living creature."

Loriel strode and Dweneth followed, as eager to keep up as I had been as a child.

"Lustre, delicacy, warmth, and durability, with the added benefit that it can be replicated at will, in virtually any amount, once the pattern has been stored. Look you . . ."

When had Loriel found time to study Hraregh? I wondered, and how did she know it was the tongue Dweneth found most comfortable? My grandmother would never cease to amaze me. My commscreen did not need me for the moment; I eavesdropped.

". . . the Kelibek, I do believe, have always made and worn the finest silks?"

Dweneth murmured some assent. Loriel was taking her

on a tour of the facturing museum; the array of some thousand years' machinery must have seemed overwhelming.

"Drowned Kelibek sailors in legion washed ashore on Four Greater in what would have been your twelfth century . . ."

"There was a war, I think," from Dweneth.

"Is there not always?" came mildly, from Loriel. "But look you, preserved in that statis case: the surviving fragment of a Kelibek shirt, of the finest silk, watermarked and figured, enduring though its owner is long dust.

"There are moths and butterflies aplenty on our isles," Loriel went on, "though it was against our philosophy to rob them of the very life-thread which nurtured their rebirth. Imagine our astonishment when chemanalysis of the sailor's shirt revealed its composition! We were quick to synth a replicate, which is what that second swatch is. Can you tell the difference?"

"Not by looking at it." A hiss of depressurization, and Loriel had placed it in her hand; I heard Dweneth gasp. "But Mistress Loriel, if it truly is so old . . ."

"Easily replicated." Loriel dismissed it. "As you will see. How does it feel?"

"As real as the first. My mother owned a dressing gown of Keli silk the color of emeralds and so soft . . ."

"And she died when you were young."

No one else could dare this as could Loriel. The statis case repressurized and the two moved on, Loriel's long arm easily about Dweneth's shoulder; it was a People's custom, and no Other would speak it amiss, not even here in public.

"The next phase became to replicate the chemical formula for use in the earliest synthers . . ."

Only Loriel could transform dry fact into a kind of singing history. Punctuated by two pairs of footsteps, her voice faded. Childlike, curious, I followed.

". . . we had always grown plant fibers for our clothing. The first synthers did little more than soften the raw product, remove the seeds and clean it . . ." She would demonstrate from

336

one of the machines in the fabrics room, roaring and clanking, part of the deluxe tour for infant-schoolers. "Later there were machines to spin the fiber into thread, and then the weavers . . ."

Her voice was lost for some minutes beneath the grind and clank of these earlier devices as she demonstrated. When at last they stilled, Dweneth was speaking.

". . . an entire village of carders, spinners, weavers. And in the larger cities are the facturies, where women spend their whole lives hunched over looms and never see the light of day. Your machines, Mistress Loriel, could change all that."

"Only if those who owned the facturies had the wisdom to understand that People relieved of menial work can be found more optimal pursuits," Loriel pointed out. "But that is the realm of sociologists, not me. As to the next phase . . ."

There followed the glide-and-clank of an early synther as Loriel showed Dweneth how to program it for fabric, size, and color.

". . . you see? Now, work that lever there . . ."

Whirr, glide, slither, and an exclamation of surprise as the length of raw, unselvaged cloth delivered itself to Dweneth's hand.

"Remarkable! Don't tell me there is more!"

"This model is over three centuries old, and made the fabric only. One needed additional pattern-cutters and sewing machines to make the finished garment." A gesture would encompass these devices in their places about the room. "Quite primitive and time-consuming. Nowadays . . ."

Leaping three centuries, she sat Dweneth at the console of a contemporary synther; I could see the bright head bent over the keyboard as Loriel's fingers guided hers, as Loriel's face betrayed the flicker of a smile, as with the touch of a final keypad—

"Yet, I wonder," Loriel interjected as Dweneth stayed her hand. "The rose is an excellent complement to your coloring, but so plain. Neither ornament nor pattern? Come, choose the colors and the modes that please you; we have no limits here. I am told you prided yourself on your colors in your own world. Choose what will please a child too long hurt and left unhealing."

No one else could possibly have gotten away with that, not even within Dweneth's awe of OtherWhere. Loriel was counting on her great age and the reverence Dweneth had for her. Showoff! I thought, not for the first time, wondering if she'd gone too far.

"Lingri said you were not Telepath," Dweneth said quite softly.

"Nor am I," said Loriel. "It needs no Telepath nor even psychologist nor healer to see in you a childhood too soon ended. One so hesitant to believe the best of anything, without fear . . ."

Had Loriel ever seen any but an infant weep? The rest I could not hear; would not if I could. Let Loriel and Dweneth have their privacy. I crept away, damping the soul-thread as far as I dared, and returned me to my work. Yet, I could see what followed.

Dweneth would dry her eyes on the backs of her hands, touch the keypad, and the synther would ply its trade, presenting her with a finished garment that might have sprung from *Faerie*. She would smile, and Loriel would approve. A small miracle, presaging a greater one. I would be back at my commscreen completing an entry on trade agreements, when a message would scroll down the Incoming on my screen. Loriel was bringing Dweneth to Three Greater, where the psych-healers were.

At last the *History* was completed. It was thorough, succinct, and would ideally explain all that wanted explaining, while at the same time offending no one. More to the point, its final form would be no larger than a Plalan holytestament, and could be carried anywhere.

All well and good. But how to print it in such quantities as the Matriarchy required, in fourteen languages and alphabets, with real ink on real paper, clothbound and seeming authentic? The primitive printing presses in our museums that would be contemporary with what People had were as incomprehensible to me as synthers were to Dweneth. I might have called upon Thrasim's expertise, assuming he could translate our alien gadgetry, but even had he got them going, these old hand-presses were far too slow, producing two pages at a time at best. The task would take months, unless . . .

I sat amid the guts of one machine, dismantling it, ink on my nose and pondering. If I could rig an adaptor into the hand-press's mechanism without overtaxing it, connect it with a century-old hard-disk processor which—

"Simplicity itself."

I all but toppled the printer on him in my surprise. "Father!"

"An interconnector between the later modem and the impression cylinder of the earlier model, adapted into the flatbed of the earliest hand-press, here . . ." Hello, yourself, I thought, as he crawled beneath the machine to join me and was soon as ink-stained as I. ". . . and a consequent addition of electroplates—retaining, of course, the effect of the manually set handcut letter-die so that the resulting printout does not look too modern—we then cheat with a paper-feeder from a two-hundred-year-old platen offset model, or we shall be slicing our fingers and printing dead air for want of a sufficiently rapid paper access—there! If I may have that micro-spanner . . . and we shall have to shim this section slightly to assure that it is level . . ."

I sat back on my heels and watched my miracle of a parent flourish in his element. That long-ago day when Loriel and I had talked of creatures being all brain, we had touched upon artificial intelligence as well.

"Someday it may be possible for machines to think," Loriel had said. "Oh, not only in the passive manner computers serve us now, but true cognitive process. Someday, too, it may be feasible to transfer living mind into a machine, as when a body grows too old to support a still-active brain. Shall I tell you whose research is foremost in that area, and who is also the first volunteer for such experiment, should it occur within his lifetime?"

Even as a child I had not been surprised to learn it was Evere.

"There!" he triumphed at last, crawling out from inside some monstrous hybrid device no technology had wrought upon the World before or since. "In which language shall we conduct our trial run?"

"Father!" I touched his arm to prevent his activating a machine no doubt as noisy as it was monstrous; the gesture was more of Dweneth to Dain than Lingri to Evere, and startled us both. "What are you doing here?"

"Did I neglect to tell you?" He scratched anOther ear thoughtfully, getting printers' ink on it. "A 'request' from the Matriarchy, not unlike the request made of you, to leave my work and come here. None else remembers how to work these ancient printers. Think you this creature will serve?"

"Only if the Matriarchy sees the end results and not the monster that bred them." My irony was affection, and Evere took it as such.

"I leave the monster in your capable hands," he said, his mind already returning to his hermitage and his work.

No greeting, no farewell. Evere returned to his work and I to mine. His assistance had saved me weeks. Within a day his jury-rigged press produced more copies of the *History* than a hand-press in a year.

One more step remained.

Droghen, now quite whole and striding unassisted down the corridors, arrived before the Council, which managed to draw upon sufficient panoply out of the ancient times to impress him, though I found myself disquieted by the sight of usually dignified Matriarchs bedecked in pompous hats and cobble-trailing habits more suited, so it seemed to me, to one of Dweneth's Comedies. As to their own discomfiture,

WiseGovin's face alone, to borrow a player's phrase, was worth the price of admission.

"Droghen Droghiad d'Droghia!" Jeijinn, orating, had never been in better form. "You have shown yourself to be our best enlightened hope in bringing our existence and our nature across the sea to your awaiting People. To put it pragmatically: you are here, the rest of your world's rulers are not, and we cannot by any reasonable means lure them individually to our shores.

"We charge you, therefore, Droghen d'Droghia, who have asked publicly what return you might make to us in exchange for the life we have restored to you: to return to that World, and make what peace is necessary to address the Fourteen Tribes. Tell them of us, and of what you have encountered here among us. Offer yourself and your whole heart as testament to your words.

"We have for our part provided you with this *History* of our race, printed by methods unknown in your world, to offer as verification. Tell your peers among the Fourteen Tribes that they are as welcome here as you were, so long as they come weaponless and in peace. It is all we ask, Droghen-Gerim, but it is no small thing. It may prove to be your life's longest labor."

"What if I refuse?" Droghen roared back, not so bedazzled either by the person of Jeijinn or the pomp and circumstance surrounding her, that he had ceased to be Droghen.

Jeijinn questioned this with a gesture.

"Can you return to your realm and never speak of us? Can you explain what sorcery healed your heart, or resist the urge to bring our knowledge as improvement to your world? Can you stop the mouths of sailors who, after a drink or two, will have wondrous tales to tell, embellished by their never having set foot in our cities, the more accurately to tell them? Further, Droghen-Gerim, can you never set sail across the sea again, without wondering where else you might encounter Others?"

To her credit, Jeijinn's understanding of xenopsych was flawless, and she hid her inner trembling well. Far more could go wrong than right with this endeavor. Had ever Other risked so much?

But as I read Jeijinn, Rau was reading Droghen:

"He's seeing himself in the history books," he whispered to me from our now-habitual place in the gallery. " 'Droghen Who Spoke Peace to the World.' It mightily appeals to him. Well done, Lingri-*ala*, well done!"

As if, I thought, it had to do with me.

"A journey of such magnitude might consume my natural life," Droghen hedged, perhaps hoping to negotiate a skimmer, to make his journey swifter. But the Matriarchy was relying on precisely the length of that journey, to grant us more time.

"Which life would elsewhere have expired upon our shores the morning you arrived," Jeijinn countered, making to step from the Chair as if this exchange bored her. Were Others such poor actors after all? I wished Dweneth were here.

"I might stay forever, Jeijinn Matriarch," Droghen dared, "if you would be my Queen."

To her credit, Jeijinn held her mask, though her step did falter. In a minim she had weighed the merits of such sacrifice of one for the sake of many. But she knew no queen could keep this man ashore for long. And what if Mantuu or the Kelibek made land upon the morrow? Jeijinn gave no answer, merely favored Droghen with her coolest gaze, and the Droghiad blushed like a child.

"You're a hard woman, Jeijinn ElvenQueen!" he roared. "But, finally, you win!"

Where are the likes of Droghen-Gerim now? There is no longer any Droghia; it has been swallowed live and whole by some improbable overlordship bred of the People's Purist Praesidium, its canals choked with refuse and the occasional mutilated corpse. At one time the dead were only Others, executed in the undercity and left to drift out to sea with the tide, to be mourned there by the *bRi*. No longer. The overlordship has begun to feed upon itself, the dead are all People, and only time will answer.

I did not stay in the gallery to hear Droghen's speech of hope and alliance, but repaired to the strand to watch Thrasim and his crew load the *History* into the *Foremost's* hold.

"Do you save me room as well, Thrasim-one!" I called to him with careful irony, as the small boat plied back and forth with stacks of oilcloth-wrapped books. Skimmers would have been that much faster, but the sailors feared them still. "I'll share with Dweneth if you're pressed, else I'll want a private berth!"

――――――

"Speech of the Candidate for the Purist Party before the
People's Praesidium"
(from *Beer Gardens and Ballot Boxes*, volume 7, number 11; 18 Kos 1631 P.A.)

They glory in subverting everything we cherish . . .
What they do not subvert, they pervert . . .
What they do not pervert, they undermine . . .
What they do not undermine, they deride . . .
What they do not deride, they sneer at . . .

What were we, before they came? Were we free and natural and our own determinators? Have we the courage to be such things again? Then we must free ourselves of them!

How can we, you ask, when they are everywhere? They have intertwined themselves about our every endeavor—twisting, throttling, parasitical—choking the life out of every hope and dream that once was ours!

Until we rid ourselves of this Eternal Other—this mincing, nancing, dream-eyed, grotesque-eared, bloodless thing that sucks our lifeblood from us—we shall not be free!

Let us free ourselves from this Eternal Other! Thrust its coils from our necks that we may breathe again! Pluck its vampire teeth from our throats that we may live again! Untwist the twining thorn-trees of its influence from our governments and exchequers, leach its poisons from our hospitals and laboratories. Better to live without the "improvements" they say they alone have given us—with no mention of our own labors and contributions!—than submit to being their minions any longer.

Seek out this eternal, infernal Other! Smash its face into the pavement! Rape its body, rend its mind! Kill its children and its old, drive it back into the sea! Rip its tongue out of our libraries, burn its books and treatises! Rip its bloodless heart out and nail it to the crossroads as a warning! Let there be no more Eternal Other, but only a mound of stinking corpses, unnatural even in death.

sixteen

Lingri Inept had as usual spoken too soon. By definition of their task, Monitors were free to return to crossover once they'd been debriefed. My duty to Others was fulfilled in the *History:* it seemed logical that I should return in Droghen's train to assist in its distribution. I need only send Chior my refusal of the bonding-suit, take the telfer to Three Greater to fetch Dweneth, and—

"The Council may have freed you, but the Telepathy dictates you remain." Jeijinn showed me the hardcopy with the official sigil. "The soul-thread must be studied. There are Monitors aplenty, and more enlisting since the People's arrival. The work will continue, but in your absence. Daughter . . ."

How long since she had called me that? Doubtless I was not yet weaned, for I could not recall a single instance. The trace of a scar still crossed one clavicle above the neck of her gown, greenish in this light. Still empathizing with the sailors' plights, WiseJeijinn? She had ordered the healers aboard the ships while Thrasim was still untangling the cat; the instant each man was cut down from the triangle he was swathed in pseudoskin and tranquilized. The sailors healed, but Jeijinn suffered still. An empath would not survive a day in crossover, I realized. Perversely, I wished I could embrace her.

"Daughter . . ." Again. ". . . take this not so grievously. It is for your own sake. It is not known but that you carry some Empath's gift as well, which may have been what caused the aging. My error, perhaps, in not stating my empathy in your gene-file. But if I had, you might have been restricted from making crossover. Acquiesce to this, for your own sake."

Acquiesce? I had no choice. Unusual psychic phenomena were the realm of psychologists and Telepaths, and as my growing years had been subsumed to testing, so would my time now, will I, nill I. Telepaths owned no timesense; they might detain me for a day or for a lifetime. As I would not take the hardcopy from her, Jeijinn placed it on her desk.

"This summons pertains only to me, and not to Dweneth?"

"Ideally the Telepaths would prefer to study you both, but as she is not Other, she cannot be kept here."

It was all that I could ask for. I took the 'copy from the desk.

"As it pleases you, Mother, and as it frees Dweneth, I will acquiesce."

To say more would endanger both our Disciplines. If I lingered longer she would be obliged to have me spend the night, but where? In the visitors' suite or in my childhood's rooms? My time in OtherWhere had been divided between Jeijinn, Loriel, Evere, and Rau; I had never had home of my own. I would not tax Jeijinn with the dilemma. I took the telfer to Three Greater.

Droghen's ships would not sail until tomorrow; I had time to say my farewells. But how say farewell to Dweneth? She had said no more about the soul-thread. If she were to return with Droghen, and I remain among the Telepaths, would it stretch a sea-wide?

"I'm not going."

She sat on her players' trunk, swinging her legs to contain

346

her excitement. Doubtless I should have felt it resonate from here to the Citadel.

"Indeed?"

"I've been given the run of the hospices—watching, learning. What knowledge Others have amazes me, and when I think what it could do for my world, if People could learn these things . . ."

She began to pace, speaking very slowly, breathing deeply to calm herself.

"I have asked, and been accepted, as applicant at the teaching hospice. There was much concern at first about the haphazard of my learning, and much tutoring is needed . . . but I have passed the 'scans and pretests, and my intelligence is deemed 'quite high.' "

She did not add "for People," but I knew she knew it had been thought where it had not been said.

"It may take me twice as long, and I must master everything from Othertongue to table manners, I suppose . . . even Loriel, for all her patience, chided me for hanging washing on the window-ledges—well!"

She caught her breath and giggled before she could say the last, not quite believing it herself.

"But I've been accepted. I'm going to be a healer!"

And with those words she—

No. Ah, no! Say not what even a nonTelepath can hear, through walls that cry to me with a message that signifies the beginning of the end! I am summoned . . . it is too soon . . . and for what horrendous reason . . .

We are a nation bereft of children.

How it happened comes to us in fragments. An outcry among the surviving Telepaths. The transmission of a Zanti merchantman to a hidden receiver in the Citadel abruptly broken off. *bRi*-rumor. I have been called away from my chronicle to *bRi*-speak; WiseChior cannot be found.

A three-hour journey in a rowboat wrought from a depowered skimmer, eluding the patrols, slipping under the sensor webs, brings me to the beach at Four Greater, in the Forbidden Zone. To merely set foot on the island is to invite death, but it is the place the *bRi* have chosen to meet with us, and Others gather on the shores from everywhere. If their children's lives are lost, as they assume, their own lives matter little. I glean what information I can from them, then motion the boat away that I might have free access to the *bRi*.

For some moments I must gather myself. I am no longer accustomed to crowds, to voices, to the turmoil of Other minds, *bRi*-minds, all seeking diverse things. Perhaps at long last I understand what Telepaths experience. Too late.

Too late for everything. The one who came for me and rowed the boat here gave me no name; I do not know him. He rowed without speaking, a welcome thing, for I was able to continue my chronicle in my mind, perhaps the only place I may compose it henceforth. I step ankle-deep into the surf.

"*bRi*-Mother," I trill out over the waves, farcalling the lead-female of the pod showing their moonlit flukes where the deep begins. I judge her age and status by the number of scars her encounters with Peoples' fishing trawlers have etched upon her back. "*bRi*-Mother, speak me!"

She heels over, flank gleaming in moonlight as she considers my urgency. What else would cause me to breach both our etiquettes and ask her assistance outright? Will she answer? I await her pleasure.

I feel the stares of Others at my back. Lingri Inept, Lingri unkempt, her fingers ink-stained, clothing rumpled, hair all in straggles down her back and blowing into her mouth as she trills and farcalls against Stormseason winds, her arms outstretched cruciform in a gesture too dramatic for their taste—oblivious, pale, slovenly Lingri is their last, best hope, now that Chior has disappeared, to learn what has become of their children. Let them stare. They need me.

The *bRi*-female's curiosity gets the better of her. She swims leisurely toward the shore. I stand now waist-deep in the too-cold surf, forcing my teeth not to chatter as I trill to her.

"*bRi*-Mother—!"

My urgent tone frightens her and she flinches from my outstretched hand, backswimming, scolding. I bow my head beneath her tirade to acknowledge its truth, backstep out of the water to sit on my heels in the squish and grit of sodden sand, my hands resting palm-upward on my knees to show my receptivity.

"Bad-One!" the *bRi* scolds me. "Hurry-One, Shout-One, Push-One! Drown-One, Eat-too-much-One, Bad-One!" It seems endless, exhausting her vocabulary. "Bad-One!" a final time.

I acknowledge her truth in silence, making the humble-gesture. I am without shame, so long as she will tell me what Others need to know.

They have retreated from the shoreline to crouch behind the stone jetty, concealing themselves from my display before this presapient creature, or perhaps only mindful of patrol boats. If the Guard roars by now, I am the only one dead— a laser burn bubbling in wet sand. No matter. I will remain here until the *bRi* speaks to me, or until I succumb to exposure. The *bRi* knows this. For all my bad manners, she does not wish me harm. Her scolding exhausted, she pulls her great bulk up the sand beside me, her great domed head a daunting pressure against my thigh.

"ssSpeak!"

"My children, *bRi*-Mother, You-Who-Know . . ." I emulate *bRi* humble-gesture again, the full-out gesture, stretching my body out beside hers, hair sopping like seaweed, grit in my eyes and mouth, shameless. I will strip off my sodden garments and swim the night with her, if that be her price. She knows this. Her bottle nose nudges me upright, not ungently.

"ssSpeakk!"

"All my children, *bRi*-Mother. Those-who-went-away. Speak-me of my children, You-Who-Know." My hand rests

349

on her back amid the scars, *bRi*-courtesy. "Gone, *bRi*-Mother? All gone?"

"Gone!" she confirms after an eternal moment, a single sibilant syllable in her tongue.

She nods her huge head, drenching me. I shiver. Sh-hush! the surf sighs. Otherminds groan, behind me on the beach. Some move away, already mourning; they will know no more. But I am Lingri Chronicler; I must know it all.

"How, *bRi*-Mother, how? Did you see?"

The children and their Zanti saviors both? I wonder. All of them, gone? How?

"Gone. All-gone," the *bRi* informs me. "Fireflyers. Thunderwands. Longteeth. Bad!"

War planes. Rifles and swords still—primitive, brutal. A bloodbath. Lasers would have been swifter, more merciful. Why?

"No-swim after. All-sink. Sea bad-taste!" the *bRi* squeaks, commiserating. How many kin has she also lost in like manner? "Blood-in-sea bad-taste. Cold, cold, cold. No warm-thing more. Gone!"

How long do I remain after the *bRi* have gone? I cannot see or hear past the voices and the faces. Small Luctah, who danced so well. Jedor who showed such promise in the higher mathematics. Tiaka, whom I taught to sing. How many more whose names I might not know, but whose absence now sings along the lines of Otherconsciousness, lost?

And Joreth, my son, who is/was no longer a child. I shall not think of this.

A simple action, signifying much. I retrieved the transcript of my unparenting from the corner where my former spouse had flung it, handed it to Redrec Younger, father of my child.

"My error," I said, voice and hand trembling. "For by this, I have no son!"

Who nevertheless heard all, and followed me.

350

"Mum no! Mum, wait! Is it me? What did I do? Don't leave me—!"

Common sense, nay Discipline, told me: Turn not, respond not, do not stop. No good can come of any conversation here. Let Joreth loathe me all his days, so long as I do not prolong this. Perverse, I turned.

"Joreth . . ." His name clutched at my heart; I could not breathe. Do not weep! Let him forget this moment or, if he must remember, let it be in the absence of tears.

But the tears were his, streaming from those Redrec-green eyes, cracking his newfound man-voice. He seized my hands, clutched at my shoulders and I reeled with holding his rampant thoughts at bay.

"Mum, tell me why! I know I've failed you as anOther, but I didn't think you'd hate me for it! Tell me what to change and I will change it!"

"It has not to do with you," I started. No, this was not what I wanted to say, but it was said, and wounded him. "Let your father try to explain—I cannot. Joreth, whatever else, know that it is nothing of hate and nothing you have done, only that I love you, and for that I can no longer name you son."

Bewilderment strove with pain on that near-man's face, but the tears, at least, had stopped. Did he begin to understand? He scrubbed the tears away.

"You may say you have no son!" he cried. "I'll always have a mother!"

I freed one hand to place it on his lips.

"So it may be. But say she died when you were young, and never speak her name, not even in your thoughts. If ever you loved her, do this much for her."

It made no sense in anyone's philosophy. He pulled away and did not answer, might have run from me as he always had before when a half-breed's childhood proved too painful. But from this moment, childhood ended.

"What will happen to you?" he asked more quietly. "What will you do, where will you go?"

He had barely begun school when the Purists first emerged as the shadow of the threat they had now fully become. He had lived in that shadow most of his life, and knew better than to ask any Other her itinerary. He remembered this, and hung his head.

"I'm sorry. I know I'm not supposed to ask, so no one can ask me. Or—rip it out of me." He rubbed the tear-tracks from his face, and would not cry again. With childhood's end came vincibility. "But this is not forever. Whatever I can guess about where you are, I'll keep it to myself, I swear. And I'll find you when it's over, when it's safe."

What if it's never over? I dared not thwart his innocent's faith with that.

"I'll come for you, Mum, when it's over. I'll come for you, no matter what!"

But it was never safe, and I never saw him after. Nevertheless, I will always cherish the thought.

We are a species bereft of children, saving those few whose parents refused to surrender them to what we thought was safety, who cling to them still, hungry and cheerless, in the labyrinths of One Greater. How long before these too are gone? How long for any of us, and why prolong it? Why do the Purists not finish what they have begun? How long—

"WiseLingri . . ." Otherhands wrap a cloak about my shoulders, which have forgotten what it is to be warm and dry. Otherhands raise me to my feet, linger longer than the task requires—a People's gesture, affection. I turn toward the face and do not recognize it.

"The patrols will be by soon," he says. "We must go."

"Of course."

By his accent he is originally from Two Greater, the Windwardmost island. He is of an age to have sent his child or children with the Zanti. I dare not ask how many, or their names, but touch his hand where it rests still on my shoulder.

"I grieve with thee."

352

He turns his face away, damp with tears. It was People who taught Others how to weep.

"Our gratitude," he manages, "you have done so much!"

What have I done but what has been given to me to do, and it not enough? I shudder beneath the borrowed cloak, which can no longer warm me. Dweneth! I think, I cry. Dearheart, hear me: I despair!

How did it happen?

Succinctly: Droghen's ships returned within five years of their departure, in the vanguard of a fleet of such disparate fellow-travelers as Kelibek and Mantuul, though it was Thrasim, not Droghen, who now ruled Droghia.

Within those five years, those Others who could not reconcile themselves to the inevitable, took themselves and their opinions to Two Greater and the outermost of the Lesser isles and attempted to hold themselves apart.

This second encounter between People and Others was nothing like the first, but that is a tale for later, if there is to be a later.

Within that same five years, Dweneth passed her doctorals, and was licensed to practice general healing, with specialties in obstetrics and pediatrics. Within the same eventful five years the Telepathy and I at last came to a parting of the ways. Little did I know that simultaneously Dweneth and Lerius began a joining of the ways whose outcome I still do not fully understand.

The untoward aging I had brought back from crossover never evidenced itself again, but I had lost nearly a year I was never to regain, and there would be no way to determine my mating cycle until the first one was upon me. This made any thought of bonding at best problematical. But it freed me of Chior, who was among the separatists relocated on Two Greater. And my teacher Rau made one more crossover, this time in the direction of Kelibesh, and was eventually reported missing.

353

This second encounter, five years after the first, brought about the Pact Between the Two, as the earliest agreements between People and Others were named, and ten years followed in which policy was made, unmade, and made again, to determine what place Others were to take in the larger World. In truth, most of us would have preferred to remain where we were, offering our knowledge and expertise from a careful distance. But the People demanded our presence, and we went.

We became a nation of administrators.

Our best scientists, our best agronomists, our best healers and teachers, linguists and economists, were soon scattered about the World. Philosophers, sociologists, engineers, and crafters departed in the second wave. In time only the very old, the very young, recluses like Evere, and the Telepaths remained on the Archipelago. All of us in some wise became engaged in service to the People.

The People's best artists, linguists, players, and all but one musician brought their talents to the Archipelago, and if it was true that People would never be the same, neither would we. The changes wrought were never painless, never without misunderstandings, hand-wringing, and stress, and no individual among us was unmoved by what was lost in what was gained. We had survived the Thousand-Year and were perhaps better prepared for radical change. But some People found the changes intolerable, and the rift began.

Perhaps it was only partly that. Perhaps it was as simple as that we lived twice as long as they did still, and no amount of medical advance or genetic engineering could close the gap. There is no People that does not in some wise crave immortality. The majority's unslakable longing for what they could not have may have been all that made the difference.

At first we were their pets, their darlings, and they could not get enough of us. They emulated our manners, and compared our lore and axioms to theirs, parroted our philosophies, embraced us in a paroxysm of cultural exchange, and many a play and poem and popular novel extolled our virtues and the wonders of the Glorious Era of Cooperation which lay ahead.

Our Legend and what survived of our poetry were soon translated into every People's tongue, and courses in our language became mandatory in all the universities. Vegetarian and animal sufferage cults arose everywhere: in some places, religions and class structures began to blur and melt.

Perhaps we should have spoken out then against this blurring of diversity, but who would have listened? Soon, rare was the city or backwater that did not boast its representative Other. How often did I alone hear the phrase, "Well, but some of my best friends are Others . . ."? But finally someone, somewhere, had enough. The backlash began.

Still we might have abandoned all our works and returned to the Archipelago without protest. Our initial thought had been to set up a functioning technology to be left in the People's hands as we went on our way. Few of us ever intended to live all our lives among the People, but at first they would not let us go, and later they could not.

Some few had intermarried, as improbable as our mating cycles may have rendered this. Some fewer of these, through genetic splicing, produced the rare intermix offspring. Had People dictated that we must all return overnight to our part of the World, this might have proved difficult, but not insurmountable. But no such order was ever issued, though we certainly, from the most highly placed government official to the lowliest librarian, would have obeyed it, slipped quietly out into the night and gone. But those in charge gave no warning, and stayed at our posts until the last.

The need for a scapegoat was, in hindsight, inevitable. The party calling itself the People's Purist Praesidium was by its own admission comprised of the "scrapings and leavings" of the Fourteen Tribes—the disgruntled and disenfranchised, the has-beens and never-will-bes. Had they not had Others to victimize they would have preyed upon their own. Even in this, we served.

Documentation of how and why the Purists began first to preach against us, then to systematically exclude us, then to detain us, round us up and exterminate us, finally to drive the remnant of us back to the Archipelago where we were ever willing to retreat of our own accord, exists in plethora everywhere in the World, and I shall not be accused of redundancy here. Let the dominant culture's histories be as inaccurate as their leaders dictate, the fact remains: we were driven out, everyone among the People who ever had traffic with us suffered. The Purists will not be content until we and all our works are no more. Within one of their own generations, they hope to be able to state that we never existed, and rewrite the past in their own image. There is nothing I, or any Other, can do to prevent this. Yet I try.

They began to round us up, I say: first individually, then wholesale. Most of us were treated as anonymous numbers— Others, enemies, names or identities of no consequence. But some of us merited more special ferreting out than the rest, and Lingri was among them—because I had been a Monitor, because, historically, I had been with Droghen's ships which precipitated the changes, because I had a half-breed son, and because of a host of Other crimes, not all of them spurious. I was stopped in the wood called Gloom, barely running distance from the shore. *bRi* fed here at this time of year, and I had hoped to get away.

There was no trial; I had expected none. I was Lingri, and by that definition one of their greatest prizes. At least no one else was incriminated with me.

Better that I had remained anonymous, shot down in the streets of some large city, torn into unrecognizability by wildcurs like so many Others. Better even that they had hanged or crucified me; it would have been over, and less trouble to any number of People. Instead they chose to make a particular example of me and, having a record of my weaknesses, used leather. Poor fools!

First they drugged me. I could not but note the refinement in the pressure-hypo—Dweneth's doing; she owned the patent—as it entered my arm. They stripped me and wrapped me

356

in raw, untanned leather, still dripping from the carcass, and hung me up at the crossroads to dry, a sign about my neck: THUS DIE THE ENEMIES OF THE PEOPLE!

Odds are I should have stayed unconscious until sufficient toxins entered my system to overload autonomic functions and stop my heart. But Lingri Inept did not abide by even natural law.

"Cut her down! And strip that stuff off her, quickly! Waste no time on finesse, damnit, do it!"

So old, that voice—so weary, tremulous. Ah, Dweneth, no! Do not be so old, I plead with thee! How had she found me, how?

"How . . . find me?"

"Shut up! Lie still." Blurred rapid movement all about me; I could not see. "You're all over blisters and rubbing them off every time you move. Oh God, why this? Lekko, my bag— set it here where I can reach it. Oh God, look at you!"

Her tears splashed my face, stinging; my body was unfeeling. Shock. Blisters, like third-degree burns, had formed wherever the rawhide touched.

"Dwen . . ." I touched her face. Like parchment. The red-gold hair had gone snow white. Ah, Dwen! She was ninety years old, as I was, but so different!

"Still in great shape, damn you, old Stick! Don't look a day over forty. Don't you die on me or I'll know the reason why . . ."

I woke in a whitewashed room. Bright sunlight, fresh cracks in thick plaster walls from seismic waves set up after nuclear testing. Tubes, catheters, scanners. Cocooned from the neck down in some fluffy, numbing stuff.

"—can piss on my own, thank you!" Dignified words with which to return to the World.

"You could if we'd let you up, but we won't now, will we?" One of Dweneth's prize nurses, as tough as she was. "Never mind. I've changed urine bags before, not squeamish. Wish you had real blood, though. That's the creepy part!"

357

"Thank you!" I grimaced. Sleep again, and Dweneth.
"Where—?"

"My Grenni hospice. Flew you in under the radar. Intensive care." She took my free hand, the one not tangled in tubes and wires, in her own. "Silly Stick, still trying to get yourself killed. How many times is it now I've saved your life?"

"I have lost count," I lied.

"You'll never be even with me for this one!"

"We'll see."

I freed my hand to touch her face again.

"Still beautiful! You'll have to let me go, you know. Have you a cellar, until I can walk?"

"Don't talk rot! They'd expect you in a cellar. Up here in the sunlight, you're just one more patient. Too skinny, mayhap, and there's always your color—! But I've even put vegetable dye in your bloodpak."

So she had; I'd been too befogged to notice.

"Think of everything, bless you! Dwen—you'll still have to let me go."

"*Graaxshit!* I've more patients than you want looking after!" She pulled herself painfully to her feet. "And don't harass my nurses, either!"

"You should be retired . . ." I murmured.

She turned on me; nothing wrong with her hearing. "And do what? Sit and wait for the World to end? I'll meet that on my feet, thank you! Behave!"

"You're wheezing," I observed; she came every few hours to change my dressings herself.

"It's called old age!" she said crossly. "Not something your kind understood then or now and probably, really, if you scrape all the rest of the detritus and bombast off it, the reason mine are killing yours."

" 'Mine and yours,' even now?"

She threw the last bloodied dressing into the basin. An autonurse wheeled it away, clanking disconsolately. A warped flywheel, no doubt, and no one on this side to fix it.

"Mine and yours, always. Only difference is I loathe them both, now. We never should have met—yours and mine, you and me. I might have died in a peaceful world. Squalid and too soon, mayhap, but peaceful. What else matters?"

She had yet to apply fresh dressings; I managed to sit up.

"Is that how you truly feel?"

"About yours and mine, yes! About you and me?" She sighed, tugged at the snow-white hair at her temples, hugged herself for want of hugging me. "Oh love, oh Dearheart, how? Sometimes I can't separate your memories from mine anymore. Pure senility. We've traveled the same way for so long. Even if it was hemispheres apart, it was always headed in the same direction. How else did I know where to find you?"

"I severed the soul-thread some time ago . . ." I reproached her.

Her ancient face was wry. "Oh, you think so?"

I listened, felt it resonating. She was with me to the last.

"I see. Then do me one last favor?"

The room became too quiet, the World too quiet, listening to us.

"A 'last' one? I've pulled you through. You'll survive this one in spite of yourself. Or do I look that old to you?"

"Yes." I was cruel, but then she'd always known I could be. "Frankly I know not how much time you may have left. That's why I'm asking now."

Her face crumpled; I had hurt her deeply. Would she weep?

"I have no tears left. Used 'em all up taking you down from the cross. Right, then. What's your favor?"

"Betray me. Turn me in."

"What? I must be getting deaf."

"A commcall to the Purist Police—anonymous, if you like. Or tell them who you are. The headlines will be wonderful, and they'll shower your hospices with grants and favors. You'll be designated a hero, and live your remaining years in peace. Betray me."

She scowled at the mediscanner to keep from scowling at me.

"Have to change your medication; this one's making you stupid! 'Betray me.' *I'm* the one who's getting senile. What rot is this?"

"Do you recall what happened in Tilar Town when the PP learned they were harboring Others? Down to the last babe and ancient? I think they even killed the livestock, because they'd hidden them in the barns. Then scorched the soil with nuclears so it won't be safe for a millennium. What will they do to your People if they find me in your hospice?"

"Not to worry!" She would not look at me. "I've alibis bought and paid for all around, and my People will back me up."

"I will not have you lie for me—"

"—since when? How often have I done before?"

"—or endanger lives for my one life." I was halfway up by then, and she lacked the strength to stop me. "You will do this for me, else have no part of me. I'll rip the tubes out and depart this instant. Will you have that on your healer's conscience? Dweneth-one, as you once loved me—"

"No!"

"—betray me!"

"Never! No!"

When last I saw her, neither of us could speak. I found myself as I find myself, ashore in the land of my birth, alone in a windowless room, scratching the end of everything on a finite scrap of paper.

But the end has not quite happened yet. Is it Soliah again who taps on my wall, summoning me to it? I go.

All that remain of Others gather on the beach, not far from where then-Droghen's ships made their landing eighty years ago. One supposes we must ring the island 'round, for there is no break in the line that faces, silent, out to sea. Thrasim's magic ring after all, impenetrable. Still, we are so few. And even that is about to change. Everyone seems to know it but Lingri.

"Gayat will bring your chronicle," Jisra Matriarch approaches to inform me. I can see the too-thin son of a Telepath struggling with a stasis case alone the way I have come. "It is decided. We will not permit the People to take any more of our lives. We will not await their final onslaught. As our lives belong to us, we will decide for them."

"What consensus is this?" I demand against the wind. "No one has consulted me. I must finish my chronicle!"

"And so you shall!" Jisra shouts at me. Doubtless even she did not know she owned such voice. "For you are to be the last!"

Slowly it dawns on me. There was wind along the inner ways of the city as I walked here—most unusual. Unused telfer cars swung perilously above my head, their cables dragging. The last of the weather-shields has fallen, then. Stormseason is upon us, and every Other living is gathered on the beach.

We are gathered here today, down to the last ancient and the few surviving children, to walk into the sea and put an end to it. No further weight of responsibility be on the People's souls if we by our own volition swim out as far as weariness will take us into the rising swells Stormseason brings, swim until we can swim no farther, and let the sea take us. All but Lingri, who is to stand mute on the shore, witness and chronicler, write it all down, seal it in the waiting stasis case, which will preserve it in the event it is ever found. Others think of everything. Except they have not thought of me.

"No one has consulted me!" I repeat; I too can shout, but Jisra already knows this. "What Discipline is this? Has everyone here consented? Even the children? How can they know what choice they make?"

"Every one." Jisra has her back to me, perhaps measuring how far out she will swim, to lead the rest. "Some reluctantly, but all agreed. If you like it not, remain, and live, however long you are permitted. None will survive to reproach you. Either way, you are to be the last."

She moves away toward the unbroken circle—full-circle, first since the Thousand-Year—as does Gayat, dropping the

361

stasis case at my feet, sidling away as if my lust for life might be contagious. I seek what Others here I may yet know—Soliah there, her tattoos defiant in the weak Stormseason sun; Lerius, last of the elder Telepaths, still alive somehow, barely corporeal enough to walk. Shall I presume to speak, or leave them to the peace they have reconciled themselves to?

For only the second time within my life are Others all agreed, and all we can agree upon is that what we are must end. Perversity, thy name is Other!

Thus it begins, will I, nill I. Even as the first few, Jisra leading, brave the waves, I do not know what I will do. Stay and continue my chronicle? Stay beyond its completion, last of my kind? I do not wish the appelation, as I never desired any of those thrust upon me in the past—Speaker for the Old Ones, She Who Brought the People, Lingri WiseOne, Lingri Chronicler. Let me die as I have lived, Lingri Inept, my only epitaph: "She meant well."

They walk into the sea and I cannot stop them. The younger Matriarchs go first, to lend strength to the ancients and the last of the children. Those of middle years, as I, wait on the shore as witness. Gayat turns to me once, shrugging a Telepath's shrug, as if to say: It is all one, this realm or the next. He takes an old one's hand and turns away from me—he thinks—forever. The only decisive act he will ever perform, poor Telepath.

At first there is only silence and the steady stream of Others, encumbered by their clothing, wading out until their feet lose bottom, then beginning their final swim. Long slender arms ply the uneasy waves, streaming heads, predominantly dark-haired and long-eared, bob toward an unreachable horizon. Sea-birds, disturbed in their feeding, plummet and screech, while farther out, the *bRi* . . .

The *bRi*. No one has considered the *bRi*, who intuit at once what we are about and will have none of it. It is not unknown for a pod to beach itself in despair when calves are killed. So the *bRi* interpret our present seaward flight, as a reverse air-

362

swimmers' suicide. But however great their despair, they would never permit all of their number to die; nor will they us. Our error, for our long intercourse with the creatures. They will not let us die.

I bear witness to the absurdity that follows—an awkward, undignified shoving match between Others intent upon continuing out to sea and larger, more powerful *bRi* nudging and jostling them back to shore. The sea is turmoil, churning waves and limbs, the ear-splitting cry of *bRi* farcalling their alarums. And then a sail.

A sail? Illusion. My eyes, too long in darkness, cannot be trusted. But the younger ones see it, too.

A sail of canvas, patched and worn, presaging a wooden galleon of Droghen-Gerim's era. A further absurdity. Is this how the People's final armada will arrive, forerunned by an antique sailing ship?

Those nearest shore pause in their exodus, step back, regain the land to watch transfixed. No one cries out, but only murmurs, and the murmurs rise like sea-swell. "A sail . . . sail . . . ship . . . what can it . . . can it mean?"

The ship looms now, and *bRi* surround it, unusual in itself. Generations of hunting have at last convinced *bRi* to avoid the People's ships. Why not this one? What do they know that we ashore cannot?

The ship looms, and we can see she's Peopled. Figures aboard scurry to man lifeboats, lowering—to retrieve our swimming Others from the waves! Not to strike them back, nor fire upon them, but to rescue them! Is it only to gather us for the final, concentrated slaughter? What does it mean?

The ship looms alone and, as if no time has passed, is suddenly upon us, navigated unerringly into the natural harbor of One Greater as if its pilot knows the way. An agile male in antique Doghian garb leaps the gunwale to the jetty. People, broad-shouldered, moving along the beach to question Others casually, as if present at a Marketfest and not mass suicide. But I am wrong. There is desperation in that voice, and I know it well.

"Which is Lingri?" I hear him cry. "Lingri—is she among you?"

Do I speak aloud or only think it? "Joreth."

He swings about, his face delighted. "Mother? Mum!"

And before that host of Others sweeps me up into his arms—am I so frail or is he so strong?—whirls me about, laughing, hugging. A world weeps, but my son still laughs. Later I will ask how he managed to forgive that world, and me.

There is, apparently, to be a later.

"What is your number?" Joreth asks Jisra, recognizing her authority. Too late, he remembers my dignity and sets me on my feet. "How many survivors on the Archipelago?"

"Nine thousand, four hundred thirteen." The voice is Lerius's—a croak. He keeps the soul-threads alive in his subconscious.

Joreth hears this solemnly, as we do who are among that number.

"So few! Our plan can accommodate many times that. But can it succeed with so few?"

His question is for a second newcomer, arrived less urgently from the looming ship. Silent, hooded, she remains unintroduced to us, but not entirely unknowable. She, I say, seeing the form beneath the voluminous robe, the small hands barely visible beneath belled sleeves. Small hands, small fingers, alarmingly familiar to me. She is more solid than anOther; People too or, like my son, an Intermix.

My son. How dare I even think it?

The newcomer seems to be calculating something. "Our plan"—what might that mean? All Others have returned now, the last straggling out of the water, out of breath and curious. A growing murmur explains the presence of the newcomers to those too far back in the crowd to hear directly. From their ring around the island, Others gather, waiting. No further sound but surf, and as little movement. Suddenly Lerius sways on his feet; the silent one has been studying him.

"Barely, husband," she answers Joreth at last. "Only just. Nevertheless, we must try."

364

Something wrenches in my soul. There was only one, I thought, who owned that voice. I was wrong. Knowing her Joreth's wife startles me less than what those small hands reveal as she reaches to throw back her hood—tumbled redgold hair and a face I have lived too long to see.

It is Dweneth's face—her face, her hands, her voice—not as she would be now, did she still live, but as she was when I first knew her. Only her eyes—a Telepath's eyes—are nothing Dweneth. They look past me at Lerius.

"Father," she says aloud, having staggered him by speaking it in his mind. I think I know the answer, but dare not think it through. This stranger-Dweneth turns from Lerius to Jisra and me now, deferential.

"My name is Dwiri."

Lerius totters. A sodden, sea-spewn Gayat must go to him and help him sit. But Dwiri pays no heed, waits for me to speak what she can read in my mind.

"Dwiri—Dweneth'sDaughter."

Her smile is Dweneth's, radiant. "Yes, how did you know?"

I know because her very existence defies the norm; her mother would have been eighty when she was born. But Lerius's paternity explains everything, I think. There was a year when Dweneth, infatuated with him as she had been from the moment she encountered him on the beach, had him all to herself, and neither spoke of it after. Dweneth's ultimate gene-splicing experiment stands before me—living, breathing, embodying her mother, and married to my son. After so much sorrow, I cannot bear this happiness.

It is short-lived.

"Your mother—?" I ask, though I have known the answer for some time.

The Dweneth-smile fades, extinguishes. "Dead. More than a year. But peacefully. I will tell you—"

Joreth's hands are on her shoulders, affectionate. "Not now. We have not time."

She touches his hand, smiles fleetingly. "Of course not. Later. There is much we must do."

Joreth explains, his voice rising to include the Others.

"There are islands, near the Windward polar cap, uncharted by any People. The ship can carry the sick and elderly. The rest will find the current surprisingly warm this time of year. Whatever you can salvage that will make a vessel . . . the strongest can take turns swimming with the *bRi* . . ."

"And when the People come and find our islands empty—?" Jisra, practical.

Joreth gestures toward the sea. "They will assume you have done what you were about to do, before we told the *bRi* to stop you."

I am horrified. "You *told* them?"

Joreth grins at me. "Intermixes change the rules, Mother, you know that. Chastise me later. We have work to do!"

He brings Jisra aboard in conference, to provide the Matriarch with precise coordinates of these mysterious islands, their size and shape and habitability, and how Others will reach them. How does he know these things, my sheltered musician's son? Where has he been, what learning, in this decade I have not seen him? So many questions, no time for answers.

The news soon rings One Greater around. No infonet is needed, only Other to Other, mouth to ear, to say what marvel has arrived. We gather, the remnant of us—nine thousand, four hundred thirteen precisely—to learn what we must do.

It is Stormseason in our latitudes, but warmer to Windward this time of year, and we will be following the warmcurrent. The early part of the journey will be bearable, before the waters grow too cold. Yet the distance is overlong—my journey to Rau's island, multiplied twenty-fold, and with unknown dangers. Under less dire circumstances it would be madness. Add questions of food and rest and shelter, the likelihood of searchnets . . .

"All taken care of," Dwiri assures me, smiling. I must grow accustomed to having my thoughts read once again, and by one who looks like this. Preparations are underway.

Whatever is not metal and will float is carried out of the Citadel and pressed into service. The youngest and strongest, led by Jisra, set out first on a vast flotilla companioned by more *bRi* than even I have ever seen before, two flanking each makeshift craft no matter how small. Course set, each little boat keeping in sight of the one before and the one after, they embark the afternoon long. Forlorn and dignified at once, this wave-flung exile, its beginning vanishing in mist as its end still hugs the shores, one little boat at a time.

The ancient galleon will go last, to guard the rear and carry our supplies. Its crew has been debarking bit by bit, to companion Others in their flimsy craft. Still ashore, I record all this; my chronicle, apparently, is coming with us. Something occurs to me.

"Have you weapons aboard?" I demand, springing up the gangplank in order to seem agile, seeking out my son in the aft compartments.

"Don't ask me what you'd rather not have answered," Joreth brazens. "How well can you steer?"

He has heard the tale of how Droghen's ships arrived here. "Some skills are never lost. But I am as able to go with the flotilla. Why have me take up space?"

"We've better uses for you here," Joreth says in his old don't-cross-me tone. Does he mean he can't bear to part with me, or that he has old hurts to settle? I take the helm for the first watch.

"Heading?" I ask. It is a leap of faith. Islands, near the polar regions—barren, uncharted, cold. How ever will we live?

Joreth grins, gestures to where the small craft bob and vanish.

"Follow the Others!" he cries, and we are on our way.

As with much else about their everyday lives, People and Others measure time in differing ways.

The People employ one unified calendar, which was established under the Plalan Ascendancy, a sun-worshiping, slave-trading society which endured for approximately eight hundred years before falling into decline. Droghen-Gerim's arrival on the Other Archipelago occurs in the year 1563 P.A. [Plalan Ascendancy].

Others honor three concurrent time-lines. First is their Old Calendar, which extends back approximately 500,000 years, to the age of the most ancient artifacts found on the Archipelago, and assumed to be of Other manufacture. This Old Calendar is used in scholarly and scientific notation, counting backward from the year Zero (see below), and designated with the suffix BT-Y ("Before the Thousand-Year").

The Thousand-Year marks the beginning, or "Year Zero" of the second time-line. It is considered the most significant event in Other history. Having nearly destroyed themselves as a species in a series of wars on their Archipelago, Others at last agreed to set aside their so-called "negative passions" and began to master the Disciplines of the Inscape. Others' technological era begins with this Year Zero of the Thousand-Year.

The Thousand-Year was intended to be precisely what the name implies: a millennium within which Others hoped to achieve true Discipline. But while they did achieve one thousand years of peace, Others were not satisfied that they were truly Disciplined within that time, nor were they prepared to undertake the task of redating every event which transpired after the first millennium, to reflect a second Year Zero. Consequently, a third time-line was designated to begin at the "Thousandth-Year" or T-Y1000. Both the system of dating and the striving for true Discipline continued uninterrupted.

The fact that Lingri was coincidentally born in the Thousand-Year is not considered unduly significant. Many Other children were born in that year, each of whom achieved their own measure of fulfillment, and Others subscribe neither to superstition nor to fate.